The Xothic Legend Cycle

The Complete Mythos Fiction of Lin Carter

Chaosium Mythos Fiction

Robert Bloch's Mysteries of the Worm
Cthulhu's Heirs
The Book of Iod
Made in Goatswood
The Dunwich Cycle
The Disciples of Cthulhu 2nd revised edition
The Cthulhu Cycle
The Necronomicon
The Hastur Cycle 2nd revised edition

Call of Cthulhu® Fiction

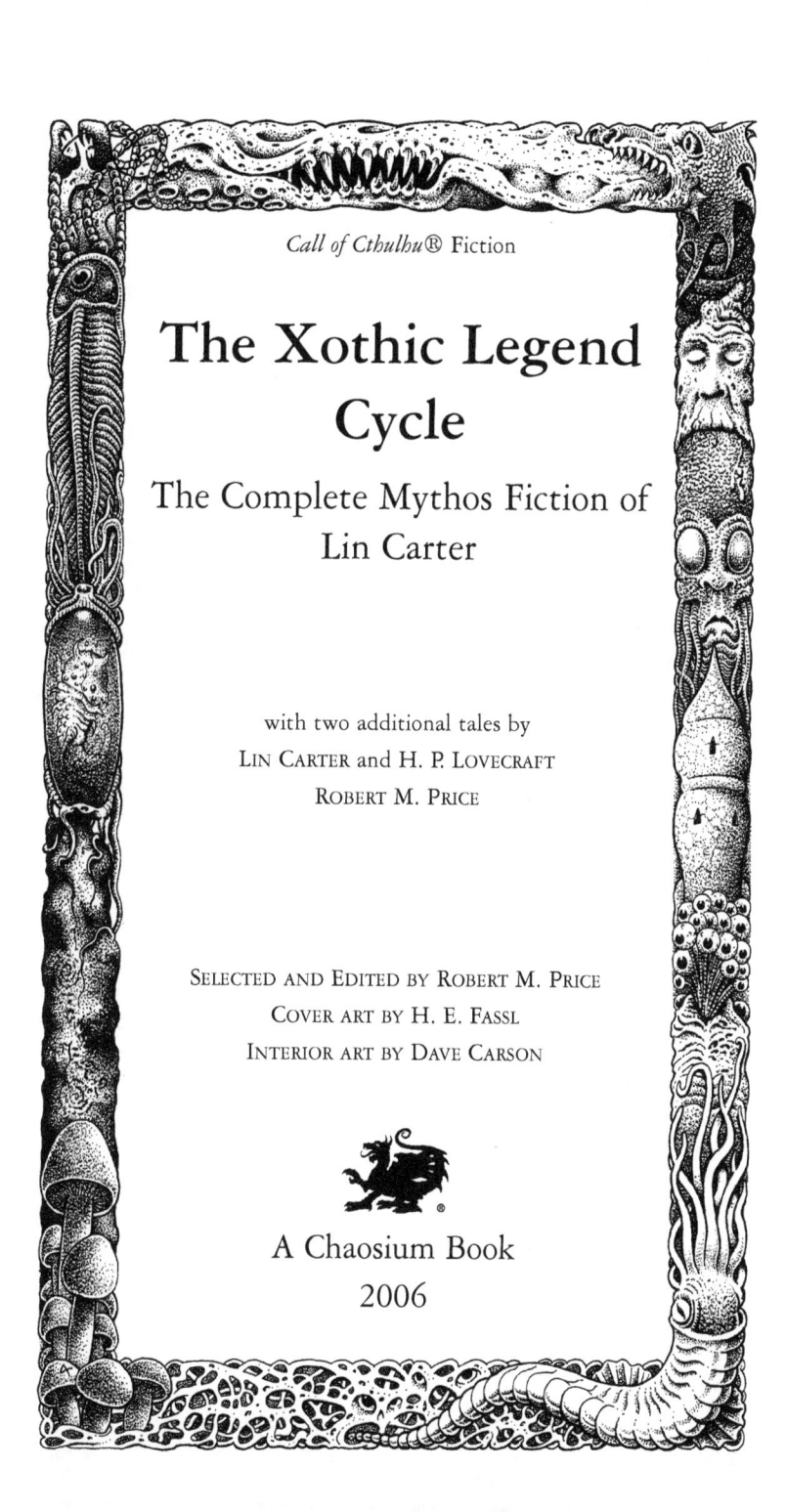

The Xothic Legend Cycle

The Complete Mythos Fiction of Lin Carter

with two additional tales by
Lin Carter and H. P. Lovecraft
Robert M. Price

Selected and Edited by Robert M. Price
Cover art by H. E. Fassl
Interior art by Dave Carson

A Chaosium Book
2006

The Xothic Legend Cycle is published by Chaosium, Inc.

This book is copyrighted as a whole by Chaosium, Inc., ©1997, 2006; all rights reserved.

"The Red Offering" (as "The Offering") ©1982 by Lin Carter for *Crypt of Cthulhu* #7. "The Dweller in the Tomb" ©1971 by August Derleth for *Dark Things*. "The Thing in the Pit" ©1980 by Lin Carter for *Lost Worlds*. "Out of the Ages" ©1975 by April R. Derleth and Walden W. Derleth for *Nameless Places*. "The Horror in the Gallery" (as "Zoth-Ommog") ©1976 by Edward P. Berglund for *The Disciples of Cthulhu*. "The Winfield Heritance" ©1981 by Lin Carter for *Weird Tales* #3. "Perchance to Dream" ©1988 by Cryptic Publications for *Crypt of Cthulhu* #56. "Strange Manuscript Found in the Vermont Woods" ©1988 by Cryptic Publications for *Crypt of Cthulhu* #54. "Dreams from R'lyeh" ©1964, 1965, 1967 by The Terminus, Owlswick, & Ft. Mudge Electrick Street Railway Gazette for *Amra*. "Something in the Moonlight" © 1980 by Lin Carter for *Weird Tales* #2. "The Fishers from Outside" ©1988 by Cryptic Publications for *Crypt of Cthulhu* #54. "Behind the Mask" ©1987 by Lin Carter for *Crypt of Cthulhu* #47. "The Strange Doom of Enos Harker" ©1989, 1996 by Cryptic Publications for *Crypt of Cthulhu* #69 (original fragment) and for *The Xothic Legend Cycle* (completed version). "The Bell in the Tower" ©1989 by Cryptic Publications. "The Soul of the Devil-Bought" ©1996 by Robert M. Price for *Cthulhu Cultus* #5; appears here by permission of the author. All Lin Carter material appears by permission of Robert M. Price, literary executor for Lin Carter.

Cover art by H. E. Fassl. Interior art by Dave Carson. "The Fishers from Outside" illustration by Lin Carter. Cover layout by Eric Vogt. Editing and interior layout by Janice Sellers. Editor-in-chief Lynn Willis. Proofreading by James Naureckas and Tod Briggs.

The reproduction of material from within this book for the purposes of personal or corporate profit, by photographic, digital, or other methods of electronic storage and retrieval, is prohibited.

Please address questions and comments concerning this book, as well as requests for free notices of Chaosium publications, by mail to Chaosium Inc., 22568 Mission Blvd. #423, Hayward CA 94541, U.S.A. Also visit our web page at:

www.chaosium.com

FIRST EDITION

2 3 4 5 6 7 8 9 10

Chaosium Publication 6013. Published in February 1997, reprinted June 2006.

ISBN 0-56882-095-6

Printed in USA.

Contents

INTRODUCTION *Robert M. Price* vii

THE RED OFFERING *Lin Carter* 1

THE DWELLER IN THE TOMB *Lin Carter* 6

THE THING IN THE PIT *Lin Carter* 17

OUT OF THE AGES *Lin Carter* 27

THE HORROR IN THE GALLERY *Lin Carter* 49

THE WINFIELD HERITAGE *Lin Carter* 95

PERCHANCE TO DREAM *Lin Carter* 116

STRANGE MANUSCRIPT FOUND IN THE VERMONT
WOODS *Lin Carter* 127

DREAMS FROM R'LYEH *Lin Carter* 144

SOMETHING IN THE MOONLIGHT *Lin Carter* 165

THE FISHERS FROM OUTSIDE *Lin Carter* 179

BEHIND THE MASK *Lin Carter* 194

THE STRANGE DOOM OF ENOS HARKER
Lin Carter and Robert M. Price 209

THE BELL IN THE TOWER
Lin Carter and H. P. Lovecraft 204

THE SOUL OF THE DEVIL-BOUGHT
Robert M. Price 219

For Robert Bloch and
Frank Belknap Long
… and, of course,
for August Derleth.

[dedication by Lin Carter]

Xothic Romance

Terrors Out of Time

THE PRESENT collection provides a generous portion of Lin Carter's work in the Cthulhu Mythos. What it excludes in the main is his considerable body of stories written in the form of chapters from the *Necronomicon*, the *Book of Eibon*, and the *Pnakotic Manuscripts*. Most of these should appear either in the Chaosium *Necronomicon* or in a projected volume, *The Book of Eibon* by Clark Ashton Smith and Lin Carter. What *The Xothic Legend Cycle* includes is the set of his Mythos stories set in the modern day, usually contemporary with the Lovecraft and Derleth stories upon which they are based.

Of these Lin had segregated a group of five ("The Thing in the Pit", "The Dweller in the Tomb", "Out of the Ages", "Zoth-Ommog", and "The Winfield Heritance") to comprise the chapters of an episodic novel resembling Derleth's *The Trail of Cthulhu* (available again from Carroll & Graf). These stories appeared in the mid-seventies in a handful of anthologies, and it was not easy for the interested reader to sit down and read them together. This novel he eventually submitted to Arkham House under the collective title *The Terror Out of Time*, a title that Lovecraft neglected to choose from the paradigmatic table, but just as easily might have. (The title did appear, however, on a collection of some of the pulp stories of Lovecraft's collaborator/revision client Clifford M. Eddy, Jr.) This was a doomed effort, since following the passing of August Derleth, Arkham House seemed to repeat the fate of poor Amos Tuttle, undergoing a horrific transformation after death. Arkham House, it seemed, was no longer very keen on publishing, or even tolerating, that Cthulhu Mythos stuff. It was as if the American Bible Society had kept their name but decided to quit wasting their time publishing scripture! Thus *The Terror Out of Time* was born out of time and found no home.

I have included these stories, in some cases substituting earlier working titles Lin had used for the stories, which seem more fitting to me. Hence, "Zoth-Ommog" has been restored to "The Horror in the Gallery", while I have retained the published title for "The Thing in the Pit", instead of changing it to "Zanthu", as Lin intended for the book publication. Partly this is because I am not quite publishing the collection he intended, as is evident from the simple fact that these stories do not stand alone. They premiered as individual stories, and that is how they appear here, flanked by several other tales, some of which have quite as much mutual interconnection with the *Terror Out of Time* tales as these do among themselves. Most of them participate in that elder lore Lin called the Xothic legend cycle. This refers to the alien star Xoth where Cthulhu's three offspring were spawned. It is patently obvious that Ghatanothoa, the chief bogey of Lovecraft's "Out of the Aeons", is Cthulhu under another name, so Lin, determined to harmonize the two stories (that is, to find some way of placing both in the same narrative universe), decided that Ghatanothoa must be the son of Cthulhu. The other two are Carter creations *de novo*: Zoth-Ommog and Ythogtha. The entities are connected, by means of the discovery of their images and of certain ancient manuscripts (the *Zanthu Tablets* and the *Ponape*

Scripture) containing their lore, with the Sanbourne Institute of Pacific Antiquities. Characters whose names and adventures reverberate throughout the whole group of tales include explorers Abner Exekiel Hoag and Harold Hadley Copeland, curators Henry Stephenson Blaine, Arthur Wilcox Hodgkins, and Bryant Hoskins, together with various latter-day Blaines and Hoags, etc.

Lin Carter's contribution to the Cthulhu Mythos, one can see, is quite extensive, contributing new entities, books, and eerie locations to the Mythos megatext which seem to me on a par with the Mythos work of Ramsey Campbell. I believe that fact will become clear to any who have missed it, now that the whole Xothic cycle is available in one volume. Even readers already familiar with the original published versions are in for a treat, since Lin made numerous changes and expansions in the versions I have used here.

The Copeland Bequest

Lin Carter once styled himself not only a member of what he dubbed "The New Lovecraft Circle", but even as "the Last Disciple." That might seem both an arrogant and a short-sighted boast, as if he were Hegel announcing that philosophy had reached its final acme with him, or the Prophet Muhammad proclaiming himself the Seal of the Prophets. But that would be the wrong way to see it. When Lin Carter claimed to be the Last Disciple, it was a trick of perspective, like one of those posters which show the United States from the chauvinistic viewpoint of a New Yorker or a Bostonian. From where Lin Carter was standing, the whole genre of Cthulhu Mythos fiction seemed to be a great and mighty Ganges flowing toward him. Or think of it as a chain of tradition of which he found himself the inheritor. It all seemed to have aimed itself at him as its destination with the seeming inevitability that hindsight lends to random events.

Lin Carter saw himself as the fortunate possessor of a great inheritance, left to him by the likes of Lovecraft, Derleth, Bloch, Henry Kuttner, Clark Ashton Smith, Frank Belknap Long, and Robert E. Howard. Thus he was much like the typical protagonist of his own or Derleth's Mythos tales: the scion of a doomed line, inheriting a legacy that is either a blessing or a curse, depending on which side you're on. In fact, the single, central theme of his Cthulhu Mythos tales is the widening wake of "the Copeland Bequest", a collection of Pacific Island relics and idols brought back by archaeologist Harold Hadley Copeland and bequeathed to the Sanbourne Institute of Pacific Antiquities. Everyone it touches it marks for terrible doom, so that history repeats itself again and again. Even this standard feature of Mythos fiction can be understood as an allegory of reading for Carter's *oeuvre*: By writing pastiches, simply reshuffling the deck and retelling the old stories of Lovecraft and Derleth, Lin was doing what modern Structuralist and Post-structuralist poetics tells us is happening with every literary text. To read or to reread a text is to rewrite the text.

Lin Carter's stories are much like the ancient Targums, the Aramaic paraphrases of the Hebrew Bible dating from around the first centuries B.C.E. and C.E. Most Jews in the Holy Land no longer commonly spoke Hebrew, the language of the Bible, so for their benefit paraphrases, something like today's Living Bible, were prepared in Aramaic, the sister language to Hebrew, which most Jews were then speaking. What is important for today's scholars about these paraphrases is that they preserve popular interpretations of the scriptures. They are fossils of ancient reader response. We read the scriptures for ourselves, but we must not suppose that the ancients read what we do when they perused the same text. Each community of interpreters has its own set of lenses through which it reads the same text, with widely variant results. We all unwittingly bring presuppositions to the texts. When we see an ancient reader recording in a paraphrase of the scripture what he thought the scripture meant, we have a priceless window into the way the text was being understood then.

In the late 1970's and early 1980's, Lin Carter revived *Weird Tales* as a series of paperback anthologies. He lovingly recreated the unique magazine, not necessarily as it *was*, but as he remembered reading and enjoying it, and pleasant memory distorts. In the same way, his Derlethian fiction is a record of what he read when he read the tales of Lovecraft and Derleth years before. He had really rewritten the stories years before, when he read and reread them in his youth. It was years later that he formalized it by putting pen to paper. For a similar case, take the difference between the book and the movie named *Psycho II*. The book was Bloch's own sequel to his original *Psycho*. The movie (like its own sequels) was the sequel, not so much to the original novel or even to the original film (quite close to the novel), but rather to the movie as viewers remembered it, a sequel to the *legend* of *Psycho* (as Marc A. Cerasini pointed out to me). To tell you the truth, I preferred the movie version of *Psycho II*.

So Carter was trying to pass onto you the Mythos as he himself knew it and loved it. Some readers recoil, they think, because Carter (or Lumley or Derleth) has dared to rewrite Lovecraft or the Mythos. In fact what they cannot stomach is the fact that it is Carter's rewriting which is on the printed page rather than their own, which they naively equate with "the real HPL."

Let me be a bit more specific about the matter of rewriting the earlier fictions of one's predecessors. There are two points to get straight here, about Lin Carter's stories and about anyone else's. The first is that, as Gerard Genette shows us, any pastiche is also a parody, an exaggeration of the original writer's or story's most characteristic marks. If you decide to write a Conan pastiche, chances are you are going to wind up having the mighty Cimmerian swear "By Crom!" a few more times than Howard did per story. You will probably increase the quotient of "skull-cleaving" blows, etc. Since the smaller details of the warp and woof of Howard's style work so well, hypnotizing you as you read, you cannot quite identify or explain them, and thus you cannot quite take aim at them to imitate them in your pastiche. To compensate, you lean more heavily on the most obvious stylistic trademarks and hope the reader will think it sounds like the real thing. This is of course the reason, also, for the way many fan Mythos pastiches turn out. As immature writers, their authors cannot account for what it is in Lovecraft's stories that grabs them so. So they go overboard with the most blatantly obvious feature, the Mythos names and monsters. The pitiful result only makes it all the more obvious that this was never really the secret at all.

The other thing about rewriting, pastiching, is this: It is like trying to reduplicate the results of a favorite recipe you got from your mom or grandmom. You are using pretty much the same ingredients, but it's not an exact science. It is human imperfection that allows for human individuality. And that's good! That way, even several writers who are trying their best to imitate Lovecraft, let's take the young Ramsey Campbell, the young Henry Kuttner, and the young Robert Bloch, each has his own unique spin. So does Lin Carter. If his tales were exactly like Lovecraft's stories, they would *be* Lovecraft's stories, which, one senses, is what some critics really want. They would like all Lovecraftian fiction besides Lovecraft's to be reduced to nullity; they wish anyone else never to have written. I don't.

As to the how of the thing, I must repair to the Structuralists again. Not that there is no one else from whom to learn it; Lester Dent, with his Mad Libs-like plot board, was already doing Structuralism without knowing it. But I think Claude Levi-Strauss and Vladimir Propp have drawn some helpful maps for us better to know what we're trying to do when we write. Levi-Strauss stressed the importance of the paradigmatic axis along which a story is told. That is, a plot may be almost endlessly repeated without the reader not noticing or at least not caring much, in tale after tale. The story is not monotonous as long as the Mad Lib blanks are filled in with different options every time. The author has something like a grammatical paradigm before him every time he sits down to write. Who's the hero going to be? Choose from "male" or "female." "Old" or "young." Will the hero be a cowboy? A spy? A swordsman? An average Joe forced into heroism by circumstances? Take your pick. There will be some wrong to redress. What sort will it be? Kidnaping of a maiden? Of a child? Theft of a magic medallion? Or a magic sword? By whom? An evil wizard? An estranged husband? Etc. The various options available in the paradigm are what give the story much of its variety, even if the plot does not vary. Again, read any dozen or three dozen Doc Savage novels: You'll find the same set of narrative roles divided up among a new set of names each time. But so flexible was Lester Dent's imagination that it never grew tiresome!

The plot is plotted (no coincidence!) along the syntagmic axis. This is the train of logic that carries things along, the narrative syntax, like the governing structure of single sentences. The path proceeds through this set of windings and not that. Even here, what you do is choose from the set of options at each plot juncture: victory? Defeat? Temporary setback? Apparent defeat that is later revealed as a victory? There is an infinite number of possible combinations as the writer reshuffles the deck each time, spinning the wheel again for every narrative.

Cthulhu Mythos stories tend to vary more along the paradigmatic axis than along the syntagmic axis. That is, having read your Lovecraft or your Derleth, you have a pretty good sense of *what* is finally going to happen, though maybe not yet to *whom* it will happen. Will the doomed delver be a Miskatonic University prof this time? An antiquarian? A genealogist? What sort of secret will he discover? An ancient tablet? An ancestral diary? A forbidden book? And whose unwelcome attention is he going to attract? An ancient sorcerer (like Joseph Curwen, Keziah Mason, Ephraim Waite?), an Old One? If so, will it be Cthulhu, Tsathoggua, Shub-Niggurath? Narrathoth? Does it matter?

One way to mark the difference between traditional Lovecraftian writing and the New Wave is that the latter dares to experiment more with the syntagmic axis. Different sorts of things happen in Campbell's collection *New Tales of the Cthulhu Mythos* than did in Derleth's *Tales of the Cthulhu Mythos*. You're off the scale with both axes left dangling when you get to Creation Press' collection *Starry Wisdom*.

Lin Carter, though, was definitely a traditionalist. He just shakes up the paradigmatic dice, whispers "Yig eyes!", and lets 'er rip. But you know the game he's playing. It's the one he's always played, with the same rules, the same narrative syntax.

Subtext and Superstructure

One trait of Carter's did prove an Achilles Heel, at least when it came to his Cthulhu Mythos fiction. He shared the fan's enthusiasm for the jots and tittles of the Mythos as a system of lore, just as Trekkies pore over those manuals of the imaginary schematics of the Enterprise. To me, Star Trek lover that I am, that seems a bit much. One might view the sort of thing some of us Lovecraftians do, like compiling Mythos glossaries and theogonies, in the same light. I have that fascinated fixation on Mythos lore myself, in case you hadn't noticed. I do not consider it a fault, as long as you don't let it run away with you. How do you know when you are in danger of letting it run away with you? I'd say one major symptom is when you start writing stories about the Cthulhu Mythos instead of stories that merely utilize the Cthulhu Mythos. Sometimes, I admit, Lin Carter very definitely did the former.

David C. Schultz maintains that the Mythos is only a set of atmospheric props and should never be brought to center stage. This is the flaw for which Fritz Leiber excoriated Brian Lumley's *The Transition of Titus Crow*. I think Schultz is entirely correct. Being fascinated with Mythos lore in no way means you think that the stories should be about that lore. But Lin Carter *did* think so. He would even say up front that he wrote a particular story just to get some new Mythos items in print (and thus admitted to the official canon). This is like when a monkish pal of Erasmus asked him why the critical Greek text of the New Testament he was compiling (it was the first one after the Medieval use of the Latin Vulgate) did not contain 1 John 5:17b ("For there are three that bear witness in heaven, the Father, the Word, and the Spirit, and these three are one."), the single biblical passage in support of the dogma of the Trinity. Erasmus replied that, though he was as Trinitarian as the next guy, he had to admit that the passage was not found in any ancient Greek manuscript known to him. It must have been penciled into the Vulgate to provide after-the-fact evidence for the doctrine. So he had to omit it. He agreed to include it after all if his friend could turn up a Greek manuscript containing the text. It wasn't long before he did, though Erasmus suspected it was not in fact more ancient than a few days! In the same way, Lin was not above writing out a tale of the Mythos to provide a scriptural citation for a piece of theology he had just dreamed up.

I know it's a tightrope we all sometimes walk; so much so that to some it must seem there is no difference between a story that *uses* the Mythos and one that is *about* the Mythos. After all, the collection you are reading, like all its fellows in this series, does not contain randomly selected horror fiction, maybe a little Hawthorne here, a little Stoker there. No, what we have here is a bunch of stories whose supposed virtue lies precisely in their being "Cthulhu Mythos" tales. So aren't the stories really about the Mythos? Aren't we playing a pathetic game of self-deception when we pretend stories are not about the Mythos but only utilize it, sounding almost as if we regretted its presence but are able to tolerate it as long as it doesn't become too obtrusive?

I would prefer to put it a bit differently than the venerable Schultz does. I would say that the Cthulhuvian lore functions as a subtext for the rest of any story in which it appears. I am assuming Michael Riffaterre's concept of subtext in his book *Fictional Truth*. What gives a fictional narrative its ring of truth? Deep down, Riffaterre argues, we all take for granted the correspondence theory of truth. That is, we imagine that "true" statements are those which accurately correspond to the way things are. Historians should report "history as it actually happened", as the dictum of Franz Overbeck had it. Art should be strictly representational, even superreal, not that crap by Picasso. This is where the larger literary category of verisimilitude comes in: A story cannot draw the reader into a "temporary willing suspension of disbelief" (Coleridge) unless it answers, for the most part, to the rules of reality as the reader defines it. A reading public who believed much more in divine providence than we do might find Charles Dickens' wild coincidences less jolting than we do. When we find ourselves saying, "Oh come on now!" we know the author has lost us, has fumbled the ball. He has forfeited verisimilitude and the reader rudely awakens to the fact that he is just spending his time reading some story some guy made up.

The use of a subtext provides a hidden layer of symbols with which the surface narrative text will resonate, and to which it will seem to correspond. The subtext might be a set of conventional assumptions or sentiments which the reader can be expected to hold. Then the surface events of a horror tale will ring against them like the hammers moved by the piano keys striking on the strings inside. Stephen King does this quite well, e.g., in *Pet Sematary* by erecting the superstructure of the zombie tale (which by itself would be mighty hard to take seriously) upon the hidden foundation of a subtext of real-life tragedy: the horrendous aftermath of the mundane death of a child. The latter is a horror only too real to any reader who has been close to a real-life case of it.

In its opening chapters, the Gospel of Matthew depicts the Messiah as being born miraculously of a virgin, fleeing persecution by repairing to Egypt, entertaining magi from Parthia who have timed his birth from their star charts, etc. All this is built upon a subtext, a substructure of scripture citations ("This happened so as to fulfill the scripture, saying, 'Out of Egypt I have called my son' [Hosea 11:1]"). These fictive events would have sounded scarcely more credible to the ancients than they do to us, except that Matthew undergirded them with a subtext layer of scripture-citation. Did those Old Testament texts really foretell the gospel events? Hell, no! It's a trick! Literary sleight-of-hand. Lovecraft's tales work the same way. They lay a groundwork of ancient myths (of Cthulhu, etc.) of which glimpses surface in the story once present-day events start to seem to correspond to them. The air of menace in "The Call of Cthulhu" would dissipate quickly if we were to remove all the references to the ancient cult of the Old Ones, the *Necronomicon*, the Eskimo diabolists, the theosophical Masters in Tibet, etc. If all we knew was that some castaway on Gilligan's Island suddenly had a big green octopus-man chasing him, it would look as stupid as that idiot flick *Yog, the Terror from Beyond Space*. Mythos tales work best when the Mythos is seen but not heard. It stays a subtext. It does its indispensable work behind the scenes. But if we drag it out on stage, it ceases being the subtext. If the subtext becomes the story, we are in trouble, because the Mythos can no longer be taken for granted as hoary and ominous background. In the foreground it will be seen for what it is, like the Great Oz once he is forced to emerge from behind his curtain. With the Mythos on stage, it finds itself dangling in the air, twisting in the wind, because it has no subtext of its own on which to rely. Or does it?

August Derleth brought the Mythos into the spotlight in his Mythos tales, with Laban Shrewsbury and Seneca Lapham giving windy disquisitions on its details and conundrums. Derleth seemed to know he had to try to set the Mythos against some subtext of its own, and to serve this purpose he invoked genuine mythology, usually ancient Greek, biblical, and Polynesian. He hoped the Mythos, which was now itself the great bogey, would ring true against the ancient tales of the Titans, Satan's fall, and a bunch of frog totems. Famously, this failed. He sank the *Titanic*, because all these myth cycles were already so familiar to the reader that, far from lending exotic and esoteric ambiance to the Mythos, they tended to reduce the Mythos to the contemptuously familiar, to make it mundane textbook fodder. Derleth played taxidermist and taxonomist: He killed and stuffed the Mythos so as to install it safely and motionlessly in its place in the museum exhibit.

Lin Carter, too, has flipped the boat over. He has, like Derleth, made the Mythos the protagonist of the story (at least sometimes), and for his new substitute subtext Carter employs *the previous Mythos fiction of Derleth and Lovecraft*. If the story rings true, it is ringing off the bell of the stories it is retelling. As Tzvetan Todorov says, all parodies, pastiches, and plagiarisms, to be understood and appreciated for what they are, must be seen as translucent to their source material. If not, then it's like an in-joke that you happen not to be in on. "I guess you had to be there." Thus, Lin Carter's stories strike readers in one of two ways: You think, "This story was a lot better when Derleth wrote it!" or "Hey, this is the real thing! Just like Derleth!" It's like a mystery story when someone is searching for a secret panel in the wall by tapping against one section of the wall, then another. When the echo sounds thick, immediate and pat, you know your tap is just resonating through the solid wall going away from you. When it sounds hollow, like an echo, it means your tap has passed through intervening air and is coming back as an echo from a farther, inner wall. Voila! If you like Carter's Mythos pastiches, you're measuring the distance between Carter's story and its Lovecraftian or Derlethian source/subtext, and it rings true. If Carter's story seems flat and pat, it is likely because it seems to lie directly atop its source, like a layer of sheet rock.

It Came from the Margins

A quick survey of Lin Carter's Mythos fiction, such as I give in the chapter "The Statement of Lin Carter", in my book *Lin Carter: A Look behind His Imaginary Worlds* (Borgo Press), reveals that Carter was very selective in his choices of which portions of Lovecraft's canon he would take as his chief inspirations. He did not start in the center but rather at the margins. What I mean is that his own Mythos tales often tend to be sequels to stories from particular categories of tales in which Lovecraft's genius was diluted with the influence of others. For instance, some of the stories in this collection branch off Lovecraft's revision tales, stories ghost-written for a client, perhaps based on some minimal plot-germ supplied him by Hazel Heald or Zealia Bishop. While the prose in these tales is usually 100% Lovecraft, one can sense a certain lack of seriousness, a tendency toward self-parody and pulp magazine extravagance, that does not characterize the stories he knew would appear under his own byline. It is this "Lovecraft on vacation", this frivolous alter-ego Lovecraft, that Carter recognized as a kindred spirit.

Another favorite Lovecraft source for Carter was "Through the Gates of the Silver Key", the collaboration between HPL and E. Hoffmann Price. This was not something Lovecraft would ever have written by himself, and even in its finished form it contains large amounts of prose and conceptuality from Price. It is not straight Lovecraft. Since Lin was not planning to write straight Lovecraft (who could?), this collaboration appealed to him as a kind of prototype for what he did plan to do: a mix of Lovecraft and his own stuff.

"Straying" even farther into deuterocanonical territory, Lin Carter found to his liking certain of August Derleth's "posthumous collaborations" with Lovecraft. These are stories (now available in two paperback volumes from Carroll & Graf, *The Lurker at the Threshold* and *The Watchers Out of Time*) in which Derleth did no more than to choose some idea from Lovecraft's Commonplace Book and write a tale of his own based on it. They are like a can of Slice or Sunkist: They make a great noise about being refreshing citrus drinks, but the label reveals that they contain but a molecule or two of actual juice. In *The Lurker at the Threshold*, Derleth had actually incorporated a couple of pages of Lovecraft's prose, extended notes for three different stories he might have gotten around to writing someday. Carter was, again, much influenced by this novella. Another Derleth tale that attracted him was "The Return of Hastur", one that made no pretense of containing Lovecraft verbiage, but which was, to some degree, written under Lovecraft's supervision, as was "The Lair of the Star-Spawn", the title of which HPL even supplied. These foundational stories of the emergent Derleth Mythos proved seminal for Carter as well.

Remember, Lin Carter was not so much interested in Lovecraft's work in its own right, but rather as the root of the Cthulhu Mythos. Thus when he staked his claim to mine the rich acres of Lovecraft's texts, the section he chose was right on the border, where others had already prospected. Or to return to our earlier categories, he had his own reading of Lovecraft, to be sure (and you will be surprised to see how close it is to that of Richard L. Tierney and Dirk W. Mosig if you read Lin's *Lovecraft: A Look behind the "Cthulhu Mythos"*, a new edition of which, revised and corrected by yours truly, will soon be available from Borgo Press). Lin was also well aware that there were other readings of Lovecraft, such as Derleth's, and he wanted to draw upon all of them. Lovecraft's were not the only set of bony shoulders he stood upon, and unlike many others of whom the same is true, he knew it.

Happy Magic!
Robert M. Price
August (Derleth) 24, 1996

THIS one Lin Carter wrote especially for my magazine *Crypt of Cthulhu* (#7, Lammas 1982). Though "The Red Offering" leads off this collection, it was by no means the first of these tales to be written. The five stories making up the projected novel *The Terror out of Time* had all already been written and published, but "The Red Offering" is something of a prequel, in which certain motifs occurring in other stories of the Xothic cycle are retroactively anticipated. For instance, the notion of the red offering itself is now seen to begin and to round off the *Terror out of Time* sequence, occurring as it does in both "The Red Offering" and "The Winfield Heritance." The notion implicit in "Out of the Ages" that Harold Hadley Copeland was the reincarnation of the Muvian hierophant Zanthu is (implicitly) elaborated in this tale, in which the eerie archaeological delvings of both men proceed along fate-driven parallel lines.

Speaking of parallel lines, it is tempting to trace one here with Carter's Conan tale "The Thing in the Crypt" (in the Lancer/Ace collection *Conan*). As in Carter's Simrana tale "The Laughter of Han" (apparently no relation to the "Dark Han" of Mythos obscurity), "The Red Offering" shows us the other side of the ethos of the sword-&-sorcery genre. In his tales of Conan and Thongor, Carter always had the steel-thewed hero triumph over skinny sorcerers and animated mummies, whereas in his horror tales set in analogous milieux, it is the Mythos equivalent of Dalendus Vool or Thoth-Ammon who wins.

The title "The Red Offering" appeared atop a surviving draft of this story, though for the *Crypt of Cthulhu* appearance he had shortened it to simply "The Offering." I have chosen to go back to Lin's original, literally more colorful, title. Another difference from the published version is that, in the draft, the lost item sought by Zanthu was not the Black Seal of Iraan, but rather the ancient scripture *The Rituals of Yhe*. A later reference to the same book has also vanished, this time in favor of another old text, the *Ygoth Records*. In closing, let me conjure up Lin Carter's shade, as eager to tell a story now as it was then, when this note was subjoined to the story:

Author's Note: S.T. Joshi has discovered evidence in Lovecraft's letters that H.P.L. had a hand in rewriting one of Henry S. Whitehead's stories, "Bothon." The story is partly laid in Mu, and, comparing the text of that tale with another Muvian yarn, also one of Lovecraft's revision jobs ("Out of the Aeons" [written for Zealia Bishop]), I feel certain that Joshi is correct. Such Muvian place names as Ghua, Aglad-Dho, Yish and Knan, and the Gyaa-Hua submen certainly sound like the place names in the Heald story (K'naa, Yaddith-Gho, etc.) and like some of the names in another Lovecraft revision job, "The Mound" (Yoth, K'n-yan, Nith)—and there is a striking similarity between the Gyaa-Yothn submen in "The Mound" and the Gyaa-Hua submen in "Bothon." So I have written this new story, incorporating the names that seem most Lovecraftian in "Bothon," together with previously-established place names from "Out of the Aeons" and my earlier Muvian story "The Thing in the Pit," which also purports to be a translation from the *Zanthu Tablets*.

The Seven Lost Signs of Terror and the Words of Fear are taken from yet another revision story, [William] Lumley's "The Diary of Alonzo Typer," while such phrases as the Bottomless Well of Yuggugon, the dark tarn of Kyagoph, the onyx sea cliffs of Kho, etc., are drawn from Lovecraft's letters, as is the Black Seal of Iraan itself.

The Red Offering

by Lin Carter

NOTE: The narrative which follows is an extract from the disturbing and debatable *Zanthu Tablets*, a brochure published at San Francisco in 1916 by the late Professor Harold Hadley Copeland, consisting of his shocking and conjectural translation from the primal Naacal of certain inscribed stone records found in the tomb of a prehistoric shaman by the survivor of the ill-fated Copeland-Ellington expedition to Central Asia (1916).

The narrative is taken from Tablet VII, Side 1, Lines 12 through 148.

* * *

FROM my earliest youth, I, Zanthu, had considered myself a devotee of mighty Ythogtha, the Abomination in the Abyss, and even dared aspire to the highest position in what remnants remained of the cult of that Dark Divinity, in whose service the founders of my house had prospered and had waxed prestigious in the land of G'thuu, northernmost of the nine realms into which the continent of Mu was divided. Even in these sorry latter days when the cult of Ythogtha had sadly lapsed into desuetude, while that of the detestable Ghatanothoa waxed mighty in the land, I persevered in my determination to achieve the hierophantic throne itself.

My ambition was fostered by certain apparitions or locutions which visited my slumbers during those nights when the Moon is absent from the skies and it has been of old the wont of Ythogtha to trouble the dreams of men. It is not given to human hands to set down in words the Indescribable, so suffice it to say that more than once in my youth a Shape of Darkness rose up within my sleeping brain and I heard a Voice vast and echoing, yet fainter than a whisper, which repeated over and over these menacing and enigmatic words, whose meaning I was not to unriddle for many years:

You must make the Red Offering.
You must make the Red Offering.
You must make the Red Offering.

But more on this enigma which haunted my youthful dreams I will later speak.

Now, the last high priest of my order had perished untold centuries ago, a victim to the unrelenting persecutions which the worshipers of the Monster on the Mount visited upon the rival cults whose very existence they deemed a challenge to their theological supremacy. The hierophantic throne thus vacant, with no contender daring to exert his claim thereunto, my path seemed clear: but into such neglect and disarray had the cult of Ythogtha fallen, I knew not by what unequivocal authority to bolster my claim.

Now, most precious and sacrosanct among the thaumaturgical treasures of Mu was that immemorial and long-lost talisman known to men as the Black Seal. It had of old been the most prized possession of the elder conjurer Iraan, for upon that mystery-fraught sigil were inscribed the Seven Lost Signs of Terror, which hold power coercive of any Dweller in the cosmos or in the unknowable and nameless regions beyond. Were I to secure into my possession the Black Seal of Iraan, the hierophantic throne would be mine, for I could then summon the Presence of the god himself to ratify my claim.

* * *

THUS it came to pass that, my tutelage under the wise H'mog complete, I rose up and, together with my younger brother Kuth, departed from the land of my birth and eloigned into those southern lands once frequented by the potent conjurer. In truth, we made an odd, ill-matched pair, my brother and myself, for I was unprepossessing of appearance, while Kuth was tall and fair of face, and desirable to women, whereas I was not. Neither were we the best of friends, for Kuth had won the heart of the maiden Yeena, for whom I lusted above all of the young women of G'thuu; nonetheless, I required the strength and courage of my brother Kuth to see us through the innumerable vicissitudes of our long journey, which was beset with perils, while he wished to wallow in the wine shops of the southern cities, and to enjoy the embrace of women.

We passed the onyx sea cliffs of Kho, the sandy wastes of Ylagh, where we went with care ever wary of the frightful Noogs. Entering into the central eastern province of Ghua, we skirted the dark tarn of Kyagoph and avoided those ill-rumored mountains that hide the bottomless well of Yuguggon. In the fullness of time we passed through the Black Wood and came to the Hills of Ninghom at the Hour of the Singing of the Green Vapour, and stood upon the heights thereof and gazed down for a time upon the squat and monolithic turrets of Aglad-Dho.

From this ancient city are ruled the lands of the southeast, among them Yish and Knan, and in this old metropolis standeth yet the eldermost upon Earth of all of the temples of Shub-Niggurath the Mighty Mother. Aye, it was forth from this very temple, ages before, that the rash T'yog ventured on the first steps of his fruitless quest to limit for all time to come the fearful power of Ghatanothoa.

Thus we came down to the ancient city and secured rooms in the hostelry, and while my tall brother swaggered forth to drown his thirst with wine and to sate less mentionable appetites with the flesh of dancing girls, I sought the archives of the temples. In the shrines of Nug and Yeb found I many rare tomes and treatises, but none that recorded aught of the history of the conjurer Iraan or of the Black Seal. But under the copper domes of Shub-Niggurath's temple, I discovered at length a copy of the *Ygoth Records* wherein that famous sorcerer, a disciple of Iraan, made revelation of many things not heretofore known to me concerning the last days of his master, even unto the secret place of his burial, which was a tomb situated in the very midst of the Desolation of Voor. A dreadful excitement seized my heart as I perused the very words which revealed the secret for which I so long had sought:

> Amidst the Desolation of Voor, in the land of Yish, there lies buried in a tomb of black marble, guarded by seven avenues of granite monsters, the mummy of wise Iraan, which guardeth for all time the Black Seal which the Outer Ones brought down from Yuggoth on the Rim before the first men walked the world; and thereon are recorded the Seven Lost Signs of Terror and the Words of Fear.

* * *

WITH trembling hands I reverently closed the covers of the *Ygoth Records*, which were bound between two plaques carven of the *tlath* wood which is sacred to the Mighty Mother. I rose up and went forth into the wilderness of Yish with my brother Kuth and a number of shambling Gyaa-Hua, the bestial submen we of Mu used in that time for slaves and servitors, and discovered at length the tomb. Many and fearful were the hazards which confronted us on that last journey, but at length it was done.

While our slaves, cowering and whimpering, pried timidly at the immense slab of black marble which shielded from the light of day the last resting-place of the conjurer Iraan, I tried to avert mine eyes from the dreadful signs and warnings cut deep into the stone by long-dead hands. After a time, my brother impatiently thrust aside the moaning Gyaa-Hua and tested the might of his strong arms and shoulders against that massive weight. Ere long it fell to the ground, shattering into seven great fragments against the pave, and the mummy was revealed.

A gaunt and desiccated thing it was, for many centuries had passed since last the face of Iraan had looked upon the day, but I cared naught for that, for there, clasped in bony talons against its naked ribs, the hands of the ancient conjurer clenched to its bosom the Black Seal of unknown metal brought down from the stars when the Earth was but newly formed.

A shrill wailing came from our slaves, where they huddled some distance away, for in truth had the sorcerer Ygoth warned that his dead master guarded for all time the Seal. Even as Kuth and I bent to wrest the Black Seal from its grasp, the dried lids of Iraan flew open and eyes of red fire glared awfully into our own. Those claw-like hands flew up to close about the very throat of Kuth, who gave voice to a cry of unutterable terror, and locked his own brawny hands about those skeletal wrists, striving to break their merciless grip.

Strong and young was my tall brother, but the withered horror in the tomb possessed preternatural vigor; his eyes popped, his tongue lolled, and his face blackened. He cast me an imploring look from eyes bright with terror. But the mummy had released the Seal in order to battle against the desecrators who had disturbed its rest, so I prudently snatched up the sigil and bore it to a place of safety amidst our baggage, some distance apart, where the hairy submen grovelled and whined. There I lingered for a little time, striving to master my fears and to still my labouring heart.

When I cautiously drew near the tomb again, Kuth was dead, crushed to gory ruin against the bony ribs of the mummy, whose crimson-soaked remains had already begun to crumble into dust beneath the merciless rays of the sun, and which was sustained no longer by that unnatural animation.

We hastily buried my brother's corpse beneath the sands of Voor, and fled from that accursed place, returning to the city; and my heart was filled with a cruel and bitter joy: for I had made the Red Offering, and now the hierophantic throne was mine.

And so was the maiden Yeena ...

IN an early page of notes for "the Ythogtha Tales", Lin Carter called this story "The Inhabitant of the Crypt." For its planned appearance as part of the episodic novel *The Terror Out of Time* he had intended to change the title to "Zanthu." I have chosen to stick with the title borne by the story in its only publication thus far, in the 1971 Arkham House anthology *Dark Things*, where it was called "The Dweller in the Tomb." It is likely enough that Lin borrowed the title for this story from one of Robert E. Howard's Conrad and Kirowan stories, "The Dwellers under the Tombs" (included in the 1978 Berkley collection *Black Canaan*).

On the other hand, it is an obvious choice from the paradigm of possible Lovecraft/*Weird Tales* horror titles, all constructed on the same syntagmic scheme: a participial noun followed by a spatial preposition, followed in turn by an ominous-sounding location. It's easy, just like that old *Mad* magazine gag inviting you to write your own Bob Dylan song by picking one cliché Dylan term from column A, another from column B, a third from column C, etc., since all the songs were so much alike that the words were nearly interchangeable. First, pick your noun: the Horror, the Lurker, the Haunter, the Whisperer, the Colour, the Shadow, the Dweller, the Inhabitant. Next, choose your preposition: at, on, over, under, out of, in. Next, your location: Red Hook, Warrendown, the Graveyard, Time, Space, the Ages, the Aeons, Darkness, the Dark, the Threshold, the Tomb, the Lake, Innsmouth, the Gulf. Presto! You're a Mythos writer!

This story, and the four others that with it were intended to be *The Terror Out of Time*, are being published in this book with Lin's intended revisions. These revised versions appear in print for the first time.

The Dweller in the Tomb

by Lin Carter

NOTE by Henry Stephenson Blaine, Ph.D., curator of the Manuscripts Collection of the Sanbourne Institute of Pacific Antiquities in Santiago, California:

THE following extract from the journals of the Copeland-Ellington expedition to central Asia (1913), made by Harold Hadley Copeland, the expedition's only survivor, were discovered during a routine inventory of Professor Copeland's papers, which were bequeathed by his estate to the Sanbourne Institute in April 1928. It is hardly necessary for me to remark that Professor Copeland's is a very distinguished name in the field of Pacific archaeology. His great text, *Prehistory in the Pacific: A Preliminary Investigation with Reference to the Myth Patterns of Southeast Asia* (1902), remains the standard classic in its field and has been an inspiration to at least two generations of scholars who have followed in his footsteps—myself but the least among many. Even his *Polynesian Mythology, with a Note on the Cthulhu Legend Cycle* (1906), although it reflects his unfortunate and growing enthusiasm for questionable occult "theories", which led to the regrettable erosion of his scholarly reputation and is perhaps indicative of the mental aberrations which dominated his declining years, remains to this day a massive workof scientific research. It is even possible, I think, to admire the monumental scholarship that went into his *The Prehistoric Pacific in the Light of the* Ponape Scripture (1911), although even the kindest critic cannot but regret that Professor Copeland's developing mania led him to accept too readily flimsy theories of a bygone Pacific civilization of absurdly remote antiquity based insecurely on doubtful documents and the lore of obscure cult survivals—a presumably ancient and highly advanced civilization, of which the enigmatic Easter Island images and the megalithic ruined cities of Ponape and Nan-Matal are assumed mere vestiges.

The reader of this issue of the *Journal of Pacific Antiquities*, in which the directors have seen fit to include the following excerpta, must be aware that the publication of that particular work in 1911 led to a rather hasty prejudging of Professor Copeland's admitted aberration and to his being requested to resign from the Pacific Area Archaeological Association, of which he was a cofounder and a past president.

In all his colorful career, however, no episode is more controversial than the central Asian expedition of 1913 and the discovery of the so-called "Zanthu Tablets", reputedly in the stone tomb of a prehistoric wizard in the mountain country north of the Tsang plateau region. The expedition was lost, Ellington having died of red-water fever only a few days out from the advance station at Sangup-Koy; Copeland himself was near death when, three months later, emaciated from advanced starvation and in a raving, incoherent state due to hysteria and deprivation, he was discovered in the dunes beyond the Russian meteorological outpost at Kovortny on the borders of the Chian province of Mongolia. Slowly recovering his health, Professor Copeland unfortunately published, in a privately printed brochure issued in 1916, a conjectural and fragmentary translation of the Zanthu Tablets. The edition contained material so shocking, chaotic, and revolutionary, so thoroughly at odds with even the most imaginative theories yet set forth on early Pacific civilizations, that not only was the booklet officially suppressed, but the resultant public outcry, from press and pulpit alike, occasioned the final extinction of what little remained of his scientific reputation.

Amid the widespread publicity surrounding the discovery and translation of the debatable and blasphemous Zanthu Tablets, no reasonably authentic account has been published to this day concerning the course of the ill-fated expedition itself, nor of the peculiar circumstances precedent and subsequent to the opening of the famous tomb of the prehistoric Central Asian shaman. Professor Copeland's own account, from his unedited journals, herewith follows. Some will see in these disjointed passages only the psychotic spewings of a diseased brain; others, perhaps more deeply versed in certain obscure texts of ancient lore and in the surviving myth patterns of little-known Pacific and Asian cults, may find troubling hints of a primordial and frightening truth.

—H. Stephenson Blaine
June 1928

Journal of the Copeland-Ellington Expedition, 1913

Sept. 22.
Thirty-one days out of Sangup-Koy. Made about fifteen miles today, more or less, despite dwindling supplies of water—thank the Lord for creating camels! Still weak from lingering traces of fever, but medical supplies low, too. Since Ellington died, native bearers have become distinctly uneasy and are growing ever more troublesome ... muttering about tomb-guarding *dugpas* again, and most reluctant to travel after sundown. Must have a stern talk with Champo-Yaa; remind him, as chief guide, it's up to him to keep his boys in line and on the move. Took samples from eroded stone rubble at base of cliffs today; examination in my tent tonight over reeking oil-lamp most disturbing. Expected at least some fossils of rudimentary fish, primitive mollusks, coral, or the like, prob. dating from Silurian or Ordovician, but *no signs of fossilized life whatsoever*. Surely, this tableland cannot be *that* old! Cold very intense tonight, air most penetrating, and wind in the distant peaks horribly suggestive of *howling* ... but Champo-Yaa swears there are no wolves in these regions.

Sept. 23.
Only about thirteen miles today, alas! Traveling in these loose dry sands very difficult going, even for the camels, and the air itself is so incredibly dry that it sucks the very moisture out of the lining of our throats. Spotted the eleventh landmark right on schedule: cairn-like mound of rubble circling central spire with a cloven pinnacle. *Ponape Scripture*'s directions to the burial ground remarkably precise, even after all of the elapsed millennia. My book (when and if I find the tomb of Zanthu) should set the scientific world on its ear and astound the so-called "experts." Pack of damned fools: evidence of primal Mu is written on the labyrinthine walls of immemorial Nan-Matal and Matal-Nim, to say nothing of the *aku-aku* monoliths on Easter Island. Surprising that the Kester Library has never gotten around to publishing an edition of the *Scripture*: the scientific find of the century, if only the blind, stubborn fools dared to set aside their preconceptions and prejudices long enough to face the facts squarely. (Shall certainly dedicate my eventual book on the Zanthu find to that gallant and pioneering ship's master, Captain Abner Exekiel Hoag, who found the book on Ponape during his voyage to the South Seas circa 1734, and brought the document home with him to Arkham, Mass., where his half-breed Polynesian-Asiatic bodyservant translated the Naacal for him ... come to think of it, perhaps it would be better to dedicate the book to the memory of Imash-Mo, High Priest of Ghatanothoa on Mu itself, and to his continuators, who recorded the prehistoric myth-cycle in the first place. Without them, there would have been no *Ponape Scripture* for Capt. Hoag to discover.) ... Bad night, more nightmares of howling

shapes lurking atop snowy summits crowned with weird architectural remains that looked weathered as if by *millions* of years ... aftermath of my bout of fever, no doubt, and after all, what harm can come from mere dreams?

Sept. 24.
Managed only twelve miles today. Reserves of water getting very low—damn whoever it was that slashed the goatskin waterbags during night of the 18th! Thought it was some sort of animal, from the way the bags were mangled, cut to ribbons as if some beast had *chewed* them with his fangs. But now I'm not so sure. May have been those lazy, superstitious fools, my native bearers. Surly, troublesome louts! Thought I would turn back to Sangup-Koy if they destroyed supplies of water. Fortunately, there is the snow, although Champo-Yaa seems oddly reluctant to drink it ... bearers growing more restive and unruly every day—gave me surly looks today, and overheard them muttering amongst themselves of *peling* (bad word—something like "foreigner-devil") when I tried to urge them forward. But I will not turn back; I walk in the steps of brave and stalwart gentlemen—Steelbraith, Talman, McWilliams, Henley, Holmes. Only poor Richardson and the unfortunate Clark Ulman have gone as far as I into this forbidden Tsang Plateau region; I shall yet outdo them all, or die in the attempt. Remnants of fever lingering in my system, or lack of purified water beginning to take its toll, I fear. Disturbing dreams again, and curious hallucinatory waking visions during the day: like stone outcroppings along summits which begin to take on the appearance of *unthinkably vast, inhumanly angled, cyclopean masonry*. Probably due to the combined effects of eye strain (wind bitterly cold and horribly dry), dehydration, cumulative fatigue, etc. Perhaps even mirage effects. But the natives see something too along the ridge-line—began whimpering and mumbling among themselves—something about "Old Ones" or "Primal Ones." May have a showdown soon; either that or wholesale desertions. Sleeping with revolver under my pillow tonight.

Pray God—no more of those horrible dreams.

Sept. 28 or 29.
Five more bearers deserted during night. Stupid beggars tried to make it appear they had been *bodily dragged away*—obviously in attempt to frighten their fellows into taking similar flight. Well, seems to have worked, or at any rate the remainder *pretend* to be dreadfully afraid of—something. I am not fooled easily, however, and had another little "talk" with Champo-Yaa. (Still and all, if they were faking the signs, how the devil did they manage to carve those hideously suggestive claw-like marks in the flint-hard rock? Clever swine, these Asian native hill tribes! But they are mad if they believe they can scare me into turning back; nothing will do that, I will go forward even if I must continue the journey alone.)

Hallucinations, or mirage effects, growing more frequent along the ridge. Distinct suggestions of tremendous fortifications on the peaks—huge crenelated walls and squat, thick turrets, but of such incredibly vast proportions as to hint they are the work of giants, not of men. Odd architectural style, too: nothing Chinese or even Tibetan about them. Curiously suggestive of the cyclopean masonry on Ponape and of certain horribly old ruins in Peru. Also oddly reminiscent of certain things mentioned in that abominable *Necronomicon* I foolishly read in Cambridge back in my student days. Vile book, gave me bad dreams for weeks!

... Bearers whispering of *dugpas* (tomb-guarding ghoul-like things) again, and, along toward sunset, one of the men squealed and dropped his load, swearing he had glimpsed something up above amid the "ruins"— thought I caught a glimpse of something moving myself, but it must have been that cursed eye strain. Whoever heard of an animal part lizard, part crustacean, bigger than a grizzly, and—*winged*? Just another illusion brought on by fatigue, nervous strain, weakened eyes, and the fever—but all the bearers began grunting fearfully something that sounded like *"Mi-go! Mi-go!"* and would not stir from their tracks one step until I showed them the revolver. ...

Must remember to keep up this journal; have been forgetful recently. Not even certain which day it is, not that it matters much.

About Oct. 1
... This land is more ancient than I could have dreamed; wind has scoured sand and desiccated soil away to lay bare the hill slopes, revealing strata of amazing antiquity—Cambrian, certainly, if not indeed *pre*-Cambrian— incredible to realize that this region of central Asia has been above the waves for five hundred million years, perhaps as much as a *thousand* million ... surely it must be one of the oldest continually exposed portions of land area on Earth. ... Suffering terribly from cold and the haunting stillness, also thirst. Snow tastes "bad" again, as if contaminated with some foulness. ... down to five bearers only by now, since Champo-Yaa deserted, or disappeared, or was carried off ... no water at all for eleven days now ... drinking the blood of the camels ... wind like a whetted knife, and more *howling* in the hills ... but no single sign of life for a hundred miles and more, as if all of this immense region has been sterile since Time began. ...

—That unknown range of mountains closer now, looming monstrously huge, virtually Himalayan ... weird vistas of bare, black, jagged, fang-like peaks marching across supernal sunset skies to the north; sky an amazing sight, a blazing panorama of sulfurous and flame-lit vapors ... somehow, the colossal vista of snow-laden, black peaks and under-lit cloud effects horribly suggestive of a growing and gathering menace, as if with each day I struggle on I draw closer to some stupendous ancient secret those nameless and uncharted ranges have been guarding like a colossal wall for hundreds of thousands of aeons ... oddest of all is the peculiar and haunting sensation of *remembering* ... doubtless after-effects of that lingering fever and this omnipresent thirst, but—*I could swear that I have seen this region before, either in a previous life, or within old, half-forgotten dreams.*

About Oct. 3rd or 4th.
Horrible day—hunger, gnawing cold—thirst a continual torment—snow deposits still polluted and undrinkable—perhaps the uncanny sterility of this region, its total lack of living things, of even the most rudimentary forms of life, due to some inexplicable *contamination?*—one step after another, boots crunching through dry crystalline sand—Richardson never got this far, turned aside in the hills, searching for some strange, sealed, forbidden cave which was supposedly guarded by degenerate worshipers of that abominable Chaugnar idol ... tortured him to death, I believe, poor, brave man!—remember now that Ulman brought back a horrible stone Thing from this region—something so chillingly *suggestive*, so nauseatingly *obscene*, that I believe the Manhattan Museum of Fine Arts people never dared put it on public exhibition. ...

This must be the most horribly ancient land on Earth—ghastly place of horrid cold, utterly lifeless, dry, desiccated, no other desert region this bleak and barren, none known to me, anyway ... remember cryptic and frightful hints in the obscure Mu Sang prophecies ... shadowy whispers of age-old survivals from the blasphemous Elder World, hideous hybrids from the squirming ooze of primal swamps ... old gods and demons and darkling horrors that lurk and linger on in the dim, forgotten corners of this bleak legended region of unthinkable and terrifying antiquity. ...

Odd, how that chance reading of the *Ponape Scripture* years ago has changed my entire life—from the day I first unwisely peered into those curious, thick-fibered pages of palm-leaf parchment, bound between crumbling boards of wood hewn from what some experts unhesitatingly swear is an extinct species of prehistoric cycad or tree-fern, and then first studied the Hoag translation, I have been unable to think of anything else but to locate the tomb of the wizard-priest Zanthu, who fled from the destruction of antique Mu, bearing with him the Elder Lore. And to think that Zanthu himself passed this way, flying over this same harsh and desolate ice plateau of dead sand and frozen shadows! ... The quest has been like an obsession with me, as if to the fanaticism of the dedicated scientist was added the blind, unquestioning faith of the occultist or the mystic. ... Dreams very disturbing, and more howling in the hills to all sides, and from that enormous range of unmapped and nameless mountains that loom dead ahead. ...

A bit later.
Have lost much weight and depleted my strength from short rations and fatigue, but thank God thirst no longer a problem, now that we are into the high snows, queer chemical contamination no longer noticeable—it was old von Junzt that confirmed me on my path; his data on Mu, in the copy of the *Unaussprechlichen Kulten* they keep (for some reason) under lock and key at the Huntington, completely corroborates information in the *Ponape Scripture*. ...

Found myself thinking lately about certain obscure old books and their puzzling hints as to the fantastic antiquity of all this Tsang Plateau region of Asia—dim whispers of elder horrors that seeped down from the stars when the planet was young and molten, or terrible Visitants from beyond the universe itself, uninvited Things that wandered here through interdimensional "gates"—started to remember baffling remarks in that damnable *Necronomicon* I puzzled my way through so many years ago ... did not the Mad Arab himself, old Abdul Alhazred, whisper suggestively that remote and mythic Leng was thought by some to be located somewhere in this dark corner of forbidden Asia? Horrible, prehuman Leng, guarded by the Tcho-Tcho people, and the shantaks, and the Abom. Mi-Go who haunt the hills? ... Terrible, fragmentary legends of weird, inhuman shapes shambling amid the unbroken snow of polar summits, threshing tentacles in the moonlight, shrill ululations that come from no human or bestial throat—gliding pillars of quaking protoplasmic jelly, somehow strayed from other worlds and far dimensions—what is that awful passage from the nightmarish pages of the *Necronomicon* about "portals to Beyond, and Things from Outside that sometimes stray through the shadowy Gates to stalk through earthly snows" ... antique Leng is coterminous both with obscure regions of High Asia and with other worlds and spheres and planes of existence ... *why do I seem to recognize all this landscape, as if I had seen it before, long ago, as though from another, earlier life?*

God! I am mad or going mad ... cannot endure for much longer these torments of the mind, body and soul ... near the limits of my strength and sanity ... last three bearers half-insane themselves with superstitious fear by now; have to drive them on before me all day at gun-point. ...

Much later.
Horrible blind battle in snow—bearers dead or run off—middle of the night, frightful shrill ululation from the frigid darkness, terribly close; snatched up gun and flashlight and plunged out into the moonlight to glimpse bearers battling hulking crustacean-lizard monsters, horribly huge—*they had no faces, but somehow they saw me*—had already torn one poor native (poor devil!) limb from limb, the hot blood glistening black on fresh snow in the gray moonlight—came stalking toward me, dreadfully real in the dim light, paying no attention to the gun in my hand ... but most curi-

ous and frightening of all, when the flashlight momentarily revealed *my face*, the monsters whipped about—waddled away, and all the while squealing as in mindless panic—but why should such brutes be afraid of *me*?

2 days later.
Into the nameless mountains at last, trudging forward alone, dragging my supplies and records behind me on improvised sledge. ... Two more encounters with the winged lizard-things since that first, shocking scene; each time, they fled blundering and squealing from the very sight of me (perhaps I am the first white man they have ever seen?)—Shot one of them, but didn't succeed in killing it. God forgive me, *I had to drink its slimy, nauseous, stinking blood*, no snow at this height ... hallucinations virtually continuous now, night and day, almost at the end of my strength—queer architectural effects along the skyline clearly visible, though I am half-blind from cold and dryness of the air, so only blurred glimpses of geometrical stone cube sections clinging to the heights above me, worn and weathered as if hundreds or thousands of millions of years had gone by since unthinkable hands first reared them. ... Down into the gullies and ravines amid the foothills now. ... Stone outcroppings unbelievable, *Azoic, I swear it!* Most horrible ancient piece of continuously exposed land surface on this planet ...

If genuine ruins, works of sentience, then these terraced cyclopean walls and fortifications that seem to throng about the fang-sharp, frightful peaks are, must be, the oldest worked stone artifacts known to science ... older by innumerable ages than dark Lhasa or the labyrinthine ruined cities on Ponape ... surely, survivals of immemorial Mu *or of something older even than Mu*—titanic glyphs, or suggestions of glyphs, along the stretch of the terraced battlements, uncannily suggestive of the uncouth R'lyehian characters found in Alhazred and von Junzt. ... I am going on somehow; God help me, there is no going back now. ...

Later.
... Must be very near the location of the Zanthu tomb by this time—curse the black day I ever dared peer within the shockingly suggestive pages of the *Ponape Scripture* they keep hidden away in the archives of the Kester Library, and found the clue that put me on the track of the wizard's tomb and the trove of inscribed tablets supposedly buried with him, rumored to contain frightful lore from the Elder Records. ... If any eye but mine should ever peruse these scribbled pages, listen to me: *some things we were not meant to discover.* ...

Later (same day).
Have been thinking about those grim, unholy revelations hinted at in Alhazred: I tell you, the old Arab *knew*, damn him! ... Trudging on through this black realm of icy shadow and whistling wind and horribly ancient rock ... there are incredible survivals that would blast the mind of men, if con-

fronted face to face, and grisly cults linger in these forgotten regions, whereof the grim Chaugnar-worshipers poor Richardson found are the *least frightful* (doesn't Alhazred himself whisper of a corpse-eating cult somewhere in Leng?) ... flaming skies, and Something hidden away behind a wall of black mountains that march across the north like the ramparts of some fantastic, sky-tall barrier built by the Elder Gods to hide and hold prisoned an unthinkable terror ... what gigantic secret have these frozen hills kept hidden for five hundred million years? The shadowy aura of some tremendous revelation of mind-withering magnitude haunts my feverish and disordered brain—*some horrible and unguessed-at Truth which men were never meant to know*. ...

—Food gone; crawling forward on hands and knees now; I can suck moisture from the unpolluted snow, thank God, but nothing to eat ... chewing on the leather straps of the sledge ... if only I could shoot another of those crustacean-things, but the faceless, squealing monstrosities avoid coming near, although they linger on the fortified heights ... I would do more this time than merely drink its filthy blood.

Much later.
I have found the necropolis in a narrow, mountain-walled valley. It is older than the foundation stones of Ur, or the eldermost of the pyramids. Atlantis was not uprisen from the steaming seas when these low, crude, flat-roofed stone tombs were built ... no living thing can have been here for unguessed millennia, but I do not like those nine-clawed pawprints in the age-old snows ... deep-cut, enormous glyphs above the sunken doorway to each tomb in Naacal, Tsath-yo, and R'lyehian; if the wizard lies in this buryingground, I will find him. ... What do you suppose it was that he did, that made the *Ponape Scripture* curse his name so dreadfully? What unthinkable cosmic blasphemy did he perpetrate, that made Them come down from Glyu-Vho, to drown all of primordial Mu beneath the boiling waves? ... (*Later.*) I have found the tomb, his name deeply but hastily scratched in the old weathered stone above the crumbling lintel—*Iä! Cthulhu!* Give me the strength to somehow force the stone slab of the door .... I have crawled inside; nothing but blackness and stale, vitiated air ... can hear nothing, not even the wind nor that accursed and constant howling from the heights ... the sepulcher itself is rectangular and very heavy, with a stone lid that seems to weigh a ton. ... I do not care for the inscription cut around the edges of the lid, and avert my eyes hastily from the Name writ there in warning. ... Ah! the lid is off at last. ... I must pause to rest, must conserve my strength ... very weak; heart laboring ... now, shine the flashlight within—*there*! Ten black jade tablets, narrowly incised with row upon row of tiny characters that resemble hieratic Naacal ... skeletal hands clutch them to the bony rib cage of the mummified thing .... I must shine the light around to see if Zanthu bore to his grave other artifacts or talismans of interest to science—

Oh, God. God. Why did it all seem so horribly *familiar* to me? I should never have tried to come this far ... "some things we were not meant to discover!" Almost, I could laugh at my own words, now. ... The wind outside is horribly cold, the howling shrill in my ears ... clutch the stone tablets to my breast, icy chill against the flesh under my furs ... out into the hills again, to the desolate sands of the plateau beyond. ... I will die here in the lonely places of Tsang, I think, but not in that shunned valley of prehistoric tombs, not *there!* ... God, let me shut it out of my mind ... let me forget the unforgettable ... *THAT FACE!* ... that awful moment of shattering revelation ... the light of my torch shining upward, past withered bony thorax a-dangle with leathery shreds of dried and ancient flesh ... that skull, whereon the flesh had dried, but the features were still recognizable ... how my horrified shrieks rang and rang and died in shuddering echoes in that closed stone room ... I am quite mad ... my brain throbs and *burns* ... slogging on, the dead crystals of sand whispering about my heavy boots ... but who could blame me? How could I have known? ... "some things we were not meant to discover" ... O, God, the mummy's face ... O, God, O, God, O, God, I should have guessed. *For the face was my own.*

HERE is another translation from the shocking *Zanthu Tablets*, one of Lin's own contributions to the Mythos. They seem intended as a Muvian counterpart to Lovecraft's Lomarian *Pnakotic Manuscripts* and Richard F. Searight's *Eltdown Shards*. In the early notes for these stories, Lin had envisioned two tales, "The Tablets from the Tomb" and "The Thing in the Pit." The first would have read much like the present version of "The Thing in the Pit", save that it would have ended with Zanthu fleeing the destruction he had unwittingly unleashed, hoping to make it to Leng or Shamballah. The single premise of the story, the priestling's attempt to vindicate his patron deity against the tyrannical cult of Ghatanothoa, is lifted bodily from Lovecraft's "Out of the Aeons", specifically the subnarrative of the doomed attempt of T'yog to invade the sanctuary of Ghatanothoa.

In the original planned version of the second story, "The Thing in the Pit" (just a note, not an extant draft), the action jumps ahead into the modern world. Here is the note: "Submarine volcanic activity temporarily heaves above the waves a portion of a drowned prehistoric continent off Ponape. Dr. Henry Stephenson Blaine, then at Ponape with the Sanbourne Institute Research Vessel *Evans*, is the first to reach the island. Finds mighty chasm, etc. Sailors retreat, firing at monstrous paw which reaches up from the Chasm (it can only be the Abyss of G'than-yu, mentioned in the shuddersome documents of fabulous antiquity)."

This protostory is about three fourths "The Madness from the Sea" (third part of "The Call of Cthulhu") and one fourth "Under the Pyramids" (published as "Imprisoned with the Pharaohs"). Carter finally decided to dump the "Call of Cthulhu" elements, but this left him little story. So he salvaged the bit about the paw and tacked it onto Zanthu's own account.

One observation on a minor feature occurring in both "The Thing in the Pit" and "The Red Offering": Zanthu makes sure to introduce himself by name, "I, Zanthu." (Alhazred does likewise in Lin's *Episodes from the* Necronomicon). Why should the author identify himself twice in the same work? A genuine ancient author would not, which is why so many ancient writings are anonymous, as well as why many more are instead pseudonymous. On the one hand, even if there were a reason for such "station identification" once, there wouldn't be twice in the same work. The reason both "The Red Offering" and "The Thing in the Pit" have Zanthu refer to himself in the first person is that they are, obviously, two separate stories pretending to be excerpts from a single work. Each must identify itself as the work of Zanthu. Actually, Lin could have been satisfied with tagging each tale as Zanthu's in the fictive editor's notes he supplied to each story. The interior self-reference becomes redundant. It is nonetheless revealing. The reason for such a reference, whether once or twice, is that the narrator (as distinct from the author) is by nature a part of the story, himself a character in it (or at least on its margins, as a friend of a protagonist, for example), whereas the author exists outside the narrative universe of the story. Thus the author must use the very voice of the narrator in order to name the narrator for the reader's benefit. What this means is that an "I, Zanthu" or "I, Claudius" sort of reference is an immediate dead giveaway as to the fictive character of what you are reading.

So what? Is there anyone that imagines he is reading a factual narrative when he peruses "The Thing in the Pit?" (Lin did once tell me he received an earnest letter from a fan asking where the transporter beam to Callisto could be found in the Cambodian jungle. The poor fool was apparently planning to go there and give it a try.) The thing is, once you can establish the self-reference as a mark of fiction by studying its occurrence in a piece of admitted fiction, you are forewarned what to conclude when you start running across it in covert fictions, including ancient pseudepigraphs (epistles, narratives, revelations) using the name of a renowned authority of the past as a pseudonym so as to gain a hearing for one's own work. Sometimes the use of the name was pure forgery, other times more of a dedication to the memory of the great man. When we read in the Infancy Gospel of Thomas, "I, Thomas the Israelite, tell unto you, even all the brethren that are of the Gentiles, to make known unto you the works of the childhood of our Lord Jesus Christ and his mighty deeds," or in the Book of the Resurrection of Christ, "Believe me, my brethren the holy apostles, I, Bartholomew, beheld the Son of God on the chariot of the Cherubim," we are reading the words of someone "protesting too much", someone making a claim, an assertion of authorship, something an author writing under his own name feels no need to do. When we read a text in which the writer is implicitly defensive about his identity, we know we are reading a fictive claim. The author's is that guilty conscience that needs no accusation. He has anticipated it and thus given the game away. The Bible contains several such spurious claims to authorship: "When I, Daniel, had seen the vision" (Daniel 8:15); "I, John, your brother, who share with you the tribulation and the kingdom" (Revelation 1:9); "I, Jesus, have sent my angel to you with this testimony" (ibid, 22:16); "I, Paul, myself entreat you" (2 Corinthians 10:1).

This revealing little detail strikingly confirms a much-debated observation made by Käte Hamburger (yeah, that's her name) in her marvelous book *The Logic of Literature*. She enumerates several defining marks of fictional narrative, separating it from autobiographical narrative on the one hand and historical reporting on the other. One is a certain distancing device called "the epic preterite", the use of the past tense for recounting up-to-the-minute action, with genuine past references retreating to the pluperfect tense: "Conan swung the broadsword he had taken from Zarono" really means "Conan now swings the broadsword he took from Zarono." Another is the presence of verbs of situation, describing the specifics of a scene in a way the historian could never know (which is why Captain Picard scoffs at the phony time-traveling historian from the future, who remarks that the exact position of Picard's command chair would be a matter of scholarly debate).

In short, the story is told not from the perspective of the narrator but rather from that of the narrated character. When the narrator is not supposed to be that character, when the narrative is third person, the fictive nature of the whole is evident. But what about overtly fictive first-person narration? Hamburger claims that such narrative is in a sense not fiction at all, since it really employs the technique of autobiography. This is why occasionally we are not sure whether a first-person narrative is fictive, factual, or some mixture of both. "Marcel", the narrator of *In Search of Lost Time* (*Remembrance of Things Past*) sometimes seems to be the same as Marcel Proust the author, sometimes not. Is Robert E. Howard's *Post Oaks and Sand Roughs* an autobiographical novel, or a fictive novel using some autobiographical material here and there, in the manner of Lovecraft's *The Case of Charles Dexter Ward*?

Hamburger has taken considerable heat for this claim, which seems *prima facie* absurd ("What do you mean it's not fiction?!"), but she has merely expressed it in a peculiar way. It might be better to say that first-person fictive narration is the exception that proves the rule she has enunciated concerning the mode of fictive narration. Another way of saying it is to see fictive first-person narrative as a kind of pseudepigraphy, fiction posing as genuine first-person writing, or at least adopting the fiction of providing someone else's first-person account. So we end where we began, since Lin Carter's uses of the false self-reference device occur precisely in "ancient" pseudepigrapha, stories purporting to be excerpts from an ancient text. The formal pretense is the same, though the intent is not; in the case of overt fictions we are able to tell there is no desire to deceive. Joseph Smith no doubt did mean his readers to understand the *Book of Mormon* to be a genuine ancient document. Ditto for Madame Blavatsky and the *Stanzas of Dzyan*. Obviously not with Lin Carter's *Zanthu Tablets*, a counterpart to Smith's golden tablets of Mormon and Moroni, or Lin's *Ponape Scripture*, a clear analog to Blavatsky's own palm-papyrus codex.

"The Thing in the Pit" first appeared in Lin Carter's collection *Lost Worlds* (DAW Books, 1980).

The Thing in the Pit

by Lin Carter

THE mythological narrative which follows is taken from the disturbing and debatable translation made by Professor Copeland three years after his return from central Asia. His brochure, *The* Zanthu Tablets: *A Conjectural Translation* (1916), was published at his own expense after being rejected by the academic firms which had printed his earlier, more scholarly works. Widely condemned as unsubstantiated "ravings" by his scientific colleagues, the brochure was swiftly suppressed by the authorities. The present editors make no claims for the validity of Copeland's "translation." It must be remembered that the professor returned from Asia, his health, both mental and physical, broken by the terrible privations he endured in 1913, and that he died raving in an asylum only ten years after seeing his "translation" through press. His final manuscript, *The Civilization of Mu: A Reconstruction in Light of Recent Discoveries, with a Synoptic Comparison of the* R'lyeh Text *and the* Ponape Scripture (circa 1917-1926), remains to this day unpublished—and unpublishable.

We have prefaced this extract from the *Zanthu Tablets* with a note from Copeland's own introduction.

From the Preface to the Translation
"Upon prolonged study I became firmly convinced that my initial impressions were thoroughly accurate, and that the *Tablets* were indeed inscribed in an elder hieratic variant of the primal Naacal language. It is regretful that, with the death of poor, much-maligned Churchward, the last man who could have possibly attempted a decent translation of so obscure a variant was lost to the scientific community. Hoping that a chance existed that the Colonel had left a key or some manner of Naacal glossary among his papers, I hastened to contact his estate and, with time and great cooperation which I am pleased to acknowledge here, a clue to the inscriptions was indeed unearthed in his files.

"What follows, however, is correctly termed a 'conjectural' translation, and to this qualification I should perhaps add 'fragmentary' as well: for although the inscriptions are complete, my respect for the public sanity is such that I would not care to subject wholesome, healthy minds to the full depravity, the hideous blasphemies, set down by the hand of the long-dead, accursed wizard-priest of the Abomination Ythogtha, whose tomb I opened, perhaps unwisely, in 1913.

"Let it be said now and in this place, once and for all, that the matter which I have named 'the Xothic legend-cycle'—which is to say, the myth-sequence of the Xothic Triad (Ghatanothoa, Ythogtha, and Zoth-Ommog)—has at its secret core a chaotic and cosmic blasphemy so appalling in its ultimate depravity and in the magnitude of its bearings upon human and prehuman evolution as to stun even the detached and dispassionate scholar."

FROM THE ZANTHU TABLETS
Tablet IX, Side 2, Lines 30 through 174

I.

THE innumerable iniquities of Yaa-Thobboth, hierophant of Ghatanothoa, the Monster on the Mount, I, Zanthu, wizard and last surviving priest of Ythogtha, the Abomination in the Abyss, have endured for long with uncomplaining and stoical fortitude. But this last, supreme, and ultimate affront I could not let pass in silence, nor could I forebear from the action I will describe.

For uncountable millennia, the fortunes of my cult had languished and waned, even as, during the same intervals of time, the rise to affluence and popularity of the rival cults which celebrate the vile Monstrosity that dwelleth ever atop the mysterious and untrodden heights of Yaddith-Gho had enjoyed an unbroken succession of triumphs. It was now many millennia since that legended Year of the Red Moon[1], when the rash and impudent T'yog, high priest of the Old Ones, and votary of Shub-Niggurath the Mighty Mother, sought with ultimate futility to whelm and break asunder for all time to come the power of Ghatanothoa, in which vain and perilous attempt the unfortunate T'yog came to so unthinkable and shuddersome an end that even that dread chronicle, the *Ghorl Nigraal*, did not dare whisper a single hint or slightest rumor of his fate.

It can easily be seen that the disastrous failure of the gallant, if incautious, T'yog was sufficient to overawe any other from making a similar attempt in all the ages since the Year of the Red Moon to my own epoch, for during the cycles which have lapsed from the era of T'yog to this day, none other has tried. And the rise to power and unquestioned authority of the cult of Ghatanothoa has been loathsomely smooth and rapid.

That this was, in very large part, the doing of Imash-Mo can easily be demonstrated. For upon the horrible demise of the unfortunate T'yog, gloatfully and hastily seizing upon the moment, the infamous Imash-Mo, who was high priest of Ghatanothoa in his day, proclaimed to all the Nine Kingdoms that his loathsome and noxious divinity was thus proven supreme over all the thousand gods of primordial and everlasting Mu. And, alas, Imash-Mo had long since gained ascendancy over the weak and easily swayed Thabou, king of the province of K'naa, wherein rose the demon-possessed mountain of Yaddith-Gho; and King Thabou hastened to ratify the supremacy of Ghatanothoa even over the might of Cthulhu, the Lord of R'lyeh, himself.

Lustrum by lustrum, cycle by cycle, the wealth, power, and following of the cult of Ythogtha declined thereafter, even as did all of the other of the thousand cults of primal Mu. In vain did my priestly predecessors warn that the vengeance of the affronted gods would someday smite the Nine Kingdoms of Mu, and mayhap trample all of the mighty continent beneath the green and seething waves of Ocean, as ancient prophecies reiterated was to be our eventual and transcendent Doom. But naught could avert or even retard the remorseless decline of the worship of Ythogtha.

II.

WHEN I, in my turn, assumed the scarlet pontificals and the brazen rod of my office, in the Year of the Whispering Shadow[2], I swore by the Gray Ritual of Khif, by the Vooric Sign, by the Weedy Monolith, and by the might and glory of potent and terrible Ythogtha, that my god should achieve His triumph and His revenge during my pontificate.

Alas, I had reckoned without the cunning and the ambition of Yaa-Thobboth! For no sooner had the brazen rod been set into my grasp and the *Thirty-one Secret Rituals of Yhe* been given over to my keeping, than the villainous high priest of Ghatanothoa let pass the ultimate and unforgivable affront against the dignity of my office and the splendor of my god.

For this Yaa-Thobboth had at length prevailed upon the palsied and enfeebled Shommog, monarch over K'naa, and a writ was proclaimed which set under ban and interdict any other form of worship of the Great Old Ones than that approved by the followers of Ghatanothoa. The copper gates of the temple of Shub-Niggurath were sealed; the greenly lit adyta of Cthulhu were deserted; and, temple by temple, across the breadth of the Nine Kingdoms, the supreme power of Ghatanothoa the Monster on the Mount was proclaimed.

Now King Shommog was regnant over the province of K'naa while I and my few acolytes dwelt in the land of G'thuu to the north, beyond the River of Worms and the Carven Basalt Cliffs and the Catacombs of Thul. But great had the authority of K'naa grown in the eleven thousand years since the reign of King Thabou and the hierophancy of Imash-Mo, and in these moon-dim, latter days, the power of my land of G'thuu was shrunken and seldom did mine own monarch, the degenerate Nuggog-ying, dare oppose the will or whim of the King of K'naa. Thus it seemed inevitable that the last vestige of reverence for the Abomination in the Abyss should gutter and die, and in the very pontificate of one who had sworn by dread and terrible oaths to restore Him to the heights of His former and tremendous might.

III.

IN despair, I withdrew to the crumbling ruins of my palace which stood of old upon the very brink of that profound and shadowy chasm, the Abyss of Yhe, wherein the victorious Elder Gods had hurled the great Ythogtha and had sealed Him therein forever under the potency of the Elder Sign and wherein to this day unbreakable bonds of psychic force imprison Him, even as foul Ghatanothoa is pent and imprisoned in that immemorial and cyclopean citadel atop Mount Yaddith-Gho, and Great Cthulhu slumbers in his Sunken City on the ocean-whelmed and aeon-lost Black Island, and terrible Zoth-Ommog lies chained amid the Deep beyond the Isle of the Sacred Stone Cities.[3]

Even in the uttermost nadir of my despair, it were unwise for me to neglect the awful duties of my sacerdotal office and thus I turned from a dreary contemplation of this most dire of all the thousand iniquities of the infamous Yaa-Thobboth to that scrutiny and study of the *Thirty-one Rituals* demanded of my office. This precious document, of which the Earth affords no single other copy[4], and which dates from the most extreme and legended antiquity, was indited by the very hand of Niggoum-Zhog, the First Prophet, himself, in the dim aeons before the Old Ones had yet dreamt of creating man. The Secret Rituals themselves were inscribed in fiery and metallic inks upon leaves of parchment fashioned from *pthagon* membrane, and bound between twin and carven and gem-studded plates of unthinkably rare and precious *lagh* metal brought hither from dark Yuggoth where it rolls upon the Rim in the most remote of terrestrial aeons by the shadowy Elder Ones. My seething brain a roiling chaos of incoherent images, I perused one by one the Thirty-one Secret Rituals of Yhe, and in the last, most potent and terrific of them all, I found the answer to my dilemma.

For that Thirty-first Ritual contained the dread and portentous formula which is called "The Key That Openeth the Door to Yhe", and which the primal and elder Prophet warns is not to be spoken aloud save in the final extremity of ultimate Doom.

Therein, in my madness and desperation, I found the answer for which I sought—*aii, n'ghaa xuthoggon R'lyeh! Iä Ythogtha!* A million generations yet unborn shall curse my name!

IV.

AND thus was I resolved to open the Door to Yhe, by which term is meant to render null the strictures of the Elder Sign and to release the Primal One, the Abomination in the Abyss, from the chains of psychic force which have imprisoned Him in the depths of the great Chasm for innumerable aeons.

To set free Ythogtha from His Abyss would be at a single stroke to render Him the most awesomely powerful of all the thousand gods of antique Mu, and to thus elevate myself, as His hierophant and prophet, as the supreme and most potent priest in all of the Nine Kingdoms.

The ambitions of Yaa-Thobboth would thus be ground into the dust before my feet; the too easily dominated King Shommog would in a breath be divested of all authority, to the elevation of mine own monarch, Nuggog-ying; the wealth and might of the province of K'naa would drain away like shallow mud before the sucking tides, and my own realm of G'thuu would achieve ultimate prominence over the kingdoms of Mu. What man dares condemn me, if, in the last extremity of my need, I dared set my hand against the tremendous decree of the Elder Gods themselves!

Thus I went down the Hidden Stair to the ultimate and most secret crypt, burrowed deep into the bowels of the planet beneath the age-crumbling foundations of my palace, and there I caused my mute Rmoahal slaves to open the ponderous trapdoor, one single massy slab of hewn and polished onyx, revealing a black depth from which blew ever a chill and noxious wind.

And, steeling my soul, I called upon the power of the Xothic Key, and summoned slithering from his black and noisome burrows the Father of Worms himself, even undying and putrescent Ubb, leader and progenitor of the dreaded Yuggya—the loathly and prehuman servitors of my god, who squirm and slither in the slime about His feet.

Like a great, glistening mass of putrid whitish jelly was Father Ubb, and his squat and quivering trunk supported naught but a swollen and rounded head wherein drooled and quivered ever a pink-rimmed, obscene orifice lined with triple rows of adamantine fangs. Now the Yuggya serve my lord Ythogtha and His Brother, Zoth-Ommog, even as the Deep Ones serve Cthulhu and the Tcho-Tchos their lords, Zhar and Lloigor; and as the Flame-Creatures strive ever to free Cthugha and the Serpentmen of Valusia sought to unchain their lord, Yig, so do the Yuggya tirelessly gnaw at the bonds that hold Ythogtha and Zoth-Ommog.

Emerging at length pale and shaken from my converse with Father Ubb, whose unholy vileness and stench is even that of Abhoth Itself, I gained the upper air with relief. But I had won the aid of the Burrowers Beneath to my great endeavor, and together we swore to open the Door to Yhe, though we incur the wrath of the Elder Gods upon remote and rubescent Glyu-Vho![5]

I chose the Day of the Writhing of the Aurora as most efficacious for my terrific endeavor; and thence to the brink of the mighty Abyss of Yhe went I forth, with my few frightened acolytes in my train, and in the Hour of the Singing of the Green Vapor I stood upon the cliffs overlooking the profound and gloom-veiled depths of the chasm and made the Scarlet Sacrifice while behind me arose the wailing chorus of my acolytes in the uncouth and alien rhythms of the Yuggya Chants.

I performed the Red Ablution; I brandished the Xothic Key; I traced upon the trembling air in characters of living and supernal fire the Hieroglyphs of Yrr; I performed the Quaar Exorcism; I called upon the Dholes in aeon-forgotten Aklo; I employed the lore of the Forbidden Litany; I summoned the Xlath Entities from beyond the extraspatial region of Asymmetrical Etheric Polarity.

I adored the Black Flame in a manner which makes my soul shrink and shudder within me to this hour; I called upon all of the gods of archaic Mu—upon the Great Ones (saving only the noxious and tyrannical Ghatanothoa), and upon the Lesser Ones, upon Yig the Serpent-Father, and shadowy Nug, and Yeb of the Whispering Mists, upon Iod the Shining Hunter, and Vorvadoss of Bel-Yarnak, the Troubler of the Sands—and upon Him Who Is To Come, and upon Father Dagon and Mother Hydra, who rule the Deep Ones who are His servants in the green sea.

And I uttered in a great voice The Name Which Is Not Ever To Be Uttered Aloud ....

Above me the stars trembled and burned pale as waxen tapers in an icy and miasmic draught ... all save for the scarlet burning eye of Glyu-Vho, which blazed more brightly than before.

Beneath my heel, the Earth shook with tremors; and from the dimly lit west, where titanic mountains march the breadth of Mu, deep subterraneous thunders mumbled and cold black craters burst redly into flame, filling angry heaven with seething smoke.

My acolytes huddled before me, white faces hidden in shaking hands. And there was a great silence upon the Earth for seven breaths of time.

V.

AND then my heart leapt up within me for horrid and blasphemous joy, for Lo! I had released the first of the seven bonds that had, from the immemorial depths of forgotten time, held prisoner the Abomination in the Abyss.

And *He* lifted Himself above the brink of the vast chasm of Yhe and gazed down upon His arch-hierophant.

Very terrible was Ythogtha to the sight of men, and more huge than my mind could scarcely accept.

Like a black glistening moon He rose above the brink, a gigantic hemisphere of quaking slime, vaster than any mountain. Faceless and neckless was He, save that from His front a terrific beak thrust forth. Cruel and terrible and curved was this beak of blackest adamant, and it measured many thousands of paces in its length.

And then, half a league further along the brink of the chasm, a second hemispheric, black, glistening, beaked head rose into sight—and another!—and then yet a fourth mountainous and colossal beaked head rose above the lip of the Abyss!

And then it was true terror smote me to the heart, for I saw and knew my lord in His awfulness ... and we trembling mortals were dwarfed by Him, like motes before the ponderous *yakith* lizard were we ... and, suddenly, horribly, I knew what I had done.

The acolyte huddled at my feet knew in the same instant, and squealed shockingly, and wallowed in squalid and gutless terror, wriggling from before the altar of the Abomination ... to flee, staggering and stumbling, white to the lips, with wide, mad, staring eyes that burned with pale fire like sick moons ... and I, too, quailed to the depths of my being, and turned on palsied and trembling limbs, hurling from me with sudden horror the loathsome volume of the Rituals, which fell into the Abyss from which ultimate and mind-blasting Nightmare had but part-way emerged ... and I ran—*ran*—while the Earth shook and great crevices opened to split the land asunder ... ran, while mountain after mountain erupted in flame and thunder, and the sea boiled madly, and a great terrible shaft of unearthly light burned down the star-gulfs from distant and blazing Glyu-Vho ... ran, even as down that terrific star-beam descended, from the remote star that flamed like a wrathful and revenging Eye athwart the smoke-veiled and volcano-shaken west, terrible great Things like terrific Towers of Flame ... which I knew to be either the Elder Gods or Their servants ... while sky-tall and burning Towers swept the Abyss with their lightnings—and I fled through the gates of Yu-Haddoth, where dwelleth my king, but which lay now in smoking ruin, shaken by the great tremors of the Earth—and I scourged the panic-stricken multitudes before me—*who knew not the true nature of the mon-*

strous and inconceivable Thing I had almost freed—drove them shrieking into the vidya vahans, the ancient sky chariots of elder and doom-fraught Mu ... while the ground shook and the towers fell and mountain after mountain erupted in thunderous flames ... and we fled through the storm-torn skies and across the wind-lashed waves ... fled all that unending night of flame and doom and chaos, while behind our sky-borne keels immemorial and terror-haunted Mu crumbled under the mighty waves that beat in from the angry sea, and broke apart, shaken to its unstable core by the convulsions of outraged nature, lashed by starry fires of the Elder Gods ... on we flew at length into a distant land near the Hidden Gates of elder Shamballah itself ... but mere distance can not erase from my terror-frozen brain the ultimate glimpse of nethermost Hell that shook my soul when I saw ... and knew ... that vast and beaked and mountainous Head of the Thing in the Pit ... *that awful and aeon-accursed Thing whose unthinkably prodigious FINGERTIPS I had seen* ....

Translator's Notes

1. Friedrich Wilhelm von Junzt, in his impressively researched *Unaussprechlichen Kulten* (XXI, 307), identifies this date as B.C. 173,148.

2. Evidence in the *Ponape Scripture* (particularly the astronomical data in Versicle 9759) suggests this date may be equivalent to roughly B.C. 161,844; vonJunzt does not include any reference to this period, as his commentary breaks off several millennia earlier.

3. The cryptic and horrible *Ponape Scripture* says that Ghatanothoa, Ythogtha, and Zoth-Ommog are "the Sons of the mighty Cthulhu, Lord of the Watery Abyss and dread and awful Potentate of drowned R'lyeh." While neither the *Scripture* nor any other text of elder lore known to me records the planet wherefrom Cthulhu descended to this world, the *Scripture* says of the origin of his three sons: "The Spawn of Cthulhu came down from remote and ultra-telluric Xoth, the dim green double sun that glitters like a daemonic eye in the blacknesses beyond Abbith, to whelm and reign over the steaming fens and bubbling slime-pits of the mist-veiled dawn aeons of this Earth, and it was in primordial and shadowy Mu that They were great." Von Junzt (XXI, 29-a) cannot identify Xoth save to say that it lies in the same star cluster as Zaoth, Abbith, and Ymar. The reference to the "Isle of the Sacred Stone Cities" and the Deep that lies off its shores, together with geographical data hinted at earlier in the *Zanthu Tablets*, enables me to identify tentatively the place whereat Zoth-Ommog the Dweller in the Deep lies imprisoned as a submarine chasm off Ponape.

4. The hierophant Zanthu is in error here, for the surviving fragments of the Susran myth cycle list a copy of "the *Yhe Rituals* from elder Mu" as among the necromantic tomes in the library of the great magician Malygris, according to the inventory recorded by the sorcerer Nygron, and an incredibly ancient copy of the *Rituals* was in the possession of the Saracen wizard Yakthoob, Alhazred's mentor, according to the Irem chapter of the *Necronomicon* (Narrative II). A copy, perhaps the same Yakthoobic redaction, is rumored to have been found in a sealed tomb in Egypt about 1903.

5. In an often-quoted passage of the *Necronomicon*, Alhazred identifies this name, which is primal Naacal, as that of the star known to the Arabic astronomers of his day as *Ibt al Janzah*, which is to say, Betelgeuse.

IN "The Dweller in the Tomb", we read the journal entries of Harold Hadley Copeland, thus seeing what he sees only shortly after he himself sees it. What we are seeing is an eerily ineluctable process whereby, even against impossible odds of hardship, Copeland is irresistibly drawn to a predetermined conclusion/destination. What is the nature of that fate? It is that his own soul's history must repeat itself. At the climax he recognizes that Zanthu is himself in an earlier incarnation, and that his mission was simply to replay his own actions from this earlier life. He says he "should have guessed it", because he was already very close to experiencing his moments of ominous anticipation as memories. By reading his journal we are reliving his story, which in turn was a reliving of his own story as Zanthu. This makes Carter's retitling significant in retrospect. Why is the adventure of Harold Hadley Copeland called by the name of Zanthu? Why isn't it named for the actual protagonist? It is—Copeland is Zanthu! ("So why'd you nix Carter's title change, Price?" Because I happen to like Mythos stories with corny, campy titles better than those with a single piece of mute glossolalia as a title. I've done the same thing with "Zoth-Ommog", as you'll note.)

"The Thing in the Pit" is presented as a rediscovered first-person memoir of horrific events of the remote past, making it a window on the past. "Out of the Ages", on the other hand, is another case of infinite regress. Here we are reading another journal, a dream diary by Henry Stephenson Blaine, so we are leeching off his perceptions. Through his dreams Blaine himself seems to be reliving ancient perceptions, visions, of the ocean-depth blasphemies that are slowly but surely making their insidious return through the whole story cycle. In the next installment, "The Horror in the Gallery" ("Zoth-Ommog"), we see yet more, but through still a different window. We read over narrator Hodgkins' shoulder as he reconstructs the outlines of the "Alhazredic demonology" from the pages of shunned texts, including the *Necronomicon*. Finally, in "The Winfield Heritance", we will join the narrator as he begins to relive the spiritual seduction that befell his late uncle once he takes possession of his ancestral home. Each rare and evil volume he discovers hidden away behind the library shelves and within the furniture of secret rooms brings him further down the perilous path to the past.

Lin had originally intended to spread the events of this story over two tales. The first would have been "The Papers of Stephenson Blaine", a collation of Mythos data derived from (= divided among) various sources, including Copeland's journals, ancient grimoires, etc., much of which probably wound up in "The Horror in the Gallery"/"Zoth-Ommog" instead. The second was "Out of the Ages", of which the notes say, "Abhorrent idol from the waters off Ponape, brought back in 1937 by Stephenson Blaine from his expedition to Yhe, causes strange dreams of weird landscapes and curious suggestions ... this too is from the Blaine papers." Here Blaine would have been a doublet of Copeland, rather than, as he turned out to be, the inheritor of the aftermath of Copeland's discoveries.

Let no one think that the obvious borrowing of the title "Out of the Ages" means Carter unimaginatively copied from Lovecraft's "Out of the Aeons." The similarity is so obvious that surely we are meant to mark it and to understand it as a salute to the flagship revision tale which has inspired the whole Xothic cycle. This tale first appeared in the Arkham House anthology *Nameless Places* in 1975.

Out of the Ages

by Lin Carter

THIS manuscript was found among the papers of Dr. H. Stephenson Blaine, then Curator of Manuscripts at the Sanbourne Institute, in 1928. It would seem to be pages from a journal or diary which Dr. Blaine had been keeping shortly prior to his unfortunate collapse. A note by Mr. Arthur Wilcox Hodgkins, Dr. Blaine's assistant, who later succeeded him to the Curatorship, suggests that the material seemed to have some bearing on the deterioration of his health in the months prior to his nervous breakdown. Mr. Hodgkins therefore passed the manuscript along to the physician in charge of Dr. Blaine's case, from whom this copy was obtained.

From the Papers of Stephenson Blaine

AS Curator of the Manuscripts Collection at the Sanbourne Institute of Pacific Antiquities in Santiago, California, it was my pleasure and duty to conduct a general inventory of the Copeland Bequest, which was awarded the Institute by the estate of the late Professor Harold Hadley Copeland in 1928, two years after his lamentable demise in a mental institution in San Francisco.

The bequest was long and eagerly anticipated by the members of the staff at Sanbourne, and, in particular, by myself. When it arrived at last, we discovered the bequest to consist of several large trunks of miscellaneous and unsorted papers (including at least one book-length unpublished manuscript), and a modest but highly selective collection of artifacts which the Professor had accumulated over the many years of his long, distinguished career.

Dismissing my assistants, I devoted the remainder of the day to cataloguing the contents of the trunks and boxes. I decided to examine the artifacts and antiquities first of all, as the Directors of the Institute were most anxious to place the more choice and interesting articles from the Copeland

Collection on public exhibition during the forthcoming 1928 season. With excitement and great anticipation, I began my work.

I opened the packing case containing the artifacts collection with mingled emotions. Beyond mere curiosity as to what I should find therein, my predominant feelings were those of regretful respect. The Professor had been twice my own age, and I had never known him on a personal level, but no scientist can work in any area of the prehistory, archeology, myth patterns, or folklore of the Pacific islanders for long without encountering the work of Harold Hadley Copeland. His is undoubtedly the most distinguished name in the young field of the study of Pacific antiquities, and such has been the case ever since the first publication of his monumental book, *Prehistory in the Pacific: A Preliminary Investigation with Reference to the Myth Patterns of Southeast Asia* (1902), a book which remains the classic of its field and which has proved a source of inspiration to at least two generations of scientists, including myself. And there is much that is admirable, even brilliant, in his *Polynesian Mythology, with a Note on the Cthulhu Legend Cycle* (1906), although, as I have written elsewhere, "it reflects his unfortunate and growing enthusiasm for questionable occult theories, which led to the regrettable erosion of his scholarly reputation and is perhaps indicative of the mental aberration which dominated his declining years", to which I added that it "remains to this day a massive work of scientific research."

From that high-water mark, however, the Professor rapidly declined. His unfortunate mania centered about a bygone Pacific civilization of extreme antiquity, of which the mysterious stone images on Easter Island and the megalithic ruined cities of Ponape are mere vestiges. From what little I then knew of his mania, it focused upon certain patterns of myth found commonly throughout Micronesia and most of the more populous Pacific islands, which concerned a numerous pantheon of gods or devils or evil spirits of extraterrestrial origin who came down to this world in remote ages and dominated the planet in the pre-Pleistocene.

In particular, he was interested in those deities who had their dominion over his beloved ancient Pacific. Native legends described them as completely non-human, unlike even the beasts, and as generally aquatic in nature. They had fought some sort of war with another group of cosmic gods from the stars, had been defeated, and, in some manner, thrown either into exile or into trance-like slumber, from which at some unknown future date they would awake, arise, and attempt the conquest of the earth again. A ludicrous myth, surely, although with a surprising sophistication to it; not at all the sort of thing one would expect from the imagination of primitive islanders.

With Professor Copeland's third major text, alas, it became obvious that his obsession had assumed the overwhelming proportions of a mania. Still, there is much that can be admired in that book, *The Prehistoric Pacific in the Light of the* Ponape Scripture (1911), and it is a monumental work of sheer scholarship. Two years following publication of this book, he led an expedition into the depths of Asia, and in 1916 he published, in a privately printed brochure, his "conjectural translation" of the ancient stone tablets he had found in the tomb of a prehistoric central Asian shaman. The shocking and blasphemous nature of his *Zanthu Tablets* led to official suppression; the Professor himself was asked to resign from the archaeological association of which he had been cofounder and past president. His decline from that point on was rapid.

Unpacking the artifacts, I found a typed list in a file folder, which described and attempted to date them. I reproduce it here.

1) *Tapa* cloth, Tonga Islands, *circa* 1897. Note 5-pointed star motif. (Eld. Sign?)
2) "Fisherman's god" image, Cook Islanders, about 1900. Native name: *Zatamaga* (? Zatamagwa—ref. #7)
3) Sepik River Valley figure, New Guinea, date unk. but after 1895. Note cone-shaped torso, suggestion of tentacles, mane-like hair.
4) Carven shell pendant, Papua. 1902? Octopoidal head.
5) Carven stone door-jamb or *talé*, New Caledonia, *circa* 1892. Note 5-pointed star motif *in conjunction* with serpent-maned head—native name "Hommogah"
6) Bushy-maned and bearded wooden mask, Ambrym origin, New Hebrides, date unk. Note suggestion of *tentacles*, not hair: "Medusa" motif observed in Carolines, New Guinea (Sepik R. area), also Marquesas.
7) Stone *tiki*, Marquesas, about 1904, but motif common in prev. generations, says Tillinghast. Note snaky hair, pyramidal body. Native name: *"Z'otomogo"* or *"Zatamagwa."*
8) Carven lintel, New Zealand, *very old* Maori (bef. 1800?). Cone or pyramid body, surmounted by wavy-maned head. Note "Medusa" motif, as in #6. Old shaman called it "Sothamogha."
9) Basalt image, Easter Island, undatable. *No* similarity to giant *aku aku* heads found on outer slopes of Rano-raraku; natives call it "god of ocean deeps" (Cthulhu? Zoth-Ommog?)
10) Frag. lavastone bas-relief, S. Indo-China, perhaps Khmer? Used as idol for degenerate native cult in Singapore, *circa* 1900-1905. Cult-name "Z'mog" attached to central fig.; note serpentine hair motif.
11) Devil-mask, Sepik Riv. area, N. Guinea. Non-human, octopoid head, pyramid or cone body, tentacular arms.

> Missionaries in area report fighting native cult for 30 years; Rev. H. Wallace says native god named "Zhmog-yaa."

As for the artifacts on this list, described in the notes, they were for the most part excellent examples of South or Central Pacific native workmanship. Design motifs, however, were quite unusual and suggested sources in Pacific myth and legend unfamiliar to me. There was nothing about the stone images and carvings, the wooden masks or woven cloth samples, that seemed particularly bizarre or frightening ... except that, taken together in this proximity, they suggested a surprising and even disconcerting similarity of theme and design, which became all the more enigmatic when you consider the enormous distances involved.

That is to say, there is nothing really uncanny about a lavastone basrelief fragment such as #10, which, if the Professor is correct in assigning Khmer origin, must come from the jungles of Cambodia; nor is there anything frightful or unnatural about the stone *tiki*, #7 on the Professor's list, which is clearly of Marquesan craftsmanship.

What *is* a trifle disturbing, however, is to examine them in the light of *distance* ... for there are more than *eight thousand miles of ocean* between the Marquesas and Cambodia ... and it seemed perplexing, if not virtually inconceivable, that two so widely separated cultures could have carved images of a snaky-maned divinity with names so amazingly similar as *Z'otomogo* and *Z'mog*.

* * *

As for the twelfth item on the inventory—that was much more surprising than all the rest put together. The Professor's notation read as follows:

> 12) Jade image, workmanship unidentified; disc. by native diver off Ponape, 1909. Note inscription on base (*not* Naacal— Tsath-yo or R'lyehian?). *Definitely represents Zoth-Ommog!*

This particular artifact arrested my attention almost immediately. Indeed, among the jumble of carved and painted wood and crudely cut stonework, it stood out dramatically. As the "Ponape figurine" has never been photographed or displayed, I shall describe it in some detail, for it is most remarkable.

In the first place, it is an extraordinary rarity to find worked jade articles of such size among native Pacific artworks—unless they be mere trade craft exports from China, such being commonly found. This particular image or idol was certainly not of Chinese workmanship ... indeed, both from style and technique, to say nothing of craftsmanship, it is completely unique.

Briefly, the figurine, including base, stands about nineteen inches tall and is of worked and polished jade of an unfamiliar type. I am no authority on Chinese jade carvings, but I have never seen this sort of jade before anywhere. It is greasy gray-white, flecked or mottled with irregular spots of deep dark green, and both extremely dense and heavy. The image itself is not only non-humanoid, but virtually non-objective—hauntingly suggestive of some of the weird carved figures of the little-known amateur sculptor Clark Ashton Smith—and in detail and finish, to say nothing of conception and sophistication, weirdly reminiscent of the brilliant if degenerate work produced by the famed San Francisco sculptor Cyprian Sincaul.

It represents a peculiar creature with a body shaped like a broad-based, truncated cone. A flat, blunt, wedge-shaped, vaguely reptilian head surmounts this conical torso, and the head is almost entirely hidden behind swirling tresses. This hair, or beard and mane, consists of thickly carved and coiling ropes, like serpents or worms, and the workmanship is so uncannily naturalistic that you could almost *swear* the slithering tendrils are in motion. Through this repulsive Medusa-mane of ropy tendrils, two fierce, serpent-like eyes glare in a horrible mingling of both cold, inhuman mockery ... and what I can only describe as *gloating menace*.

The technique of the unknown sculptor is one of astonishing sophistication: There is not the slightest hint of the primitive about this puzzling and vaguely repellent figurine. It must have taken exceptional talent, virtual genius, to catch that expression of leering, icy, alien menace in the stubborn medium of slick, heavy jade. But caught it the artist has ... to an almost disquieting degree.

The base upon which this truncated, conical body rests is carved from the same unfamiliar speckled jade, and it is oddly angled, as if the sculptor's culture possessed a completely non-Euclidean geometry. Deeply and cleanly cut in one side of this odd-angled base are two exceedingly complex hieroglyphs in no language known to me, symbols which bear no similarity to Chinese ideographs, Egyptian glyphs, Arabic characters, Sanskrit, or even common forms of Mesopotamian cuneiform, and certainly no slightest resemblance to any southern or central Pacific native writing known to me.

Rising from overlapping folds at the base of the image's neck, four bluntly tapering limbs or appendages rise from the torso. They are flat and resemble the arms of the common echinoderm of the class *asteroidea*—the familiar starfish of our California beaches—with the rather peculiar exception that the underside of these broad, flat, narrowing limbs bear row upon row of disc-like suckers. Remarkable how the unknown artist has combined suggestions of starfish and squid or octopi in his central conception ... and extraordinary, the cold sensation of unease amounting to a sort of psychic warning of *actual physical danger* I receive from the briefest contemplation of this idol! The combination of that fixed, gloating stare from those soulless, snake-like eyes half-veiled behind the coiling, worm-like tangle of its hair ... and those weird, bending arms or tentacles, half-raised and half-extended as ... as if to clutch their prey! ... well, it is quite unsettling.

* * *

PUTTING aside the jade figurine, I next turned to a cursory perusal of the miscellaneous manuscripts. I first leafed through the manila folder which had been inserted in the packing case which had contained the artifact collection, and whose first page consisted of the annotated listing of the collection.

Leafing rapidly through the bulky folder, I discovered its contents to be heterogeneous indeed, consisting of some personal letters from Professor Copeland to various institutions such as the Curator of Rare Books at the British Museum, the Bibliothèque Nationale in Paris, universities and libraries here in the United States; there were also bundles of newspaper clippings from a vast range of papers (generally having nothing in common, outside of the fact that they concerned missing or sunken ships in the Pacific, or news accounts of the temporary emergence of sunken islands of volcanic nature), and several pages of notes clipped together and bearing the heading *Notes on the Xothic Legend Cycle, with References to the* R'lyeh Text *and Other Books.*

The first page consisted of a list, in phonetic spelling, of the variant names of the aquatic deity whose representations in the plastic arts the Professor had collected so assiduously. As noted earlier, it was most surprising that cultures so widely scattered should share a divinity in common, or at least the very similar names the Professor had noted down—"Zatamaga", "Hommogah", "Z'otomogo", "Sothamogha", "Z'mog", and so on—were so similar as to strongly suggest a common religious figure shared by obscure cults across the breadth of the Pacific.

The Professor had next tabulated the physical elements of this being as shown in the various artworks. In summation, they tallied in amazing detail with the appearance of the jade figurine I had set aside atop my filing cabinet.

Next he had carefully traced the two complicated hieroglyphs onto a sheet of notepaper, and underneath these followed a list of the phonemes contained in the composite name to which he had attached symbols from several languages I was not familiar with. These symbols were arranged in neat columns, and the columns were headed with odd, uncouth labels— which, from context, must be the names of languages. If so, they are of languages unlisted in Havering's *Alphabets of the World, Ancient and Modern*— "Naacal"—"Hieratic Naacal"—"Tsath-yo"—"R'lyehian"—"Senzar"—

"Conjectural Aklo"—and others, several of them, not one of which was known to me. His purpose here was clear: He was attempting to find the phonetic meaning of the two Ponape figurine glyphs by comparison with similar phonemes in presumably culturally related tongues. The file folder bore no evidence of success in this endeavor.

Next followed a sequence of letters to and from officials at various institutions. The Professor was attempting to obtain certain obscure books, obviously of considerable rarity, either on library loan or in copy. I reproduce a specimen of this correspondence at random below:

MISKATONIC UNIVERSITY LIBRARY

Arkham, Massachusetts
Office of the Librarian
September 3rd, 1907

Dear Professor:

We are in receipt of your letter of August 29th, requesting information on the availability of the Necronomicon of Abdul Alhazred on interlibrary loan.

The Librarian begs me to inform you that the Kester Library is correct in its information. We have indeed a copy, in excellent state, of the Latin translation made by Olaus Wormius in the edition published in Spain in the Seventeenth Century, and to our knowledge this is the only copy of the "complete" *Necronomicon* (i.e., the Spanish edition of Wormius) at present in this country. Only five copies, in fact, are known to exist in the entire world.

The extreme rarity of this volume is such that the University Board of Regents has strictly forbidden us to circulate our Alhazred on interlibrary loan, although it is available for personal examination to qualified scholars within the premises of the Library itself.

Since you are at present located in California, and a trip to Massachusetts might be difficult to one of your busy schedule, the Librarian suggests you contact Dr. Foster at the Huntington Library in your own state. I believe the Huntington possesses a *Necronomicon* in manuscript copy, but cannot be certain.

Yours most sincerely,

Thaddeus Pressley, Jun.
For the Librarian

After this came a series of notations in Professor Copeland's own hand, which appear to be a summary of correspondence missing from this file:

Sept. 17th. Contacted Huntington but they have not *Nec.*
    Suggest Brit. Mus. Huntington has *Unaussprechlichen Kulten*, however, in 1840 Düsseldorf edition, so may be worth a trip

after all, since von Junzt has much data on Mu, and I suspect Z-O may turn out to be Muvian.

Oct. 11. Obtained good copies of relevant passages from *Nec.* courtesy of Wallingford in London, but must be from incomplete 15th Century black-letter edition done in Germany—same edition Kester Lib. in Salem has. *Must have Nec.* passages concerning Xothic data in complete form!

Oct. 20. Writing today to Lib. Univ. Buenos Aires, Lib. of Univ. of Lima, Peru, and Bib. Nat. in Paris. Spanish edition reputedly in Buenos Aires and Paris; while Lima supposed to have the Italian edition of Theodorus Philetas' Greek trans.

These entries were followed by long passages in several different handwritings, of odd, rhythmic, seemingly mythological narratives. They are far too lengthy and obscure for me to bother copying them into this record, but as Copeland obviously found something important missing from certain of them—something which other copyists had eventually supplied—I will jot down the shortest of these, as follows:

Necronomicon, Bk. II, Chap. vii (excerpt): "And it was done then as it had been promised aforetime, that He [*i.e., Cthulhu*] was taken by Those whom He had defied, and was plunged into the nethermost depths beneath the Sea, and They placed Him within the barnacled Tower that is said to rise amidst the great ruin that is the Sunken City [*R'lyeh*], and He was sealed within by the Elder Sign; and, raging at Those who had imprisoned Him, He further earned Their wrath, and They, descending upon Him for the second time, didst impose upon Him the semblance of Death, but left Him dreaming there beneath the Great Waters, and returned to that place from whence They had come, which is named Glyu-Vho, or Ibt al Janzah as we would say [*i.e., name Arabic astronomers of Alhazred's day used for the star we call Betelgeuze*], and which is amongst the stars, the which looketh upon Earth from that season when the leaves fall to that season when the sowers-of-the-soil are accustomed once again to their fields. And there shall He lie dreaming forever in His House At R'lyeh, unto which withouten pause they who served Him swam, and didst strive against every obstacle, but then disposed themselves to await His Awakening, for that they had no power against the Elder Sign and were fearful of its great potency; but they knew that the Cycle returneth, and that He shall be freed to seize upon the Earth again and make it His Kingdom, and thus to defy the Elder Gods once more. And to His Brethren it chanced likewise, that They were taken by Those whom They too had defied and were hurled into banishment; Him Who Is Not To Be Named [*i.e., Hastur*] was thrust into the Outermost Emptiness that is beyond the Stars, and with the Others it was the same, until at last was the Earth free of Them, and Those who had come hither in the form of Towers of Flame returned whence They had come, and were seen on this World no more, and on all of the Earth peace came and was unbroken, yet ever the Minions of the Old Ones gathered and planned and sought ways whereby to free their Masters, and lingered whilst Men came to search into the Secret and Forbidden Places and fumble at the Gates. [*Note: German edition text ends here and goes on to passage beg. 'But it shall not always be thus'; whereas Spanish text continues with following portion omitted in blackletter edition.*] And thus He slept unbroken ages by, whilst in the Dark City [*i.e., Carcosa*], against whose dim shores the cloud-waves break, Him Who Is Not To Be Named roared and writhed in His fetters, and in black, lightless N'kai, deep within the secret places that gape and yawn beneath the Earth, the Black Thing [*prob. Tsathoggua*] lay enchained, and Abhoth too, the Unclean One, even as didst They all, nor was it within Their power to free Themselves from the strictures imposed upon Them by the Lords of Glyu-Vho [*the 'Elder Gods'*], aye, and thus while aeons lapse Ythogtha howls ever from his Abyss, and Ghatanothoa from His Mount, and Zoth-Ommog from His Deep, which is under the Great Waters off the Isle of the Sacred Stone Cities [*?Yhe*], and all Their Brethren, helpless as are They to free Themselves, and hungry for that freedom to which in the passing of ages They shall attain. In the meanwhile They lurk ever just beyond the threshold which They cannot pass, and hideous beyond the comprehension of mortal minds is the Vengeance that fills Their troubled dreams. CHAP. VIII. But it shall not be always thus, for it is written that the Cycle shall in time return in its appointed Round. ..."

* * *

AS I find that mythological mumbo-jumbo interminable, I shall let this single sample suffice, it being the briefest of them all. From the context and appearance of the documents, I gather that the Professor found a friendly colleague willing to copy the passages he desired from a copy of this book, the *Necronomicon*, most likely at the Bibliothèque Nationale, from the Paris letterhead on the notepaper used. This scholarly friend would seem to have been familiar with this curious mythology, for his parenthetical interpolations indicate a close familiarity with the symbolism used.

It was apparent to me that it would be the labor of many days sorting through this mélange, so I set the folder aside for the remainder of the afternoon and bent my attention to the other duties which awaited me. Ever and anon, however, I had the distinct feeling of *eyes upon the back of my neck*—a distinctly uncomfortable sensation, doubly so as there was no other person in the room with me at the time.

Finishing work early, I went home that night to my lodgings in Curwen Street in a strange mood of depression and vague unease—although why I should feel depressed or uneasy I cannot say, unless it was from thinking of Professor Copeland's unhappy fate. He spent the last eight years of his life in a madhouse, and died screaming of things coming down from the stars to wipe all earth clean of life in order to house their own hellish spawn.

In bed I somehow could not keep my mind on the book I was reading—I am lamentably addicted to "thrillers", and was halfway through a novel by one Richard Marsh called *The Beetle*, which I had been devouring with relish. Unable to fix my attention on the page, I took from the briefcase the manila file folder from the Copeland Papers which contained the data on the "Xothic Legend-Cycle" and turned again to perusing the documents, having brought both folder and jade figurine home with me for further study.

There was page after page of mythological material laboriously hand-copied from books with the most strange and unwholesome titles imaginable—-the Comte d'Erlette's *Cultes des Goules*, Ludvig Prinn's *De Vermis Mysteriis*, something called the *Pnakotic Manuscript*, the *Ponape Scripture*, von Junzt's *Unaussprechlichen Kulten*, many more pages copied from the *Necronomicon*, some typed material from Wynorth's *Tangaroa, and Other Pacific Myths*, the *R'lyeh Text*, and some material which appeared to be from a dissertation or unpublished manuscript by one Dr. Laban Shrewsbury of Miskatonic, of whom I had heard vaguely.

As for the copied material itself, I could make no sense out of it—more confused and chaotic mystical nonsense had never spewed from a disarranged intellect! What is one to make of incoherent ravings about gods or devils with such unpronounceable names as Cthulhu, Yog-Sothoth, Ghatanothoa, Lloigor, Y'golonak, Shub-Niggurath, Hastur, Idh-yaa, Ythogtha, Azathoth, Ithaqua, Glaaki, Tsathoggua, Iod, Yig, Gol-goroth, Nyarlathotep, Ubbo-Sathla, and so on?

In the main, the Professor seemed to have attempted to isolate in one place all the scattered references to *four* of these demons or divinities from the full range of this immense literature. The beings in which he was interested were Cthulhu, Ghatanothoa, Ythogtha, and Zoth-Ommog; to a lesser extent he was also gathering references to Yig, Shub-Niggurath, Vorvadoss, Nug, and Yeb. I gathered from some of the material through which I leafed rapidly that these various beings were known to obscure cults scattered all over the world—there were references to "black Zimbabwe" and "weed-grown Y'ha-nthlei", to the Plateau of Leng somewhere in Asia, to certain ancient ruins in Yucatan and Peru, to a certain region in the unexplored deserts of Australia, to a primordial city of "the Yuggoth-spawn" in Antarctica—of all places!—and to the myths of the Wendigo, or Wind-Walker, common among the North Pacific Indian tribes of Canada and Alaska, to the Tcho-Tcho people of Burma, to the "Abominable Mi-Go", which I assumed from the context refers to the so-called Abominable Snowmen of the Himalayas, to "Fabulous Irem, City of Pillars", which I recalled from my boyish reading of the *Arabian Nights* and the *Rubaiyat*, and thus doubtless belongs to Islamic legendry.

The members of the "Great Old Ones" (as the devil-beings from the stars were most commonly called), upon which Copeland had fixed his attention, were those gods of primal and legended Mu, and in particular, some sort of trinity composed of Ghatanothoa, Ythogtha, and Zoth-Ommog. These beings were supposed to be brothers, and had for their sire that same Cthulhu of whom I had seen such frequent mention in these excerpts from the literature. One quotation in particular seemed central and pertinent; it came from a remarkable manuscript which, according to Copeland's notes, had been inscribed "in the Elder Aeon", on some sort of palm-leaf parchment, and which had been discovered during diggings on Ponape about 1734 by a Yankee trader, one Captain Abner Exekiel Hoag of Arkham, Mass. Hoag's bodyservant, obviously a half-breed Polynesian or Oriental (Copeland calls him a "hybrid human/Deep One"—whatever that means!) translated this ancient book-scroll from "the primal Naacal" and it was circulated secretly to certain cultists and occult students in the United States, Europe, and Asia for many years. Eventually both the original parchment and a copy of the translation somehow got into the Kester Library, from which the Professor obtained his texts.

At any rate, the key quotation came from this so-called *Ponape Scripture*, which I will copy out here:

> As for Ghatanothoa, the Thing on the Mount, He and His Brethren, Ythogtha, the Abomination in the Abyss, and Zoth-Ommog, the Dweller in the Deep, are the Sons of the mighty Cthulhu, Lord of the Watery Abyss and dread and awful Potentate of drowned R'lyeh; and, like unto Their Terrible Sire, Who yet shall come again in future time, They have Their Dominion over the great fish and the serpents of the Deeps, and They too be sealed away under the terrific spell of the Elder Sign for that They dared to challenge Them From Glyu-Vho for the domain of the Earth. Sons be They to great Cthulhu and His Spouse, Idh-yaa, with Whom He copulated awesomely in the nightmare darknesses between the Stars, and these Three, the Spawn of Cthulhu, came down from remote and ultra-telluric Xoth, the dim green double sun that glitters like a daemonic eye in the blacknesses beyond Abbith, to whelm and reign over the steaming fens and bubbling slime-pits of the mist-veiled dawn aeons of this Earth, and it was in primordial and shadowy Mu that They were great.

I set the folder aside as weariness began to creep over me.
That night I did not have wholesome dreams.

* * *

IN a desultory fashion, over the next three months or so, I worked my way through the various notes and documents. One by one the pieces in this puzzle began to fall into place.

This Demon Trinity, and its dread Sire, interested Copeland most because the Pacific was the area of their greatest power. Obviously, in his explorations, researches and excavations, he had come across this cult or its remains, which had led him on and on through the mazes of this weird and horrible mythology.

As for the name wherewith he had labeled the cult material, the derivation was obvious. "Xothic", because the legends centered around three devil gods engendered by Cthulhu upon an entity who dwelt upon or near the double star the cultists knew as Xoth. Ghatanothoa and Ythogtha and Zoth-Ommog, and perhaps Cthulhu and his monstrous mate, Idh-yaa, as well, had come down from space to this world in the dawn ages and their empire had covered that primal Pacific civilization known to the occultists as Mu. When Mu broke up and submerged—oh, I have dipped into the wild pages of Colonel Churchward, too!—their worship and their legends lingered on among certain degenerate cult survivals of the most staggering antiquity.

It was to the task of chronicling this dread, prehistoric empire (which reputable scientists, needless to say, shrug off as mere legend-mongering), that Copeland had devoted the labor of his final years. Among the miscellaneous papers of the bequest was a vast, untidy bundle of manuscript, in length the size of a weighty tome, which thankfully was left still unfinished at the Professor's death. I say "thankfully left unfinished", because I have—to the considerable detriment of my wholesome slumber—actually dared to glance into the chaotic pages of screaming lunacy which comprise this monumental work—the spewings of a mad brain, a diseased intelligence—the wild ravings of a once-brilliant mind sadly gone teetering over the brink of cataclysmic insanity.

Few eyes, I think, save for my own, will ever have peered into this final production of a blighted, once productive, career. This particular work, to which the Professor affixed the title of *The Civilization of Mu: A Reconstruction in the Light of Recent Discoveries, with A Synoptic Comparison of the* R'lyeh Text *and the* Ponape Scripture—this manuscript, I say, for all that it is an incoherent jumble of hideous blasphemy and nightmarish cosmic speculation, yet traces the rise and decay and destruction of a civilization which, however imaginary, however purely mythical, does at least provide a seemingly viable hypothesis whereby to account for the puzzling and cyclopean masonry wherewith so very many of the jungle-clad Pacific islands are mysteriously and unaccountably encumbered.

The collapse of this primal or prehuman race, and the destruction of the so-called "Lost Continent" which some even now conjecture to have been its cradle, was (in poor Copeland's view) *survived* by obscure, shadowy cults which worshiped with decadent rites these Xothic demon gods.

This mysterious survival, his documents reiterate again and again, was simply because the Demon Trinity and their Sire had not perished after all in the destruction of Mu, indeed, could not of their very nature die or be slain, but somehow lived on eternally under the trance-state forced upon them by their adversaries, the Elder Gods. In this supernal trance-state, they live forever but are impotent to act: *except that in dreams they could somehow sway and infect with madness the minds of men.* Those men whose mental natures were somehow susceptible to their insidious influence, whether drawn thereto by scholarly curiosity, the lust for unholy power, or a certain artistic sensitivity amounting almost to innate instability, they could pervert to their worship ... like Faust, tempted from the study of Divinity by desire for the promised powers of black magic.

It was a hideously suggestive premise, and weirdly persuasive. But something about it bothered me, like the missing piece to a jigsaw puzzle. Some fact was lacking from the mosaic which Harold Hadley Copeland had so ingeniously constructed—*why did the sleeping devil-gods even need human converts?*

That was the unanswered question that baffled me and stuck in my craw. Of what conceivable use were fragile, ephemeral, mortal men to such as the Xothic Triad and their Sire?

The answer came to me quite suddenly, in a flash of recollection that left me oddly uneasy. It had been lurking in my mind all the while ... suggested by that first interminable quotation from the blasphemous and shocking *Necronomicon*, a passage which I have already copied out at length into this journal, but will repeat here: "Yet ever the Minions of the Old Ones gathered and planned and sought ways whereby to free their Masters, and lingered whilst Men came to search into the Secret and Forbidden Places *and fumble at the Gates.*"

I understood it at once—the Elder Sign, whatever it was, was a material thing, some sort of talisman or sigil, imbued with psychic force which repelled both the Old Ones and their unhuman Minions—*but did not repulse men.* It was men and men alone who could open the "Gates" and set the Old Ones free!

* * *

VERY much of Copeland's research had been geographical, trying to pin down the location of the imprisoned Old Ones in the Pacific area. There was quite a sheaf of newspaper clippings—inexplicable to me when I first leafed through them, though now they took on an ominous and sinister meaning.

These clippings were fastened together with a paperclip in three bundles, tagged "R'lyeh", "Yhe", and "Z-O; Ponape." The bundle marked "R'lyeh" was by far the bulkiest and must have contained thirty or more news items, going as far back as 1879. The most recent clipping was from the *Sydney Bulletin* for April 18, 1925. Under the headline "Mystery Derelict Found at Sea" were details of a confused and seemingly innocuous maritime tragedy concerning a two-masted schooner, the *Emma*, which sailed into the unknown from Auckland on February 20th, three years ago; on the twelfth day of the following month, a lone survivor was rescued from the waves by the Morrison Company freighter *Vigilant*. This man, a Norwegian named Gustaf Johansen, told of encountering a ship manned by villainous Kanakas and half-castes, of a battle at sea, followed by the discovery of an unknown island not found on any chart. To this yellowed newspaper clipping were attached some typewritten papers—the text of a sort of diary by the sailor Johansen—obtained, surprisingly enough, by the grand-nephew of one of my old teachers, George Gammell Angell, Professor Emeritus of Semitic Languages at Brown University; both Gammell and his grand-nephew had, it seemed, interested themselves in much the same sort of borderline studies as had formed Professor Copeland's chief preoccupation. I shall not go into the text of the Johansen narrative in any length—he describes their sightings of the unmapped island at about S. Latitude 47° 9', W. Longitude 126° 43'—their landing on a coastline of mingled mud, ooze, and weed-grown blocks of enormous stone masonry—a confused and nightmarish struggle with enormous things he shudderingly refuses to describe.

This reference to latitude and longitude Copeland underscored heavily with his fountain pen.

Turning back to the earliest clipping, a yellowed scrap of newsprint from the *Boston Register*, dated November 15, 1879, I read that certain articles from a prehistoric tomb were to be on public display in the Cabot Museum, Boston; these articles had been found on May 11, 1878, by crewmen from the freighter *Eridanus*, bound from Wellington, New Zealand, to Valparaiso, Chile, which had sighted "a new island unmarked on any chart and evidently of volcanic origin." The newspaper article gave latitude and longitude readings identical with those the *Sydney Bulletin* printed in its story about the schooner *Emma*—forty-seven years later!

The second bundle of news clippings, only half as thick as the first, contained much similar material, but located infrequent emergences from the deeps of an island containing a great chasm some thousands of miles to the south of the "R'lyeh emergences."

It was the third bundle, however, which caught my attention the most. These clippings, about a dozen in all, were about odd disappearances of sailing ships in the waters off Ponape. The earliest of these told of the disappearance at sea of the whaling ship *Nebuchadnezzar*, out of New Bedford, which vanished in the vicinity of Ponape with all hands in 1864. No storm was reported in the vicinity of Ponape—no storm anywhere in the Pacific on the date in question for a thousand miles—*nothing but a peculiar, heavy, low-lying bank of fog.*

A more recent clipping, from the *Singapore Times* for April 8, 1911, discussed the mysterious disappearance with all hands of the French warship *Versailles*. Again, no storm was reported, but heavy fog had overlaid the waters off Ponape.

One clipping in particular the Professor had marked with a large exclamation point. It came from the *Honolulu Sentinel* for June 17, 1922, and told a nightmarish and rambling story of a fleet of fishing boats manned by Ponape natives caught in a thick fog off the island and attacked by *monstrous and horrible sea slugs, swollen to fantastic proportions*, which slithered into the boats in some cases, catching the native fishermen in their mouths and dragging them over the side. More than forty unfortunates were lost in this manner, and the survivors, who were hospitalized in states ranging from incoherent raving hysteria to complete catatonic shock, repeated over and over again the meaningless word or exclamation "Hug!" or "Ugh!"

In the margin of this story, in Copeland's hand, was written: "*Yuggya!* See *Zan. Tab.*, IX, 2, lines 120-150." This note referred to the puzzling and cryptic set of inscribed tablets Professor Copeland had brought back from the prehistoric stone tomb of a priest or wizard in the Tsang Plateau region of central Asia in 1913. I recalled that the publication in 1916 of his brochure *The* Zanthu Tablets: *A Conjectural Translation*, with its unholy and repulsive picture of the dawn age of civilization, had been thunderously condemned as "cosmic blasphemy" from press and pulpit, and had given the death-blow to his scientific reputation. Two years later he was committed to a madhouse; eight years after, he died raving.

We had a copy of the *Zanthu Tablets* in our library section, although I had never dared look within its innocuous green leatherette cover; I did so now, however, and quickly found the passage to which the handwritten note refers. It is close to the end of the ninth tablet—there are ten in all—and the relevant passage must be that in which the hierophant Zanthu invokes "the Father of Worms ... even undying and putrescent Ubb, leader and progenitor of the dreaded Yuggya—the loathly and prehuman servitors of (Ythogtha), who squirm and slither in the slime about His feet."

But the central passage reads thusly: "The Yuggya serve my lord Ythogtha and His Brother, Zoth-Ommog, even as the Deep Ones serve

Cthulhu and the Tcho-Tchos their lords, Zhar and Lloigor; and as the Flame-Creatures strive ever to free Cthugha and the Serpentmen of Valusia sought to unchain their lord, Yig, so do the Yuggya tirelessly gnaw at the bonds that hold Ythogtha and Zoth-Ommog."

This reminded me of something in one of those lengthy and chaotic passages from the *Necronomicon*. I turned to those manuscripts and found the quotation—"Within the five-pointed Star carven of grey stone from ancient Mnar lies armor against witches and daemons, against the Deep Ones, the Dholes, *the Yuggs*, the Voormis, the Tcho-Tcho, the Abominable Mi-Go, the Shoggoths, the Valusians, and all such people and beings who serve the Great Old Ones and their Spawn."

I put away the Copeland papers with a little shudder of disgust. The fascination this repulsive and chaotic mythology had begun to exert on my imagination was distinctly unhealthy: I had been sleeping badly these past several nights, and my dreams—nightmares really—I, who have not had nightmares since I was an adolescent!—my dreams (which never, upon waking, could I remember in detail, save that they were *frightful*) were filled with shadowy terrors that left me weak and shaken at dawn. It was time I forgot about poor mad Copeland and his horror gods and their slithering horde of worm-like worshipers, and turned my mind to sane and sunlit matters.

Shoving the papers away with a determined gesture, I reached for my pipe ... and found myself staring directly into the carved glare of gloating, icy menace some unknown genius had sculpted in that weirdly horrible idol from Zoth-Ommog's waters.

* * *

*N*OTE *by Arthur Wilcox Hodgkins: Up to this point Dr. Blaine's manuscript is neatly written, on consecutively numbered sheets of office stationery, and develops a chronological narrative that is logical and coherent, although it betrays a level of emotional uneasiness just below the narrative surface. However, at this point the neat, logical portion of the manuscript ends abruptly, and the hastily scrawled and clumsily scribbled pages which follow are in no particular order, and describe the rapid and frightful degeneration of his mind toward a final, shattering climax of mad ravings. I have attempted to sort the following fragments into some sort of order, based on internal evidence, but without much success.*

* * *

(DREAM ONE)
Extraordinary and terrifying dream tonight—first one I can remember clearly enough to set down. Dim, moonlit vistas of stone city of Cyclopean architecture—titanic stone blocks graven with sprawling and monstrously uncouth glyphs—rows of immense pylons marching the length of flagstone-paved squares—ziggurats or angular pyramids with smoky flames at summits, like altar fires.

Hooded and robed shapes about the upmost tiers of one colossal pyramid, and the sound of rhythmic chanting—over and over, the same inexplicable phrase—woke suddenly, dripping with cold sweat, with the irresistible urge to write down what I had heard (which is why I am describing the dream). Probably utterly meaningless, but here goes—

The phrase is: *"Ph'nglui mglw'nafh Cthulhu R'lyeh wgah'nagl fhtagn."*

*

(DREAM TWO?)
Tonight I returned again in my dreams to that Cyclopean stone city of monstrous angular pyramids and tall pylons, and to the vision of queer, squat, robed and hooded celebrants worshiping at some awful Rite ... the Moon seized my attention ... it was frightfully huge, and its shining face oddly unmarked by the many craters which pockmark its visage in our day ... it made me wonder (in my dream) if this was a vision of some remote, pre-Cambrian era—just then a horrible flying Thing flashed across the silver face of the full Moon—ribbed, membranous wings and hideously elongated beak or proboscis—*surely a living pteranodon of the remote Mesozoic skies*!

*

(PERHAPS DREAM 3 OR 4)
—I am in an immense building of monolithic stone, the blocks perhaps sixty or seventy feet on a side ... it is a colossal hall, lined with monstrous huge columns, like the hypostyle hall at Karnak ... and like the colonnades of Karnak, the pillars are covered with weird ideographs in some unknown, surely not human, language.

I am approaching the great altar, which is rayed like a starfish, hollowed and scooped out in the center, and filled with some red fluid (blood?). My attention wanders to the vast bas-relief cut on the wall behind this curious star-shaped altar, and with a thrill of unearthly and mind-chilling horror I recognize thereupon the ghastly likeness of that primordial jade image from the waters off Ponape—but *ten thousand times more huge*, and incredibly detailed, with almost photographic clarity—*oh my God!* The thought suddenly seizes me that *it is a likeness done from a living model*—I awake screaming, my throat raw, with my housekeeper clutching her kimono about her bosom and asking me if I am well. Well? I hardly know ... such dreams as this cannot originate in my mind ... *unless put there by Another!*

*

(DREAM 4; PERHAPS 3)
On another night, I find myself approaching a great monolithic temple on the summit of an immense height. It is again night, and an evil, sickly moon leers down through coiling medusa-mists ... people are all about me as I ascend the height—weeping, kneeling, huddled. *They are not quite completely human*—squat, hunched, anthropoid, with very much more body hair than is normal today, almost amounting to a pelt. There is a vaguely Asiatic look to them, lemon-yellow skin, slanted eyes black and liquid, prognathous jaws and heavy brow-ridges.

The worshipers are striving to avert some threatened doom or punishment, perhaps natural; and as I advance up the long slope (covered, I notice, with what looks like Jurassic conifers!), the ground shudders beneath my heel and thunder growls in the mist-veiled sky—suddenly, a line of black mountains on the horizon burst into flame, one by one! A *range of volcanoes*, sulfurously alit in sequence, like a row of candles ignited in turn by some unseen Hand! The people around me—or subhumans—are moaning some hellish, grunting litany—"Idh-yaa, Ythogtha; Cthulhu; Nug—"

Suddenly a crevice opens in the earth at my very feet—world deep, black as the Pit itself! It fills rapidly with gurgling slime and the hunched and moaning worshipers shrink back in nameless dread from the *immense, wet, glistening, white, pulpy, worm-like*—I can not stand it; I force myself awake ....

*

(DREAM 5)
In this dream I am descending slowly through graduated levels of green light, which grow steadily more dim; it is as if I am sinking (or being drawn down?) into the depths of the ocean. The sensation of cold wet darkness pressing upon me is stifling, oppressive ... then I am floating above a mounded plain of slick black mud. It is drowned in green-black gloom, and little is visible ... now I approach a truly immense crater or chasm in the ocean's floor ... I glide over the lip and descend, it seems, for a very long time ... the crater seems to be miles deep ... the last vestiges of emerald light slowly fade into utter and abysmal blackness.

When at last I reach the floor of the great depression I can somehow see again—I think the oily ooze that covers the crater floor is dimly phosphorescent with decay or radioactivity ... now I am nearing a huge mound in the center of the crater ... it resolves gradually out of the all-but-impenetrable gloom ... it is a structure of some kind, but it has not the workmanship of human hands, the stone blocks are Cyclopean, and the rows of truncated pillars are ... it is the Temple of which I have dreamed, and dreamed, and dreamed, before! *It is the House of Zoth-Ommog*—oh Christ save me—that sickening *light*! That gloom-piercing light that blazes from the Elder Sign on the Door—*No, damn you, I will not touch it* ... remove it ... release ...—*I must WAKE UP*—

*

(DREAM 6 OR 7)
The drug that Wollstone prescribed has done me no good at all, I perceive, for I have now for seven consecutive nights dreamed the same dream, precisely identical in all respects: I am standing in my nightclothes on the beach at Wexton Pier on the outskirts of Santiago; I am shivering with the cold, but brimming with a weird and terrible exaltation ... clenched in my hands is a sheet of written matter—something I searched and searched for in the Copeland papers—the Invocation of the Yuggya—the Great Invocation from the damnable and loathsome copy of the *Yuggya Chants* that raving idiot Copeland purchased from the Lascar sailor on the San Francisco waterfront—oh, God, I am going to *read it aloud*—with a terrific effort of will that leaves me shaking and gasping with exhaustion, I wrench myself awake ... I must burn that copy of the Invocation—yes, and the filthy old book, too! I ... *must* ....

*

(DREAM 7; PERHAPS 6)
Tonight as I fell asleep, I passed into a very deep slumber as if drugged, although I have taken none of the prescription the last two nights, fearing the after-effects, which leave me lax and unresponsive and curiously lacking in will. ... From this heavy slumber I came gradually half-awake within my dream, and *Someone was whispering to me in a soft, guttural, seductive voice*—*had been* whispering to me for a long time before I wrenched myself half-awake—suddenly I awoke completely, found myself trembling before the wide-open window, incoherently repeating over and over, "No! No! *I will not do it!"*

But what was the window doing *open?* Surely, I closed and locked it before retiring—as I do every night, when the wind blows in from the sea ... and what was that slime or jelly smeared all over the window-sill—like slime from a snail-track, but if so, it was the very Father of all Snails ....

I must see a doctor—*soon.*

•

(DREAM 8)

My condition is steadily deteriorating; now, somnambulism is included among my symptoms, for Mrs. Wilkins says she has found me walking in my sleep seven times in the past week and a half, and once she found me lurching down the driveway toward the street ... I asked her (half-dreading to hear the answer), which direction was I heading? She says the Waterfront—*toward the Pier.*

I must burn that Invocation; and the horrible ancient book I copied it from; and I would to God I had not let the Directors persuade me to print that lengthy narrative from Copeland's translation of the *Zanthu Tablets* or that hellishly suggestive excerpt from his Asian diary in the *Journal of Pacific Antiquities*! Why in God's name didn't I tell them how much I know—*I could at least have hinted at the mind-blasting TRUTH behind his cursed Xothic legend-cycle!*

Some things we were not meant to know.

Some things it is ... dangerous to learn ....

Last night the Voice came again and whispered to me for hours as I lay half-conscious. ... Oh, I would like to see far Addith where the Metal Brains dwell, and Zaoth with its old books cut on plates of *lagh* metal from Yuggoth, books that predate the creation of the earth by thirty-seven million years. ... God help me, I would like to see primal and doom-fraught Mu before the Towers of Fire from Betelgeuze whelmed and trampled it down beneath the rolling waves ... the Yuggya can disembody my thought-lattice (they whisper) and set me free in time and space ... to visit Celaeno and Yith and Ymar, and horrible Shaggai ... *but I will not be the agent of the Old Ones, nor burden my soul with the massive guilt of the slaughter of this planet* ... which will certainly follow if I do Their bidding, and loose frightful Zoth-Ommog from his Deep ... *Our Father which art in Heaven, hallowed be thy Name—*

* * *

POSTSCRIPT: On the night of August 3rd, a Santiago police car saw a man in white pyjamas standing knee-deep in the surf near Wexton Pier, apparently reading a letter by the light of a match. Approaching him, Officers Harlow and Kellar shone their flashlights in his face. He seemed to be asleep, but the blinding light awakened him and he realized suddenly where he was and what he was doing. Paying no attention to the patrolmen, he suddenly, with white, shaking fingers, touched the burning match to the sheet of closely written paper he held, and hurled the blazing sheet into the dark, foaming waters. In that same instant, following the flight of the burning paper, Officer Kellar turned his light on the black waters, and reports that he glimpsed something enormous, round and slick, and white—but not remotely suggestive of a human body, he is certain.

At that moment, the wild-eyed man—later identified as Henry Stephenson Blaine, Ph.D., manuscript collection curator for the Sanbourne Institute in this city—apparently saw the thing in the surf—and much clearer than did either of the officers. For he staggered back with a horrible wailing screech that one of the officers, who has been both a prison guard at San Quentin and a security guard for an insane asylum, describes as the cry of a damned soul—"the most horrible sound I ever heard come from a human throat," he said, swearing and pale.

As the two patrolmen waded out to him, Dr. Blaine fell on his knees in the foaming surf and clapped both hands over his face, covering his eyes, screaming hoarsely: "God! God! Horrible—*I have seen a Yugg! A Yugg!—Jesus—God—a Yugg!—God—Iä! Zoth-Ommog!—cf'ayak ghaaa yrrl'th tho-Yuggya! Yaaaaaa-n'gh—*"

The police closed with him and grappled with him; he reportedly made no resistance, but was so shaken with uncontrollable spasms of trembling that he could not stand and had to be carried to the patrol car. Along the way, he babbled with desperate urgency to his two captors—or rescuers: "I am mad or going mad—get to Hodgkins at the Institute—the stone thing from Ponape—God damn that mad fool, Copeland!—tell Hodgkins—the jade idol must be destroyed—*must be smashed, d'you hear me?*—Kill it, kill it, kill it, *killllllllllll—*"

Dr. Blaine then collapsed in utter exhaustion and was admitted to Mercy Hospital Psychiatric Emergency Ward at 3 o'clock in the morning. He has been there now for two months; in all that time he has not spoken a single word, except for a gobbling sound he repeats over and over, which sounds like, "Yugg—Yugg-Yugg!"

He is now kept under forcible restraint for his own protection.

I have perused the manuscript found among the papers on his desk and forwarded to me by his assistant, Mr. Hodgkins. I have reached, and can reach, no final conclusion regarding it and its chaotic contents.

With one remark found therein I heartily concur.

Some things we were not meant to know; and some things it is dangerous to learn. To which, recalling the horror and loathing suggested in the patient's data on the monstrous worm-things he calls "Yuggs", one of which he believes he saw clearly in the blaze of the policeman's flashlight: *Some things it is death and madness to see.*

For since that night of cataclysmic horror Dr. Blaine has attempted to blind himself eleven times.

(signed) Robinson Dambler, M.D.
Physician-in-Charge

THIS tale, which had early borne as a working title "The Horror in the Gallery", then "The Terror Out of Time", wound up appearing first in Edward Paul Berglund's 1976 anthology *The Disciples of Cthulhu* under the title "Zoth-Ommog." I am glad to have the chance to restore one of the earlier titles, which is superior despite, or rather perhaps because of, its obvious derivation from the title of Lovecraft's "The Horror in the Museum" (though in fact it has almost nothing in common with that tale, being far more reminiscent of, "Out of the Aeons." As a gaffe in the first edition of Carter's *Lovecraft: A Look behind the "Cthulhu Mythos"* [Ballantine/Starmont/Borgo] reveals, Lin seems to have found it easy to confuse the two tales, since both have sections set in a museum.). The title "The Horror in the Gallery" signals the campy nostalgia of the whole enterprise, unlike "Zoth-Ommog," which tells the reader exactly nothing. That Lin opted for this latter title perhaps reflects his not-so-hidden agenda in writing these stories: to fill in gaps he saw in the Mythos as currently outlined. The data, the system, was more important than the story, which existed simply as a vehicle for getting the new data into print. The story "Zoth-Ommog" is titled simply for the piece of Mythos data it embodies.

Yet this story rises above its underlying motivation. More than a little inspired, I suspect, by Fritz Leiber's tribute to HPL, "To Arkham and the Stars" (see my anthology *Tales of the Lovecraft Mythos*, Fedogan & Bremer, 1990), this story represents a radical departure in narrative technique from the approaches evident in the previous stories in this sequence. "The Thing in the Pit" and "The Red Offering" are both cast in Carter's pseudo-Dunsanian archaic style, while "The Dweller in the Tomb" and "Out of the Ages" both employ the narrative shortcut of the journal or diary, throwing a bunch of narrative fragments at us rather in the manner of a set of story notes, which is finally all such a "story" is. "The Horror in the Gallery", by contrast, tries (and succeeds, in my judgment) to enclose the story and the reader in a distinct and convincing narrative world of sufficient texture and color. It must be, and is, sustained by the weaving of a continuous narrative web of scene as well as summary, process as well as conclusion.

The end of the story, hackneyed though it seems, is on another level semiotically quite appropriate. When Hodgkins resolves the situation by simply throwing the star stone at the idol, we have the basic plot syntax stripped down to the bare bone: The whole story is a simple process (disguised as complex by the twists and turns of the narrative discourse) of two symbol systems pursuing a collision path. At that last moment, all the fiendish lore of the "Alhazredic Demonology" meets the wisdom of the Elder Gods (larger-than-life shadows cast by the Miskatonic savants whose advice Hodgkins seeks) head on, and all superfluities such as characters, narrative motivation, etc. drop away like booster rockets. The bare symbols themselves—the Elder Sign and the Old One idol—must finally clash, and one must annihilate the other.

Or perhaps both must annihilate each other like matter and anti-matter, and this is the moral of the story. The forces in opposition really do not have any ultimate moral reference in human terms. The Old Ones are not devils with the Elder Gods playing angels. Rather, they are an utterly alien factor aloof to and unmindful to us, but dangerous to us, like nuclear energy if we dare get in its way. The genuine Lovecraftian character of this bleak vision need hardly be pointed out, though most might not expect to see it in Lin Carter.

The Horror in the Gallery

by Lin Carter

THE following document is part of the Santiago County Police Homicide File G029-02. It was taken down in dictation by public stenographer R. A. Wallis from oral testimony voluntarily given under oath on the afternoon of March 29, 1929. Sheriff Homer Tate Watkins was the questioning officer; Patrolman Wilbur J. Barlow was the witness. The file was held in the "Open" section until six months after the above date, and since then has been filed under "Unsolved" in the County Criminal Courts Building, Santiago, California. We are grateful to the Public Prosecutor's Office of the state government for permission to include here this previously unpublished deposition.

* * * * *

Prefatory note attached to Document 2, Homicide File G029-02: The deposition herein filed as Document 2 was taken down by public stenographer R. A. Wallis from oral testimony voluntarily given under oath on the afternoon of March 29, 1929. Sheriff Homer Tate Watkins was questioning officer; Patrolman Wilbur J. Barlow, witness. This file is to be held in the "Open" section until six (6) months after the above date, and will then be filed under "Unsolved" in the Santiago County Criminal Courts Bldg., Santiago, California.

DEPOSITION OF ARTHUR WILCOX HODGKINS, 1929

AS regards the murder of the night watchman, Emiliano Gonzalez, I know nothing for I was not present to witness the crime. But as to the death of the unknown intruder, who seems to have been some sort of Polynesian or Mongoloid mixed breed, I have much to say, for I saw it happen. But little of what I can tell you will be believed, I fear. It is all I can do to believe it myself, for all that I saw it with my own eyes.

Sheriff Watkins has apprised me of my right to keep silent or to have the lawyer of my choice present while I gave this testimony, but I have chosen to tell everything I know regarding these two deaths and the fire which enveloped the South Gallery, even if this sworn deposition should later be used as evidence against me. As I am innocent of all crimes except that of ignorance, I have nothing to fear.

My name is Arthur Wilcox Hodgkins. I am 29 years old, and I reside at 34 Mission Street, this city. For the past four years I have worked at the Sanbourne Institute of Pacific Antiquities, first as a library clerk, then as Assistant to the Curator of the Manuscripts Collection of the Institute. My direct superior was Dr. Henry Stephenson Blaine; when he was unexpectedly taken ill, about seven months ago, the directors of the Institute requested me to fill the role of temporary Curator of Manuscripts until such time as Dr. Blaine should be well enough to resume his rightful duties.

Because everything I am going to reveal at this time has its genesis in Dr. Blaine's unfortunate illness, and in certain events which preceded and were subsequent to that illness, I must begin my statement with what may seem to you officers to be irrelevant material. I am sorry to have to take up so much of your time, but it is imperative that you permit me to tell my story in my own way.

I.

TO anyone who knew him as well as I did, or who worked by his side day in and day out, it was distressingly obvious that Dr. Blaine's nervous breakdown had been impending for some time. His features, normally tranquil, became increasingly pallid and worn, as if he were suffering under great strain and tension during the months immediately preceding his mental collapse. The change was perhaps most visible in his manner, which was usually genial and affable; but more and more he seemed distracted, inattentive to his work, unaware of his surroundings. Many times I came upon him musing over a brown manila file folder he had recently begun keeping; he had never shown me the contents of this folder, but it was marked "Copeland Notes/Xothic Legend Cycle" in ink on the tab. It was not until much later that I gained any idea as to what this inscription referred.

Whenever I happened to interrupt his study of this particular file, he would start guiltily, eye me with something resembling suspicion, and at times abruptly ask what I was doing there. Then he would hurriedly stuff the file back in the bottom drawer of his desk—a drawer he always kept locked.

As I have said, there was no question in my mind that Dr. Blaine was suffering under enormous nervous strain, due to causes completely unknown to me. But it was not until that terrible night in August that I gained any notion of just how serious his condition actually was. Whenever I happened to inquire as to his health, he would set the question aside with some seemingly casual remark to the effect that he was "sleeping badly" or "had a lot on his mind these days." From time to time he complained of bad dreams. As his condition rapidly deteriorated, he did in fact display the signs of insomnia in his trembling hands, pale face, red-rimmed eyes, and lack of ability to concentrate.

Then, at 3 o'clock in the morning of August 4, 1928, he was admitted to the Psychiatric Emergency Ward of Mercy Hospital in a state of shock resembling catatonia. Dr. Robinson Dambler, the physician in charge of his case, said he seemed to be in a condition of complete nervous collapse. He appeared to have lost the power of coherent speech, repeating over and over again the meaningless and singularly bestial sounds, *"Yugg ... Yugg ... Yugg."* He resisted every attempt at communication, and, during the next two months or so, had to be held in continuous restraint, having made several frenzied attempts at self-mutilation. Early in October he was committed to Dunhill Sanitarium, under treatment by the renowned Dr. Harrington J. Colby, a distinguished specialist in nervous disorders of this type.

I wish I could convey to you how shocked and horrified I was at the news of his nervous breakdown. I profoundly admired and esteemed Dr. Blaine as an eminent scholar and a scientist of high repute in his field. Even more than this, I regarded him as my friend, despite the considerable difference in our ages.

As requested by the directors, I assumed temporary curatorship, and for some months was too deeply immersed in handling my double burden of work to inquire more than cursorily into his condition. I have to admit that during the several weeks immediately prior to his breakdown, Dr. Blaine had neglected his duties, and our files were in the most slovenly condition. We had been engaged in cataloguing items from the Copeland bequest, with an eye toward a public display of the art treasures recently bequeathed to us. The directors had most urgently wished to place the Copeland Collection of Central Pacific and Polynesian Antiquities on display during the 1928 season, and the South Gallery had been cleared with that purpose in mind; but this proved simply impossible, due to Dr. Blaine's neglect of his duties during the final phase of his illness. The task of completing the preliminary cataloguing devolved upon me.

I suppose I should explain to you officers that the Copeland bequest was the largest and most important acquisition the Sanbourne Institute had ever received since it was first established to house the great Carlton

Sanbourne collection itself. Professor Copeland, who died in 1926, was the most distinguished archaeologist in the field of Pacific prehistory, and the fruits of his long and remarkable career lay in the unique collection of artifacts he had built up over half a century of field research. It was composed of several steamer trunks filled with unsorted papers, correspondence, articles clipped from learned quarterlies, unorganized notes and private journals, and several partially complete manuscripts, including one of book length. The artifacts themselves occupied numerous packing crates, and ranged from examples of Tonga Island *tapa*-cloth weaving to idols and stone images, some of considerable size and weight. The work involved in sorting, identifying, labeling, and classifying this enormous miscellany occupied me for several months.

The most baffling item in the entire collection, however, remained unclassifiable and stubbornly resisted all attempts to identify either the nature of its composition of the style or period of its workmanship. This singular artifact had reputedly been brought up from the depths of the sea off Ponape in 1909 by a native diver. It had attained considerable notoriety in the popular press as "the Ponape figurine", because in some manner it was intimately connected with Dr. Blaine's collapse. News stories told how he had raved that it must be destroyed when he had been taken into custody on the night of August third; muck-raking journalists had dug up the slanderous account of Professor Copeland, its discoverer, and repeated yet again the sensationalist accounts of how he had died a babbling maniac in a San Francisco mental institution. These specialists in "yellow journalism" even had the temerity to drag poor Dr. Blaine's unfortunate condition into their Sunday supplement horror stories. I recall the headline of one, "PONAPE FIGURINE CLAIMS SECOND VICTIM", which outraged and disgusted me.

Thereafter, there was no keeping the story quiet. Reporters concocted a ridiculous account of the figurine's mysterious origins, adding in elements borrowed from the "King Tut's Curse" news stories that had filled the columns of the less reputable press after the opening of the tomb of the Pharaoh Tut-ankh-ammon only five years before. You will perhaps recall the field day the press enjoyed after Lord Carnarvon and Howard Carter opened the burial chamber in 1923, which was followed by a series of mysterious deaths of several members of the expedition, including Lord Carnarvon himself, who died two weeks later. The reverberations of this sensational story had all but died down when Dr. Blaine's breakdown became newsworthy; and the muck-rakers delighted in drawing sinister parallels between the curse on a pharaoh's tomb, which some believed had brought many men to a premature death, and the curse on a mysterious Ponape antiquity, which, it was now being rumored, had brought two distinguished scholars to madness.

The lamentable items continued to appear in the public press, much to the distress of everyone connected with the Institute.

* * *

FROM time to time we received word from the authorities at the sanitarium of Dr. Blaine's progress. By mid-January of 1929 he began responding favorably to Dr. Colby's regimen of treatment, and by the first of March we were delighted to learn that he was able to speak coherently and to recognize people around him, although these lucid intervals were but of brief duration.

On March 3rd I received a telephone call from Dr. Colby, apprising me that my friend was temporarily himself again, although it could not be predicted just how long the interlude of sanity would last. Dr. Blaine was calling me urgently, in a very agitated manner, and the sanitarium staff were of the opinion that it might be salubrious were I to visit him, so that his agitation could be eased and his mind unburdened of whatever matter he desperately desired to reveal to me. I replied that I would come at once.

I motored through the hills, following a winding road, the next morning. Arriving at the sanitarium about ten o'clock, I was taken to Harrington Colby at once. He was a tall, fit-looking man in his late forties with a manner both affable and authoritative. He cautioned me against saying anything that might upset Dr. Blaine, advising me merely to agree to do whatever it was he wished of me. Then he led me into a sunny, pleasant ward that looked out on rolling hills, and left me alone with Dr. Blaine.

It was all I could do to greet Dr. Blaine in a casual manner. He seemed to have aged ten years in the six months since his collapse. Hair that had been flecked with iron gray was now streaked with silver-white; he had lost forty or fifty pounds, his face was gaunt and lined, his once-robust figure curiously and horribly shrunken as he crouched in the chair, his trembling hands like pallid, withered claws.

His eyes were haunted and his voice tremulous as he greeted me.

"Hodgkins? Is that you? ... you look so different, I ... listen to me, Hodgkins ... I must know ... is the Ponape figurine yet on public display? ... please God, say it is not!"

I greeted him quietly, said I hoped he was feeling better, and assured him the artifact had not yet been put on display in the South Gallery.

"Thank God for that!" he cried in a weak, quavering voice; then, clutching my arm in a grip numbingly strong, he fixed his eyes on mine. The shadow of some indescribable horror filled those fine eyes with cold fear.

"The figurine must never be shown, Hodgkins ... *never*, do you understand? ... it must be destroyed, if the sanity of mankind is to survive ... but you must be extremely careful how you manage it ... there is a terrible force locked in the substance of the figurine ... a force which we do not dare release ... listen to me, boy! The *Necronomicon* has the secret ... you must locate a copy of the *Necronomicon* ... try the Miskatonic University Library in Arkham, Massachusetts ... they have a copy of the Spanish edition ... Hodgkins, in the bottom drawer of my desk you will find my file of notes on the Xothic legend cycle ... the drawer is locked, but you will find the key to it in the little teakwood box from New Guinea on the shelf beside the window where I keep the lava tomb figures from Easter Island ... *read the file carefully, before doing anything else!* Promise me that you will follow my instructions to the letter, my boy ... until you have absorbed the data in my file, little of this will make any sense to you ... so promise!"

Needless to say I understood absolutely none of this, but he was so pitifully insistent that I swore to do my best to obey his instructions. It was the least I could do, and my words seemed to reassure him. He grew calmer, and much of the tension left his features. We chatted a little on general matters concerning the Institute; shortly thereafter Dr. Colby entered the ward and intimated to me that his patient had had enough excitement for today. I left the sanitarium a few minutes later, after extracting from the physician his promise to keep me informed on the progress of the treatments.

II.

THE afternoon was spent at the Institute, finishing up a few last matters concerning the coming exhibition of the Copeland Collection. I did not again think of Dr. Blaine's urgent insistence that I study the material in his private file until just before I left for the day; recalling his words, and my own promise, I found the key where he had hidden it, unlocked the drawer, and took out the file.

That evening after dinner, I stretched out in an easy chair in my lodgings and began going through the bulging folder. It was filled with heterogeneous material, typewritten and handwritten notes, lists and summaries, packets of newspaper clippings, lengthy abstracts from scholarly works largely unfamiliar to me, and various items of personal correspondence, all bundled together without the slightest semblance of method or order. I could see it would take me quite a while to make head or tail out of all this.

Leafing through the papers, however, I got a general impression from the miscellany. It would seem that Professor Copeland had begun the file, for his spidery hand was unmistakable. He had started collecting newspaper clippings, and had been ordering his notes. The Copeland material formed the basic nucleus of the file. Dr. Blaine had obviously performed extensive work in organizing, collating, and extending the original Copeland material, for his bold yet neat Spencerian hand, quite familiar to me, could be seen throughout the mass of notes, clippings, and manuscript in the form of copious annotations, summaries, and marginal glosses. I glanced quickly through the material that evening, and studied it more closely and in detail for the next several days, so I can give you an accurate overall outline of its central thesis.

It seems that Professor Copeland had gone to the island of Ponape in the Carolines early in 1909, chasing down elusive clues as to a legendary, prehistoric Pacific civilization of vast antiquity. He had first encountered rumors of this lost civilization years earlier, while researching his monumental study *Polynesian Mythology, with a Note on the Cthulhu Legend Cycle* (1906). While compiling data for that great work of scholarship he had become intrigued by frequent references in the native folklore and literature to a "lost homeland" long since vanished beneath the waves. The old Maori *Chant of Eternity*, the magnificent but enigmatic Samoan *Creation Song*, and similar works abound in cryptic allusions to a mysterious lost land called variously "Ha-wa-iki" or "Maui", which last name was puzzlingly reminiscent of the legendary "Mu."

Ponape was the most likely site for Copeland's opening research on the lost civilization; a mountainous, heavily jungled island, largest of the islands in the Carolines group, it has long been famous for its mysterious and unexplained ruined cities of curious blue stone. These twin megalithic cities, called Nan-Matal and Metalanim, first aroused the bewildered curiosity of European explorers in 1826, when they were discovered by a shipwrecked Irish sailor named O'Connell or O'Connor. It is now a hundred years since the first European glimpsed the cyclopean, basaltic ruined cities of blue stone, and we have as yet no reliable clue to the mystery of their origin.

On Ponape, Copeland heard whispers of certain curious rites that had lingered from time immemorial among the jungle natives; they worshiped a "Water-Being" they called "Lord of the Abyss", and it was rumored the secret rituals included human sacrifice. Copeland was intrigued by how closely these bloody rites paralleled the ancient Semitic worship of the Philistine fish-god Dagon, and he was even more intrigued when, questioning a native "ghost-doctor" about the secret cult, he discovered that the Ponape natives knew all about Dagon, whom they termed "leader of the Deep Ones." It was not Dagon they worshiped, the ghost-doctor confided to him, but one far greater and more terrible even than Dagon, indeed, the *very son of Him whom Dagon and the Deep Ones served*.

Copeland learned that the sea-god cult had existed in the jungled depths of Ponape for uncounted ages, but had only within recent months grown enormously. The factor had been the discovery of a jade idol, brought up by a native diver from the offshore waters early in that same year. The wizards of the sea-god cult recognized the idol as the very likeness of their god, whom they called *Sothmogg*. Now Copeland knew he was on the trail of something very interesting, for he had found traces of the sinister, secretive worship of a marine devil-god of similar name all over the Pacific. The Cook Islanders worshiped him as *Zatamaga*, the "fisherman's god"; on New Caledonia they venerated him under the name of *Hommogah*; in the Marquesas, the natives knew him as *Z'otomogo*, or *Zatamagwa*; in New Zealand, the Maori shamans knew him as *Sothamogha*; natives in the Sepik River region of New Guinea called him *Zhmog-yaa*; and even in South Indo-China, degenerate native cults worshiped a being called *Z'mog*.

It was Copeland's theory that this enigmatic sea god of Ponape was none other than *Zoth-Ommog*, the Dweller in the Deeps, one of the three sons of Cthulhu who had been mighty gods in elder Mu before the cataclysm destroyed that shadow-haunted and primal continent in prehistoric times ... Zoth-Ommog, whose name lingers yet in the sealed, forbidden pages of certain inconceivably ancient books which are preserved under lock and key and armed guard in a handful of the world's great libraries.

Somehow or other, Copeland got possession of the jade statuette, to which his notes refer as "the Ponape Figurine." As he began to delve yet deeper into the enormous literature of this obscure mythology, he learned of strange and terrible things. At Cambridge, he dipped into the horrendous pages of the loathsome *Necronomicon* itself, the weird and half-mythic "bible" of this ancient mythology. He made another discovery as well: that a mysterious manuscript or document had come to light on Ponape back in 1734, nearly a century before the ancient stone cities had been first discovered. This book, a handwritten codex of frightful antiquity, had been found by a Yankee sea trader, a Captain Abner Exekiel Hoag, who brought it back to his home port, Arkham, Massachusetts, where it was translated for him by a half-breed Polynesian-Asiatic servant. The codex, which was known as the "Ponape Scripture", is now in the Kester Library in Salem.

Copeland studied this *Ponape Scripture* in Salem, and delved into other hideously suggestive and rightfully suppressed books at Cambridge and at Miskatonic. In time he produced the book he had been researching on Ponape. It was entitled *The Prehistoric Pacific in the Light of the* Ponape Scripture (1911), and it was a death-blow to his scientific reputation. But by then he was deeply immersed in his studies of the age-old, worldwide mythos he had so oddly stumbled upon, and the Xothic file contained his working notes on that subject.

The basic premise of this mythology was that early men had worshiped a pantheon or family of divinities that had come down from the stars when the earth was young. These beings were essentially malign and had ruled man through fear, being more demons than gods; the most common term for them was "the Old Ones", and they were not even remotely anthropomorphic. They had some innate correspondence to the four elements of earth, air, fire, and water: For example, the chief divinity, a winged, octopus-headed monstrosity named Cthulhu, was a sea elemental; his half-brother, Hastur, was an air elemental; another, Cthugha, was a fire elemental; and so on. These were known as "the Great Old Ones", and subservient to them was a second group of minor entities which Copeland called "the Lesser Old Ones"; this second group was composed of the beings who served the Great Old Ones as leaders of their minions or servants. For example, the minions of Cthulhu were called the "Deep Ones", led by "Father Dagon and Mother Hydra", and the minions of Cthugha were the so-called "Flame-Creatures", whose leader, Fthaggua, dwelt on a world called Ktynga; the great air elemental, Hastur, was served by the "Outer Ones", under their leader, N'gha-Kthun. These beings were identified with the famous "Abominable Mi-Go" of Himalayan folklore and Nepalese hill legend, in a note in Dr. Blaine's hand.

Reading further, I learned that these gods or demons rather resembled the fallen angels of Old Testament lore, having warred against and been defeated by a superior, rival pantheon called "the Elder Gods", who either banished them to distant stars (as Cthugha to Fomalhaut and Hastur to Aldebaran), or imprisoned them at various places upon the earth. Cthulhu himself they locked away in a sunken stone city called R'lyeh beneath the Pacific; his son Ghatanothoa they sealed within a mountain on Mu. His second son, Ythogtha, was imprisoned in a chasm in Yhe, a Muvian province, while Zoth-Ommog lay enchained beneath the ocean off the "Island of the Sacred Stone Cities", which Copeland had identified to his own satisfaction as being Ponape itself. An interlineation at this point stated that Cthulhu had fathered these three godlings on a female entity named Idh-yaa, who dwelt on or near the "dim green double star, Xoth" in the aeons before his descent to this planet. Hence, I assume, the term "Xothic legend cycle" when collating material bearing upon Cthulhu and his "spawn."

As for the twin leaders of this rebellion, Azathoth the "Demon-Sultan" and Ubbo-Sathla the "Unbegotten Source", they were reduced to idiocy by the Elder Gods, who thrust Azathoth beyond the physical universe into primal chaos from which he can never return, while Ubbo-Sathla they confined forever at a subterranean place referred to only as "gray-litten Y'qaa."

Several factors concerning this account intrigued me at once. In the first place, this mythology bore not the slightest resemblance to any of the native Pacific religions; indeed, the more I came to think about it, these banished or imprisoned gods of evil far more closely correspond to common Indo-European mythologies than to the Pacific island religions, which was quite odd and curious. Reading of banished Hastur and imprisoned Cthulhu and his spawn reminded me at once of the fallen archangel, Lucifer, in the Old Testament, of the titan Prometheus in the Greek myths, and of Norse legends of the imprisoned Loki and his chained children, the wolf Fenris and the gigantic serpent, Iormungandar.

Indeed, from the simple outline of the myths in this Xothic legend cycle, I would most naturally have considered the entire myth structure an example of notions borrowed from earlier legends; but Copeland's notes were quite firm on the point that the Cthulhu mythology predated the Indo-European civilizations by vast geological epochs of time, which seemed to me completely incredible.

Then, too, there was the extraterrestrial origin of the Great Old Ones, which was an astonishingly sophisticated notion for primitive island cults to have conceived. The notion of the gods of the Cthulhu pantheon as cosmic demons from distant stars and planets seemed like something drawn from the scientific romances of E. E. Smith or Ray Cummings, such as filled the pages of Mr. Gernsback's new magazine, *Amazing Stories*, a pulp periodical which I had been occasionally picking up at my local newsstand for the last year or two to beguile my leisure with some casual entertainment.

The Copeland notes, as organized by Dr. Blaine, centered largely about Cthulhu in particular and his Xothic spawn, rather to the neglect of the other members of the pantheon. Copeland drew surprisingly convincing parallels between this tentacled monstrosity, chained in his stone city at the bottom of the sea, and the horribly amorphous god of the ocean depths, the horrible Kon, Lord of the Earthquake, venerated by the pre-Incan tribes of Peru; and also to the repulsive "Devourer", the war god of the Quicha religion, and to the Incan divinity Huitzilopochtli. It was his opinion, reiterated over and over, that Cthulhu was the *original monster* behind these "later" mythical beings—the prototype from which they gradually evolved, after the collapse of the empire of primal Mu, destroyed in some prehistoric cataclysm. This contention, by the way, he supported with a wealth of scholarly data which was, superficially at least, most impressive.

Another element which greatly intrigued me was that despite the obscurity of this cult it had apparently been the object of study by scholars in different parts of the world for a long time. Both Copeland's original notes and Blaine's additions thereto mentioned any number of scholarly authorities—the Flemish wizard, Ludvig Prinn, a German scientist named von Junzt, an American professor named Dr. Laban Shrewsbury, a titled European demonologist, the Comte d'Erlette, and others. Scholarly investigation of this Cthulhu mythos had seemingly been going on all over the world for some centuries, but in a secretive and surreptitious manner. And I could not help wondering why the subject was surrounded with such secrecy. The oddest item of all was the book to which Dr. Blaine had attached such prime importance during our brief interview at the Sanitarium—the *Necronomicon* itself. The title, of course, is Greek, but the book itself, apparently the "Bible" of the Cthulhu cult, had been written by an Arab writer no less than *eleven centuries* ago!

There seemed to be no genuine grounds for questioning the extreme antiquity of this mysterious mythos, for I found copious documentation for the dates of some of these scholars in standard reference works. But the lack of open, international discussion of this mythos was completely baffling; for centuries, it seemed, there had existed an enormous conspiracy of silence about Cthulhu, his sons and brethren, and their minions and worshipers. I have to admit I found this mysterious secrecy enigmatic, disturbing, and frightfully *suggestive* ....

* * *

OUT of this mass of material, one portion in particular caught my attention. It was a sheaf of manuscript clipped together under the heading *"Ponape Figurine."*

The first page, in Copeland's hand, consisted of data concerning the figurine: weight, specific gravity, measurements, and so on. This was followed by Copeland's notes on the hieroglyphic inscription cut into the base of the image—an inscription he tentatively identified as either "Tsath-yo" or "R'lyehian." I had never heard of either of these languages, if that is what they were supposed to be, but obviously the term "R'lyehian" was derived from "R'lyeh", which was the name of the submerged stone city in which Cthulhu supposedly lay imprisoned. Copeland tentatively identified the figurine as an image of Zoth-Ommog, the Dweller in the Deeps, one of the three sons of Cthulhu; Copeland's notation was that the entity was chained beneath the sea *in a submarine chasm off the island of Ponape.*

There was something disturbingly suggestive in these facts, when mentioned in juxtaposition. The demon-god from the stars, sealed in a chasm beneath the waters off Ponape ... and an image of that same divinity, brought up by a native diver from those identical waters ....

The implications of the coincidence were strangely frightening, so much so that I felt a sudden curious reluctance to read any further in the file that night. The remainder of the papers did not look very inviting, anyway. They consisted of long, meaningless excerpts from books with wild, nightmarish titles like *Cultes des Goules, De Vermis Mysteriis*, and so on. Some inner urge, like an unheard voice, seemed almost to be warning me to read no further. It was an odd, and a rather unsettling, sensation.

I suddenly realized that I was very sleepy. I could hardly keep my eyes open and my body yearned for the warm, soft oblivion of sleep. I put the sheaf of notes clipped together under the heading of "Ponape Figurine" back in the folder with the rest of the material and, promising to continue my further investigations tomorrow, decided to turn in and call it a day.

My dreams that night were not ... pleasant.

I am not the sort of person who usually pays any attention to dreams, and rarely, upon awakening, can I recall the shape or sequence of my nocturnal visions, but that night one image filled my dreams, making them hideous, and remained horribly fresh in my mind the next morning.

It was ... *a face*. Again and again, through the tumbling mists of my dream that face leered out at me with cold and evil eyes, intent and watchful.

The face was not remotely human. It bore the stamp of cruel mockery, of vicious gloating, of inhuman and fiendish glee.

It was a face I knew, a face I had seen before. But in my dreams I knew it not; indeed, it was not until the following day, when I awoke with morning feeling drained and enervated from a night of feverish and chaotic slumber, that I could recall where I had seen that cruel visage of malignant horror before. And when I did in fact remember, a thrill of inexplicable dread went through me.

It was the face of the Ponape figurine.

III.

THAT morning I brought the Blaine/Copeland file back to my office at the Institute so that I could complete my cursory examination of it, once my morning's work was out of the way.

The first thing I did was to take out the figurine itself. We kept it in the office safe, together with another item from the Copeland bequest we did not intend to put on public display, as its authenticity had not yet been established. This second item was the dubious and controversial *Zanthu Tablets*, which Professor Copeland had reputedly discovered in the stone tomb of a prehistoric shaman in the mountainous territory north of the Tsang plateau region of central Asia during his ill-fated expedition of 1913. It will perhaps be recalled that it was the ill-advised publication of his shocking and chaotic "conjectural translation" of the *Tablets* in the form of a privately printed brochure in 1916 that had aroused such a public outcry, from press and pulpit alike, as to impair irreparably his scientific reputation. This set of twelve black jade tablets, narrowly incised on both sides with row upon row of minute characters in an unknown language which Copeland's notes refer to as "hieratic Naacal", we deemed too notoriously dubious to include in our forthcoming display.

The figurine itself is a most unusual artifact, quite unlike any other sculpture of native workmanship ever found in the Pacific area. It stands nearly nineteen inches high and is exquisitely carved of glossy, highly polished jade of an unfamiliar type not yet identified. The stone itself is a greasy, grayish-white, mottled with irregular patches of dark green, and it is harder and more dense than any other known variety of jade.

The artistry of the carving is surprisingly sophisticated for a region whose sculptural attainments seldom rise above crude, geometrical bas-reliefs and rough, anthropomorphic idol-making. As Dr. Blaine's notes on the figurine remark, it is "not only non-humanoid, but virtually non-objective—hauntingly suggestive of some of the weird carven figures of the little-known amateur sculptor, Clark Ashton Smith—and in detail and finish, to say nothing of conception, ... weirdly reminiscent of the brilliant if degenerate work produced by the famed San Francisco sculptor, Cyprian Sincaul." Dr. Blaine's notes on the figurine are succinct and well phrased to the point where I can hardly hope to improve upon them, so I shall simply quote them directly:

"It represents a peculiar creature with a body shaped like a broad-based, truncated cone. A flat, blunt, wedge-shaped, vaguely reptilian head surmounts this conical torso, and the head is almost entirely hidden behind swirling tresses. This hair, or beard and mane, consists of thickly carved and coiling ropes, like serpents or worms, and the workmanship is so uncannily naturalistic that you could almost swear the slithering tendrils are in motion. Through this repulsive Medusa-mane of ropy tendrils, two fierce, serpent-like eyes glare in a horrible mingling of cold, inhuman mockery and what I can only describe as gloating menace. ... The base upon which this truncated, conical body rests is carved from the same unfamiliar speckled jade, and it is oddly angled, as if the sculptor's culture possessed a completely non-Euclidean geometry. Deeply and cleanly cut in one side of this odd-angled base are two exceedingly complex hieroglyphs in no language known to me, symbols which bear no similarity to either Chinese ideographs, Egyptian glyphs, Arabic characters, Sanskrit, or even common forms of Mesopotamian cuneiform, and certainly no slightest resemblance to any Southern or Central Pacific native writing known to me."

Dr. Blaine's notes on the Ponape figurine conclude thusly: "Rising from overlapping folds at the base of the image's neck, four bluntly tapering limbs or appendages rise. ... They are flat and resemble the arms of the common echinoderm of the class *asteroidea*—the familiar starfish of our California beaches—with the rather peculiar exception that the underside of these broad, flat, narrowing limbs bear row upon row of disc-like suckers ... the unknown artist has combined suggestions of starfish and squid or octopi in his central conception."

Dr. Blaine's description is admirably scientific, but what he cannot suggest is the curiously horrible sensation of distinct *unease* the observer feels when he looks upon the mysterious figurine. The sensation is quite literally horrible: Something in the cold, fixed, *knowing* glare of those reptilian eyes of carved, lustrous stone, and some uncanny hint of *physical menace* in the way the jade tentacles seem to lift and reach, as if striving to seize and entangle the helpless observer in their loathsome coils, is ... quite thoroughly unnerving, and has to be experienced to be believed.

Handling the stone thing was suddenly repugnant. The cold, slick, greasy surface was repellent to the touch, and the sluggish, leaden weight of it suddenly seemed overpoweringly unpleasant. I put the ugly thing down atop the safe and turned with an irrepressible shudder of uneasiness to a scrutiny of the notes.

I had abandoned my study of the file on the figurine the night before at the point at which Professor Copeland had inserted several lengthy and incomprehensible excerpts quoted from scholarly or mythological texts. I read these with intense curiosity, mingled, I must admit, with slight amusement and contempt, for the farrago of superstitious mumbo-jumbo sounded like the spewings of a mad brain. Nevertheless, remembering Blaine's urgent warnings about the danger that lurked in the Ponape figurine, I must say I found a singularly ominous undertone pervading the excerpts.

The first item was a quotation copied from Ludvig Prinn's *De Vermis Mysteriis*. It ran as follows:

"Byatis, the serpent-bearded, the god of forgetfulness, came with the Great Old Ones from the stars, called by obeisances made to his image"— this passage was heavily underscored, probably by Professor Copeland. It continued: "which was brought by the Deep Ones to Earth. He may be called by the touching of his image by a living being." That passage was underscored, as well. "His gaze brings darkness of the mind; and it is told that those who look upon his eye will be forced to walk into his clutches. He feasts upon those who stray to him, and from those upon whom he feasts he draws a part of their vitality, and so grows vaster. For there is this about those images of the Great Old Ones brought down from the stars when all the Earth was young, that a psychic link connects such as Byatis or Han to their images, and they that worship the Great Old Ones and who serve them on this plane may communicate with their Masters through such eidola; but a fate darkling and terrible beyond belief is reserved for they who unwittingly possess such idols from Beyond, for them the Old Ones drain of vitality through this psychic link, and their dreams are made hideous with nightmare glimpses of the Ultimate Pit."

The passage from Prinn's book broke off there. I mused over it, and suddenly I recalled the long weeks Dr. Blaine had studied the Ponape figurine, which Professor Copeland had believed an image of Zoth-Ommog, and how he had complained of bad dreams during those weeks of proximity to the figurine.

The next quotation was from a book called *Revelations of Glaaki*, or from a part of it, which Professor Copeland referred to as "the suppressed twelfth volume", whatever he meant by that cryptic remark. This second quotation, also, was a frenzied babbling of weird names and meaningless symbols, and it had much of the sinister nightmarish tone of certain volumes of the Biblical apocrypha. It went as follows, beginning apparently in the very middle of a sentence:

> ... so may Y'golonac return to walk among men and await that time when the earth is cleared off and Cthulhu rises from his tomb among the weeds, Glaaki thrusts open the crystal trapdoor, the brood of Eihort are born into daylight, Shub-Niggurath strides forth to smash the moon-lens, Byatis bursts forth from his prison, Daoloth tears away illusion to expose the reality concealed behind, Aphoom Zhah rises from the bowels of Yarak at the ultimate and boreal pole, Ghatanothoa emerges from his crypt beneath the mountain-top fortress of Yaddith-Gho in eldritch Mu, and Zoth-Ommog ascends from the ocean deeps. *Iä! Nyarlathotep!* By their very images shall ye conjure them.

The third of these excerpts was the most inexplicable of all; it had been taken from a book by the Comte d'Erlette, the *Cultes des Goules*, and it went thusly:

> There is a Terror lurks in carven stone: not without reason do the children of the wastes shun horrible and thousand-columned Irem, whereof each pillar bears up an eidolon of Those Who Dwell Afar, and it is not idle superstition that bids the beholder shudder when he looks upon the monstrous and brooding Sphinx, remembering that tenebrous and frightful thing whereof it is but a simulacrum. But more to be shunned and dreaded even than these are those images brought down from Beyond ere the first Men slunk whimpering through the steaming fens of the primal Earth; for those eidola are imbued with a loathsome curse, and betimes they drain the strength of men, or fill their minds with loathsome and seductive dreams; and some whisper that the Outside Ones can be summoned hither through their very images; but I pray this last be but idle legend, for if it be truth, then the World stands in horrendous peril until such star-brought idols be destroyed to the last one.

To this final quotation there was affixed, as a marginal gloss in Professor Copeland's spidery script, a note which Dr. Blaine had underscored three times: "*Cf. NEC. III, xvii.*"

This, I suddenly realized, was the single item of transcendent import to which poor, deranged Dr. Blaine had pitiably strove to direct my attention. This clue told me exactly where in the pages of that mysterious *Necronomicon* could be found the ritual or formula whereby the Ponape figurine could safely be destroyed!

So significant did this fact appear that I took out my pocket notebook on the spot and copied down that marginal gloss in full, so that I could not mislay the information.

And, even as I did so, an indescribable feeling of being *watched* came over me. The skin literally *crept* at the nape of my neck, and an inexplicable paralysis of overwhelming fear seized me. The pressure of cold, unseen, malignant eyes from somewhere behind me was simply unmistakable.

Someone ... or something ... was watching me, with a chilling, completely evil, calculating glare.

I turned around suddenly, and looked into cold, carved eyes of lifeless stone. It was the jade image of Zoth-Ommog, which I had left on top of the office safe.

I forced a shaky laugh, and tried to shrug off the distinct feeling of uneasiness. *But I could have sworn that when I put the image down earlier, it had been facing the other way.*

* * *

FOR the next week or so I was too deeply immersed in my official duties to return to a further study of the Xothic legend cycle. The directors of the Institute had met in formal session several times during this interval, and the trend of these meetings was singularly disturbing to me.

To put it bluntly, it was in the process of being decided that the display of the Copeland collection should after all include the Ponape figurine! It was the feeling of the directors that public interest in the notorious figurine, whipped up by regrettably sensational newspaper articles, would bring the public to the Institute in droves, curious to see for themselves the mysterious idol whose ancient "curse" had driven two famous scholars insane.

Although I cannot quite explain why, I must admit I was appalled at this decision and did my best to argue the directors out of it. In this attempt I failed resoundingly, for I could offer no factual evidence as to the unwisdom of this act. What, after all, could I say—that one man, who had died a raving maniac, had scribbled down some notes on an obscure mythology—notes which seemed to suggest that a weird and supernatural danger hovered about the bit of sculpture? Or could I argue that another man, still confined to a sanitarium because of a nervous breakdown, had uttered some vague, hysterical warnings against displaying the statuette? Obviously, I could hardly use these arguments, based on superstition and hysteria, to counter the decision of the directors. In fact, I could find no basis to justify my own feeling of uneasiness at the thought of exposing the figurine before a curious and sensation-hungry public; surely, even I did not accept this occult nonsense to be literally true!

Or—did I?

Despite my own lack of conviction, I argued as eloquently as I could against the decision. I tried to convey the notion that to put the Ponape figurine on public display would be premature—that its authenticity had yet to be fully established—that to display a questionable piece would be mere sensation-mongering, mere headline-hunting. To these arguments, the directors listened courteously, but nothing I could say swayed their opinion in the slightest degree.

In the meantime, I redoubled my efforts to locate a copy of the *Necronomicon*. I fired off telegrams by the dozen, and the replies that came trickling back were unanimously disappointing. None of the universities in the state seemed to possess a copy of this fabulously rare volume, and none of the great private libraries or collections would admit to owning it, either. My desperation to find the *Necronomicon* must have seeped through the formal phraseology of my missives, for some of the libraries replied in sympathetic, helpful tones to my queries. Of these, the Huntington was most friendly, advising me to try the British Museum, the Kester Library in Salem, or the Miskatonic library in Arkham. The note from the Huntington helpfully added that they did, at least, have a copy of the *Unaussprechlichen Kulten* of von Junzt, which reputedly discussed a range of material parallel to much of the substance of the *Necronomicon*. I was grateful for their helpfulness at the Huntington, but the last thing I needed was the von Junzt; a copy of the 1840 Düsseldorf edition of the *Unaussprechlichen Kulten* had been found among Professor Copeland's papers, and was currently in the library of the Institute, although I had not yet had the opportunity to look into it.

The Huntington's suggestion that I try the library of Miskatonic University in Arkham, Massachusetts, recalled to mind Dr. Blaine's identical stricture. I sent off a wire to the university library, inquiring if they possessed the *Necronomicon*, and seeking to arrange an interlibrary loan. A day or two later I received a friendly reply from the librarian at Miskatonic, a Dr. Henry Armitage, which said that their collection did indeed include a copy of the *Necronomicon* in the Latin version of Olaus Wormius, printed in Spain during the seventeenth century, but that it was simply too rare and valuable to be permitted to leave the collection. Dr. Armitage added that Miskatonic possessed the only copy of the complete edition known to exist in America, and that there had been numerous attempts in recent years to purchase it from the library, and even to steal the precious volume. His reply was affable and friendly, adding that if it was at all possible for me to visit Arkham, he would be delighted to permit me to examine the *Necronomicon* at my leisure.

By this time it had become clear to me that if I was going to study the *Necronomicon*'s recipe for the destruction of the figurine, I was indeed going to have to make the long trip from Santiago to Arkham, Mass. And, in fact,

I could see a way to do it. For the Institute still owed me two weeks' vacation, as I had volunteered to give up my vacation and stay on duty the previous year, when Dr. Blaine had suffered his nervous collapse.

Now that my work on organizing and classifying the Copeland bequest was finished, the Institute actually had no pressing need of my services, and could well afford to give me the next two weeks off for a brief vacation from my duties. I wasted no time in making such a request of the directors, and received their favorable reply. I then dispatched a wire to Dr. Armitage, informing him of my trip, and began looking up railroad schedules.

IV.

THE trip was long and slow and time-consuming. I took a bus to Los Angeles and caught the east-bound train there, changing trains in Denver and again in Chicago, and one last time in Boston, where I boarded a local for the last leg of my journey.

I had taken a private compartment all the way, and, thinking I would need something to read during the long trip, I had brought along in my briefcase Professor Copeland's copy of the rare *Unaussprechlichen Kulten* of von Junzt. In abstracting this book from the Institute's files, I suppose I was guilty of a technical irregularity, but it was hardly likely to be missed, as no one on the staff knew or cared to know what it was.

I examined the book with some curiosity. It was a big quarto, bound in dark leather with rust-eaten iron hasps. I had looked the book's history up and had learned this was the original binding, and that only a half dozen known copies of this first edition are extant. Von Junzt, or, to give his full name, Friedrich Wilhelm von Junzt, had been born at Cologne in 1795, taught as a professor of Occultism and Metaphysics at the famous University of Wurttemberg, and died under singularly curious circumstances in Düsseldorf in 1839, just before his monumental book appeared in print for the first time. There was a cheap and faulty "pirated" edition published by Bridewell in 1845, and a heavily expurgated version in English appeared in 1909 from Golden Goblin Press in New York City.

I opened it at random; it was in German, of course, and the paper was in quite good condition considering that the volume was nearly a century old, although the pages were somewhat smudged and stained. As I flipped through the front matter my eye was caught by the name "Abdul Alhazred" on page ix. Alhazred, of course, was the Muslim demonologist whose chief claim to fame was his authoring of the *Necronomicon*; I read the passage which contained this reference to him, which began *"es steht zweifel, dass dieses Buch ist die Grundlage der Okkulteliteratur"*, and was amused to see what von

Junzt had to say about Alhazred's reputed insanity, which was more than a trifle ironic in light of the fact that many of his learned colleagues of the time had thought von Junzt quite seriously deranged himself.

Before long I found myself thoroughly engrossed in the turgid prose of the great German occultist. His book discussed many weird and curious cults which survived in the remoter corners of the world, such as the Thuggee murder-cults of India and the Dacoits of Burma and the corpse-eating cult of further Thibet, but centrally the book concerned itself with a worldwide network of secret societies who served or worshiped the Great Old Ones. The opening part of this central section of the book was an essay of considerable length which traced the descent of the Old Ones from their mighty parents or progenitors (von Junzt remained ambiguous as to their sex) who were named Azathoth and Ubbo-Sathla, names I recollected had been mentioned in the Copeland notes. This essay, which ran to something like ninety pages of text, was called the "Narrative of the Elder World", and was partly a translation of the third book of the *Livre d'Ivon*, a book written or translated by a 13th Century Norman-French scholar called Gaspard du Nord, and partly an annotation or exegesis of the third book, which von Junzt had put together by collating the *Livre d'Ivon* text with comparable data given in the Latin *Necronomicon*. Although interminable, written in the long-winded style typical of classic Germanic scholarship, this account of the basic mythology contained a considerable amount of material that was new to me, and much that was not to be found in the Blaine/Copeland notes.

From my earlier study of the Copeland file on the Xothic material I already knew that the professor had long strove to obtain a copy of von Junzt's famous (or perhaps infamous) tome. Now, as I delved deeper, I found that von Junzt's book was invaluable to scholars of this mythology because, of all those who had studied or written upon this legend cycle, it was von Junzt alone who had had unlimited access to certain unthinkably old and fantastically rare mythological works which contained precious information on the details of the mythos not available to the later writers on this subject.

Among these exceedingly rare books was one known as the *Pnakotic Manuscripts* which, like the du Nord book, had never been printed and was circulated in manuscript only among the cultists. The *Pnakotic Manuscripts* was, however, unthinkably more ancient than the *Livre d'Ivon*, or *Book of Eibon* as it is sometimes known. The traditional account of the origins of the *Manuscripts* (which von Junzt solemnly repeats without comment) claims that the earliest chapters were reputedly set down before the first forms of life had come into existence on this Earth, the authors supposedly a mysterious extraterrestrial race of mental entities from "Yith" who came to this planet long before the advent of human or even mammalian life, and who dwelt somewhere in primordial Australia in a cyclopean stone city known to subsequent races as "Pnakotus", a name which was believed to mean something in the nature of "The City of the Archives." From this name, Pnakotus, obviously, the title *Pnakotic Manuscripts* was presumably derived.

Yet another sourcebook, even more terrifyingly ancient and alien, was believed to have been used by the German occultist—that dread chronicle, the *Ghorl Nigräl*, whose ultra-telluric origin is the secret of one of the most horrible of the dark myths locked within the dim pages of the *Book of Eibon*. There it is called *The Book of Night*, and it is told that the clawed, snouted, nonhuman wizard Zkauba, on a world called Yaddith of the Five Moons, thieved it from the monstrous Dholes. Von Junzt records of this *Ghorl Nigräl* that only one copy has ever been brought down to this planet from frightful Yaddith in all the immeasurable ages of Earth's existence in this part of space. This single copy is hidden somewhere in the black depths of Asia, at a place called Yian-Ho; there the book is whispered of in a thousand legends as "the hidden legacy of eon-old Leng." According to Gottfried Mülder, a scientist who accompanied von Junzt on his travels, and who contributed a foreword to the *Unaussprechlichen Kulten*, von Junzt was the only completely human entity who has been permitted to peruse this horribly ancient book whose origins, if truly given, are so alien as to stagger the imagination. To examine the *Ghorl Nigräl*, von Junzt had to venture to a remote, obscure, ill-reputed stone monastery somewhere in the interior of China, to which a train of yellow masked and robed and "oddly-misshapen" monks bore the precious codex from its secret hiding place for his perusal, in return for a certain price so repugnant and horrible that Mülder shudderingly refused to discuss it and went to his deathbed with the secret locked within him. This same Mülder, long after the death of von Junzt, whereof such odd and frightful stories were whispered, wrote an attempted reconstruction of what he remembered von Junzt telling him about the contents of this mysterious book, using Mesmerism and something which sounds like self-hypnosis to obtain perfect recall. His book, *The Secret Mysteries of Asia, with a Commentary on the* Ghorl Nigräl, was published at Mülder's own expense at Leipzig in 1847; copies are exceptionally rare, for the authorities seized and burned almost the entire printing, and Mülder himself narrowly escaped hanging by fleeing to Metzengerstein, where he died in a madhouse eleven years later.

* * *

THE copy of the *Unaussprechlichen Kulten* which Copeland had purchased from a dealer in rare books in Prague proved exceptionally interesting. The "Black Book" as it is sometimes called (the title translates as "Nameless Cults"), contains a vast wealth of material not even hinted at in the Copeland file. The old-fashioned black-letter text was difficult to read, but the strange marvels therein were so enthralling that I persevered.

According to von Junzt's account, the planet Earth was not originally a part of this physical universe at all, but originated in another, totally alien plane or dimension of being, that wherein the race of benevolent divinities known as the Elder Gods were supreme. The Elder Gods, near the very beginning of time, decided to create a subrace of lesser entities to be their slaves and thus brought into being the twin monstrosities, Azathoth and Ubbo-Sathla. These two beings, which seemed to be androgynous or multi-sexual, were to spawn a host of minor godlings who would serve the Elder Gods. But Azathoth and Ubbo-Sathla rebelled against their masters, and it was Ubbo-Sathla who stole from the Gods that aeon-old library of hieroglyph-engraved stone tablets, the Elder Records, which he hid away in his gray-lit abode of Y'qaa, deep within the earth. When the Elder Gods rose up in their wrath to seek out the place where the immemorial library lay concealed, Ubbo-Sathla evoked the cosmic powers he had learned from study of the Records, and Earth and its primal denizen fell from their original plane or dimension into our own universe, followed not long thereafter by Azathoth and the first-born of his spawn, Nyarlathotep, Yog-Sothoth, Cxaxukluth, and yet other primordial entities. According to von Junzt, Earth fell into our present universe "untold vingtillions of aeons ago."

This account of the rebellion of the original Great Old Ones was followed by a lengthy and detailed description of the descent and genealogy of the Great Old Ones, revealing much information unavailable to Copeland. According to von Junzt, Azathoth and his spawn traversed the stellar immensitudes from the edge of our universe to the region wherein Earth now resided, and along the way spawned yet other beings of their hellish breed. Yog-Sothoth, for example, first mated with a female denizen of a world called Vhoorl, which lay "deep in the twenty-third nebula", thus fathering Cthulhu; later, he mated with a second divinity at a place not named, fathering Cthulhu's half-brother, Hastur the Unspeakable.

Hastur, in turn, mated with a divinity named Shub-Niggurath, to spawn three sons named Ithaqua, Lloigor, and Zhar, who were air elementals similar to their terrible sire. Cthulhu himself mated with an entity named Idh-yaa at a place called Xoth, thus fathering Ghatanothoa, Ythogtha, and Zoth-Ommog, who accompanied their mighty sire down to Earth in later aeons, as I already knew from the Copeland file. As well, the fire elemental Cthugha spawned, on a world circling the star Fomalhaut, another fire elemental like himself named Aphoom Zhah, who descended to Earth, coming down in remote arctic regions. There was much more genealogical information than this given in the prolix pages of von Junzt, but I lack the time to discuss it in further detail. Let it suffice to say that the Great Old Ones grew numerous and when they entered this region of space, they invested Earth and three solar planets, among which was Mars, which became the dominion of Vulthoom, third of the sons of Yog-Sothoth. Cthulhu and his spawn took the Pacific for their empire, while Tsathoggua, the son of Ghizguth, took primal Hyperborea; Aphoom Zhah and his spawn extended their dominion over the regions of the ultimate boreal pole.

Earth at that time was ruled by a race of entities known as the Primordial Ones, described by von Junzt as "winged, crinoid-headed, semi-vegetable denizens of paleogean Antarctica", against whom certain of the Great Old Ones, principally Cthulhu and his Xothic spawn, warred. Not long thereafter another race contested with them for the supremacy of Earth, the so-called "Great Race of Yith", a swarm of purely mental entities who voyaged to this planet through time and space, assuming the bodies of a cone-shaped race already resident in primal Australia. The Great Race unleashed frightful weapons of terrific potency against the Old Ones, and even managed to drive them underground into enormous caverns for a time. But here the Old Ones encountered their lost brethren, the spawn of Ubbo-Sathla, and their power was vastly augmented. For during the numberless ages, Ubbo-Sathla had begotten many offspring as he wallowed in his gray-lit abyss of Y'qaa, and among these were Zulchequon and Abhoth, Nyogtha and Yig, Atlach-Nacha and Byatis and dark Han. Before long the Old Ones burst from the depths of the earth to challenge the Great Race, but by that time the Elder Gods had entered this universe and, centering their power about the star Betelgeuse, descended into this solar system to punish their former slaves for their iniquitous rebellion. The Great Race abandoned Earth, fleeing first to Jupiter, and next to a dark star in Taurus; their eventual goal, says von Junzt, is given in the *Pnakotic Manuscripts* as the future age of a post-human beetle race here on Earth. When life becomes extinct upon this planet, they will migrate to inhabit a race of bulbous vegetable entities on Mercury.

The Great Old Ones transported the Elder Records to a planet of the star Celaeno for safekeeping and fought mightily against the Elder Gods, but were defeated, as Copeland's notes had already informed me. But the *Unaussprechlichen Kulten* gave a much more detailed account of the banishment or imprisonment of the Great Old Ones than that contained in Copeland's cursory summary. Nyarlathotep, for example, lies enchained on "the World of Seven Suns", which von Junzt equates with the "shadow-haunted Abbith to which the *Pnakotic Manuscripts* so cryptically allude"; Hastur they sealed in the "cloudy depths" of Lake Hali, at Carcosa, on a world near Aldebaran in the constellation of the Hyades; while his brother, Vulthoom, together with his minions, the Aihais, and Ta-Vho-Shai their leader, the Elder Gods prisoned in the cavernous abyss of Ravormos, on Mars, beneath the age-old city of Ignar-Vath. Cthugha was sealed away on a planet encircling the star Fomalhaut, as I had already learned, but von

Junzt added the datum that his chief minion, Fthaggua, and the Flame-Creatures, or "Fire-Vampires" as the *Necronomicon* calls them, were banished to a distant world—Ktynga, it is called—and von Junzt tentatively identifies it with Norby's Comet, a stellar object in the vicinity of Antares which some astronomers believe will approach perilously close to our own planet some four centuries from now. As well, I might add, it was to "nightmarish Yaddith", a world near Deneb, that Shub-Niggurath was banished; while Lloigor and Zhar, two of the sons of Hastur, lie enchained beneath a ruined city in the jungles of Burma, served by their loathly minions, the Tcho-Tcho people, whose leader is E-poh.

As for the spawn of Ubbo-Sathla, several of them—such as Abhoth the Unclean, the spider-god Atlach-Nacha, and Zulchequon—are imprisoned with him, or near him, in primal caverns far beneath the earth, while Nyogtha was driven from this world, and is penned on a lightless world near the star Arcturus. But most of the Lesser Old Ones, it would seem, are *not* imprisoned, and work ever to free their masters from the bondage of the Elder Sign. Among these are Dagon and Hydra, who dwell on the ocean's floor, either in sunken R'lyeh or at a place called "many-columned Y'ha-nthlei", and Ubb, leader of the repulsive yuggs, who serve Ythogtha and Zoth-Ommog, and who also dwell beneath the sea. Naggoob, the "Father of Ghouls", chieftain of the servitors of Nyogtha the Dweller in Darkness, is also free, as are Quumyagga, leader of the shantaks; Sss'haa, chief of the serpentmen or Valusians who serve Yig, Father of Serpents; and Rlim Shaikorth, leader of the Cold Ones who are the minions of Aphoom Zhah ....

Hour after hour, as my train roared on across the prairies through the gathering darkness, I read ever deeper in this hellish and blasphemous forbidden lore, gripped by a sick fascination I can neither excuse nor explain. Finally I could read no more and turned shudderingly from the hypnotic pages of the old book to seek my bunk, and my feverish and nightmare-ridden dreams.

V.

ARKHAM, Massachusetts is an ancient Colonial town northeast of Boston on the bleak north Atlantic coast. Back in the dark days of the grim witchcraft hysteria, it had an evil reputation among the sober, God-fearing Puritan divines, and earned a notoriety second only to Salem as a center of the secret witch-covens. Of course, those days have long since passed by, but terrible legends are still whispered of the decaying old seaport and of its neighboring towns, Dunwich and Innsmouth and Kingsport. Back in the great days of the Yankee clipper ships, it was a rich and populous and bustling center of the sea trade; those days, too, have passed by, and today it is a crumbling backwater, slumping into a decay from which it will most likely never rise.

The Boston-Arkham local followed the curve of the Miskatonic River, and we entered Arkham at dusk on March the twentieth when the sky was a smoky crimson conflagration in the west. The town was drowned in a haze, with only the peaked church spires thrusting up against the darkening sky. The transition from sparsely wooded hills and scattered farms to the bleak, red-brick warehouses and commercial buildings along Water Street was quite abrupt. I got off at the B&M Station at the corner of High Lane and Garrison Street, and found a sleepy-eyed porter to carry my bag through the drafty, echoing, cavernous barn of a terminal to a small taxicab stand on the street. The cab was an old rattle-trap of a much-abused Model T, but the driver was a garrulous old character with side whiskers, so talkative as to belie the legend that all backwoods Yankees from this corner of the country were cantankerous and close-mouthed, suspicious of strangers.

Dr. Armitage had been kind enough to arrange rooms for me at the Athenaeum Club, so I asked the cabman to drive me there. We crossed the river by the Garrison Street Bridge to the southern section of town, my driver pointing out the local sights along the way. The Athenaeum Club was on Church Street, two blocks away from the university itself. The wind was raw and cold, the sky leaden, the streets and sidewalks heaped with snow. I shivered through my topcoat, this being my first experience with a New England winter.

My rooms were spacious and elegant; I unpacked swiftly, aware of feeling famished. There had been no dining car on the Boston-Arkham local and I had eaten nothing since lunch. It was too late in the evening for the club dining parlor to be still open, but the gentleman at the desk directed me to an excellent old restaurant at the foot of French Hill, only a brisk walk away. I retired early and, next morning, rose early, for my appointment with Dr. Armitage was to be at ten o'clock. It was a gray, dull day, the wind raw, the air bitterly cold. Gusts of sleet swept the narrow old streets, and the wind that blew off the river pierced my garments like a knife.

Arkham was an old, old town, and the signs and tokens of its Colonial past lay all about me as I strode down Church Street to the university quadrangle. To every side I saw buildings of amazing antiquity—many of them doubtless mansions built by the great 18th-century Arkham merchants, wealthy from the India trade. Some of the houses I passed undoubtedly dated to the Restoration, or even to Charles I. The street was an antiquarian's dream: rows of dormer windows, occasionally a fine old gambrel roof, peaked and overhanging gables, diamond-paned windows, doors with old brass knockers and fanlights above the lintels, and many of the roofs bore quaint "widows' walks." I passed Christ Church, one of the local landmarks, with its classic Georgian facade and steeple. Some of the alleyways were still cobbled, and I glimpsed gaslight fixtures through one window as I passed. Over all, however, brooded neglect and moldering decay, the tawdry and faded gloom of a city long past its prime.

Miskatonic University occupies an entire block, facing on the main business thoroughfare, Church Street, between West and Garrison. Most of the buildings are Georgian, but were restored sometime in the late 19th century, and badly, by someone with a hideous taste for Victorian Gothic. I entered by the huge wrought-iron front gate, framed between ugly red-brick columns, where a guard directed me to the faculty lounge where I was to meet Dr. Armitage, which lay across the snow-heaped quadrangle.

The faculty lounge was a long room, oak-paneled, with a superb fireplace of Georgian marble, and old, gilt-framed paintings of former deans and presidents frowning down on Florentine marble-topped tables neatly strewn with scholarly journals and on large, comfortable chairs upholstered in dark leather. Dr. Armitage was a large, ruddy-cheeked man with silver hair and keen blue eyes of piercing intensity which could as easily twinkle with good-humored zest as turn frosty with stern reproof. I had looked him up in the academic directories and knew that he had taken his M.A. degree here at Miskatonic and his doctorate at Princeton, and had as well an honorary Litt.D. from Johns Hopkins. Among the several books or pamphlets to his credit was a celebrated monograph titled *Notes Toward a Bibliography of World Occultism, Mysticism, and Magic*, which the Miskatonic University Press had issued in 1927.

The doctor greeted me warmly, wringing my hand in a firm and virile grip which belied the years evident in his silver locks. In an expansive and genial manner he hastened to introduce me to several of his colleagues, among them a fine-looking older man of ascetic and aristocratic mien who was Dr. Seneca Lapham of the Anthropology Department, Professor William Dyer the geologist, Dr. Ferdinand Ashley of the Department of Ancient History, and a young literature instructor named Wilmarth, an amateur folklorist of some note, as well as a young psychology instructor a year or two older than myself named Peaslee. The name seemed familiar, and before long I realized that he must be the son of Nathaniel Wingate Peaslee, former Professor of Political Economy here at Miskatonic, who had suffered a classic attack of amnesia a dozen or so years back, much written up in the newspapers and scientific journals of the day.

I accompanied Armitage and Dr. Lapham to the librarian's office, after a bracing cup of steaming tea. The university library is a very large red-brick building, situated at the southeast corner of the block, at the corner of Garrison and College Streets. A huge dog is kept chained at the foot of the

Italian marble steps leading up to the main entrance—a bull mastiff, I believe. He rose at our approach and regarded us levelly, not exactly in a menacing manner, but warily, as if ascertaining just who we were, with an eye toward inquiring if we had legitimate business here.

"Good boy, Cerberus, that's a good fellow," Armitage greeted him; satisfied, the great dog settled down once again, permitting us to pass. We entered a dim hall whose arched ceiling was adorned with faded frescoes. Marble busts done in the classic manner were placed on pedestals at intervals along the length of the hall, and among them I recognized Thoreau, Longfellow, Washington Irving, Walt Whitman, Whittier, and James Russell Lowell. There was one I did not recognize, a stern-lipped fellow with a stony glare. I inquired as to his identity. Dr. Armitage chuckled, and patted the marble pate as he passed it.

"That staunch old Puritan, Cotton Mather," he chuckled. "A bit out of place in such literary company, perhaps, but we could hardly do without him—Arkham and Salem were his favorite hunting grounds, in the old witchcraft days!"

We mounted a curving stair with gleaming mahogany banister and superb 18th-century carved posts, and were ushered into the librarian's office, crowded with filing cabinets and cluttered with books and papers. Armitage cleared off chairs for Dr. Lapham and myself, bade us sit, and seated himself behind a huge cluttered desk. He unlocked the bottom drawer, removing therefrom a large quarto volume, bound in cracked, ancient black leather and sealed with rust-eaten hasps, which he placed on the desk before him. A thrill of tremulous excitement rose within me at the sight of the old book.

I knew at once it was the *Necronomicon*.

* * *

DR. Armitage fixed me with an intent but friendly eye.

"Now, young Hodgkins, the first thing I want to say is that you may speak freely before Dr. Lapham and myself. We have a very good idea of your problem, and why it is so urgent that you consult the *Necronomicon*, and you need not be shy about discussing such matters in front of us. Neither of us will laugh at you ... God knows, we are both horribly familiar with these matters. This concerns the Great Old Ones, does it not? In particular, Zoth-Ommog, the son of great Cthulhu, whose jadeite image poor mad Copeland fetched back from Ponape—"

"How in the world did you know?" I blurted in astonishment. Armitage grinned, and Dr. Lapham leaned over to touch my arm.

"Mr. Hodgkins, I assure you that both Armitage and I have a deplorable taste for the more sensational newspapers—not that Stephenson Blaine's story has not found its way even into the staid columns of the

Boston *Globe*—and the Arkham *Advertiser*, our local paper, as well. I am 'sitting in' on this conference because Armitage knows I have made a private study of the Cthulhu pantheon for many years, and may well have something of merit to contribute. Your problem is, we deduce from the pages of the *Necronomicon* your inquiry informed us you wish to study, the problem of safely destroying the Ponape figurine. It is indeed a serious problem, and you should feel free to speak openly on the subject."

"Yes," Dr. Armitage nodded. "We have here at the library perhaps the greatest collection of books and documents regarding the Cthulhu mythology that exists in the entire world—probably the finest and most comprehensive collection ever compiled. Beside old Alhazred, we have Prinn and von Junzt, the *Pnakotic Manuscripts*, the Norman French version of the *Book of Eibon*, the *Celaeno Fragments*, *Cultes des Goules*, both the *R'lyeh Text* and the *Dhol Chants*, the *Hsan*, the *Cabala of Saboth* and the Egyptian *Black Rites*, Porta, Remigius, a manuscript copy of Winters-Hall's translation of *The Sussex Manuscript*, a few pages of the *Invocation to Dagon*, and other works as well. Needless to say, more than a few members of the faculty have studied this literature over the years. Indeed, until he disappeared under rather mysterious circumstances back in 1915, one of our fellow faculty members, Dr. Laban Shrewsbury of the Philosophy Department, enjoyed a reputation as perhaps the greatest living authority on the Cthulhu myth cycle. Among the other books, our collection includes his authoritative study, *An Investigation into the Myth Patterns of Latter-day Primitives, with Especial Reference to the R'lyeh Text*, which the University Press first issued in 1913. A great pity Shrewsbury isn't here; his advice on your problem would be invaluable!"

Dr. Seneca Lapham expressed his agreement. "However, between Armitage and myself, we can undoubtedly be of some help. Now, I don't exactly know how much of the literature of the mythology you have studied, young fellow, but I can assure you that if the Ponape figurine is, after all, one of the images brought down from the stars as would seem likely, then the problem of safely disposing of it is a serious one. As the *Necronomicon* will tell you, those likenesses of the Great Old Ones which were not made on this Earth are very dangerous to meddle with, potentially lethal, in fact. The surviving cults which worship the Old Ones can summon their Masters to manifest themselves physically on this plane by means of certain rituals performed before such images; the peril to human civilization such manifestations entail should be obvious. Luckily, the physical manifestations of the Old Ones on this plane are of temporary duration, with the exception of Nyarlathotep the Crawling Chaos—"

Armitage interrupted at this point, complaining that we were wasting valuable time in fruitless discussion. "The important question we must decide is how the figurine can best be destroyed," he said impatiently. "Let us concentrate on that. Now, one method that comes to mind is to invoke the aid of an opposing entity—perhaps you know the Comte d'Erlette's classification system, Mr. Hodgkins, which sorts the various Old Ones into four groups identified with the four elements of the Medieval mystics? Well, according to this system, certain of the entities are fundamentally in opposition to certain of their brethren, and their aid may be invoked against the manifestations of their rivals. Cthugha, for instance, as a fire elemental, has been successfully invoked against such earth elementals as Shub-Niggurath, Nyogtha, Tsathoggua, and even Nyarlathotep. By this process of reasoning, the air elementals, such as Hastur or Ithaqua, may be invoked against sea elementals, like your Zoth-Ommog. A possibility exists in this—"

Dr. Lapham nodded. "I agree; moreover, Hastur is rather ambiguous in his dealings with men, and has never seemed overtly hostile to them. However, why don't we permit this young man to peruse the *Necronomicon* at his leisure; the star-stone exorcism Alhazred recommends may after all be the best answer to his problem."

"Very well," Armitage said. He tapped the large, leather-bound volume on the desk before him. "Knowing your stay here was to be of brief duration, I removed the *Necronomicon* from the Rare Book Room the first thing this morning. I have inserted a marker at the passage you were interested in, young man, and a second marker indicates a relevant entry you should examine. Now, please make yourself at home—you'll find pen and ink and paper right there on the desk, if you wish to take notes—Lapham and I will be back in an hour or so to continue this discussion. Oh, the text is in 17th-century Latin, and is printed in German black-letter ... I hope that will not offer you any difficulties? Excellent, excellent! Well, just make yourself at home, then; come along, Lapham."

The door closed behind them, and I was alone with the famous *Necronomicon* at last.

VI.

THE heavy old book was bound in thick black leather, much cracked and flaking with age. It was sealed with hinges and a lock of rust-eaten iron, in the manner of books printed in Europe during the 17th century. I opened it gingerly, and was appalled at the noxious miasma of decay that arose to my nostrils from the withered, stained, and yellowed pages; nevertheless, I had come too far to hesitate now. Mastering the involuntary spasm of nausea that welled up in me as I breathed in the almost palpable reek of corruption that arose from the ancient and moldering tome, I pored over the thickly printed pages.

The translator, I knew, had been the Danish scholar Olaus Wormius, born in Jutland and subsequently famed for his Greek and Latin studies. He had from some unknown source obtained a copy of the rare Greek translation of the *Necronomicon*, which the Byzantine scholar Theodorus Philetas had secretly made from the original Arabic about A.D. 950. The text Wormius had used for his own Latin version was, in all likelihood, that of the original Constantinople edition later banned by the Patriarch Michael. The Wormius translation had itself only been published twice, the first printing having been a black-letter edition published in Germany around the year 1400, the second being the Spanish edition of 1622.

Glancing through the volume I was surprised to discover that, regardless of the large size of the quarto pages (which were about nine and one-half by twelve inches), rather less wordage appeared on each page than you might have expected from its proportions. This was due to the deep margins and gutters used by the printer, and also to the thick and clumsy black-letter type. Curious, I counted the words on two or three pages at random, finding them to average about three hundred and seventy-five words each.

The narratives contained in the first book, being personal accounts from the early years of Alhazred's own career of various uncanny experiences and magical or occult experiments, did not occupy me for very long. I soon turned to the page at which Dr. Armitage had inserted the first marker, which was page 177, midway into Book IV, and began slowly to translate the old Latin, with considerable help from a crumbling, yellowed manuscript of Dee's English version of the same passage, which Dr. Armitage had set out for me and which I was often forced to consult on some of the more difficult parts. The page read as follows, as best as I can recall:

> There is no curse that has no cure and no ill against which no remedy exists. The Elder Gods dwell remote and aloof from the affairs of men, yet They have not abandoned us to the wrath of Them from Outside and Their abominable minions: for within the five-pointed star carven of gray stone from ancient Mnar lies armor against witches and demons, against the Deep Ones, the Dholes, the Voormis, the Tcho-Tcho, the Abominable Mi-Go, the Shoggoths, the Valusians, and all such peoples and beings who serve the Great Old Ones and Their spawn; but it is less potent against the Great Old Ones Themselves. He who possesses the five-pointed star shall find himself able to command all beings who creep, swim, crawl, walk, or fly, even to the Source from which there is no returning. In the land of Yhe as in great R'lyeh, in Y'ha-nthlei as in Yoth, in Yuggoth as in Zothique, in N'kai as in K'n-yan, in Kadath-in-the-Cold-Waste as at the Lake of Hali, in Carcosa as in Ib, it shall have power; but even as the stars wane and grow cold, even as suns die and the spaces between the stars grow more great, so wanes the power of all things—of the five-pointed star-stone as of the spells put upon the Great Old Ones by the benign

Elder Gods: and there comes a time, as once there was a time, when it shall be shown that:
> That is not dead which can eternal lie
> And with strange aeons even Death may die.
But the time is not yet come, and still the star-stone from Mnar, marked with that sigil that is the Elder Sign, holds strong against the rage of Them it prisons, and against the wiles of those servants and minions who would set their masters free.

This passage, I must confess, meant but little to me. I had seen "Mnar" and "the Elder Sign" mentioned in the copy of von Junzt I had been reading on the train, but I had no inkling as to what these terms were supposed to mean.

The second passage which Dr. Armitage had marked with a slip of paper came a bit earlier in the volume, about midway through the seventeenth chapter of Book III, commencing on page 142. Recalling that cryptic note in Dr. Blaine's hand, *Cf. NEC. III, xvii*, which I had noticed in the Xothic file, I realized with some excitement that this must be the key and central reference to which he had with such urgency directed my attention. It was considerably lengthier than the other entry, so I copied it out on the sheaf of notepaper which Dr. Armitage had so thoughtfully supplied, and studied it later during my homeward journey to such an extent that my memory retains it word for word. It went thusly:

> Of the coming-down of the Great Old Ones from the stars, it is written in the *Book of Eibon* that the first who came hither was the black thing, even Tsathoggua, who came hence from dim Cykranosh not long after the creation of life on this planet. Not through the starry spaces came Tsathoggua, but by the dimensions that lie between them, and of his advent upon this planet, the place thereof was the unlitten and subterraneous gulf of N'kai, wherein whose gloomy depths he lingered for innumerable cycles, as Eibon saith, before emerging into the upper world. And after this it was the Great Cthulhu came hither next, and all his Spawn from distant Xoth, and the Deep Ones and the loathsome Yuggs who be their minions; and Shub-Niggurath from nightmare-rumored Yaddith, and all they that serve her, even the Little People of the Wood.

> But of the Great Old Ones begotten by Azathoth in the prime, not all came down to this Earth, for Him Who Is Not To Be Named lurks ever on that dark world near Aldebaran in the Hyades, and it was his sons who descended hither in his place. Likewise, Cthugha chose for his abode the star Fomalhaut, whereupon he begat the dread Aphoom Zhah; and Cthugha abideth yet on Fomalhaut, and the Fire-Vampires that serve him; but as for Aphoom Zhah, he descended to this Earth and dwelleth yet in his frozen realm. And terrible Vulthoom, that awful thing that be brother to black Tsathoggua, he descended upon dying Mars in his might, which world he chose for his dominion ....

I could not help shuddering at the incoherent raving of the madman who had broken the silence of the ages, to speak of such abominations. But the passage held little that I had not already learned, so I skipped on down the page until my attention was arrested by the following passage:

> Now it is also written of those of the Begotten of Azathoth who abide not within the secret places of the Earth, that when the Great Old Ones came down from the stars in the misty prime They brought the image and likeness of their brethren with Them. In this wise, it was the Outer Ones that serve Hastur the Unspeakable, brought down the Shining Trapezohedron from dark Yuggoth on the Rim, whereupon had it been fashioned with curious art in the days ere the Earth had yet brought forth its first life. And it was through the Shining Trapezohedron, that is the very talisman of dread Nyarlathotep, that the Great Old Ones summoned to Their aid the might of the Crawling Chaos in the hour of Their great need, what time the Elder Gods came hither in Their wrath.
>
> Likewise, it was the Deep Ones who carried to this world the awful likeness of serpent-bearded Byatis, son of Yig, whereby was He worshipped, first by the shadowy Valusians before the advent of man on this planet, and yet later by the dwellers in primal Mu ....

This, obviously, was the information Dr. Blaine had desperately urged me to read. True, it corroborated the information I had already learned in the quotation from Ludvig Prinn, included in the Copeland notes. I read on, and with mounting excitement.

> For the Great Old Ones had foreseen the day and the hour of their need, when that they must summon to Their side those of their awesome Brethren who had taken far worlds for the place of their abiding, and had brought hither these images for this very purpose. Now of these star-made eidola, little there is that is known to men; it is said they were wrought by strange talismanic art, and that the sorcerers and the wizards of this terrene sphere are not deemed worthy by the Great Old Ones to be instructed in the secrets thereof.
>
> But it is whispered in certain old, forbidden books an awesome power lurks within such images, and that through them, as through windows in time and space, Those that dwell afar can sometimes be evoked, as They were when that it came to pass, in the fullness of time, the Elder Gods descended on this world in their wrath.

My hands were trembling as I laboriously copied out this passage, translating it roughly into English; and my brows were beaded with cold globules of perspiration. For I knew I stood on the very threshold of the hidden truth I had come so far to discover. I read on, no longer quite able to dismiss these chaotic passages as the disgusting spewings of a diseased brain:

> And there be those that worship the Great Old Ones through their image and likeness, but of this ye must be wary, for such eidola be uncanny, and

betimes are known to drink the lives of they that handle them unwisely, or who seek through such images to summon to this sphere Those far-off and better left undisturbed. Neither is it wholly within the knowledge of men to destroy such images, and many there be that sought the destruction thereof, who found their own destruction; but against such images from beyond the stars the Elder Sign hath very great power, although ye must beware lest in the conflict betwixt That which you evoke to destroy and the likeness of That which slumbereth afar, you be not consumed and swallowed up, or be yourself destroyed thereby, and that utterly, even to your immortal soul.

I stared at the words I had hurriedly rendered into English, my mind numb with a haunting surmise.

VII.

IT was some little while after this that Dr. Armitage returned to his office, accompanied as before by Dr. Seneca Lapham, and also by a youngish man of about my own age who was introduced to me as Mr. Winfield Phillips, an assistant of Dr. Lapham's.

I came slowly out of my trance and fumbled with words, striving to return young Phillips' amiable greeting in a natural manner. Dr. Armitage observed my bemused condition with one keen glance, and smiled grimly.

"I perceive, young man, that you have taken a bit of a shock. Tush, boy, don't be ashamed—better men than you or I have been unsettled by things they found in the nightmarish pages of Alhazred! It is a book that should never have been written; having been written, it is a book that deserves burning—and I say this in all solemnity, I, a scholar, a man who loves books and who serves them. But the world is not conducted for our pleasure, young Hodgkins—as the reader of the *Necronomicon* very soon discovers!"

I regarded the old gentleman in a bemused manner. The implications of his words were, well—*frightening*. From his sympathetic manner, and the import of his remarks, I deduced that there was after all a certain element of profound and terrible cosmic truth lurking behind these ancient and darkling myths. Already had I half-convinced myself of this in my own mind, for all the apparent madness of the notion; to hear it soberly confirmed from another opened yawning gulfs and fissures in the comfortable pattern of ordinary life wherein I had spent my days heretofore—gulfs whereby one might glimpse gigantic and hideously suggestive Shapes which slithered and crept and hid behind the mask and sham of so-called "reality." The very next words which the librarian uttered proved my half-fears beyond a doubt.

"Yes, young Hodgkins, it is more than merely an old, forgotten, primitive mythology we are dealing with here, but something infinitely more real and ghastly and strong," the old man said soberly. He glanced at Dr. Lapham and the younger man, Phillips. "All of us in this room have had some experience with the terrible truth behind these old superstitions, so we have all come to the juncture at which you now stand; and we understand the feelings which you must be suffering right now. Be at ease, young fellow: You are among friends."

Dr. Lapham cleared his throat at this point and spoke up in quiet, measured tones.

"You must understand, sir, that exactly how *much* truth lies behind these chaotic old legends we do not, at present, know. And that the legends themselves, and the books which remain our primary records on this matter, were concocted by superstitious and primitive minds unacquainted with the sophisticated concepts of modern physics and astronomy is evident. We cannot, as yet, take the legendary account seriously, as exact and literal statements of historical or scientific fact. We must look behind the legends, interpreting them according to the light of modern knowledge."

"Quite right," Armitage agreed. "We are not dealing with gods or demons or supernatural forces, my boy—clear all that mystical rubbish out of your head! Whatever the so-called Old Ones are, and whatever the nature and extent of their powers, they are neither divine nor infernal. And, surely, there is nothing of the *supernatural* about them. I have found that it helps to conceive of them as extraterrestrial creatures, the former inhabitants of other planets or star systems, who came here ages ago and who now slumber in the far places of the globe in something akin to suspended animation, as with Cthulhu himself, for instance. Alhazred speaks of this monster as 'asleep and dreaming.' This is a decently accurate description of a state of vitality in stasis, when you consider that Alhazred lacked the proper scientific terminology to describe such a condition. And also let me point out that highly intelligent though these creatures undoubtedly are—to have been able to traverse somehow the immense stellar distances—they are not remotely manlike and suffer from none of the limitations of our own fragile and short-lived fleshly habitations. We have considerable evidence to suggest they are not even composed of the same kind of matter as we are, and share few, if any, of our senses. Their normal lifespan, perhaps, is to be measured in geological epochs, rather than in the biblical three score years and ten."

By this time my mind was whirling with confusion, as you may well imagine. Struggling to conquer my revulsion at these stark and unpalatable facts, and to think clearly, I stammered out some query to the effect of how such creatures might be destroyed. Dr. Armitage looked troubled.

"We have come to the reluctant conclusion, young man, that they *cannot* in fact be destroyed. If they were capable of death or destruction, doubtless the opposing race, the so-called 'Elder Gods', would have slain or destroyed them, rather than imprisoning or banishing them, as all pertinent texts agree was their ultimate disposition. However, incapable of dissolution as they seem to be, the peculiar structure of the unknown types of matter of which they are composed seems to include a built-in defect—an Achilles' heel, if you will. That is to say, some unknown and immeasurable form of radiation, or fields of force, apparently has the power to inhibit them profoundly. Let me show you."

He went over to a large veneer filing cabinet, such as we used back at the Institute for the storage of small and frangible artifacts, and drew out a flat tray lined with velvet, which he brought back to the desk. A large number of small mineral objects were displayed on the velvet-lined tray; these were bits of dark gray stone or crystalline mineral, each of which was in the shape of a conventional five-pointed star. I could not, at first, make out whether these stone objects were natural or manufactured, but in the center of some of them had been cut an oval symbol or design like an Egyptian *cartouche*. This carved symbol seemed emblematic of the human eye, or so it looked to the casual glance. The objects, or artifacts, varied in size from star-shaped stones so small that you might have covered them with a ten-cent piece, to ones large enough to be the size of the hand with fingers outstretched. Only the larger ones bore the central eye-like cartouche.

"Go ahead, handle them if you like, they are harmless to beings composed of normal terrene matter," Dr. Armitage urged. I took up one of the stones and hefted it curiously in my palm. To the touch it was slick and smooth and cold, resembling crystal; but the stony substance was opaque, and surprisingly heavy. Heavier, I would say, than flint or ironstone; almost as heavy as a similarly sized piece of lead would have been. To the touch the stone gave off the faintest, almost imperceptible, tingle, as if it were somehow imbued with a slight electrical charge. No geologist, I was baffled at the nature of the composition of the thing.

"You know what these are, of course?" asked Armitage.

"One of the star-stones from Mnar, I guess," I said, shrugging, "as described in the passages from the *Necronomicon* I have just been reading."

"Precisely! Or such, at least, is our own supposition," nodded Armitage. "These were found in the northeastern parts of Mesopotamia, in a region we suspect but cannot prove to have been the approximate site of ancient Mnar. As yet, no trace of an urban site has been found, but subsequent excavations may yet unearth one—either the city of Sarnath or of Ib, as the urban centers are named in Alhazred. Literally hundreds of these star-stones have thus far been unearthed, scattered along a wandering southerly route which seems to have been that followed by some ancient migration—"

"Obviously the route followed by the Kishite migration," suggested Lapham. "Alhazred's fourth book describes how the followers of the prophet Kish fled from Sarnath before its destruction, bearing the star-stones as a means of protection given them by the Elder Gods—"

"Yes, yes," said Armitage gruffly, "but we are back dealing with mythology again, my dear Lapham, and none of these matters have yet been satisfactorily established. There may never have been a city such as Sarnath, or a prophet named Kish, save in legend; all we know is that the star-stones truly exist, because we have found them."

"Oh, very well, you doubting Thomas!" chuckled Lapham. "But at least we know that the star-stones and their powers against the Old Ones were known and used from very ancient times. Miskatonic's 1910 expedition to Mesopotamia found ample evidence that the star-stones had been dug up time and again, over the ages—some of the excavations suggested Assyrian and Babylonian dates, others early dynastic Egyptian and even medieval Persian. It is quite obvious that many peoples throughout antiquity knew of the protective properties of the stones from Mnar, and dug them up as defenses against the monsters of Alhazredic demonology—"

At that point, just as the discussion seemed on the brink of degenerating into an abstruse, and rather acerbic, scholarly dispute, young Winfield Phillips diplomatically suggested we all go down to the faculty dining hall for luncheon.

* * *

THE dining hall was spacious and well appointed, the walls paneled in native oak, hand-rubbed to a glowing patina, and adorned with stiff, formal portraits of elderly professors of the university. We lunched on what appeared to be a traditional New England dish, clam chowder. Never having tasted the succulent stew before, as it is seldom served in Southern California, I was curious and also a trifle cautious; needless to say, I found it delicious.

Seneca Lapham and Henry Armitage argued over the meal as to the mode whereby the star-stones might be employed to nullify the malign influences radiated by, or centered within, the Ponape figurine. It seemed from this discussion that a considerable portion of their knowledge of the Alhazredic demonology was, after all, merely conjectural or theoretical. Dr. Lapham was of the opinion that simply placing the stone from Mnar in close proximity to the jade idol would counteract or negate its noxious influences. The silver-haired librarian, however, demurred: He voiced his opinion that the star-stone must be employed in some manner of ritual in order to render the statuette harmless. Young Winfield Phillips had little to offer to either side of the debate, and devoted himself largely to the steaming broth before him.

That afternoon, Dr. Lapham having canceled a scheduled lecture, we spent huddled together in the rare books room of the great library, poring over Alhazred, du Nord, Prinn, d'Erlette, Shrewsbury, and the other main authorities on this weird, uncanny mythology. If any such ritual as the one about which Armitage theorized actually existed, it was not to be found in the major reference works to hand.

I fretted the hours by, worried that my long journey into northern New England had been in vain, fearing that every passing hour brought us and our world closer to the moment when the directors of the Sanbourne Institute might casually and unknowingly decide to exhibit the figurine publicly. When and if this occurred no one could precisely say what horrible and malignant menace might thereby be unloosed on an unsuspecting and helpless mankind. The nature of the danger poor mad Dr. Blaine feared and dreaded was still unknown to us.

That evening, as I strolled home through the bitter and wintry streets to my room at the club, my mind was a seething turmoil of shapeless fears and inarticulate terrors. I did not know what it was that I could do to avert the immense and shadowy peril which hung over us all. I only knew that I must do—something. But—*what?*

A corner newsstand caught my eye; I paused to buy a copy of the evening paper. Later, in my cozy room, dozing over the paper in the easychair, I awoke suddenly with a start. Without voluntary action my gaze fell on the open but unread newspaper spread across my lap. One black headline grew and grew in my sphere of sight until it blotted out all else.

"CURSED" IDOL TO BE SHOWN TO PUBLIC FOR 1ST TIME
Mystery Statue Goes on Display Monday in Calif.

Monday! And this was Friday evening! With all the luck and speed in the world, and the most perfect traveling connections, I could not possibly reach Santiago in time to prevent it.

VIII.

AT noon the next day, March 22nd, Armitage and Lapham bade me their anxious farewells at the railway station. I had hurriedly composed and sent off a telegram to the directors the night before, begging them to postpone until my return the unveiling of the Ponape figurine. Alas, they would think me as deranged as poor Dr. Blaine if I dared hint at my reasons for asking this delay. The best I could do to give them a valid reason for removing the figurine from the South Gallery, and returning it to the relative security of the safe in the Curator's office, was to state (quite erroneously, of course) that I had discovered new information which proved the idol to be a hoax.

I hoped—but could not be certain—that this would be sufficient. They were prudent and cautious men, I knew, who would go to extreme lengths to avoid getting the Institute mixed up in anything disreputable or shady. On the other hand, they were vitally interested in the continued success and popularity of the Institute; and public curiosity in the mystery image, fanned to a blaze by reportorial sensationalism, was at a white heat. To display the figurine would lure the public in droves, as they well knew.

My only hope lay in the possibility that their prudence would outweigh their desire for heavy popular attendance.

"Farewell, my boy," said Dr. Armitage, clasping my hand in his firm grip. His fine, aristocratic features looked strained and worried, and his keen blue eyes were shadowed with anxiety. "Let us hope that you are in time ... and that our small gift proves useful, after all!"

The "gift" of which he spoke weighed heavily in the left-hand inner breast pocket of my suit at that very moment.

I exchanged farewells, thanking Armitage and Lapham for their kindly interest, concern and generosity. Then I climbed aboard and followed the porter, laden with my bags, to the compartment. One last wave from the steam-fogged window at the two overcoated figures and they vanished behind me in the surge and clamor of departure.

* * *

OF my long trip homeward there is little enough to say. Hour by hour, mile by mile, I retraced my way across the breadth of the continent. Again I changed trains in the drafty, echoing Boston terminal; again I stared unseeingly for hours as the monotonous towns and hills, cities and suburbs, fields and plains rushed past my window.

Again, I strove to pass the hours by studying the *Unaussprechlichen Kulten*. Von Junzt proved to have little light to shed upon the mysteries of the star-shaped stone from elder Mnar, although he discussed it in several places, discoursing learnedly and at tiresome length upon its supposed efficacy against the Alhazredic demons. He seemed to have been principally concerned in settling by scholarly allusion and quotation that the so-called "Elder Sign" and "Sarnath-sigil", as well as the "Sign of Kish", were all terms which referred to the same object, and that object was none other than the star-shaped artifact of unidentified gray stone from immemorial Mnar. Whether the Elder Sign was the star-stone itself, or merely the cartouche-like emblem carved on the larger specimens of the stone, was left unclear.

This emblem or sigil I studied under a small but powerful lens I had brought with me in my case of books and writing materials. It was a curious, archaic symbol, quite unlike any other primitive or prehistoric character or glyph known to me. Under the magnifying glass it proved to be an oval, broken at either end, with something in the middle like a tower or monolith of jagged lines; or perhaps it was supposed to represent a stylized tree. At any rate, the oval *cartouche* with the vertical tower in its center resembled nothing so much as a cat's eye, save that the vertical slit pupil was, as I have said, jagged-edged.

I wondered if the symbol was supposed to suggest a burning tower ... and was suddenly reminded of a phrase from that hellish jumble of nonsense in the *Necronomicon*'s most confused and chaotic pages: "They came down out of the star-spaces unto this Earth, so that They might deal a grim and heavy judgment upon their former servants; and They went to and fro upon the Earth, terrible in Their wrath, like unto mighty Towers of Flame that walked like Men. Yea and verily was it writ of old, Terrible be the Elder Gods in Their wrath in the Hour of Their coming-hence."

Like unto mighty Towers of Flame ... is that what the sigil on the star-stones meant? Was it the seal and emblem of the Elder Gods? And did it depict Their very likeness?

My thoughts far from this place and time, I stared sightlessly from the railway carriage, through rain-swept windows blurred with steam, as the clicking wheels ate up the miles.

* * *

WHILE my journey to Massachusetts had been made in a fairly leisurely manner, schedules and connections having been arranged with comfort and convenience in mind, my trip home was quite another matter. Every factor was sacrificed to speed; it mattered little whether I could connect with a train which afforded sleeping accommodations, or a private compartment, or even a dining car. Time was the one priceless commodity, and every other consideration gave way before its urgency.

As to my state of mind during the long journey home to Southern California, I can only say that it was one of confusion. Against the most lucid and cautious arguments of logic and reason, I more than half accepted the terrible, the dreadful, the transcendent *truth* behind the grim old myths of Cthulhu and his brethren and his horribly monstrous spawn.

I had always, since my earliest years, been something of a rationalist when it came to the mystical, a materialist when it came to matters of religion, and an agnostic in dealings with the supernatural and the supernormal. Gods, ghosts, devils, magic rites—these (thought I, smugly, to myself in my abysmal but "enlightened" ignorance) belonged to the childhood of the human race. Here in the modern Industrial Age, nearly three decades into the 20th century, we had little time or patience to waste on the mumbo-jumbo of outmoded superstitions and antiquated, dying creeds.

To find men of breeding and education, men of brilliant intellect and great scholastic learning, who cautiously but soberly admitted that *such things could be* shook the flimsy foundations of my own materialistic assumptions. The fabric of the universe, as envisioned by Newton and Copernicus, Galileo and Einstein, Darwin and Freud, suddenly showed bare and cracked patches, jury-rigged scaffoldings through whose rents and holes and lacunae yawned frightful abysses of eldritch horror and ancient unholy evil. When scholars like Armitage and Lapham—yes, and Blaine and Copeland, too—had been forced to admit the reality of the supernatural, or of the ultra-terrestrial, how could I cling to the shivered fragments of my own scientific faith?

In this mood of dawning comprehension and growing belief in horrors of the primal world unguessed at in even the darkest of myths and superstitions, I retraced my journey across the continent. And at last I approached Santiago.

* * *

IT was four o'clock in the morning of March 26th. A gray, overcast morning, wintry, rain-swept, and bleak. Cold and wet were the winds that blew in from the dark Pacific, in whose unknown depths fantastic survivals might lurk from the forgotten past of this ancient planet. My eyes were red from lack of sleep, my head throbbing with fatigue, my body shivering and tense with excitement. I woke a cabman sleeping behind the wheel of his dilapidated Ford, parked in front of the railway station, and bade him drive me to the Sanbourne Institute.

"Don't open till nine, mister," he grumbled, yawning a jaw-cracking yawn. "Be all closed up at this hour."

I shook my head impatiently, climbing in the back seat and stuffing my luggage in beside me. "I work there, and I have a key. Let's go!"

"Okay, okay, hold yer horses," he muttered and began fiddling with the choke. The old Ford coughed and gurgled, then woke sluggishly to wheezing, rattling life. We pulled away from the curb and drove through dark streets empty except for a dog, snuffling at garbage cans in front of the Cozy Oak Bar & Grille. And the fog ... the cold, soft, wet fog ... that curled and coiled and floated through the dim streets like the vaporous tentacles of some immense and shadowy sea-thing.

The Institute is built well back from the road at the juncture of Sanchez and Whiteman Streets on the far side of town, an exclusive section of big estate houses called Mar del Vista. Originally, the property and the building itself had been the home of Carlton Sanbourne II, who had inherited a tuna canning fortune from his famous millionaire father. At his death the house and grounds, as well as his own world-famous collection of Pacific antiquities, had been donated to the state under a self-perpetuating foundation which established the nucleus of the present museum.

It must have been half past four in the morning when the old rattletrap of a taxi drew up before the big wrought-iron gate and let me out. I paid the driver, tipped him handsomely, and watched him drive off in a cloud of swirling fog. Then I opened the gate with my key, entered, closed the huge swinging gates behind me, parked my luggage in the gate-keeper's cottage, and went hurriedly down the drive toward the main entrance.

I let myself in by a small, unobtrusive side door used by the staff members. The building was not kept lit by night, and the halls and display rooms were thus drowned in murky gloom from which massive primitive idols bulked monstrously, like the lurking denizens of some shadowy netherworld. Just enough of the thin gray light of pre-dawn came seeping in through the tall windows for me to find my way through the maze of rooms.

I headed directly for the South Gallery where the Copeland collection would be on display. It occurred to me to call out and attract the attention of our night watchman, a Mexican-American named Emiliano Gonzalez, but for some reason I held my tongue. I cannot explain my reason for not attracting his attention. Quite certainly, I had no presentiment of the situation into which I would suddenly enter; but there was something in the very *air* of the place, a strange tension, an oddly meaningful silence that was tomb-like, which impelled me to caution and silence.

I became aware that my heart was beating, lightly but rapidly, and that my palms were wet with perspiration. My breathing came in short, shallow panting: I was—*frightened*; but—of what? All about me were the familiar glass cases, wall hangings, and statues and carvings, just as I had seen them a thousand times before. Why I should feel tension and trepidation is something I cannot explain. All I can offer by way of explanation is the supposition that, by some ethereal sense beyond the physical five, I felt an uncanny and malignant force awake and alive within the dim precincts of the museum.

Suddenly I turned a corner and found myself at the entrance to the gallery that was my goal.

And I looked on—*horror!*

IX.

FROM this point on I must exercise great care and precision in my choice of words, so that I can describe exactly what I saw and felt.

The hall was long and broad and high-ceilinged. Tall windows gave forth a view of gloom-drenched gardens and grounds. Dawn was just breaking, and the gallery itself was dimly but adequately illuminated by a pervasive, colorless light.

The artifacts from the Copeland collection were ranked along the walls and in the long glass cases, with neat tags or placards describing the provenance of each antiquity.

Directly before me—almost at my feet—lay the body of the watchman, face downward in a pool of blood. I knew at once, as if by sheer instinct, that the poor old man was dead. Something in the way he lay there, sprawled and crumpled, told me that the body was lifeless. It was like a bundle of clothing carelessly flung aside. Anything so tumbled and motionless could not possibly be alive; I did not need to see the way the back of his head was crushed in as if before the force of a brutal bludgeon, to know that the thing was a corpse.

I looked past the body ... to the very end of the hall.

The Ponape figurine stood atop a pedestal facing me eye to eye. It occupied a central position of importance in the gallery: All eyes would be drawn to it.

And it was alive.

Alive and sentient in a weird manner I find almost impossible to describe in clumsy words. The carved eyes glared with awful sentience. They were *aware*; aware and watchful ....

About the idol beat the radiations of a strange and nameless force. It was almost visible, almost palpable, that curious energy. You know how solid buildings seem to waver as waves of heat rise from the sunbaked pavement of a summer street. It was like that with the idol of Zoth-Ommog. The tall windows behind the idol *quivered* as if the very air were disturbed by a pulsing force emanating from the cold slick mass of carven stone.

The aura of force radiated outward from the idol; this was clearly visible. The ripples which distorted the background widened outward like the wavelets caused by a pebble tossed into still waters.

I sensed a tremendous force, a store of limitless cosmic energy, somehow locked within the fabric of the stone thing, as electrical energy is stored within a battery. And this force had now been—*triggered.* That which had slept dormant within the crystalline atoms of the cold stone was now violently active.

And there was something else. An intelligence—vast and deep and malignant—peered forth from the stone thing—a Mind, awesome and terrible, was now awake—aware—and *watchful!*

Suddenly, without volition on my part, there came into my mind the image of a page from that accursed and blasphemous *Necronomicon* I had so shudderingly perused back at Arkham ... and a single passage from that page stood out in my mental picture with clamorous and desperate clarity—

"It is whispered in certain old, forbidden books an awesome power lurks within such images, and that through them, as through strange windows in time and space, Those that dwell afar can sometimes be evoked and summoned hither ...."

Even in the same moment that this scrap of ancient lore rang through my brain with irresistible urgency, my eyes wavered and fell before the carved glare of the stony thing. *And I saw that which knelt before it—that which had struck down old Gonzalez, and now groveled in abasement before the Image from Beyond.*

At the first glance it looked like an ordinary man, some sort of Polynesian or Mongoloid, perhaps a half-breed. The worshiper before the idol had greasy, copper-colored skin, a bloated, chinless face with goggling, muddy-colored eyes, a mere flattened slit of a nose. He was bundled in a suit of cheap clothing, such as merchant seamen might buy in a waterfront pawnshop for a night ashore, and his head was wrapped in a piece of dark greenish cloth that resembled some sort of turban. Curiously, his hands were covered with bulky *mittens*—

But there was something about him, something in the abnormality of his crouching posture, in the odd lumpish *bulging* of his body beneath the baggy suit, something in the squat, sagging, toad-like corpulence of his slumped, slope-shouldered form, which raised the hair at the nape of my neck, filled my dry mouth with sour bile, and sent raw, unnerving horror shrieking through my brain.

That and the *smell* of him—the mingled reek of salt water and nameless decay—

He slithered about, goggling eyes glaring frog-like into my own. One mitten-covered hand fished clumsily into a baggy pocket and came out clutching a revolver. Then he came to his feet in an indescribable, boneless wriggle and pointed the revolver at me. As he did so that loosely wrapped green turban came loose, and I saw, and shrieked aloud to see it, that *he had no ears, no ears at all.*

I had no weapon, but something hard and heavy pressed against my heart—something wrapped in silken cloth, which I had carried in my inside breast pocket all the way from Arkham. With a numb hand I dragged it out, flung aside the wrappings and held it up—the gray stone starfish-shaped talisman from lost Mnar, which the followers of Kish had graven with the Elder Sign in time's dim, dark dawn.

At the sight of the star-stone the greasy-skinned man in the baggy suit cried aloud—a glutinous, gobbling sound that I swear before God came never from a human throat—and flung his arms wide as if to shield the idol of his cosmic god from profanation.

And I flung the star-stone.

What happened next I lack the words to describe. But I will try.

The star-stone struck the hideous face of the idol. And both star-stone and idol *vanished*—vanished in a soundless glare of light—light that burnt *blackly*—light that was a negation of luminance, rather then luminance itself.

The air, sucked inward by the instantaneous destruction of matter, *slapped* against itself, ruffling the *tapa* cloth wall hangings. Then, in the next eye-blink of time, *fiery lightning* lanced from the vortex of nothingness where the idol had stood an instant before.

Jagged streaks of electric fire zigzagged through the room. Windows shattered outward; I was flung to the floor; the earth shook.

Lightning touched the barrel of the revolver held by the turbaned half-breed who stood motionless as if transfixed. Touched and clung. And crawled over his bloated deformity of a body in searing rivulets of electric flame.

He writhed once, with an indescribable liquidity of motion so undulant and boneless as to drive a thrill of pure horror through my brain. Then he sagged forward on the floor. He did not fall as a man falls, but slumped gradually, like a mass of liquescent jelly, losing shape and form.

A smell came to my nostrils, as of some putrescent decay transcending all other stenches in its vile and utter rottenness.

The hall was burning; black smoke whirled around me. I was numb from head to toe as if from a paralyzing shock; I tried to move but could not, and then my brain, which had looked upon the very brink of the Pit—and beyond—failed me. And I knew nothing more until I woke, hours later, on a white bed in Mercy Hospital.

They tell me that I have suffered second-degree burns and that I am temporarily paralyzed from nervous shock. The fools have moved me to the psychiatric ward, "for further examination" as they explain, soothingly. They tell me that I murdered poor old Gonzalez the night watchman, who came upon me while I was trying to steal or destroy the Ponape figurine; but they only smile unbelievingly and shake their heads when I tell them that it was not I, but the half-breed, did the deed. They ask me where I have hidden the figurine, and why I set fire to the South Gallery, and what happened to the blunt instrument with which they claim I bludgeoned poor Gonzalez to death. But they do not answer me when I ask them about the other body … the body of the *other* man, damn it, the man who did the murder, the thing that looked and walked like a man … *why do they not tell me what became of the other man?*

* * * * *

Addendum to the Statement of Arthur Wilcox Hodgkins of 34 Mission Street, Santiago, Cal. The above statement, as transcribed from shorthand notes by R.A. Wallis, public stenographer, on March 29, 1929, concludes at this point, for here the accused lost coherence, his speech trailing off into sobbing obscenities, whereupon he was given a strong sedative and returned to the violent ward of the psychiatric wing of Mercy Hospital, from whence he was later transferred to Dunhill Sanitarium, Santiago County, under the care of Dr. Harrington J. Colby. It is believed the accused will never sufficiently recover in order to stand trial.

Appended to the above statement are the coroner's report on the body of the deceased, E. Gonzalez, and the psychiatric records of the accused. Also appended hereto: Report of Officer W. J. Whitby, the patrolman who discovered the body.

* * * * *

Extract from the Report of Officer W. J. Whitby:

2. Entered the premises at approximately 5:04 a.m. on the morning of 26 March, by forcible entry of main door. Section of premises later identified to me as South Gallery was ablaze at several points and windows at rear of hall were smashed. Used hall phone to summon Fire Department; partially extinguished blaze by means of equipment in stairwell.

3. Approximately 5:15 discovered two bodies: (1) deceased male of Spanish descent, approx. 60 yrs. old, in night watchman uniform; cause of death, injury to base of skull evidently caused by blunt instrument; (2) unconscious body of male Caucasian, approx. 30 yrs. old, suffering from effects of shock or smoke inhalation, or both.

---

7. Near base of fire-blackened empty stand at extreme end of hall, approx. 20 ft. from unconscious male Caucasian, I noticed a large pool or puddle of jelly-like fluid in copious quantities (several gallons). Nature of fluid unknown, but slimy in consistency and extremely offensive to the smell, like something long dead and rotten. Intermixed with said fluid I noticed sodden suit of clothing and something resembling pair of gloves or mittens. Unable to recover said garments, being driven from proximity to this part of South Gallery by heat of flames. Jelly-like fluid later found to have totally evaporated by time Fire Department had completely extinguished flames; clothing virtually destroyed, not burnt but rather dissolved into rags as if from immersion in acid of some kind. No bones or remnants

of human flesh were discovered. Whatever it was, it melted away like a big jellyfish which decays rapidly when exposed to open air.

(*Signed*) W. J. Whitby, P.D.
Badge # S/SC-104.

* * * * *

News item clipped from the Santiago County Sentinel, *April 10, 1929*:
"STATUE'S CURSE" CLAIMS FINAL VICTIM
Murder Suspect Ruled Insane

At a closed hearing at the Criminal Courts Building at ten o'clock this morning, Judge Maxwell J. Chase formally committed to Dunhill Sanitarium Mr. Arthur Wilcox Hodgkins of 34 Mission Street, this city, ruling him mentally incompetent to stand trial for the motiveless and brutal murder of Emil (*sic*) Gonzalez, also of this city. Gonzalez, an American citizen of Mexican descent, formerly employed as night watchman at the Sanbourne Institute of Pacific Antiquities, was found bludgeoned to death in the early morning hours of March 26th of this year. Near the corpse was discovered the unconscious body of the murder suspect, Mr. Hodgkins, apparently suffering from nervous shock. This tragedy occurred in the South Gallery of the museum wing of the Institute, within 20 feet of the pedestal on which the notorious "Ponape Figurine" had been on public display for the two days previous. ...

... County Psychiatric Officer Wilson then concluded with the opinion that Mr. Hodgkins was hopelessly insane and recommended that the Court commit the patient to Dunhill Sanitarium on a permanent basis. Judge Chase concurring, the commitment papers were signed in the presence of the three doctors. ...

... remains unsolved, as does the origin of the mysterious fire which raged unchecked for three quarters of an hour through the South Gallery. Also unsolved is the mystery of the disappearance of the infamous statuette itself, whose whereabouts remain unknown.

MANY of Lin Carter's tales in this book share the premise of the narrator or protagonist inheriting a legacy that proves to be more trouble than it's worth. (This premise was itself, of course, inherited by Carter from August Derleth and from many others.) In such stories, it is almost as if the benefactors had passed on to the next generation not their work so it might be brought to completion, but rather their own terrible fate. Lovecraft's tales "The Facts in the Case of the Late Arthur Jermyn and his Family" and "The Shadow over Innsmouth" employ this theme of the "tainted lineage" as a literal genetic transmission of non-human genes, while in other stories the inherited taint is in the form of a haunted house or a set of books. The latter is the version the theme takes in "The Winfield Heritance" (the title of which seems to have been derived from yet another tale of this type, August Derleth's "The Peabody Heritage").

This sort of story appealed to Lin Carter especially, I think, because it so closely fit the role he saw himself playing. He viewed himself (and his generation of fans, and ours) as the heirs of a tradition of blasphemous elder lore, that of Lovecraft and the Cthulhu Mythos.

As the great yogi named Berra said, "It's déjà vu all over again," when we come to the scene in which the "Hardy Boys" discover more scar(c)e manuscripts than you can shake a shoggoth at. Haven't we heard of these titles before? Of course, they're fictitious fictions, imaginary literary horrors with power to damn the soul of the reader, thus all bastard whelps of Chambers' *The King in Yellow*. Not the collection of tales he himself wrote, mind you, but rather the play which he did not write but which he wrote tales about. Don't we wish our own horror creations could have such an impact on readers and censors alike!

Lin has gathered these evocative titles from various pulp tales of horror. He has catalogued them here much as he did the Mythos grimoires in his early article "H. P. Lovecraft: The Books" (a new, updated edition of which is shortly due out from Borgo Press in the second edition of Darrell Schweitzer's *Discovering H. P. Lovecraft*). The rare and potent horror tomes he lists here are not quite heavy artillery like the *Necronomicon* or the *Livre d' Eibon*. They're no mere Arkham House or Chaosium titles either! No, they are right in the middle, written by people like HPL or CAS, but with a little help from certain Outside forces.

Now just where did Lin get these titles? Figuring it out for yourself is part of the game, a sort of "Test Your Mythos Knowledge" quiz, as if *Reader's Digest* might contain such a thing. If you want to cheat, here's the answer key. Edgar Henquist Gordon's books *Night-Gaunts* and *The Soul of Chaos* and his story "Gargoyle" are taken from Robert Bloch's "The Dark Demon." The weird magazine *Outré* is possibly derived from the amateur press zine of the same title by J. Vernon Shea. Of course, Derby's *Azathoth and Other Horrors* comes from Lovecraft's "The Thing on the Doorstep." Justin Geoffrey and his verse collection *People of the Monolith* come from Robert E. Howard's "The Black Stone." *Whispers* magazine is the fictive *Weird Tales* analog in which Randolph Carter's shocking tales, including "The Attic Window", used to appear, according to "The Unnamable." Amadeus Carson is a Henry Kuttner alter ego, the hapless renter of the Witch Room in "The Salem Horror", with his novel *Black God of Madness* reflecting his experiences in the ill-fated apartment. Michael Hayward is the author who stimulated his imagination by means of a time-vision drug in Kuttner's "The Invaders." He was only following in the staggering footsteps of Halpin Chalmers, author of *The Secret Watcher*, who used the Liao drug to abet his own creative juices in Frank Belknap Long's "The Hounds of Tindalos." Ariel Prescott's *Visions from Yaddith* appears in Carter's own "Dreams in the House of Weir" (available in *The Shub-Niggurath Cycle*). Phillip Howard is, believe it or not, Howard Phillips Lovecraft. Lin Carter is referring to Frank Belknap Long's "The Space Eaters", in which the narrator, one "Frank", refers to his pal "Howard" and his "The House of the Worm" and "The Defilers", together with the storm of protest the latter aroused among the stolid citizenry of Partridgeville. Finally, "Shaggai", "In the Vale of Pnath", "The Burrower Beneath", "The Feaster from the Stars", and "The Stairs in the Crypt" are the short stories Lovecraft attributes to his Robert Bloch analog Robert Blake in "The Haunter of the Dark."

"The Winfield Heritance" first appeared in Lin Carter (editor), *Weird Tales* #3, Zebra Books, 1981.

The Winfield Heritance

by Lin Carter

STATEMENT OF WINFIELD PHILLIPS, 1936

IN the event of my death or disappearance, I herewith request of the person into whose hands this statement shall come that he mail it without delay to Dr. Seneca Lapham, care of the Anthropology Department of Miskatonic University in the city of Arkham, Massachusetts. And, for his own safety, if not indeed his sanity of mind, I beg him to send it *unread*.

My name is Winfield Phillips, and I reside at number 86 College Street in Arkham. I am a graduate of Miskatonic University, where I majored in American literature and took for my minor the study of anthropology. Since my freshman year I have been in the employ of Dr. Lapham in the capacity of a private secretary, and have continued thereafter in that position in order to support myself while researching for a book on the Decadent movement in recent art and literature. I am twenty-nine years old, and consider myself to be sound of mind and body.

As for my soul, I am not so certain.

I.

ON the morning of June 7th, 1936, having obtained a brief leave of absence from my employer, I boarded the train for California at the B&O Station on Water Street. My purpose in undertaking a journey of such length as to traverse the entirety of the continent was partially business and partially pleasure. And, in part, from a sense of family duty.

Due to the recent death of my uncle, Hiram Stokely of Durnham Beach, California, I felt obligated to attend his funeral and to take my place at the obsequies in order that the eastern branch of the family might be represented on this solemn occasion. Uncle Hiram had been, after all, my mother's favorite brother; and, even though I had never met him, had, in fact, never seen him to my knowledge, I knew that she would have wished me to attend his burial. My late mother was a Winfield of New Hampshire, but my father was a Phillips, sprung from ancient Massachusetts stock which can be traced back to 1670, if not further. I am a descendant of the celebrated, and ever so slightly notorious, Reverend Ward Phillips, former pastor of the Second Congregationalist Church in Arkham, author of an obscure but psychologically fascinating bit of New England eccentricity called *Thaumaturgical Prodigies in the New-English Canaan*, first published at Boston in 1794 and later reprinted in rather expurgated form in 1801. It is an old family joke that the reverend doctor, in this his only known venture into the fine art of letters, literally did his "damnedest" to out-do in hellfire and brimstone mad old Cotton Mather's hellish *Magnalia* and the even more nightmarish *Wonders of the Invisible World*. If so, he succeeded admirably.

Many years before I was born, there had been some sort of trouble between my Uncle Hiram and the rest of my mother's family. I have never quite known what occasioned this breech, but the breaking-off of relations was lasting and permanent. If my mother ever knew the reason, she never confided it to me, but I can remember my aged grandfather muttering about "forbidden practices" and "books no one should ever read" whenever Uncle Hiram's name came up, which was not very often. Whatever the nature of the family scandal, Uncle Hiram moved away from Arkham, went to California, and never returned. These ancient, inbred New England families, as you may be aware, are rife with skeletons in the closet, old feuds, centuried scandals. It seems quaint, even perverse, nowadays to bear a grudge for a lifetime, but we are a proud, stubborn, stiff-necked race. Just how stiff-necked we are can be demonstrated by the fact that my uncle, as if not content with severing all relations with the family (even with my mother, who was his favorite sister), actually repudiated the family name, Winfield, adopting instead his mother's maiden name, Stokely.

At any rate, all of this happened long before I was born—before my Mother married into the Phillips family, in fact—and because of this, and of the fact that no single communication had ever passed between my uncle and myself, I had no slightest thought of ever being mentioned in my uncle's will, and had as well utterly no interest in his estate, although it was commonly known that he had become immensely wealthy since moving to distant California.

As for the element of pleasure involved in my journey, this lay in the opportunity to resume a cherished friendship with my cousin, Brian Winfield, the only son of my other uncle, Richard. We had first met, Brian and I, quite by chance, in the Widener Library at Harvard in 1927. I had been sent there by my employer to copy out some passages from a certain very rare version of a curious old volume of myths and liturgies called the *Book of Eibon*, since Harvard was lucky enough to possess the only known text of the medieval Latin translation made from the Greek by Philippus Faber. The young man seated next to me, a cheerful, freckle-faced, snub-nosed fellow with tousled sandy hair and friendly blue eyes, deep in a medical book of the most repulsive illustrations imaginable, responded to the librarian's call of "Winfield" and ambled forward to claim another book just fetched up from the stacks for his perusal. Thinking he must certainly be a relative, I took the liberty of introducing myself; later, chatting over coffee, we laid the foundations of a lasting friendship.

Brian was about five years younger than myself and had come east to study at the medical school, hoping to become a doctor. We both took to each other from the start, both equally delighted to discover we were cousins. Although my stay was a brief one, we managed to continue our friendship on weekends and during vacations. On these occasions I had come to the dorm to visit him, since his father had made him swear never to venture a foot closer to Arkham than the Boston city limits.

This afforded me no particular discomfort in traveling, of course, since Boston and Arkham are only some fifteen miles apart. But after some two years my visits to Boston had to end, for Brian flunked out of medical school because of some ridiculously boyish prank, and he went home to live again with his parent. He later studied veterinary medicine at Tate College in Buford, the county seat of Santiago County, in which Durnham Beach is located, and became a licensed veterinarian. I suppose this was quite a come-down for one who had hoped to cure cancer and win the Nobel Prize; or perhaps his father, discovering our surreptitious correspondence, demanded that it cease. At any rate, our exchange of letters dwindled and died. An infrequent card at Christmases or birthdays, and that was about it.

Until this June, when suddenly and to my delight I found in my mailbox a brief, scribbled letter in his familiar, childish hand, informing me of our uncle's death and inviting—virtually *begging*—that I come west for the funeral. I did not need much urging, and, as Dr. Lapham was willing to dispense with my services for a week or so, I went out that very afternoon and purchased my railway tickets, informing Brian by telegraph of the time of my arrival.

Besides the pleasure of resuming my acquaintance with Brian, and the family duty of attending my uncle's funeral, I had also a bit of unfinished business to clean up on behalf of Dr. Lapham. A few miles north of Durnham Beach, on the coast of Southern California, lay the town of Santiago, in which the famous Sanbourne Institute of Pacific Antiquities was situated. About seven years earlier we had been visited at Miskatonic by a gentleman named Arthur Wilcox Hodgkins, the assistant curator of the manuscripts collection at the Sanbourne Institute. This earnest and scholarly young man had implored the assistance of Dr. Lapham and certain of his colleagues in unraveling an ancient mystery which I shall not go into here, save that it involved the necessary destruction of a rare primitive idol of unknown craftsmanship, found off Ponape some decades earlier. Possession of this peculiar statuette—which gained considerable notoriety in the popular press under the rather melodramatic name of the "Ponape figurine"— was already reputed to have driven two famous scientists mad, and from Hodgkins' agitated state, threatened to unhinge his own reason as well.

Rather to my surprise, Dr. Lapham took these ravings quite seriously indeed, as did Dr. Henry Armitage, the librarian at Miskatonic. It is a measure of their concern over the potential danger to mankind in the continued existence of this so-called Ponape figurine that the two of them placed at young Hodgkins' use the fabulously rare copy of a grim, blasphemous old book called the *Necronomicon*, of which Miskatonic owns and jealously guards in a locked vault the only known copy of the "complete edition" of the book known to exist in the western hemisphere.

This book, and several other volumes of similar rarity and esoteric lore, form the central source of information the world possesses on an obscure, very ancient, and bafflingly widespread prehistoric mythology called by some the "Alhazredic demonology", from the name of the *Necronomicon*'s Arabic author, and by others the "Cthulhu Mythos", from the appellation of its most celebrated devil. Traces of the Cthulhu cult, and of other cognate cults and secret societies devoted to the worship of Cthulhu's three sons, Ghatanothoa, Ythogtha, and Zoth-Ommog, as well as his half-brother, Hastur the Unspeakable, and other gods or demons with names like Tsathoggua, Azathoth, Nyarlathotep, Daoloth, Rhan Tegoth, Lloigor, Zhar, Ithaqua, Shub-Niggurath, and so on, have persisted for ages in the far corners of the world, and are not yet entirely extinct. Linked together into a vast secret network, a sort of "occult underworld", the Cthulhu cult and its minions form, in the opinions of some authorities, little less than an enormous, and age-old, criminal conspiracy against the safety, the sanity, and the very existence of mankind.

Dr. Lapham and Dr. Armitage asked me, while visiting Santiago, where Brian was currently employed, to look into the mysterious end of Arthur Wilcox Hodgkins. He had cruelly bludgeoned an old watchman to death, set fire to the South Gallery of the museum wing of the Institute, hidden or destroyed the noxious figurine, and had been hauled off raving mad to the local sanatarium.

It would seem that there was considerably more to this wild story than one might reasonably have assumed. While assisting Dr. Lapham in his investigations of the activities of the Cthulhu cultists I have undergone a few unnerving and scientifically inexplicable experiences myself. I knew, although I tried not to believe, that there was in fact a hard, grim kernel of truth behind the nightmarish legends of this fantastic mythology. I saw enough in Billington's Wood that dark day in 1924 when Dr. Lapham and I shot and killed Ambrose Dewart and his Indian bodyservant, Quamis—or whomever it *really* was had taken over their minds, bodies, and souls—to treat these matters with caution and trepidation.

Something had driven poor Hodgkins mad. The Ponape figurine? Or what he saw in the instant in which he touched to the cold slick jadeite of the figurine the gray star-stone talisman from lost, immemorial Mnar which Dr. Armitage had entrusted to him? I did not know. But Lapham and Armitage wanted desperately to find out; they wanted to close their file on the weird and unearthly statuette they believed had come down from the black yawning gulfs between the stars when the Earth was young.

And so did I.

II.

BRIAN was there to greet me at the Santiago railway station when the train pulled in. Hatless, his sandy hair tousling in the breeze, he waved and grinned and thrust his broad shoulders through the crowd to crush my hand in his clumsy, powerful grip. He had changed very little in the years since we had last seen each other: he was still loud and boyish and irrepressible, with that joyous zest in life and boundless store of physical energy I admired and envied so much.

Collecting my bags, he tossed them into the back seat of his car, a sporty red roadster, and bade me pile in. I had been just as willing to have employed the dilapidated old taxi which was pulled up before the station, but this was even more comfortable an arrangement. While we drove to Brian's little apartment on Hidalgo Street, just off the park, we talked, renewing our acquaintance.

"Tomorrow, I'd like to motor down to Durnham Beach, so we can explore Uncle Hiram's house," said Brian as he helped me unpack. "The lawyers gave me the key to the front door, and directions on getting there."

"Haven't you ever seen it?" I asked. "Living so close to our uncle, all these years ...."

He grimaced. "Uncle Hiram didn't get along with my dad any better than he got along with the rest of the family, I guess! Anyway, I never got invited down. Queer old bird he must have been, but not a bad sort, after all. By the way—I didn't get around to mentioning it before—did you know that you and I are his beneficiaries?"

I blinked, fairly thunderstruck. "Do you mean it?"

He grinned, nodding. "Everything but the money, I'm afraid! That goes to some sort of foundation. But we can split the house, the library and furnishings. Reckon you'll be most interested in the books ... I understand our uncle had quite a library. Well, come on; let's wash up and get something to eat."

III.

THE events of the following morning I will pass over without comment. There were only a few people at the services, a couple of our uncle's old servants and a curiosity-seeker or two. The burial was done rather hastily, and I noticed it was a closed-casket service, for some reason.

After lunch, we motored down the coast. It was a brisk, bright day, and Brian drove with the top down. I could tell Brian had some news for me—he was fairly bursting with it. Finally, I asked him what was up. He gave me a mischievous sidewise glance.

"Remember, when you wrote you were coming, you asked me to find out anything I could about that 'Ponape figurine' affair?" he asked. I nodded. "Well, I got together some newspaper clippings for you—give them to you later. But I discovered something positively weird while looking into the matter ...."

And he mentioned the name of the late Professor Harold Hadley Copeland. Time was, what with all the newspaper sensationalism connected with that name, it would instantly have been familiar to the reader of Sunday supplements. But how swiftly yesterday's news becomes ancient history! I suppose few people would even recognize the name nowadays, although his death in a San Francisco mental institution was only some seven years ago.

It had been Professor Copeland who had discovered the notorious Ponape figurine, which formed the nexus about which so many strange and baffling mysteries had centered. The figurine had been part of the collection of rare Pacific antiquities and books which Copeland had left to the Sanbourne Institute in 1928. It seems that the figurine was in some way connected to an ancient, little-known cult which worshiped "Great Old Ones from the stars", whose myths and legends were presumably recorded in a number of old, seldom-found books. Several of these books Copeland had left to the Sanbourne Institute, as they bore upon the matter of his research. What I now learned from the lips of my cousin thoroughly astounded me.

"The old prof had a copy of the *Unaussprechlichen Kulten*, did you know?" asked Brian, teasingly, playing with my curiosity.

I nodded. The book, by a German scholar named von Junzt, was a principal text in the study of the cult.

"*And* some pages from the *Yuggya Chants*," he added, "and a copy of something called the *R'lyeh Text*—"

"Yes, I know all about that," I said impatiently. "Get on with it, won't you?"

"Well, Win, where do you suppose Professor Copeland got these rare books from in the first place?"

I shrugged, irritably. "How the devil should I know?"

Still smiling, Brian dropped his bombshell. "*He bought them from Uncle Hiram.*"

I'm sure my jaw must have dropped, making me look ludicrous, for after another sidewise glance, Brian began chuckling.

"Great Scott," I murmured, "what a coincidence! D'you mean to say our uncle was interested in occultism—in this Alhazredic demonology?"

He frowned, not recognizing the term. "'Alhazredic'—?"

"After the Arabic demonologist, Abdul Alhazred, author of the celebrated *Necronomicon*, one of the rarest books in the world. We have a copy back at Miskatonic, kept under lock and key. The only one in the western hemisphere."

He confessed that he had no idea about our uncle's interests, scholarly or otherwise. "But Uncle Hiram made a fortune, you know ... and he went in for book-collecting in a big way ... anything old and rare and obscure and hard to find was just his meat. He had purchasing agents all over the world working for him ... say, bet that sounds good to you, since you've inherited your pick of his books!"

I didn't say anything, feeling a bit uncomfortable. While my Uncle Hiram's death had meant nothing at all to me personally, there is something a trifle ghoulish about profiting from another man's demise. I changed the subject.

The long drive down to Durnham Beach took us by a scenic route which disclosed frequent glimpses of the rugged, rocky coast, with the smiling blue Pacific lazing beyond under clear sunlight. But, as we approached the town, the highway turned inland, and the scenery became by gradual stages oddly drab and even depressing. We passed acres of scrub pine and mud flats full of stagnant, scummed water. Then followed, for dreary miles, abandoned farms and fields where the raw, unhealthy earth, eroded by the salt breeze from the ocean, exposed beneath pitifully thin layers of topsoil nothing but dead and sterile sand. Sea birds honked and cried mournfully, as if to fit the mood of uneasy depression that had fallen over us both. Even the clear sunlight seemed vitiated and dull, although the skies were as clear as ever.

I said something about this to my cousin, and he nodded soberly.

"It's not a very healthy place," he remarked. "Town's been going downhill as far back as I can remember—especially when they started to close down the canneries and people were out of jobs. I can remember when all these farms were going strong, lots of orange groves, truck gardening ... some communities thrive and grow, and others just sort of crumble and go rotten at the heart ...."

We passed a roadsign and the name on it seemed vaguely familiar to me, like something I half-remembered reading years ago in the newspapers. I asked Brian about it. He looked grim.

"Hubble's Field? Sure, you must have read about it—ten or fifteen years ago, something like that. They found all those bodies buried there—hundreds, I think it was."

His remark sent a shiver of cold apprehension through me. Of course, I remembered the Hubble's Field atrocity—who could forget it? The county was putting in a pipeline for some reason, and when they came to excavate a certain stretch of condemned property, they began to dig up the remains of human bodies, literally hundreds, as Brian said, although from the way the bodies were dismembered and jumbled together, it was never possible to ascertain an accurate count. Somebody on the radio at the time remarked that if you took all of the mass murderers in history and put them together, you wouldn't have half as many corpses as those found buried in Hubble's Field ... oddly gruesome thing to remember! Or to think about.

"Yes, I remember something about it now," I murmured. "They never did find out who did it, or why, did they?"

Brian uttered a harsh little bark of laughter. "No, they didn't," he said shortly. "What they did find out, was that it had been going on for one hell of a long time ... the further down they dug, they began to find scraps of homespun and tanned leather and old bottles from the early settlers ... deeper down, bits and pieces of old Spanish armor were found mixed in with the skeletons ... and beneath *that*—"

He broke off, saying nothing. I nudged him.

"Beneath that—*what*?"

"Indians," he said heavily. "Lots of 'em. Infants, old people, braves, women. Way back before the Spaniards came. This was all Indian country once, of course. The Hippaway nation owned all these parts before the explorers came. Still some Hippaways around, on reservations in the mountains. But not anywhere around *here*, you can bet!"

"What do you mean?"

"Back in school I took a course in anthropology, Indian stuff. Hippaways had a name for Hubble's Field in their own language ... something like *E-choc-tah*, I think it was."

"What does it mean?" I inquired curiously.

His face looked stony. "'*The Place of Worms.*'"

Suddenly the sunlight dulled, the sky seemed to darken, and the air around us became dank and unwholesomely chill. But when I glanced up, the sky was still clear and the sun shone brightly ... but seemed weirdly unable to warm the air.

I changed the subject.

IV.

WE arrived at our uncle's house by late afternoon, after driving through what was left of the old town. Rows of dingy housing inhabited by whiskered, surly men and slatternly women and squalling brats ... storefronts shut and moldering into decay ... dirt streets cut with ruts, with scrub grass growing in many of them. And beyond the rotting wharves of the harbor, where only a small boat or two gave evidence of fishermen, loomed the abandoned warehouses and the crumbling canneries. It was hard to believe that this disintegrating ghost town had been a vigorous community in Brian's boyhood, only a dozen or fifteen years ago. It looked contaminated—poisoned, in some uncanny way—and slumping almost visibly into ruin.

"I'm certainly not surprised you've stayed away all of these years," I murmured. "The wonder is, Uncle Hiram kept on, with all his money: I'd of moved to San Francisco or somewhere—*anywhere* but Durnham Beach!"

Brian grunted assent. "Still, the house *is* grand," he mused, looking it over. And I had to admit that it was. A two-story, rambling stucco structure in the Spanish hacienda style, with red-tile roofs and chimneys, ringed about with desolate gardens gone to seed and fishponds long dry, scummed with filth and rotting leaves.

"Doesn't look like he kept the place up in recent years," I remarked.

"No, it doesn't," he said. Then he pointed to a stretch of empty field bordering the property, beyond a row of dilapidated and dying palms. "Maybe he *couldn't*," he added thoughtfully.

"What does *that* mean?"

He nodded to the empty fields: raw red clay, cut into ditches and hollows and gullies, stretched beyond the row of palms.

"Neighborhood sort of went to pot," he said sourly. "*That* is Hubble's Field ...!"

After a couple of tries, we opened the big front door with the keys from Uncle Hiram's lawyer and entered a dim, cool front hall. Suits of rusty armor stood beneath tattered banners and faded tapestries; a grand spiral staircase wound through the dimness into the upper reaches of the house. Dust lay thick and scummy on heavy, carved, antique furniture, and gusts of rain from some broken windows upstairs had turned the old carpet green with mildew.

The place had a cold, unlived-in feeling, despite its attempt at feudal grandeur. It looked like the reception hall in some high-class funeral parlor with pretensions toward Baroque.

"Well, we're here," Brian grunted. "Let's look around—explore." There were tall stained glass windows in the grand dining hall, whose heavy oak table must have seated twenty guests, if guests had ever been welcome here, and I had a queasy feeling they had not. Bronze statuary stood about on old sideboards and stone mantles, and there was quite a clutter of endtables and bric-a-brac, some fine pieces of old Indian pottery, Victorian art glass, ashtrays and brass pots. The air was musty and unwholesome, although the house had not really been closed that long: Hiram Stokely had only recently died, after all—did he have something about open windows and fresh air?

Or did the breeze that blew across Hubble's Field, where hundreds and hundreds of corpses had rotted into the earth over centuries, bear with it the taint of some miasma, some pestilence so unholy, that even in the hot summer months, Hiram Stokely had preferred to stifle behind shut windows, rather than breathe it in?

It was a question to which I really desired no answer.

We found the library on the second floor, a huge room, lined from floor to ceiling with bookshelves. I didn't really feel in the mood for evaluating my inheritance that gray and gruesome afternoon, but ran my eye cursorily over the shelves. Tooled leather bindings held standard sets of Dickens, Thackeray, Scott, the Lake poets. Doubtless, a good second-hand book dealer in San Francisco could turn a tidy profit for me, if the damp and mildew hadn't gotten to the books first.

"My God! What's that?" ejaculated Brian in startled tones. He was staring at an oil painting which hung on the paneled wall beside the door. Dim with dust and neglect, its thickly scrolled gilt frame held a shocking scene I could not quite make out in the dim light.

Peering closer, I read the little brass plate attached to the bottom of the frame. "Richard Upton Pickman," I murmured. "I've heard of him, Boston artist—"

Then I lifted my eyes to study the painting. With a distinct sense of shock I saw a dim, shadowy graveyard vault, stone walls slick with trickling moisture, pallid and bloated fungi sprouting underfoot; scores of obscenely naked, unwholesomely plump men and women, naked and filthy, with heavy clawed hands and a suggestion of dog-like muzzles about their sloping brows and distorted lower faces, were clustered about one who held a guidebook. What was so spine-chillingly ghastly about the grotesque painting was the uncanny, the virtually *photographic* realism of the artist's technique ... that, and the hellish expressions of hideous, gloating relish stamped on the fat features of the degenerate, the almost bestial, hound-muzzled faces ....

With a shudder of aversion, I dropped my gaze hastily from the oil, to scan the title of the picture.

"'Holmes, Lowell, and Longfellow Lie Buried in Mount Auburn,'" I read half-aloud.

Brian looked sick. "God, I'll sell that abomination first off!" he swore feelingly. I didn't blame him: frankly, I'd have burned the grisly thing.

We decided to stay the night, since it would have taken us hours to drive back to Santiago. We'd driven past a dingy little diner near the docks on our trip through town, but, somehow, neither of us felt like retracing our path through those rutted streets lined with tottering, decaying tenements. In a mood of festive generosity, Brian's landlady had packed us a large picnic lunch, which we had only nibbled at along the way, so we built a fire in a cavernous stone fireplace and wolfed down cold tea, ham and chicken sandwiches, and potato salad by the flickering orange light of the blaze. A thin, drizzly rain had started up; the skies were leaden and overcast; a mournful wind prowled and whimpered about the eaves. It was going to be a filthy night, and neither of us felt like crawling into bed after one look at damp, stale-smelling sheets and empty, drafty bedrooms. We fed the fire and curled up on a couple of sofas, wrapped in quilts found in an upstairs closet.

Brian was soon snoring comfortably, but I found myself unable to get relaxed enough to feel drowsy. Giving it up after a while, I stirred up the fire and lit an old hurricane lamp we'd found on the back porch, which still held plenty of oil. Then I went hunting through the shelves for something to read. Twain, Dumas, Balzac—all of the standard classics were too heavy for my gloomy mood, but surely, somewhere in among all of these thousands of embalmed masterpieces, Uncle Hiram must have tucked away a good thriller or a juicy detective story ....

On one of the lower shelves I noticed something odd: a row of books and pamphlets which stood *behind* the front row, which made me wonder if all of the bookshelves were built double ... or was this, perhaps, where Uncle Hiram had squeamishly concealed from casual public discovery a small, choice selection of "risqué" Victoriana? Grinning, I pried one of the volumes out and held it up to the light so that I could read the title.

It was *Night-Gaunts*, a novel by Edgar Henquist Gordon, published in London by Charnel House, Publishers—great heaven! I was holding in my hands an extremely rare and very valuable book. It was the first book Gordon had published and, probably because of what critics of the period had damned as its "excessive morbidity", had been a total failure, which was why the volume I held in my grasp was so sought-after by collectors of the bizarre and the fantastic.

Setting it down gently on the table, I removed the front row of books and began to take out and to examine one by one the hidden volumes they had concealed. The next one was also by Gordon, his privately published novel, *The Soul of Chaos*. This was followed by a rare copy of the obscure magazine *Outré*, the very issue which contained Gordon's famous first short story, "Gargoyle". For my projected book on Decadence in literature I had studied a photographic copy of "Gargoyle", obtained not easily and with considerable expenditure of time, and I remembered well its phantasmagoric lore of black cities on the outermost rim of space, where weird beings whisper unmentionable blasphemies from formless thrones that stand beyond the domain of matter.

The next volume was a slim volume of verse by Edward Pickman Derby entitled *Azathoth and Other Horrors*, into which I had also peered and which was a valuable first edition in a very desirable state. Paired with this was a second volume of verse, *The People of the Monolith*, by Justin Geoffrey; then came several crumbling and yellowed copies of *Outré* and another magazine called *Whispers*, which contained the famous tales of that extraordinary, overlooked young genius, Michael Hayward. But the next book was such an astonishing find that I virtually reeled backwards in slack-jawed amazement: It was the original, unpublished manuscript of Amadaeus Carson's notorious and legendary novel, *Black God of Madness*, which most authorities believed no longer to be in existence.

I had stumbled upon an amazing trove of literary treasures so fabulously rare as almost to be considered legendary.

Which made me wonder—it was only an idle, passing thought!—what other hidden treasures the house of Hiram Stokely might conceal.

V.

WHEN Brian woke to a gray and drizzly morning, and I shared with him the wonder and delight of my discoveries, he was considerably less enthralled than he might have been. I suppose it takes a liberal arts education with a deep interest in Decadent literature to appreciate fully the profundity of my discoveries, but, still, he could have showed a *little* more interest—!

"Pretty rare stuff, and really valuable, eh?" he mused, leafing through the bound manuscript of *Black God of Madness*.

"Some of these items are almost priceless," I said. "The one you're examining is not the only unpublished manuscript, either: Here's what seems to be the authentic original manuscript of Simon Maglore's celebrated, prize-winning poem 'The Witch is Hung', famous for its riot of wild imagery and eldritch color ... and here's a gem: a true first edition of Halpin Chalmers' arcane and recondite work, *The Secret Watcher*, another first edition from Charnel House in London."

"Yes, and here's another one," he muttered, looking through a slender pamphlet. "*Visions from Yaddith*, verses by Ariel Prescott, Charnel House, Publishers: London, 1927. I've heard of her; didn't she die raving in a madhouse?"

"Yes; in Oakdeane," I said briefly. "And here's the notorious January 1922 issue of *Whispers*, which contains that famous—or infamous!—tale by Randolph Carter, 'The Attic Window.' This copy could be worth hundreds to the right collector; when the story appeared, it aroused such an outcry of revulsion that every known copy of that issue was withdrawn from the newsstands."

Brian was glancing through some magazines, flaking and yellowed with age. "Who was Phillip Howard?" he murmured curiously.

"The author of several short stories that would have delighted the soul of Poe and Bierce," I declared. "'The House of the Worm' is probably the most notorious; at least one young reader, a student at Midwestern University, I believe, went insane because of it. Another of his tales is in one of the issues you're looking at: 'The Defilers', it's called; I remember an article in the *Partridgeville Gazette* as claiming the magazine received no fewer than three hundred and ten letters of outraged indignation when they published that tale."

"Didn't know Uncle had such morbid tastes in literature," he said wonderingly. Then, looking up: "What's that you've got?"

"More original manuscripts," I whispered almost reverently. "I don't suppose you've ever heard of that appalling young genius, Robert Blake? I thought not; well, he only died last year, after all ... but word is getting around about these stories." I stared at the neatly written manuscript pages of "Shaggai", "The Feaster from the Stars", "The Stairs in the Crypt", "The Burrower Beneath", and "In the Vale of Pnath."

"Someday, they must be published, for all to read," I murmured, hungrily scanning the papers.

But Brian was examining the pile in bafflement. "If they're so rare and valuable, why hide them away behind another row of books?" he asked, almost challengingly. "I always thought collectors liked to show off their treasures—*why?*"

I gave him look for look.

"I don't know," I said honestly.

* * *

WE drove to the diner for breakfast and bought some supplies for lunch, as the utilities were still turned on and it might be more pleasant to cook something than go out through the rain again. We spent the rest of the morning cataloguing the furniture and pictures; I don't know much about antiques, but everything looked pretty valuable to me. With a little luck, we would each come away from this with a sizable sum of money. The real estate value of Uncle Hiram's house was another matter; the way the town was slouching into decay—and the nearness of the house to Hubble's Field—might bring the resale value way down.

I was mulling over these things while going through my uncle's curio collection, when I was roused by a startled whoop from Brian.

"What's up?" I demanded, joining him in the library. "You just about gave me a heart attack ...."

Then my words trailed away. Brian was grinning at me excitedly, beside a door-size opening in the bookshelves. "A secret room!" he exclaimed, eyes a-gleam with boyish enthusiasm. "I was searching behind the shelves to see if there were any more concealed books, and must have triggered the mechanism. Like to've scared me out of a year's growth! Take a look ...."

I peered past his burly shoulders into a narrow, small, cramped, airless room, revealed to view when one of the bookcases had swung ajar like a door. It was so dark within the hidden chamber that, at first, all I could see was a huge piece of ancient oakwood furniture. It took me a few moments to identify it.

"My God! That's an adumbry; looks authentic, too," I gasped.

"What's—"

"Sort of a Medieval bookcase. Monks in the old monasteries used them to lay flat books too huge to stand on edge," I said absently.

"Looks like they left a few behind, then," he remarked. For there were a number of immense volumes on the low, flat shelving—books bound in vellum, wrinkled and yellowed with age, or in flaking black leather. I pulled one down, screwing up my face at the reek of ancient mildew and decay which arose from it like a palpable touch.

The next instant a pang of fearful surmise stabbed through me. I held in my hands an Elizabethan folio of fabulous age, a bound manuscript written in a crabbed hand on thick sheets of excellent parchment. And the title page bore this inscription: *Al Aziph, ye Booke of ye Arab, Call'd ye Necronomicon of Abdoul Al-hazred, Newly Englished by Me, Master Jno. Dee, of Mortlake, Doctor of ye Arts.*

Even Brian could not help but be impressed by the discovery, doubtless remembering that I had called the *Necronomicon* "one of the rarest books in the world," which indeed it was. It was worth, I suppose, thousands ... even more, if it truly was what it seemed to be. That is, I am no expert in Elizabethan or Jacobean handwriting, but the huge folio pages looked old enough to have been in Dr. Dee's own hand. *Could* this be the original manuscript?

"Here's another one," Brian muttered thoughtfully. "*Livre d'Ivon* ...."

"... *The Book of Eibon*," I said dazedly. I examined it; the ancient bound manuscript was tattered and in a disreputable condition, the pages water-stained and foxed with mildew. Still and all, the antiquated Norman French seemed legible enough ... and also, the calligraphy of the handwriting looked old enough to be in Gaspard du Nord's veritable hand ....

With repetition, I found, the shocks of discovery diminish. The mind numbs, can bear no more. There were other books on the shelves, but we did not look at them. The light from the open door revealed cabalistic designs traced in chalk on the floor; curious and oddly obscene instruments of brass, copper, or steel glittered on the topmost shelf; the air was rank with mouldering decay, stale and vitiated. Quite suddenly, I felt sick to my stomach: Now I knew, or thought I knew, why Uncle Hiram had broken off relations with his family.

It was not his doing, it was *theirs*. The Winfields were of ancient stock; rumors and whispers of disgusting witch-cult survivals in our accursed corner of New England had come to them, with whispers of certain disturbing and unsettling doings in Arkham, Innsmouth, and Dunwich.

The Winfields had cast Uncle Hiram out because he was dabbling in rituals and lore too loathsome, too blasphemous, to be tolerated.

And I am a Winfield ....

No words passed between us, but we left the secret room together, as if in obedience to the same impulse. And we left the hidden door ajar.

VI.

WE did little more the rest of that cold, drizzly day; nor did we discuss what we had found. Brian was too healthy-minded, too boyishly wholesome and normal to have read the queer old texts and the tainted literature into which I have delved more deeply than I wish I had. But he sensed the evil that lurked all about us, in the pages of those abominable old books, and that gloated down from the smirking canine faces in that grisly painting, and that breathed about the dark old house from that charnel-pit of buried horrors men call Hubble's Field.

Later, feeling a bit hungry, and oddly desirous of some human companionship, we drove through the dank drizzle back to the diner by the waterfront. Before, it had been empty, save for a slatternly girl behind the counter and a fat cook chewing on the stub of a dead cigar, bent over the steam-table. Now, though, it was half-full, and I thought the locals looked at us oddly as we went in and took a table by the blurred and greasy window. They were a disreputable lot, men with stubbled cheeks and furtive eyes, clad in filthy overalls and flannel shirts. We paid them no attention, but it seemed to me that we were a larger object of curiosity, or resentment, than we should have been, even taking into consideration the attention a "city stranger" draws in secluded, decaying backwaters like Durnham Beach.

The gum-chewing waitress leaned over the counter and said something to one of the locals. I couldn't make out her whining tones, something about "ol' Stokely place" and "Hubble's Field", but he grumbled something in reply that sounded like "Damned lotta nerve, comin' in here."

"... Git back where they came from," muttered another. A third gave a surly nod of agreement.

"Now it's gonna start all over again, *I* bet!" he growled.

More disapproving, even menacing, looks were directed at us. Brian noticed it, too. "We seem to be distinctly unpopular, Win," he observed. I nodded quickly.

"We do, indeed. Let's finish up and get out of here before there's trouble."

"Good idea," he agreed. We left and drove back through the wet, saying little, each busy with his own thoughts.

* * *

That evening Brian was browsing through one of the old books while I tried to concentrate on cataloguing the contents of the house. My mind seemed unable to focus on business, being obscurely troubled.

"Here's something odd, Win," Brian spoke up. Something in his tones made me look up sharply.

"What's that you're reading?"

"The *Necronomicon* ... listen to this! Hm, let's see—here it is: '... and the Mi-Go that are the minions of His Half-Brother, Lord Hastur, come down but rarely to the ...', no, a little further on: '... and likewise is it with the fearsome Yuggs that are the servitors of Zoth-Ommog and His Brother, Ythogtha, and that are led in That Service by Ubb, Father of Worms, they slither but seldom from their moist and fetid burrows beneath the fields where they make their loathsome lair'—wasn't that Ponape figurine you people were so concerned about supposed to be an image of Zoth-Ommog?"

I felt a queer foreboding. "It was. Is there any more?"

"Plenty. Listen to this: 'But all such as these, aye, and the Night-Gaunts, too, that be in the service of Nyarlathotep under their leader, Yeggha the Faceless Thing, and the Dholes of Yaddith, and the Nug-Soth, that serve the Mighty Mother'—I'll skip down the page—'they fret and fumble ever at the fetters of the Elder Sign, the which doth bind their Masters, and they strive ever to do That which should set Them free, even unto the Red Offering. And in this dreadful Cause they have full many times ere this seduced and bought the hearts and souls of mortal men, selecting such as be frail and vain, venal or avaricious, and thereby easily corrupted by the thirst for knowledge, or the lust for gold, or the madness for power that is man's deepest and most direful sin ....'"

We stared at each other for a moment. Then I got up and crossed to where my cousin was sitting, and examined the page over his shoulder.

I read: "Such men as these, I say, they whisper to of nights, and lure into their toils with Promises most often unfulfilled. For men they need, and that hungrily: for 'tis the hand of mortal men alone can dislodge the Elder Sign and undo the mighty ensorcellments stamped upon the prisons of the Old Ones by the Elder Gods—"

"Look at the next passage," he said in low, troubled tones.

I read on: "In particular it be those of the minions that inhabit the noisome depths beneath the Earth's crust that lure men to their dreadful service through promise of wealth; for all the ore and riches of the world be theirs to dispense, aye, mines of gold and great heaps of inestimable gems. Of these, the Yuggs, whose name the Scribe rendereth as the Worms of the Earth, are by far the most to be feared, for it is said that there be many a rich and wealthy man bestriding the proud ways of the world today, the secret of whose wealth lies in accursed treasure brought to his feet by the immense and loathsome, the white and slimy Yuggs, whereby to purchase his service to their Cause, *to the utter and most damnable betrayal of humankind, and the imperilment of the very Earth.*"

Brian's face was drawn, his eyes haunted by a fearful surmise. "Remember, we wondered where Uncle Hiram's fortune came from," he whispered.

I flinched away from his stare. "What are you suggesting?" I cried protestingly. "That's absolutely crazy—madness!"

"Is it? Remember that queer term, the 'Red Offering' ... and all those bodies out in Hubble's Field ...?"

"What are you ... trying to say?" I scoffed, but my voice was shaky and I knew that Brian could read the doubt in my eyes.

"Hubble's Field," he murmured somberly, "Ubb, Father of Worms ... the Worms of the Earth ... 'those that inhabit the noisome depths beneath the Earth's crust that lure men to their service through promise of wealth' ... Hubble's Field ... *E-choc-tah*, 'The Place of Worms' ...."

"*...Ubb's Field*," I gasped. He nodded grimly.

"Come on," said Brian briefly, springing up and heading for the secret chamber. I paused only long enough to snatch up my electric torch. Then I followed him into the Unknown ....

VII.

THE beam of my torch flashed about the plaster walls of the cramped, airless little room sending enormous shadows leaping crazily. Brian was running his hands over the walls as if searching for something. I asked him in a rather breathless voice what it was he was looking for. He shook his head numbly.

"Damned if I know," he confessed. "Another secret panel, I guess, leading maybe to another hidden room beyond this one."

At my suggestion we dragged the huge Medieval adumbry away from the wall. As the only piece of furniture in the hidden chamber, it might conceal another door, if door there was.

And there was ....

Brian's searching fingers found and pressed a button set flush into the plaster. Some mechanism concealed behind the wall squealed rustily, protesting. A black opening appeared. I shone my light within the opening, and we saw crudely hewn stone steps going down into darkness.

"That's it!" Brian breathed triumphantly.

"You're crazy," I said. "Probably just leads to the basement."

"This is Southern California," he reminded me. "Houses don't have cellars or basements like they do back east. Just hot water heaters out in back ... come on! And hold that light steady."

Propping the sliding panel open with one of the brass implements from the top shelf of the adumbry, we started down the steps, Brian leading the way.

The stone stair wound down into the depths in a spiral; air blew up from below us, sickening with the stench of mold and rot and mildew, sweetish with the smells of raw wet soil. And over all the other stenches, strangely, the salt smell of the sea.

"My God! There! *Look*—"

Strewn on the lichen-crusted steps beneath us gems glimmered and flashed in the light of the torch. Some were cut into facets and set in antique gold or silver settings, others were raw and neither cut nor polished. Interspersed among the jewels were lumps of gold ore, and silver, and worked pieces of precious metals. There were many coins scattered down the steps: I bent, picked one up, examined it, peering with dread surmise at noble Spanish profiles of ancient kings.

"No wonder he was so rich, damn him!" breathed Brian, his eyes gleaming wildly in the electric glare of the torch. "No wonder they bought his 'service' so easily ... my God! The 'Red Offerings!'"

"You still don't have any real proof," I protested. But my words rang hollowly, even to my hearing.

"*There's* all the proof I need," raged Brian, kicking with his shoe at the surface of the mold-crusted step. Gems and coins scattered, clattering. And it seemed to me that something stirred in the darkness beneath where we stood.

"Come on, let's follow this thing to the end of it." Without waiting for me to follow, he plunged recklessly down the coiling stair, rubies and sapphires crunching and squealing under his tread. While I lingered, hesitating just a little, he vanished from my sight.

Then I heard him cry out in a wrathful roar.

"There's someone down here, Win! You, there, stop—"

A moment of dead silence. The stench became overpowering, sickening. Something huge and wet and glistening white surged in the gloom beneath where I stood hesitating.

Then Brian *screamed* ... a raw shriek of ultimate horror such as I have never heard before from human lips, and hope and pray never to hear again. A scream such as that could rip and tear the lining of a man's throat—

Calling his name out, I plunged and stumbled and half-fell down the steps, slipping in the slimy muck that coated the stones.

I reached the bottom of the stair, but Brian was not there. There was nothing at all to be seen, no side passages, no doorways: nothing.

The coiling stone stair did not end, but it vanished into a black pool of slimy liquid mud which completely filled the bottom of the stairwell. Something died within me as I shone my light across the black pool. *The agitated ripples that crawled from edge to edge of the pool, as if something heavy had just fallen in* ....

Fallen, or been dragged.

* * *

I DID not stay very much longer in the huge old house so near, so fearfully near to Hubble's Field. Once the police had taken my wild and incoherent statement—which doubtless they dismissed as the ravings of a lunatic— I returned to Brian's apartment in Santiago.

I brought with me the old books. It was—it *is*—my firm intention to give them to some suitable, scholarly collection; I shall most likely donate them to the Sanbourne Institute of Pacific Antiquities, which already has Copeland's *Unaussprechlichen Kulten* and the *Zanthu Tablets*. For some reason, I linger on here; and I do not think I shall go back to my place of employment at Miskatonic. After all, with the wealth of my heritage from Uncle Hiram's estate, I need no longer work for a living and may indulge my whims.

Every night, as I hover on the brink of sleep, the Voices come—whispering, whispering. Wealth and power and forbidden knowledge they promise me, over and over ... now that I have already performed the Red Offering, I may enjoy the fruits of my—sacrifice.

In vain I protest that *it was not I* that flung or felled or drove Brian down into that horrible pool of black, liquescent mud at the bottom of the secret stair. The stair of which I said nothing to the police.

But the Voices say it does not matter: The Red Offering has been made. And it must be made again, and again, and again.

Is that what the loutish workman in the diner meant when he predicted, "Now it's gonna start all over again?" Perhaps. From the hundreds of corpses the authorities found buried in Hubble's Field, it has been going on for a very long time already.

Oh, they know too well how easy it is to seduce weak and fallible men, curse them!

The Voices whisper to me how easy it is to make the Sign of Koth, which will take me beyond the Dream-Gates where the Night-Gaunts and the Ghouls, and the Ghasts of Zin, wait to welcome me; from thence the great winged Byakhee that serve Hastur in the dark spaces between the stars linger upon my coming, to fly me to the dark star amidst the Hyades, to Carcosa beside the cloudy shores of Lake Hali, to the very foot of the Elder Throne where the King in Yellow—even He, Yhtill the Timeless One—will receive my Vow, and where I will receive the penultimate guerdon of my service, and will at length glimpse That which is hidden behind the Pallid Mask ... soon ... soon ....

I have been reading the *Necronomicon* a lot, these empty days, waiting for the nights to come and the Voices to begin.

I think I will move back to Uncle Hiram's house in Durnham Beach soon. After all, it belongs to me, now.

It, too, is part of the Winfield heritance.

THIS brief story, which first appeared in *Crypt of Cthulhu* #56 (Roodmas 1988), is a crossover between two Lin Carter series, both involving the Cthulhu Mythos. The hero—not just a protagonist this time, but a hero—is Dr. Anton Zarnak, Lin's version of Seabury Quinn's occult detective Jules de Grandin, who is even mentioned by name in this story (just as Lin's Prince Zarkon, his Doc Savage analog, hobnobbed with most of the old pulp heroes at one time or another). Zarnak made his initial appearance in Lin's first attempt at a novella, *Curse of the Black Pharaoh* (which will appear in the forthcoming Chaosium collection *The Nyarlathotep Cycle*), where, for all his occult powers and accomplishments, he somehow manages to come across as a colorless figure. Decades later Carter returned to Dr. Zarnak, sprucing him up considerably for a pair of brief tales, the one you are about to read here and "Dead of Night" (which appeared in *The Book of Iod*). I have, by the way, undertaken to continue Zarnak's adventures, one of which appears in the new Chaosium edition of Edward Paul Berglund's *The Disciples of Cthulhu*. Another appears in this collection.

The other Carter series hybridized here is, of course, the Xothic cycle. Various familiar names and associations reappear here. In fact, "Perchance to Dream" resembles an epitome of the whole Xothic series thus far: Zarnak's client is named Winfield, yet he seems to have no connection with the Winfields in "The Winfield Heritance." His inherited collection of South Pacific artifacts comes not from the Copeland bequest, nor even from Captain Hoag, but from his own sea-faring Hoag analog, Grandfather Winfield. He is plagued by a series of maddening dreams quite similar to those of Henry Stephenson Blaine (and Bryant Hoskins—see below). And the method Zarnak uses to solve Winfield's problem is the same Gordian strategy used by the unfortunate Hodgkins in "The Horror in the Gallery." In this story Lin has used his own previous Mythos stories as a motif pool in precisely the same way he elsewhere uses the work of Lovecraft and Derleth.

Finally, some readers may need to be informed that Zarnak's location on seedy River Street derives directly from the adventures of Robert E. Howard's detective Steve Harrison. The reference to Clithanus is a tip of the turban to August Derleth, who invented this mad monk and his revelations for a set of early Mythos tales (which are planned for inclusion in the forthcoming collection of Derleth's Cthulhu Mythos tales, *In Lovecraft's Shadow*, edited by Joe Wrzos and distributed by Arkham House).

Perchance to Dream

by Lin Carter

1. China Alley

THE cab drove past Fourteenth Street and continued south, driving between Chinatown and the river. This part of town was shadowy and disreputable—the streets grew narrow, crooked, the corner lamps dim, the shadows deeper, the people fewer and more furtive. There were Levantines and Turks, Portuguese, Lascars: the gutter-scrapings of half a hundred Eastern ports. The shops became smaller and their signs and windows bore inscriptions in queer Oriental letters. Heaven alone knew what crimes were plotted in these black alleys, these crumbling tenements ....

Of all these matters, Parker Winfield was all too uncomfortably aware, and with every block his taxi bore him deeper into a tangled maze of decaying slums, his discomfiture grew. *Damn* that nosy Muriel van Velt for goading him into making the appointment, which made him come into parts of the city that he had always instinctively avoided, far from the luxurious clubs and fashionable, expensive restaurants that were his usual habitat! And damn the mystery man, this seeker into strange lore and forbidden places, for daring to dwell in such a hellish neighborhood!

Fog was drifting in from the riverfront as the cab drew up to the yawning mouth of one black alley, whose gloom was feebly dispelled by a lone lamp that shone above a doorway off Levant Street.

"That's it, buddy, Number Thirteen China Alley," announced the cab driver. Parker peered at the narrow cobbled way with strong emotions of misgiving.

"You're quite sure?" he quavered. The driver nodded curtly.

"Sure. Number Thirteen China Alley, between River Street and Levant. That'll be six seventy-five."

Winfield tossed him a crisp ten-dollar bill and got out of the cab.

"How the hell do I get back?" he demanded petulantly. The driver shrugged and pressed a card into his hand.

"Call the garage—if they got a phone in there," he muttered, with a dubious glance at the one dim light that glowed above the door. Then he drove off, mist swirling in gray tendrils in his wake. Hesitantly, Parker Winfield drew his expensive topcoat more closely about him to ward off the damp and chill and entered the alley's yawning mouth. The glow of a streetlight illuminated his features, revealing a spoiled young man with lines of dissipation under watery eyes and a weak, indecisive mouth which a costly Bermuda tan did little to disguise.

The house was narrow and small, two stories in height, shouldered to either side by taller brick tenements. The door, surprisingly, was a heavy slab of polished oak with stout hinges. A small brass plaque above the doorbell bore the single word *Zarnak*. The visitor thumbed the bell and waited, wishing he had never let Muriel van Velt talk him into coming.

The door was opened by a tall man in a turban, lean and rangy, his aquiline features swarthy, hawk-like. Keen eyes sharp as dagger points scrutinized Winfield from top to toe.

"You will be Mr. Winfield," said the turbaned man in flawless English. "Pray enter; the *sahib* is expecting you."

As the door was shut behind him and steel bolts slid home, Winfield gave the servant his hat and topcoat, staring about him with vague astonishment. He had not known quite what to expect, but certainly nothing like *this*. The small foyer bore an immense bronze incense burner on a teakwood stand; Tibetan scroll paintings hung on walls covered with silk brocade; lush Persian carpets were soft underfoot.

He was ushered into a small study.

"Pray make yourself comfortable, sir; the *sahib* will attend you in one moment," said the Indian servant. Left alone, Winfield glanced with dazed eyes about the room. Furniture, evidently of antique workmanship, stood here and there, all of heavy, polished teak inlaid with ivory or mother of pearl. Damask-hung walls displayed illuminated cabinets crowded with curiosities, among them Etruscan, Hittite, Egyptian, Greek artifacts. The carpeting underfoot was ancient Ispahan, faded but still glorious. A subtle fragrance sweetened the air, rising in lazy blue whorls from the grinning jaws of a brass idol.

Bookshelves held hundreds of scholarly looking tomes; Winfield scanned them absently but they were in Latin, German, French, with titles unknown to him—*Unaussprechlichen Kulten, Livre d'Ivonis, Cultes des Goules*.

A desk, also of old, carved teak, was covered with a clutter of papers, notebooks, leather-bound volumes. Egyptian tomb-figurines of blue faience, heavy scarabs of schist, Sumerian tablets inscribed with cuneiform inscriptions, served as paperweights. Above the desk a leering devil-mask, painted scarlet, black, and gold, snarled down from the wall, symbolic gold flames coiling from fanged mouth and dilated nostrils. Winfield gaped at it.

"Tibetan," said a quiet voice from behind him. "It represents Yama, King of Demons; in prehistoric Lemuria he was worshiped as Yamath, Lord of Fire."

Winfield flinched at the unexpected voice and turned to view his host, a lean saturnine individual of indeterminate age, wrapped in a gold and purple dressing-gown. His skin was sallow, his eyes dark and hooded, his black hair seal-slick, with a dramatic streak of pure silver that zigzagged from his right temple.

"You're Zarnak, I guess," blustered Winfield rudely. His host gave a slight smile. Seating himself behind the long, cluttered desk, he gestured toward a marble-topped table where decanters of cut crystal reposed.

"To quote an old adversary rather imprecisely, I have a doctorate in medicine from Edinburgh University, a doctorate in theology from Heidelberg, a doctorate in psychology from Vienna, and a doctorate in metaphysics from Miskatonic; my guests usually address me as *Doctor* Zarnak. Please help yourself to some brandy, and tell me of what service I can be."

Probably some damnable spic or dago rotgut, thought Winfield, taking up a bell-shaped glass. But from the first gulp, Winfield felt as though he were drinking liquid gold.

"Imperial Tokay," murmured Zarnak, opening a notebook and selecting a pen. "From the cellars of the late Emperor Franz-Joseph. Now: How can I help you?"

2. The City in the Sea

"IT'S these damned dreams, you know," began Parker Winfield, settling into a chair. "Always the same damned dream, night after night ... I'm sinking under the sea: At first, the water's light green, like muttonfat jade, then darker, like turquoise, then malachite. Finally, it's a green so dark it's almost black. I ... I see huge stone blocks, thick with seaweed, slimy with mud. There's a central building, a temple of some sort; virulent green light shines through the portal, luring me toward it—"

"Does this city have a name in your dream?" inquired Doctor Zarnak. Winfield's weak mouth twisted sneeringly.

"Sure does! Nonsense, though ... 'Arlyah.'"

Zarnak made a note in a small, precise hand. "Please continue," he said softly. Winfield shrugged uncomfortably.

"That's really all there is," he admitted. "Except that in the dream, I'm damnably afraid! And every night I get nearer and nearer to that green-lit portal ... before I wake, drenched in cold perspiration. And then, there's the *chanting*, you know ... some damnable Eastern gobbledygook ... sheer mumbo-jumbo ...."

"Can you recite any of it?" asked Zarnak. The other nodded, with a small shudder.

"Certainly can: I've heard the nonsensical words often enough ... sounds like 'fuh, nug, louis, muggle, waffle, klool, yu, arlyah, waggle, naggle, fong.'"

He broke off, eyes defensive. "You must think I'm nuts! Everybody does. Tell me to see an analyst, but they're just a bunch of witch-doctors after your wallet!"

"Have you consulted a physician of any kind concerning these dreams of yours?"

Winfield nodded. "Dr. Cartwright on Park Avenue; family physician, you know."

"An excellent man," murmured Zarnak. "What was his conclusion?"

Winfield laughed harshly. "Too much champagne, too late hours, not enough exercise, rich diet ... *that* sort of thing."

"I believe that when you phoned you mentioned that it was Miss van Velt who suggested that you consult me?" Zarnak murmured meditatively.

"Yes, it was Muriel," Winfield muttered. "I thought you'd be some fancy, high-priced nerve specialist on Fifth Avenue or Sutton Place ... why in the world do you live down in this filthy neighborhood?" Winfield suddenly asked.

Zarnak smiled. "The denizens of River Street and its environs know how to mind their own business, since many of them hide guilty secrets in their hearts and a lack of curiosity about their neighbors is an excellent means of preserving their own lives. Also, I have many scholarly colleagues among the Asian populace down here, and thus access to obscure and arcane information ... but let me change the subject, if I may. You mentioned mutton-fat jade and gemstones a moment or so earlier; may I assume that you collect antiquities or rare minerals?"

Parker Winfield smirked. "Not me! Know next to nothing about that sort of stuff. But my grandfather, now, *he* collected all sorts of oddities, from all over."

"Indeed. Was your grandfather born to wealth, or did he establish the family income?" asked Zarnak.

"Gramps? He was in the China trade; all over the Pacific—Indonesia, the Carolines—"

"Ponape?" hazarded Doctor Zarnak.

"Most likely. Not sure where they are, the Carolines, but if they're in the Pacific, Gramps was there. Brought home a load of junk, Gramps did. Been in storage for years and years, since we closed the country estate and sold it off. Odd you should mention Gramps and his collection; I've been unpacking some of it, now that I've opened my new apartment. Got an extra room I've fitted out for his collection; nothing else to put in there."

"How very interesting! I should like to visit, just to compare: one antiquarian collection with another. May I call tomorrow morning?"

Winfield looked uneasy. "Thought you'd have some surefire way to get rid of my bad dreams," he complained. "Muriel said—"

Zarnak spoke soothingly. "There are one or two things I could try, but I need more information. There is nothing that I can do at this late hour, and, besides, I am expecting another visitor. But permit me to call on you tomorrow morning, and explore your new residence. There may be something about the apartment that has been causing you to have these dreams of a city in the sea."

"Ghosts, you mean!" demanded Winfield scornfully. "Think the place is haunted, do you?"

Zarnak spread his hands. "Who can say what psychic residue may have been left by former residents? I am sensitive to atmospheres; give me a chance to help you."

He rose, touched a bell. "My servant will see you out."

"Hindu, ain't he?" asked Winfield.

"Ram Singh is a Rajput," replied Zarnak. "They are a princely race of noble warriors."

"Where do you find a servant like that? My man Rufus is all right, but I'd give plenty for a fellow like the one you've got working for you—"

Zarnak asked, without expression: "Have you ever heard much of werewolves?"

Winfield stared at him. "Like in those old Lon Chaney movies, you mean? Certainly! But what's that got to do with India?"

"In India, they have were-tigers," said Zarnak tonelessly. "I was able to save Ram Singh from one. To reply to your question, you cannot hire a Rajput servant, but you can earn their lifelong gratitude and service. A Rajput chooses his own master, and not the other way around."

"Your hat and coat, sir," said Ram Singh from the doorway.

When Parker Winfield had left, Zarnak sat down at his desk to look at his notes.

After a moment, under the line of "gibberish" his visitor had heard from the chanting in his dreams, Zarnak wrote in a precise hand: *Ph'nglui mglw'nafh Cthulhu R'lyeh wgah'nagl fhtagn.*

Under the name of the sea-drowned city, which Winfield had given him, phonetically, as "Arlyah", he wrote a single name: *R'lyeh.*

Ram Singh appeared in the doorway.

"*Sahib*, the Doctor de Grandin is arriving."

An expression of pleasure crossed the saturnine features as Zarnak rose to greet his very old friend.

3. Something from Down There

AT ten o'clock in the morning of the next day, a car pulled up before a fashionable condominium off Fifth Avenue, and Zarnak, carrying a black leather briefcase that seldom left his side, emerged.

At the door of Winfield's apartment, he was greeted by a young black man neatly attired in a somber gray suit, white shirt, and narrow black tie.

"I am Doctor Anton Zarnak. I believe Mr. Winfield is expecting me."

The black man smiled and opened the door wider. "Surely! Mr. Winfield is having breakfast now, but if you'd like to join him—?"

The apartment was discreetly furnished in good modern taste, obviously by an expensive interior decorator and not the resident. The furniture was of blond wood in Swedish Modern, and the carpet was an excellent Rya. The bric-a-brac was polished aluminum and the pictures were signed lithographs.

Rufus—for that must have been his name—led Zarnak into a sunny breakfast nook where he found Parker Winfield, his face more pouched than before, with bleary, red-rimmed eyes, hunched over a table. Apparently, the younger man had indulged in a bit of alcoholic beverage after leaving China Alley. He waved a feeble hand.

"Good to see you, Doc! Help yourself ... I don't have much appetite this morning."

Zarnak inspected the sideboard: selected a rasher of Canadian bacon, an English muffin dripping with Devonshire butter and clover honey, eggs Florentine, and asked the servant for a cup of black coffee.

"More of those dreams last night?" Zarnak asked of his host, who nodded dejectedly.

"Worse than ever, Doc; I got closer to that hellish portal than ever before. Don't know how much more of this I can take before my nerves are entirely shot. Think you can help?"

"I will try," said Zarnak.

After breakfast, he asked Winfield to show him around. The apartment was a sumptuous one composed of eight rooms, of which two held the cook and Rufus. A terrace gave a sunny view of Central Park. In none of the rooms did Zarnak experience that chill *frisson* along the nerves that would have signaled, to a sensitive, the presence of malign forces. The building, it appeared, was too newly erected to have had time to acquire the psychic residue that ordinary people call "ghosts."

Nothing that Zarnak experienced alarmed or disturbed him, until his host led him into a side room where reposed Grandfather Winfield's relics of his South Sea voyages. The room was crowded with uncouth artworks, chiseled from stone or carved from wood. Most of these were obviously antiques and worth considerable sums of money. Zarnak examined them with thoughtful care.

There were pieces of tapa cloth from the Tonga Islands, charged with an odd motif like repeated five-pointed stars; curiously frog-like idols of wood or stone from the Cook Islanders; a Sepik River Valley figure from New Guinea with an odd, kraken-like fringe of waving tentacles; pendants of carved shell from Papua shaped into octopoidal heads; wooden masks from the New Hebrides with a mane of writhing serpents instead of hair; a basalt image from Easter Island depicting a peculiarly loathsome combination of frog and fish; and the fragment of a lava bas-relief from South Indochina upon which Zarnak's eyes did not linger.

His very worst suspicions were confirmed. Grimly, he went on, examining exhibit after exhibit, until he found one which arrested him in his tracks. He lingered before it, staring unwinkingly.

"Ugly creature, isn't it?" asked Parker Winfield at his elbow. "Maybe I should donate the whole lot somewhere; some of 'em give me the creeps."

"I suggest that you do," murmured Zarnak distractedly. "And I could recommend the Sanbourne Institute in Santiago, California; they have an admirable collection of this kind of ... art."

The piece upon which Anton Zarnak's attention was fixed seemed to have been hewn from jadeite. It was about eleven inches tall, and depicted a bipedal monstrosity whose hind legs resembled those of a batrachian, with forelimbs uplifted almost as if in menace, sucker-tipped, webbed hands extended toward the viewer. The head of the image was a seething mass of pseudopods or tentacles, amid which a single glaring eye could be discerned.

The symbols carved in the idol's base were in a language long vanished from human knowledge; few human beings on earth could have read them. Zarnak was one of the few.

"*Ythogtha*," he breathed.

"That's the thing's name?" inquired Winfield cheerfully.

Zarnak nodded somberly. "I don't suppose you have ever happened to look into any of the late Professor Copeland's books about the prehistoric Pacific civilizations?"

Winfield chuckled. "Not me! Not much of a reader, I'm afraid. What is it about this bugger that interests you?"

"It is quite unique. I should like to study it at length. May I borrow it for a time?"

"Well ... valuable, is it?"

"Priceless, I should say. It is probably the only piece of its kind on earth—fortunately for us. In my opinion, you will sleep much more soundly without it on the premises, and enjoy much more wholesome dreams," said Zarnak.

Winfield looked skeptical; nevertheless he insisted that Doctor Zarnak take the piece with him and keep it as long as he wished.

"Grandfather said that thing was found by a native diver somewhere in the waters off Easter Island," he remarked. "Maybe it would have been a lot better if it had stayed down below, eh?"

"Quite so," said Zarnak fervently. He had never spoken more sincerely in his life.

4. To Dream No More

ONCE back in China Alley, Zarnak examined the stony image more closely. It was made of a greasy gray stone, mottled with dark green splotches like fungus or lichen. He weighed the image, and it was abnormally heavy—heavier than lead, far heavier than any terrene mineral was supposed to be. The phrase "star-quarried stone" passed through his mind briefly.

Zarnak consulted the books in his library. First he looked into a slim, cheaply produced pamphlet which bore the title *The Zanthu Tablets* and read of Great Ythogtha, the Abomination in the Abyss, imprisoned by the Elder Gods in Yhe. Then he consulted von Junzt, and found the following passage of interest:

> Of the Spawn of Cthulhu, only Ythogtha lies prisoned in regions contiguous to sunken R'lyeh, for Yhe was once a province of Mu, and R'lyeh is not far off the submerged shores of that riven, drowned continent; and Yhe and R'lyeh are close nigh unto each other, along dimensions not numbered among the three we know.

Zarnak studied the stony image with some of the scientific instruments in his laboratory. It seemed to possess a powerful electromagnetic charge— at least, contact with the image wilted the gold leaves of the electroscope. Zarnak meditated: Such images, he knew, brought down from the stars when the earth was young, may be fashioned of an unearthly and abnormal amalgam of stone and metal, which would account for the unusual weight of the object. That such figurines may be impregnated with thought waves, even as a strip of magnetic tape can be recorded with sound waves, was also known to him from his researches. Was that the secret of the image, or did it somehow serve as the transmitter of thought waves from the lair of Ythogtha's awful Sire?

All the while, the frog-like image squatted on the laboratory table, regarding him unwinkingly with that one Medusa-like eye of cold malignancy.

The thing seemed virtually alive in some uncanny way. Almost, it seemed, the gray-green mineral surged with vitality and the writhing tendrils that mercifully masked its hideous visage seemed almost to flicker with furtive motion, when glimpsed from the corners of his eye.

At length, completing his notes, Zarnak rose and went to a steel cabinet against one wall, whose topmost drawer he unlocked with a small key. He drew forth a tray lined with black velvet whereupon reposed a number of curious objects shaped like five-pointed stars. Some had been carved from a stony mineral, either slate gray or dull green. The bottom row were of ceramic, taffy-colored, baked in a kiln and heavily glazed. These last had been manufactured for Zarnak by a sculptor friend in Seattle, and Zarnak himself had consecrated them, had energized them with power, according to an old formula he had discovered in Clithanus.

Thoughtfully, he weighed the star-shaped amulet of the Elder Gods in the palm of one hand, while his gaze brooded upon the stone image. It would be interesting to discover whether the statuette of Ythogtha had so impregnated the mind of Parker Winfield with its malign and sinister influence that the dreams continued even without the eidolon being present as a sort of "conductor."

It would also be interesting to learn what happened when one of the star stones came in physical contact with the image from Outside ....

* * *

THE dream began as all the dreams began: He was sinking slowly down through luminous water that dimmed and darkened around him into blackest gloom, lit only with that eerie emerald radiance from the ruin. He was vaguely conscious of stifling pressure from the many tons of water above him, of wet cold, of utter helplessness ....

Parker Winfield felt his body drift without volition over the murky vista of tumbled stone blocks that were matted with pallid weed and thick with slime ... the broken stone ruin came closer, ever closer. The weird green luminance waxed in strength, pulsing like the beating of some enormous heart ....

Now his dream-form was floating up the mossy, mud-thick stone steps; now the very portal of the ruin filled his vision, immense, of unthinkable antiquity, concealing God alone knew what horrible abnormality, what monstrous dweller in the depths ....

The portal *opened*: Throbbing green radiance smote Parker Winfield full in the face, blinding, dazzling him—then his dreamer's vision adjusted to the unwholesome light, and he strove to see the source of that lambent glow, which seemed throned in some vast and oddly angled chair—

Then a flash of clear, pure, golden light wiped the dreamscape away!

Winfield awoke, gasping, saturated with cold perspiration, hands shaking like willows in a wind. He stared about him with wild and haunted gaze, seeing only his own darkened bedroom, nothing more. A wave of sheer relief sluiced through him, washing away the residue of night-fear—

The telephone rang. With nerveless hands, Winfield snatched up the instrument.

"Yes?"

"Doctor Zarnak here," said the familiar voice. "Have you had another of those sea-dreams?"

"I certainly have, and worse than the ones before, although it ended differently from the others—"

Zarnak listened carefully to his client's description of the nightmare. From time to time he made small, precise notes in the book on his desk before him. When the other was finished with his recital:

"Very good. I believe I have isolated and eradicated the source of the infection, as you might call it. You shall dream no more; or, rather, such dreams as you experience from henceforward will be only the healthy dreams of normal sleep ... ah, one thing more. I regret to tell you that the jadeite image from your grandfather's collection of artifacts met with severe damage during the testing process, and I will be unable to return it. Yes; very good. And you are shipping the remainder of the collection to the Institute? Very satisfactory. Good day to you."

Zarnak replaced the instrument in its cradle, made a final note in his book, rose, and stepped silently from the room.

On the asbestos mat atop the small steel and porcelain table which had borne the jadeite image and the star-stone now reposed only a heap of fine gray ash. The sharp stench of ozone hovered in the air.

It was much better so ... and the case was one that had had, after all, a happy ending.

I HAVE always been pretty confident that August Derleth borrowed the title for his novel *The Lurker at the Threshold* from Robert Hitchins' 1911 novel of spiritualism *The Dweller on the Threshold*, and equally sure that Lin Carter derived the title of the following story, "Strange Manuscript Found in the Vermont Woods", from the anonymous 1888 lost race novel *A Strange Manuscript Found in a Copper Cylinder*. We know Derleth appreciated Hitchins' work, though he happens not to mention this particular novel by name as far as I know, while Lin Carter, being a fan of lost race novels and having written some himself, would have to have been familiar with *Strange Manuscript*. Lucky for me, both Derleth and Carter are in no position to prove me wrong.

The present tale shares certain features in common with "The Winfield Heritance"—both make passing reference to Harold Hadley Copeland and his researches, as well as to the terrible Xothic legend cycle, and both have some link with Derleth's *The Lurker at the Threshold*. It is interesting, moreover, that whereas "The Winfield Heritance" branches off from the third episode of Derleth's *Lurker*—the "Narrative of Winfield Phillips", in which the eponymous Phillips plays Dr. Parker to Seneca Lapham's Solar Pons—"Strange Manuscript" builds instead on the first and second episodes, "Billington's Wood" and "Manuscript of Stephen Bates." Not only are Seneca Lapham and Winfield Phillips not mentioned in "Strange Manuscript", but Carter has ignored the events of the third episode entirely. In that concluding segment, Derleth had arbitrarily swept away all that preceded, including the identity of the monster as Ossadogowah, the son of Tsathoggua, substituting Yog-Sothoth. Carter here has returned to the original conception of Tsathoggua, Junior. While even Lin Carter lacked the *chutzpah* to dare substitute a new conclusion to *Lurker*, something I ventured with "The Round Tower" (see *The Dunwich Cycle*), in "Strange Manuscript Found in the Ver-mont Woods" he did at least try to tie up some of the loose ends Derleth left hanging.

We ought also to note the connection between this story and Carter's *Book of Eibon* chapter, "The Feaster from the Stars", in which the same entity is conjured. "Strange Manuscript" is also woven into the fabric of the Xothic cycle by virtue of the connection of its protagonist with the Hoag family of Arkham, whose scion, Captain Abner Exekiel Hoag, first brought back the manuscript of the *Ponape Scripture*. The sonnet cycle "Dreams from R'lyeh" provides another glimpse of the heirs of this tainted line.

I have noticed an intriguing little blip in a couple of Mythos tales (maybe there are more) which may be worth pointing out, and that is the occasional presence of odd variants on familiar biblical names. I have always liked August Derleth's "Alijah [for Elijah] Billington" in *The Lurker at the Threshold*, and Lin Carter has an odd spelling of Ezekiel in the name "Abner Exekiel Hoag." Of course, as in names like "Xavier", the "X" could be said as either an "x" or a "z." I assume "Exekiel" is to be pronounced with a "z." The name "Abner Exekiel Hoag" seems to stem from two sources. "Hoag", a common enough New England name, was the last name of a friend of Lovecraft to whose collected poems HPL wrote the introduction. James E. Hoag's "To the American Flag", in fact, mistakenly appears attributed to Lovecraft in the latter's own *Collected Poems*! "Abner Exekiel" is a pair of biblical names, those of the military chief of staff for King David, who tried to dissuade him from the disastrous census of his people (2 Samuel 24), and the Exilic Jewish priest-prophet Ezekiel. Lin Carter had combined both names long before, in his Belmont novel *The Tower at the Edge of Time* (1968), where there is a mystic seer named, improbably for an Oriental, "Abdekiel."

"Strange Manuscript Found in the Vermont Woods" first appeared in *Crypt of Cthulhu* #54, Easteride 1988.

Strange Manuscript Found in the Vermont Woods

by Lin Carter

NOTE: In the early spring of 1936 the following manuscript was found buried in the snowbanks in the wood south of the village of Townshend in Windham County, Vermont, by a local farmer, one Seth Adkins. When Mr. Adkins reported the discovery of the manuscript, which he turned over to Constable Homer T. Whitlaw, he said it was found in a leather briefcase which was curiously charred as if from exposure to intense heat, and seared here and there as if from the action of some virulent acid, and was also stained with a black slime-like substance which stank horribly. He also added that the briefcase and its contents were not only buried deep under a heavy snowdrift, but were partially impacted in the still-frozen soil, as if it had fallen from an incredible height. The spring thaw, it seems, had exposed one corner of the leather case to view, attracting the farmer's attention.

Upon examining the contents of the valise, Constable Whitlaw found a sheaf of handwritten manuscript inscribed in a neat hand which eventually deteriorated into a scarcely readable scrawl, as if the later portions of the document had been scribbled hurriedly, under tension or duress. Furthermore, the edges of the several handwritten pages were *crisped* as if from exposure to severe temperature, and in places illegible due to leakage from the thawing snow.

The manuscript was written on both sides of sheets of correspondence paper embossed with the name of Winthrop Hoag, with a Boston address. Recalling the mysterious and still unexplained disappearance of a certain Winthrop Hoag from a cabin in the woods north of Arkham, Massachusetts, only three months earlier, the Constable forwarded the valise and its contents, together with an account of their discovery, to County Sheriff Wilbur F. Tate in Arkham. At Sheriff Tate's direction, the manuscript was transcribed exactly as it appears below. Certain of the words and entire passages remained illegible, even though studied by handwriting experts.

The mystery remains unsolved to this day.

Journal of Winthrop Hoag

I ARRIVED in Arkham in early fall on the Boston train and went at once to the law offices of Mr. Silas Harding, who had been my cousin Jared Fuller's lawyer until his death or disappearance seven years before, and who was the custodian of his last will and testament, in which, Harding's recent letter had informed me, I was declared sole beneficiary to his estate.

I found Mr. Harding a gaunt, silver-haired man in a dark suit, who spoke affably but with a pronounced Yankee twang. Ushering me to a seat, he explained that since the waiting period allowed by law in the case of missing persons had now expired, my cousin's property was legally mine. Said property consisted of a small cabin on a bit of land in the woods north of town, and its contents, the most valuable of which were probably certain old books which might prove worth a considerable sum in the hands of a rare book specialist.

The lawyer informed me that the cabin had been stoutly padlocked on his instructions, and the windows shuttered and barred. He had, he said, visited the property as recently as last week, and was pleased to report that the roofing was sound, the interior dry, and that the place was perfectly habitable, if lacking in certain of the civilized amenities of life.

"Is there any sort of plumbing?" I inquired. He shook his head.

"Too far out of town for that, sir! But there's a privy in the back and a decent well has been dug. Walls seem secure; you'll git good heat from the Franklin stove. There's even a goodly supply of well dried firewood under a tarpaulin in the shed. You'll need thet, come winter."

In my reply to Harding's letter informing me of my small bequest, I had stated my intention to live in the cabin, despite the nearness of winter—and they can be cruel and bitter winters, north of Arkham!—for I needed seclusion in which to prepare the notes for my master's thesis. He had written back, rather insistently, arguing against this plan on several points. It amused me that he repeated some of them now.

"You'll be snowed in, you know, for weeks at a time."

"Surely I can lay in supplies of canned goods, coffee, and the like from the nearest grocery," I said gently, humoring him a little.

"There *is* a general store on the Pike," he admitted grudgingly. "And the bus runs between Dunwich and Arkham pret' regular, 'cept in the case of blizzards. Still have to suggest you just visit the place and take your property, and go back to Boston ...."

When I pressed him for his reason, he merely muttered something about those woods "not having the best reputation", but remained close-mouthed on his meaning. When he saw I would not be swerved, he handed over the keys after requiring my signature on a few documents.

"You kin catch the bus to Dunwich at the end of River Street," he said curtly, in answering my request for directions. "Takes the Aylesbury Pike. You git off two, three miles beyond Dean's Corners, they's a mailbox by the road with 'Hoag' painted on it. Painted yer name on it myself, so you'd know. Driver'll know where t' let you off."

I thanked Harding and rose to leave. He laid a restraining hand on my arm.

"Daont' like to talk about sich matters," he said in a low voice. "But the Deep Woods, where you're goin', they have an even wust reputation than Billington's Wood just saouth."

And with that enigmatic warning, he let me leave.

* * *

DRIVING north and northwest from Arkham, the land grew wild and lonely, thickly overgrown with gnarled and ancient trees with strangely few farmhouses to be seen, at least from the Pike. There were only a few people on the bus, a slatternly middle-aged woman or two, and an old farmer in filthy overalls, so I chose my seat near the driver. He seemed in a chatty mood.

"Daoun't get many young fellers like you up this way," he drawled. "From Boston, y'say; but ain't Hoag an old Arkham name?"

"Yes, it is. From back before the Revolution, in the old sea-trading days."

"Heard tell of a Cap'n Abner Hoag onc't," the driver ruminated. "South Seas and Chiny trade, I recollect." I told him that Abner Exekiel Hoag was my direct ancestor.

"My branch of the family has lived in or around Boston since about 1912," I told him, and he seemed interested in the older Massachusetts genealogies. "Our line descends from Hiram Lapham Hoag, who moved to Lowell, near Boston, in that year. He was the younger brother of Zorad Ethan Hoag, who lived in Arkham until recently."

For some reason he became silent and taciturn at that point, and all my conversational gambits were able to elicit from him for the remainder of the trip were a few grunts or shakings of the head.

He dropped me off at my stop, where a narrow dirt road—well, hardly more than a path—wound between huge old trees. I trudged along the path and the woods pressed uncomfortably close, as if resenting with some weird sentience the intrusion of man into their ancient domain. The *Deep Woods*, Silas Harding had called them ... odd how, in this oppressive silence, the narrow way walled about by thickly grown, close-crowding trees, the name had a sinister ring to it.

The cabin my cousin had left me in his will was small enough, but it seemed livable, despite the fact that the clapboard walls could have used a few coats of paint. It stood amid a small clearing, on a patch of naked earth, and again I could not help noticing (with slight revulsion, even dismay) how disturbingly close the edge of the woods shouldered about the forlorn habitation. These feelings I resolutely dismissed from my mind; I have always been unusually sensitive to the atmosphere of lonely, wooded places.

Once within, the bars removed and shutters opened, I found the interior dry and clean. There was a small Army cot, neatly made, a rickety table with a hoop-back wooden chair drawn up before it, and even a hooked rug before the old iron stove. These, and an empty woodbox, were the sum total of the furnishings: "lacking certain of the civilized amenities of life", even as lawyer Harding had dryly remarked.

Still, I thought I could be comfortable here, even in the depths of winter. There were shelves on the wall with tin plates and cups, sparse tableware, cheap and worn, a coffee pot and two or three pots and a frying pan. I even discovered a dime-store can-opener hung from a hook on the shelf. In a corner of the one-room cabin I found a hurricane lamp in serviceable condition, although the can of kerosene which fueled it proved empty.

Unpacking my clothing and books and papers, which latter took occupation of the table, I went outside and found the well-water fresh and clean, and in the woodshed a good supply of cut and stacked firewood in fine, dry condition, as Harding had promised, together with a rusty axe for cutting more when needed.

That afternoon, I went down the Aylesbury Pike to the little general store I had noticed from the bus. It stood on the outskirts of Dean's Corners, and the proprietor was happy to sell me supplies. As I must be frugal—my funds being low, and the bequest from my cousin Jared containing no cash worth speaking of—I settled on canned pork and beans, home-bottled peaches, boxed crackers, ground coffee, ketchup, salt, and a few other things, together with some pipe tobacco.

The storekeeper, an old, withered, wiry backwoodsman named Perkins, proved helpful but very inquisitive as to what I was doing "in this neck o' th' woods." When I told him I was a cousin of Jared Fuller, and had inherited his cabin in the woods a mile or two north, he stared at me incredulously.

"Fuller, y'say? Not in th' Deep Woods?"

"Yes, I'm afraid so," I smiled. He gave me a strange, almost *frightened* look.

"Why, daoun't y'know they be even wust than Billington's Woods, saouth o' here?" he inquired in a whisper, as if fearful of being overheard, although there was no one else in the general store save him and me.

I shook my head. "'Billington's Woods' rings a bell somewhere, but I can't quite place it," I had to admit.

"Ever hear tell of a feller named Ambrose Dewart? Another one, name of Stephen Bates—Boston-man, like y'rself, I figger?" he breathed.

A slight chill passed through me. *Dewart ... Bates ...* surely, I had read about them in some sensational newspaper items eleven or twelve years ago ....

I shook my head reluctantly, not quite able to recall the details. When I asked what Perkins knew about these two individuals, he became as close-mouthed as the incommunicative bus driver. All I could get out of him was that my "goods" would be delivered "long abaout sundown-time."

* * *

THAT afternoon, rather late, it became chill and dank, so I carried some armloads of wood into the cabin and built a fire. While I was loading up my arms with logs and kindling, I noticed a shelf built against the back of the shed and a dilapidated old suitcase of scabbed and peeling leather which stood upon it. I wondered if this might not contain Cousin Jared's "books and papers", to which Silas Harding had alluded. Since I had not found these in the cabin anywhere, this was probably the fact of the matter.

I resolved to look at the contents of the suitcase later.

About sundown I became aware of a persistent honking from the Pike. I went to investigate, and found a battered old Model T Ford parked before the entrance to the path, with a leathery, gaunt driver in worn overalls behind the wheel.

"Name of Hoag?" he grunted. When I replied in the affirmative, he gestured behind him with a calloused thumb.

"Groc'ries in th' rumbleseat," he snapped. Which meant I had to carry them in by myself.

I had expected the inhabitants of these rural backwoods to be a suspicious, unfriendly lot, and thus far my expectations were certainly fulfilled.

Returning to the cabin, where my fire was burning cheerily in the stove, I cleaned and filled the lamp, trimmed the wick, and lighted it, for twilight fell quickly this time of year and the darkness was not far behind. I had scrubbed clean the pots and dishes with water from my well, and began heating my meal atop the stove. After dinner I settled down with a mug of hot black coffee and my pipe and began sorting out my notes and references by the yellow light of the hissing lamp. It was a cozy, rustic scene, like something out of Colonial times, almost, and the cabin was warm and comfortable, although, with darkness, the wind rose and moaned eerily through the stiff black boughs where the last gaudy tatters of foliage clung stubbornly against the autumnal chill.

When my fire collapsed to burning coals, I donned my heavy jacket and went to get more wood from the shed. This time I made another trip to drag forth the old suitcase. I was weary of my work and desired to turn my mind to other matters for a while; also, I was getting a bit curious to see what "old, rare" books my cousin had bequeathed to me.

Inside the suitcase I found about a dozen volumes, mostly leather-bound, flaking with age, the pages yellowed with the years. They were certainly old enough, but as most of them were in French or German or Latin, I could make little of them, not being proficient in those languages. Anyway, they looked foreboding and not particularly of interest to me, with titles like *Unaussprechlichen Kulten* and *De Vermis Mysteriis* and *Cultes des Goules*.

Two of them, however, proved to be in English. One of these was a slender brochure bound in leatherette, privately published in 1916 by a commercial printer in San Francisco; it contained Professor Harold Hadley Copeland's "disturbing and conjectural" translation of the *Zanthu Tablets* which he had reputedly discovered in the tomb of a "prehistoric" shaman somewhere in the black and secret heart of Asia. I had heard of the *Zanthu Tablets*, for the book had been much notorious in my boyhood and was denounced by press and pulpit and was finally, as I recall, officially suppressed.

Knowing what little I knew about the *Zanthu Tablets*, I assumed (correctly, as it turned out) that the other books were concerned with occultism and demonology—subjects which have never interested me in the slightest.

Opening the other book in English served but to confirm my supposition, for it was a bound manuscript, written with a quill pen, apparently, in a narrow, crabbed hand, and bore the quaint but ominous title, *Of Evill Sorceries Done in New-England of Daemons in no Humane Shape*. It had no date nor the name of its author, and the manuscript had apparently been clumsily bound by the hands of an amateur bookbinder. I leafed through it, finding nothing but the ugly, superstitious village gossip of a diseased mind—another Cotton Mather, you might say. Arkham and Salem had a lot of these "God-fearing" (so called) witch-hunters back in the *bad* old days. I tossed it aside.

At the very bottom of the suitcase I found a dog-eared, scribbled bundle of foolscap, written in my cousin's clear, bold hand. It was entitled *Diary of Jared Fuller: 1929*.

I leafed through the opening pages, and paused to read an entry so intriguing that I copy it here in this Journal.

From the Diary of Jared Fuller

Sept. 4th. At sundown, or shortly thereafter, when the constellation of Perseus rose in the sky, heard again the sound of chanting from the woods in some bestial language that should not come from human lips. Was it from the "dead place" in the Deep Woods, where the Great Stone lies, or further off? Snowfall too light to leave tracks for me to find by morning. Again, strained to make out anything of the howling, grunting, gibbering language, but one word or name repeated very frequently: *Ossadogowah*, always followed (as in some liturgical response) by a second uncouth name or whatever: *Zvilpoggua*. These wooded hills home of devil-cults and witch-covens long ago, God knows, and fiendish Indian secret societies back before the first white settlers came into these parts. No Indians around here now, of course, but the rustics hereabouts are ignorant, superstitious, inbred, degenerate—and old beliefs die hard, and are long in the dying.

Sept. 8th. Finally heard from young Wilmarth at Miskatonic, supposed to be an enthusiastic amateur folklorist of the region. Says certain Indian tribes in this region, now long gone (the Nansets, Wampanaugs, and esp. Narragansetts) worshipped—or at least knew how to summon down with spells—a sky-devil they called *Ossadogowah*; not a name but a title, it seems: "Son of Sadogowah"—whoever *he* was! Will send me photographic copies of (*phrase illegible*) next week, if possible. Suggests I try rare-book merchants in Salem, Boston, Providence, to obtain copy of something called *Of Evill Sorceries Done in New-England of Daemons in no Humane Shape*, which he read years ago and which bears on Indian devil-worship cults.

Chanting after dark again. This time, hid in the underbrush at the edge of the clearing: bestial gruntings and garglings indeed come from the "dead space" where the Stone lies. Was able to make out something of the words, but they are in no human language I know of. As follows, best as I could make them out over the roaring of the wind:

Eeeyaah! Eeeyaah nughun nuh-nuh-guy guy eeyaah
eeyaah nug-hi enyah enyah zhoggoh ffthaghun ....

Sept. 17th. Made the trip into Arkham today, but Wilmarth off on a walking tour somewhere. Ass't Librarian at Miskatonic refused me access to any of the old texts Wilmarth suggested, damn his eyes! Did, however, let me examine back files of the local papers, *Ark. Advertiser* in particular, 1921 thru '22. Ltrs. to editor about chanting heard in the woods to the north; mysterious disappearance of locals named Lew Waterbury and Jason Osborn; Osborn's body turned up later. Autopsy by County Medical Examiner sugg. corpse had been subjected to "severe changes in temperature" and had "fallen or been dropped from a great height." (Fallen from *what*? Dropped by ... *what*?)

Conditions of corpse sound dreadfully similar to the body I found in the woods, and buried hastily because of the terrible stench, *which was not that of decomposing human flesh*. Should have reported disc. to police, I know, but it was torn beyond all possibility of identification. Note that "horribly foetid black slime" found on Osborn corpse.

My eyes were getting tired from trying to read by the unsteady light of the lamp, so I put Jared's manuscript aside, carefully marking the last entry I had read, and went to bed.

But not, as it chanced, to sleep for quite some time.

* * *

AS I tossed and turned on the hard, narrow cot, it occurred to me that my cousin Jared had lost his reason. This would, of course, explain many of the weirder aspects of what I had read in his diary: chanting from the depths of the Deep Woods, having found and buried a crushed and mangled corpse, his allusions to eldritch lore. However slightly we had known each other, this seemed unlikely, for he had always seemed stable and eminently sane, to my experience.

I gave the problem up and strove to compose myself for sleep. But sleep did not come easily. For one thing, the star Algol shone like a burning green eye through the window, which was closed against the night's cold but which I had left unshuttered. Its unusually brilliant, viridian light seemed to burn through my closed lids like some unearthly searchlight from Beyond ....

When, at length, slumber overtook my weary mind, and I sank through ever-darkening layers of shadow, I still found not the repose I sought. As I hovered between wakefulness and dream, it seemed to me that a dim and distant current of rhythmical sound, like far-heard surf or distant *chanting*, persisted in intruding upon my rest. This, of course, was absurd, for the woods, as I have already noted, were abnormally silent, and the wind had died. Finally, along toward dawn, I awoke, neither rested nor refreshed.

It was then that an odd coincidence occurred to me.

Algol is a star in the constellation of Perseus ....

* * *

AFTER a meager breakfast, feeling the need for a little fresh air and some exercise before settling down again to the organization of my notes, I decided to take a tramp through the woods. I was particularly interested in finding the barren glade whereof my cousin had written in his diary, and the "Great Stone" that lay in it. Donning my winter gear, and finishing off my hot black coffee with a gulp, I left the cabin and entered the woods, striking out at pure random, not knowing in which direction I must travel to find the region my cousin's papers described.

These woods were distinctly unlike any in New England, at least within my personal experience. For one thing, all of the huge, gnarled trees seemed of unnatural, even abnormal age. In such a wood one might expect to find new saplings springing from the fertile mulch, and the skeletal and moldering remains of fallen tree trunks. Not so, however, here in the Deep Woods: No saplings were to be seen; it was as if some extraordinary source of life and vigor had prolonged the life of these ancient trees immeasurably beyond their natural span.

For another thing, the woods were uncannily, even unhealthily, silent. At this season, I would have expected the underbrush to be filled with rabbits and chipmunks, field mice and squirrels, all scampering through the crisp, dry leaves upon their small tasks and errands. Not so here in the Deep Woods, where an unwholesome silence and a distinctly odd absence of small life reigned ....

I came upon the clearing abruptly, and knew at once that this was the "dead place" Jared had described. The ground underfoot became abruptly barren of anything but sparse, unhealthy, lank grass, which grew in sickly, thin patches, as if the soil beneath it was either somehow poisonous or, for one or another reason, hostile to living things.

There in the very middle of the small open space, ringed about with a thickly crowded wall of gaunt black trees, lay half-buried in the bare soil a huge, rectangular stone—surely, the "Great Stone" of which Jared had written. I came closer to examine it: While the trunks of the trees through which I had passed were slimy with mold and moss and lichen, the enormous, brick-shaped stone was as bare of life in any visible form as if newly scrubbed clean by industrious hands.

Add one more unnatural thing about the Deep Woods, I thought uneasily to myself.

The block measured some ten feet in length and about three and a half feet in height and thickness, although it was not possible to measure the height of the stone with much certainty, so deeply was it sunken into the dead earth. As for the composition, it was of the gray granite commonly found in these parts, brought hither aeons before by the glaciers when those vast serpents of age-old Arctic ice came crawling sluggishly down across the continent.

In the exact center of the upper surface I noticed a queer shape seemingly carved therein, like a bas-relief. I had to climb up atop the stone to examine it closely, and some residium of the night's cold, not yet banished by the feeble warmth of daylight, struck bitterly and savagely through my thick gloves and heavy trousers, to sear the flesh with an almost unearthly rigor.

The carving—for it was unmistakably the work of intelligent hands—was weathered and very ancient, but so deeply had those primordial chisels gnawed into the recalcitrant granite, that the form it outlined was distinctly visible. It was a grotesque monstrosity, a gross, corpulent, toad-like thing with an obscene, swollen paunch and huge splayed, clawed feet, but without the forelimbs its toad-like shape might be expected to have. The skill of the ancient sculptor was sophisticated enough to suggest *webbing* between the spread claws of these hind legs. From a point along the back where the shoulders would have been sprouted crook-ribbed wings, like those of some monstrous bat or one of the fantastic flying reptiles of the saurian age which preceded the coming of mammalian life. Face it had none, but from the forepart of its sloped, bulging, and misshapen head slithering and snake-like tendrils sprouted, like the serpentine tresses of some hideous Medusa.

I repressed an involuntary shudder of disgust; even so, I could not help admiring the *sophistication* of the nameless sculptor's technique, in bestowing upon this grisly spawn of his unclean imagination such a lifelike air of realism. It was almost as if the sculptor had worked from *a living model*.

* * *

RETURNING home from my tramp through the woods, I felt reluctant to take up again the dreary task of organizing my notes, and passed the time before lunch by again perusing the diary of my cousin.

>From the Diary of Jared Fuller

Sept. 22nd. Rec'd today photographic copies from Wilmarth of the passages in the *Book of Eibon* he fancied I might find useful. (Or *Liber Ivonis*, I should say, since the pages are from the Latin version made by Phillipus Faber.) My Latin being very rusty, it will take me some time to render them into passable English.

In the same mail, haply, came that rare copy of the manuscript titled *Of Evill Sorceries etc.*, for which I paid that skinflint of a dealer in Salem such a high price. Relevant passages too lengthy to quote here in this diary, so I have merely marked them down [here followed page numbers which doubtless referred to the pagination of the bound manuscript I had already found in my cousin's collection; I decided to look them up later, and read on.—W.H.], but they proved *very* informative.

Howled chanting in the woods again last night, clearer than before: The frosty air of this rather early winter obviously permits far sounds to travel more easily. Searched the woods again and found, in the recent-fallen snow, those horribly huge, splayed prints as of some unthinkably prodigious Beast and splatters of stinking black ichor of indescribable foulness.

And my dreams are getting worse ....

With a shiver of distaste I set the manuscript aside and sat there for long moments, listlessly pondering on what I had read and trying to fit together some of the pieces of this weird puzzle. Finally, I dug into the heap of mouldering books and took up the bound manuscript, turning to the parts my cousin had marked. And I read:

> ... gave a very curious and Circumstantiall Relation, saying it was sometimes like a great Toad, but sometimes huge and cloudy, with no Shape, though with a Face which had Serpents grown from it. It had ye name *Ossadagowah*, which signifi'd ye child of *Sadogowah* [and here my cousin had written in the margin "Tsathoggua?"], ye which is held to be a Frightfull Spirit spoke of by antients as come down from ye Stars and being formerly worshipt in Lands to ye North. Ye *Wampanaugs* and ye *Nansets* and *Nahrrigansets* knew how to draw It out of ye Heavens, but never did so because of ye exceeding great Evilness of It. They knew also how to catch and prison It, tho' they cou'd not sent It back whence it came. It was declar'd that ye old Tribes of *Lamah* [here my cousin had scribbled another marginal gloss: "Lomar?"], who dwelt under ye Great Bear and were antiently destroy'd for their Wickedness, knew how to manage It in all Ways. Many upstart Men pretended to a Knowledge of such and divers other Outer Secrets, but none in these Parts cou'd give any Proof of truly having ye aforesaid Knowledge. It was said by some that *Ossadagowah* often went back to ye Sky from choice without any sending, but that he cou'd not come back unless Summon'd.

I closed the bound volume and returned to Jared's manuscript, but found nothing I could make sense out of, merely a series of cryptic, and (to me) meaningless jottings:

> 1. *Lomar*. Quasi-mythical ancient place in extreme north. If worshiped in Lomar, perhaps Zobna and Hyperborea also?
> 2. *Child*. If of the spawn of Tsath., also known in Hyp.? Tsath. once worshipped there. See *Lib. Ivonis*.
> 3. *Elemental*. Arctic region suggests air elemental like Ithaqua, Hastur. But Tsath. an earth elemental accord. to *Cultes des G*.
> 4. Must translate passages from Eibon *at once*.

That night, after another meager meal, I sat up drinking mug after mug of hot black coffee, waiting for Perseus to rise above the horizon, determined to find out whether the bestial howling-like chants I had *seemed* to hear in my fitful slumbers the night before were actuality or something in my dreams. For some reason, it occurred to me to turn down the wick and blow out the lamp, so that the interior of the cabin would be in darkness.

I had positioned my chair within clear view of the window. Once the familiar stars of the constellation were aloft, I left the window ajar, despite the cold breath of the night air, and listened closely. For a long time I heard nothing at all unusual, merely the wind moaning in the bare black boughs and the comfortable rustling of dying coals in the Franklin stove.

Then suddenly there came to my ears the sound of many distant voices raised in a rhythmic, if uncouth, chanting. I strained to catch the words of that chant, but could not make them out clearly. They seemed in no language I have ever heard before.

What snatches of the eerie chant I could hear bore a distinct resemblance to some of the weird mouthings Jared had scribbled down in his diary.

I went nearer to the window in order to hear the liturgy better. As I did so, with a thrill of indescribable horror I watched a vast, black shadow drift across the snow-clad clearing before the cabin, vanishing into the Deep Woods. Was it purely my imagination, my nerves wrought by the uncanny things I had read in Jared's diary and in that damnable old book, or did the shadow-shape seem cast by *something toad-like, and bloated, and obese, with huge, membranous, bat-like wings?*

* * *

I FELL asleep in the wooden chair just before dawn, and woke stiff and groggy and chilled to the bone in very late morning. After heating and devouring the remnants of my supper and huge draughts of hot coffee, the thought passed through my mind that I would be wise to leave this place at once. Surely, a few dollars would persuade Jenkins to loan me his Model T and the use of his driver, in order to transport my few possessions and Jared's books and the manuscript back to Arkham, where I could arrange to have Silas Harding sell the cabin and grounds.

Why I did not do so, I will never know. Perhaps I feared to see the knowing smirk in the pale eyes of the storekeeper, Jenkins, and to hear his leering chuckle when he learned that I was giving up and running back home to Boston.

Building up the fire a bit later, I found some old newspapers under the stacked kindling in the shed and was about to stuff them into the stove when the headline

HORROR IN BILLINGTON'S WOOD

and the names *Ambrose Dewart* and *Stephen Bates* leaped from the page to seize my attention. With hands that shook, ever so slightly, I bore the newspapers, brown and withered with age, to the table and read the news item that had caught my eye.

They related, in fragmentary fashion and without any explanation, an account of the mysterious and inexplicable disappearances of Dewart and the young Bostonian, Bates, a visiting relative, from a huge old house in Billington's Wood some miles south of my cabin, and how no trace of the missing men had come to light and the local constabulary was without a single clue. There was nothing in the straightforward newspaper account, written in dry journalese, which hinted at weird horrors from the sky, or the lingering survival into our own time of horribly ancient devil cults which should have perished or been ruthlessly exterminated generations or even centuries ago ... nothing which mentioned blasphemous and forbidden old books which any sane man would burn or bury, rather than read ... but there was a grisly *suggestiveness* which lurked behind the succinct newspaper items, with their passing reference to a Druidic-like ring of stones deep in the wood, near a crude stone tower of unknown workmanship and uncertain date, which sent a thrill of clammy fear up my spine.

I buried the newspapers in the stove, and resolved to put all of these matters out of my head.

I wish to God I had done so.

* * *

TOWARD afternoon I donned my winter gear and returned to the woods. I found again the altar-like "Great Stone" in the sterile glade, where it squatted like some loathsome altar left behind by a savage and bloodthirsty race when they receded into the dimness of mercifully forgotten ages. It was not my second sight of that massive block of stone, lying upon the earth like some toppled Druidic menhir, however, that froze me where I stood—

The snow had fallen thickly in the clearing the early evening before, and now it could be seen that the white blanket which covered the dead soil like a burial shroud was *marked and trampled* under the tread of many feet.

It was not even this—clear evidence that the cult which worshiped Ossadagowah or "Zvilpoggua" indeed gathered nightly about this stony altar—that chilled me to the bone with fear.

It was the huge marks with which the human footprints were intermingled ... *the marks of splayed, webbed feet, huger than those of any elephant that ever walked the earth, which had broken the crusted snow and left deep tracks sunken in the hard soil as if beneath the tread of ponderous, incredible weight.*

* * *

(About one and a half pages which follow are quite illegible.)

(Apparently from the diary of Jared Fuller):
 ... those passages from the Latin of Phillipus Faber, as follows:
 Of the wise Yzduggor, whom the wizards of Commoriom held in the highest repute, it was rumored that he was a devotee of the obsolete and interdicted cultus of Zvilpoggua, even he, firstborn of the spawn of

Tsathoggua and begotten by the Black Thing upon the female entity, Shathak, upon far and frozen Yaksh the seventh world [here my cousin had scribbled another gloss: "7th fr. the Sun? Neptune?"]. Therefore unto his remote, secluded dwelling-place did the fearful Vooth Raluorn forthwith eloign ...

... the eremite at length yielded grudging reply to his entreaties, and erelong did the young Commorian learn from Yzduggor's reluctant lips that presently Zvilpoggua resided upon the dark planet Yrautrom, a world circumambient about the green star Algol, and may be called down to this world during those months of the year when Algol rises about the horizon [here my cousin scribbled: "Algol is in the night sky during the fall"] whereupon it is his grisly wont to feed upon the flesh and to drink of the blood of men, wherefore is he known to sorcerers as the Feaster from the Stars. ...

At the end of his translations of these fragments, evidently from the *Book of Eibon*, my cousin had scribbled a page reference to *"Nec."*, by which he probably meant the *Necronomicon*, which he had several times named in his diary. It would appear that he had entreated the scholar Wilmarth to copy certain parts of this volume for him, and I gather now, from the context, that this was one of the books he had tried in vain to secure permission from the librarian at Miskatonic University to consult. Thereupon fol(*lowed? Manuscript illegible here for about three-quarters of a page.*)

* * *

... which appear to have been scissored from a letter, doubtless from his correspondent Wilmarth, as the handwriting is quite different from my cousin Jared's. I read:

From the Diary of Jared Fuller
... no need to laboriously translate from the Latin of Olaus Wormius, for Miskatonic owns a partial copy of John Dee's English version of the *Necronomicon*, which makes the task easier. The two passages below come from quite different portions of the volume, but as both seem relevant to the matter at hand, I will cite them here.

To Summon-Down the Feaster from the Stars, seek those nights when first Algol riseth above ye Horizon, and, if that ye be Thirteen gather'd in Coven, join hands in ye ring about ye Stone and chaunt in unison as followeth, *Iä! Iä! Iä! N'ghaa, n'n'ghai-ghai! Iä! Iä! N'ghai, n-yah, n-yah, shoggog, phthaghn! Iä! Iä! Y-hah, y-nyah, y-nyah! N'ghaa, n'n'-ghai, waphl phthaghn-Zvilpoggua! Zvilpoggua! N'gui, n'-gha'ghaa y'hah, Zvilpoggua! Ai! Ai! Ai!* And note well that ye Response to ye Name *Zvilpoggua*, the which is to be onlie chaunted by ye Coven-Master, is *Ghu-Tsathoggua*, the which doth signify ye Son of *Tsathoggua*, and ye above Name onlie may be spake forth in ye common or vulgar Tongue.

I put down the manuscript with trembling hands, then took it up again and leafed back to that earlier passage where Jared had written down what he had heard on the night of September 8, 1929 [see page 7 of the present text]. The two chants were word for word the same, until my cousin's jottings broke off; the only differences between them were that Jared Fuller had set them down *phonetically* and with little attempt at punctuation.

The pieces of the puzzle were fitting together into a dreadful and *horribly meaningful* pattern.

I must leave this place soon, very soon. They must know the cabin, situated so fearfully close to their place of worship, is once again inhabited. Surely, it was the coven-folk, or whatever I should call them, that murdered or carried off my cousin ... *they or the monstrous demon-thing they serve* ... and surely I will be the next victim.

That night I had another of those ghastly dreams that have of late haunted my troubled slumbers [apparently a reference to matter contained in the several passages illegible because of damp]. It seemed I hovered, shivering beneath the bit of ultra-telluric and bone-chilling cold, above a dark and frozen world dimly lit by the spectral light of three pallid moons. On an ice-sheathed plain rose the hoary ruins of a black city of monolithic, windowless walls ... was it a dream of Yaksh (but Neptune has only one moon, as I recall from my boyhood enthusiasm for astronomy), or of that dark world revolving about Algol, where Zvilpoggua resides?

As I drifted nearer and nearer to the black metropolis, I forced myself awake with a tremendous effort of will, and found myself drenched in cold perspiration and trembling like a frail reed in the wind. And I was *screaming* ....

Most horrible of all, my screams were echoed mockingly by a deep-lunged, howling ululation, *but whether from the Wood or from the sky I cannot tell.*

(About three paragraphs totally illegible)

... second passage from the *Necronomicon*, either raggedly cut or torn from Wilmarth's letter, and read as follows:

> ... hath the Likeness of a great Toade, black as pitch and glist'ning with foetid slime, bewing'd like ye Bat and with ye nether-limbs of ye Behemothe, splayed and clawed and Webb'd betwixt ye Toes thereof, and Face hath it naught, butte from where ye Face shouldst e'en be sprouteth a Horrid Beard of crawling tentacles. And it feasteth of the Fleshe, and Swilleth of ye Bloode of Men, but at its gluttonous Leisure, for first it is said to bear men aloft into ye Sky, and may bear them thus an hundred Leagues or more ere it will rip and tear and Feede, then dropping them to Earth far from whence it snatch'd them up.

But I can read no more. I will leave the cabin tonight, before Algol rises to peer down at me like the glaring, feral eye of some predatory beast. I will abandon everything, taking only my journal in an old briefcase. But before I leave the cabin, I intend to burn the diary of Jared Fuller ... would to God I had the time to consign to the wholesome flames those hellish old books which sane men were never meant to read.

(Four sentences illegible)

Too late—Algol almost risen. I must run for it. If I cannot catch the bus to Arkham, I dare not linger so close to the Deep Wood, but must try my luck on the Pike. Perhaps I can make it to Dean's Corners before it is too late.

I wish

(Manuscript breaks off suddenly at this point.)

* * *

NOTE: As of this date (February 15, 1983), no evidence has ever been found as to the fate or the whereabouts of Winthrop Hoag. The case remains in the "unsolved" files of the County Police.

The editor has no opinion as to the validity of the manuscript, or concerning its authorship. But one or two remarks might be useful at this juncture. It is now fairly certain that the planet Neptune has at least three moons; the existence of two such satellites has been confirmed by visual observation, and from perturbation in their orbits around their primary, the presence of a third moon is considered almost certain.

It may be of no particular consequence, but the Islamic peoples, together with certain other cultures of antiquity, held the star Algol in peculiar loathing and abhorrence. The Arabic astrologer of the VII Century, Ibrahim Al-Araq, refers to it, in those of his writings still extant, with an ambivalent phrase which scholars translate either as "the Demon Star" or "the Star from whence the Demon comes."

HERE is one of Lin Carter's two verse apocalypses in the Cthulhu Mythos. The other, mentioned in "The Winfield Heritance", is "Visions from Yaddith", and you may look it up in an earlier volume in this series, *The Shub-Niggurath Cycle*. Come to think of it, we might count his "Limericks from Yuggoth" (see *Black Forbidden Things*, Borgo Press) as a third. Anyway, it is clear that Lin's model in these poetic endeavors is Lovecraft's sonnet cycle "Fungi from Yuggoth." The "Fungi from Yuggoth" represent almost a free-associating expansion of the Commonplace Book; in it HPL was free to develop individual items of mood, particular plot germs, etc. in their own right, without trying to work them into a connected narrative context (though, reading them in another way, each poem and several two- and three-sonnet sequences can be read as mini-narratives unto themselves). Lin Carter has done the same in "Dreams from R'lyeh."

I have called "Dreams from R'lyeh" a Mythos apocalypse, or revelation. On one level, the reason for this label is obvious: The premise of the poems is that the Lord of R'lyeh sends dreams to communicate with certain sensitive individuals to make his will known and to signal his soon awakening. Beyond this I intend a comparison with the apocalypses of ancient Judaism and Christianity, including, among many others, the Revelation of John, the Book of Daniel, and Second Esdras. Apocalypses are composed in poetry, though this is not obvious to some readers, partly because of old Bible typography, in which the text is printed as a series of dense paragraphs, eliminating the poetic structure. Also, biblical poetry employed rhyme but seldom, utilizing instead various styles of parallelism. Such poetry makes up the bulk of the Old Testament prophets, the Psalms (which were hymn lyrics), the Song of Solomon (a bowdlerized Ishtar and Tammuz liturgy), the Book of Job, and most of the sayings attributed to Jesus.

Even the derivative character of "Dreams from R'lyeh" reinforces its identity as an apocalypse, rather than undermining it, since by far most of the ancient apocalypses were themselves reworkings of earlier examples of the genre, or of other biblical texts. The Revelation of John, for example, is heavily based on Daniel, Zechariah, and Ezekiel, to such an extent that one can scarcely appreciate Revelation without constant comparison with its biblical sources.

This point raises the question of the literary artificiality of a stylized "apocalypse" such as Lin Carter's. The whole thing is quite evidently a studied literary performance, as were the ancient apocalypses. Though a modicum of debate still exists on the point (see Christopher Rowland, *The Open Heaven*), the evidence of conscious literary composition of the ancient apocalypses seems overwhelming to me. That is, "John" (with Benjamin W. Bacon, I do not exempt the Book of Revelation from the universal rule of pseudonymity in apocalypses) and the others did not simply transcribe their visions. They may possibly have begun with some sort of dream or visionary experience as their initial inspiration, but even this hardly seems likely, given the location of the apocalypse genre in the larger category of scribal Wisdom Literature, which implicitly makes them complex puzzles (see Revelation 13:18). Apocalypses are written as if they were telegrams from heaven, but this is just a convention of the genre. No one should take it seriously any more than they would the chance that songs in operas or Broadway musicals actually represent anyone's mode of speech.

Yet the opposition "genuine vision" vs. "literary product" reveals itself as a false alternative when we view it from the aspect of the creative process, rather than that of genre mechanics. That is, who will deny that the poetic afflatus is itself a kind of inspiration bubbling up directly from the oracular brook of the artistic subconscious?

This is true equally of any sort of creative writing. There is another dimension of poetry in particular that seems to lend it a revelatory quality, and that is its unique diction. Cleanth Brooks condemned "the heresy of paraphrase" (*The Well-Wrought Urn: Studies in the Structure of Poetry*, chapter 11), the notion that a poem is merely one more vehicle for communicating ideas or information. Rather, "a poem should not mean, but be" (Archibald McLeish, "Ars Poetica"). As Gerard Genette says, poetic diction's unique feature and power is the "intransitivity" of its language (*Fiction and Diction*, p. 25), an only apparently referential character that is like the false depth in the flat picture plane of a painting. In poetry, therefore, it is the form which is the content. Thus a poem cannot be paraphrased.

As Nabokov says, the translator is the betrayer. This is why Muslims who call attention to the sublime poetic quality of the Qur'an also deny that any translation of the book can rightly be called the Qur'an at all. You can't pour fine old wine into new skins. Somehow it is the old skins that made it fine wine! It is only because of the logocentric bias of traditional Western theology that no one seems to have realized that the Bible is "revelatory" not because of any special informational content it may contain, but because of its poetic character. It is only to be expected that dumbed-down paraphrases like the Living Bible or the New International Version or the New Revised Standard Version just plain stink. The fools who translated them and priced them at thirty pieces of silver destroyed the one thing that made the Bible worth reading in the first place.

Sadly, it is precisely this element of poetic diction, that which makes Lovecraft's "Fungi from Yuggoth" a chilling revelation (just listen to the Fedogan & Bremer audiotape of it!), that seems to me utterly lacking in Lin Carter's "Dreams from R'lyeh." Thus I think it really belongs here as one more (prose) story in the Xothic cycle, manifestly linked to the others by internal references. This one just happens to rhyme.

"Dreams from R'lyeh" appeared originally in the Arkahm House Lin Carter collection of that same title in 1975.

Dreams from R'lyeh: A Sonnet Cycle

by Wilbur Nathaniel Hoag [1921-1944]
(edited for publication by Lin Carter)

Eternal is the Pow'r of Evil, and Infinite in its contagion! The Great Cthulhu yet hath sway o'er the minds and spirits of Men, yea, even tho' He lieth chained and ensorcelled, bound in the fetters of The Elder Sign, His malignant and loathly Mind spreadeth the dark seeds of Madness and Corruption into the dreams and Nightmares of sleeping men.
—*The Necronomicon* of Abdul Alhazred, III, 17; the Translation of Dr. John Dee, *circa* A.D. 1585.

Death is no deterrent to the mighty dead. Even in decay their vast intellects can fill our sleeping minds with nightmare visions of the Pit and ultimate insanities beyond the reach of reason.
—*Necrolatry* (The Worship of the Dead), Ivor Gorstadt; Leipzig, 1702.

"Alhazred's image of the Sleeping God leads one almost to the interpretation of Cthulhu as one of the dream-gods such as Hypnos; he is set forth as a god who infects the minds of those asleep with dark and terrifying dreams, nightmares, visions—spreading the germs of his own evil through the world through the medium of his own dreams."
—*Cthulhu in the* Necronomicon, Laban Shrewsbury, Ph.D., LL.D., etc.; from an unpublished, fragmentary manuscript written *circa* 1938-39.

Editor's Note

DR. Milton Avery Barnes, senior curator of the Manuscripts Collection of Miskatonic University in Arkham, Mass., has asked me to edit for publication the following verses which were discovered among the papers of the gifted young poet, Wilbur Nathaniel Hoag. Nearly thirty years have elapsed since the discovery of these poems, which are now published here in their final and corrected form for the first time.

The disappearance of Mr. Hoag from his ancient family home on State Street occurred during the night of September 13, 1944, and is still an unsolved mystery. He has since been declared legally dead by the County Court, however, and as he died intestate, leaving no clearly defined heirs, the Commonwealth of Massachusetts has formally bequeathed his papers and his library to the University, on whose behalf my editorial labors have been performed.

The Hoag family was established in the old seaport town of Arkham in 1693, when Isaiah Hoag and his wife and eldest son settled there from Plymouth, England. The family fortunes were built on the South Seas trading voyages of Isaiah's son, the famous "Yankee trader" Captain Abner Exekiel Hoag, who pioneered the rum and copra trade in the Pacific. Folklorists, anthropologists, and occult scholars may, however, know Captain Hoag best for his reputed discovery of the obscure and debatable *Ponape Scripture* in the Carolines *circa* 1734, which manuscript currently is in the possession of the Kester Library in Salem, Mass., and concerning which the late archaeologist Harold Hadley Copeland published his shocking and controversial book *The Prehistoric Pacific in the Light of the* Ponape Scripture (1911).

For well over two centuries, the Hoags have been prominent in Massachusetts history. Their connections with the great Marsh family have been the subject of considerable genealogical research (it was, in fact, this same Abner Exekiel Hoag who wed Bathsheba Randall Marsh in 1713, and thus became the son-in-law of the famous Captain Obed Marsh, whose exploits as a merchant skipper are part of local Arkham legend). Still later, about 1780, the Hoag family also intermarried with the old Kingsport line founded by Amos Tuttle in 1604; the house of Hoag may, then, most fittingly be set among the ancient patriarchal families of Colonial New England and in the light of their distinguished history it is exceedingly regrettable that the old line has become extinct at last.

Our poet, Wilbur Nathaniel Hoag, was of course the last of his line, and with his death or disappearance yet one more living link with the Colonial past of our country has ended. He was only a youth of twenty-three when he vanished so mysteriously, and in all the years since that time the facts of his disappearance have never been adequately explained, nor have the circumstances surrounding his death, or presumed death, ever come to light. Official queries at the time elicited from his neighbors that for some months before he vanished into the unknown, Hoag had become a virtual recluse and was seldom if ever seen, and then only during the hours of darkness. The morbid strain evident in his verses, the continual references to death and madness, the profusion of occult themes borrowed from obscure, unwholesome mythological texts, indicate an unstable intellect bordering perhaps on severe aberrance. This is a question for the psychologist, however, and our principal concern here is purely a literary one.

In preparing these sonnets for publication, I have imposed upon them an order and sequence not indicated in the original manuscript. I have been aided by the rapid degeneration of Hoag's handwriting. What I assume to be the earlier verses, those relating to his childhood, are written in a clear and classic Spencerian hand; rapidly, however, the clarity decays to a hurried scribble, and, in the latter half of the sonnets, the penmanship has become an almost animal scrawl, the pages splotched and stained by the oddest pus or slime. Indeed, the latter verses are all but illegible, and so uncouth is their ragged scrawl that I have almost fancied them indited on the page by the deformed paw of some hybrid beast, than by the scion of a fine old Arkham family.

The mystery of Hoag's disappearance—so oddly akin to the mystery of his late uncle, Zorad Ethan Hoag, murdered and repugnantly mutilated by an unknown hand (our poet makes shuddering reference to the crime in the sonnet I have numbered VII)—will probably never be solved at this late date. But the dark brilliance of his macabre verses, savoring of the more poisonously beautiful pages of Baudelaire, or Poe, or the late Rhode Island poet H. P. Lovecraft, is clearly evident in every jeweled page. Morbid these poems are, but in the phrase of H. P. Lovecraft, *Radiant with beauty, the Cup of the Ptolemies was carven of onyx.*

—Lin Carter
Miskatonic University
Arkham, Mass. 01970

I. REMEMBRANCES

I am New England born, and home to me
Is ancient Kingsport on the Harbour side.
When I was very young my Father died
And so I came to Arkham by the sea
Where Uncle Zorad and his servant, Jones,
Lived in the old house. He, my guardian,
Was a strange, silent, melancholy man
Given to dark old books and carven stones.
It was from him at last I understood
Why Kingsport people shunned our family.
"Our grandsires came in 1693,"
He said. "And even here they hate our blood.
We came from the old country to survive.
There, we were witches, to be burnt alive."

II. ARKHAM

How much I loved the city's ancient ways,
Quaint cobbled streets, fanlights above the door;
Arkham preserved a softer, gentler lore
In this day's turmoil, from lost nobler days.
I loved the crooked alleys, narrow, grey,
And gabled houses leaning all awry ...
But even then it had begun to die;
The very air was noisome with decay.
The river-mist, rank with a rotten smell,
The crowded houses, slumped, ramshackle, thin;
Arkham was like a corpse whose outward shell
Preserved a lifelike semblance, while within
Worm, mould, and maggot, in a wriggling slime
Bear witness to the leprous touch of time.

III. THE FESTIVAL

It was that month when red Aldebaran
Burned in the solstice skies arisen late,
With cryptic starry signs enconstellate,
Spelling some occult lore unguessed by man.
The shifting starlight made strange shadows flit
Among the sliding coils of mist that flowed
From the dark Miskatonic past the road.
And every night the Dagon Hall was lit.
It was a sort of church. Old malformed oaks
Grew up around it in a kind of ring.
I overheard the servant say, "The folks
Wonder, ye keep the lad from Worshipping;
Tonight is Festival." I bent to hear
My Uncle say, "He's young. Another year ...."

IV. THE OLD WOOD

Northwards from Arkham up along the coast,
The ancient woods that climb the hills around
Grow oddly thick for such unhealthy ground.
And on the hill-tops, where they grow the most,
All seem deformed and strangely overgrown
As if their roots, deep down within the earth,
Fed on the rank putrescence of some Birth
Malformed and monstrous, and best left unknown.
Even the grass grows mouldy, and a smell
Hangs in the air as though something was dead,
While bloated fungi spread their stench as well.
I asked my Uncle's servant once. He said,
"Sure, I can tell ye"—would he had not talked!
"—That is the Wood where once the Black Goat
 walked."

V. THE LOCKED ATTIC

He always kept it locked, the attic room,
And ordered me to keep away from there.
I wondered why, and one day climbed the stair
And broke the lock. A place of airless gloom
With walls and rafters that leaned oddly wrong
And crazy angles that were hard to see,
As in some alien geometry
With more dimensions than to ours belong.
But nothing frightened me, until I tried
To open up the window for some air
And found it opened from *the other side*.
I wiped the dusty pane, and saw out there—
What should not be! I screamed, and somehow knew
What awful worlds that window opened to.

VI. THE SHUNNED CHURCH

"It's been abandoned quite a spell," he said,
"That old church on the hill in back o' Hunt's.
When we was kids, we thought 'twas haunted. Once
I found out why it's still untenanted ....
One night I heard 'em talk about the place,
How it were closed on 'count of what were done
In there each Roodmass, and how there was one
Never come out, who went inside. They chased
The preacher feller out o' town, I think ....
One night the kids dared me to go inside.
It were all dark and dusty, with a stink
All through th' air, like somethin' that had died.
—I screamed and run, soon as I understood
Whose image there on the Black Altar stood!"

VII. THE LAST RITUAL

The night he died the Demon Star was high.
It hung above the house against the dark
A cold, arcane, malign and watching spark
Like some green, burning and Cycloptic eye.
They locked me in my room, but I could see
My Uncle take down that abhorrent book
At whose mad page I was forbade to look,
Gorstadt's grim volume of *Necrolatry*.
I heard them chanting (they had closed the blind),
And smelled some burning reek ophidian ...
Then all was silence ... till the screams began.
At dawn the neighbors broke the door, to find
Jones gibbering and mad. Uncle was dead.
They found his body. All except the head.

VIII. THE LIBRARY

When I was young they never let me look
Into that room kept under lock and key,
But when he died my Uncle left to me
His strange collection. Almost every book
Was old and crumbling, curiously bound
In serpent-skin, and with a rotten smell
As of some tainted and abandoned well,
Or some dead thing long buried underground.
I looked in one. And, though my blood ran cold,
I read it, page by page. The nightwind blew
About the eaves, and when red morning rolled
Up from the east, I finished. And I knew
Those old, old books were not meant to be read
By sane men. They were better burnt instead.

IX. BLACK THIRST

The yellowed pages, rotten with decay,
Crawling with loathsome symbols, fill my brain
With wild, tumultuous visions. Were I sane
I'd rise and hurl the leprous books away ...
Yet I read on, half thrilled, half in disgust,
Rapt with sick fascination to explore
The vile corruption of forbidden lore,
That leaves me weak and soiled with nameless lust.
I rise with dawn and scrub my shaking hands
And gulp strong brandy down, and try to pray,
And vow to burn these books ... another day ....
But I am like one trapped in sinking sands,
Who strayed apart far from the paths of men.
The night will come. And I will read again ....

X. THE ELDER AGE

This lore was old before the rise of Ur,
Before the pomp of Babylon was born,
Ere golden Egypt knew her golden morn,
Or Tyre, or Nineveh, or dark Sumer.
Ere any human peoples trod the earth
The blue Pacific lapped the carven walls
Of seacoast cities whose basaltic halls
Were drowned in myth before Atlantis' birth.
Lost land, thy ancient mages read the stars
And scanned necrotic hieroglyphs on scrolls
Borne hence from nighted Yuggoth where she rolls
Far on the Rim amidst fantastic wars.
Only the *Text* bears witness to thy lore,
Sunken R'lyeh, that shall rise no more.

XI. LOST R'LYEH

Long-lost and legended, R'lyeh sleeps,
Dreaming ensorcelled ages by, the while
Slow foetid waves wash round her rotting pile
Drowned in the uttermost of ocean deeps ...
Until the stars are right, when from that tomb
The awful Dead her primal ruins hide
Shall rise tremendous, as was prophesied.
Until that hour she sleeping bides her doom.
Wake not, dread ruin that the tides caress,
Thou weed-grown mass of thronged decaying spires,
Dim, phosphor-litten with putrescent fires—
Sleep on, thou whelmed, accurst necropolis!
Too soon shall from thy cyclopean fane
Cthulhu wake to walk the earth again!

XII. UNKNOWN KADATH

In what remote Hyperborean clime,
Under what alien-configured skies
Namelessly constellated, it doth rise
Is known to none. In the abyss of time
No eye hath seen the sable mountain rear
Her pinnacles. The place hath not been guessed
Where Kadath lifts her onyx-castled crest
Among the *shantak*-guarded deserts drear.
Only those dreamers roaming far afield
Beyond the lands we know, to them alone
Is far and fabulous Kadath revealed
And all her mysteries to them made known,
And *That* which lies deep in her inmost crypt—
The secret of the Pnakotic Manuscript.

XIII. ABDUL ALHAZRED

Only Alhazred of all mortal men
Hath seen far Yuggoth lost beyond the Rim.
And drowned R'lyeh where lies buried Him
Who Was Before And Who Shall Be Again.
The cloudy shore of fabulous Hali
On dread Carcosa where Hastur abides,
That caverned deep where Tsathoggua hides—
No wizard else hath known, save only he.
Alhazred *saw* ... and from that sight returned
Out of the nightmare deeps of the Abyss.
If thou wouldst know the Elder Lore he learned
And passed down from that century to this,
Read of those horrors of that primal dawn
Recorded in the *Necronomicon*.

XIV. HYPERBOREA

Far to the north an ancient kingdom lies
In frozen lands where only glaciers rule;
Beyond the Pole, beyond Ultima Thule,
The tomb-like towers of the city rise.
This is a cursed land where none dare dwell
And Silence guards the empty altars where,
In ages gone, by spell and rite and prayer
The wizard-priests unloosed the hordes of Hell.
But all the terrors of that primal year
Sleep glacier-guarded under walls of snow,
And never shall arise. And this I know.
Yet is my soul still haunted by this fear:
The thrones and empires of the world will shake
If ever ... Hyperborea ... *awake!*

XV. THE BOOK OF EIBON

In glacier-whelmed and lost Commoriom,
Aeons before Atlantis, at the Pole
Where now but black and frozen oceans roll
Their sluggish tides, and warm suns never come,
He sought the secrets of the Elder Age,
Of nightmare gods and old fantastic wars
Brought down by Tsathoggua from the stars
And chronicled on Eibon's darkling page.
Hyperborea spake his name with dread
And whispered of strange shapes and stranger light
That moved about his ebon spire one night
When thunder spoke and all the stars burned red.
Next morn it lay in ruins everywhere.
They found his Book. His body was not there ....

XVI. TSATHOGGUA

Beneath Voormithadreth the Mount of Dread
In lost Hyperborea long ago
Before the coming of eternal snow,
The wizard followed where the *shantak* led;
Down through the gulfs of those tremendous deeps,
Caverns of nightmare, where the wholesome sun
Hath never shone since first the earth begun,
To that abyss where Tsathoggua sleeps.
Eibon alone hath seen, and come back sane
From that slime pit of madness where It lies,
The Black Abomination from the skies,
Who sleepeth now but who shall wake again.
We know the truth, we who have dared to look
Into the darkling pages of his Book ....

XVII BLACK ZIMBABWE

In dreams alone I tread those jungled streets
Where shattered columns, black with hoary age,
Hint of the splendour of some crumbling page
Of history now legended. The seats
Of prehistoric majesty still stand—
The monstrous walls, the cryptic minarets
—But whose the hand that raised them? Time forgets,
Mazed in the darkness of this silent land.
Only the moon remembers, ages gone,
The glittering, barbaric Wizard-Kings
Who found the Sign and made the Offerings
In the forgotten ages of earth's dawn.
The moon alone recalls that nameless crime
That wiped them from the memory of Time.

XVIII. THE RETURN

Something is wrong tonight. Far out to sea
Strange phosphorescence flickers from below.
The ocean heaves in waves uneasy, slow,
That roil and bubble, an old prophecy
Comes back to haunt my soul ... the stars burn cold,
In patterns oddly wrong. And now the deep
Surges, like something—stirring—in its sleep!
Is this the Night the ancient books foretold?
Iä! The seas unfold! That *Shape*—'tis true!
He rises from the city old as time! ...
I *woke* ... and knew it but a dream ... yet knew
The blood-congealing truth of that old rhyme:
"That is not dead which can eternal lie,
And with strange aeons even death may die."

XIX THE SABBAT
"This is the night," the sly-faced stranger leered
—He had approached me on the lonely streets—
"This is the night the Arkham coven meets!"
Before I answered he had disappeared.
At nightfall I went down the cellar steps
And through that secret door which I had found.
It led by dark ways tunneled underground
Into a caverned abyss in the depths.
Weak with a mingled loathing and desire,
I joined the hooded throng that milled and whirled
About the standing stones, red-lit with fire
That flamed up from the bowels of the world.
One hailed me—"Azath!"—he was robed in red—
"That was your Uncle's coven-name," he said.

XX. BLACK LOTUS
The Coven-Master gave to me a phial
Of that dread opiate that is the key
To dream-gates opening upon a sea
Of acherontic vapours: mile on mile
Stretched ebon coasts untrod, wherefrom aspire
Pylons of rough-hewn stone climbing to skies
Alien-constellated, where arise
Grey mottled moons of cold and leprous fire.
My dream-self roamed the cosmic gulfs profound,
Past daemon-haunted Haddith, where in deeps
Of foul putrescence buried underground
The loathsome shoggoth hideously sleeps.
I saw—and screamed! And knew my doom of dooms,
Learning at last ... *where* the Black Lotus blooms.

XXI. THE UNSPEAKABLE

I drank the golden mead and did those things
Of which I read within the ancient book.
The wind awoke. The elms and willows shook
Before the thunder of fantastic wings.
Down from the cosmic gulfs the monster fell,
The grim, stupendous, bat-winged Byakhee,
Come from the cloudy shores of Lake Hali,
Black-furred and iron-beaked, with eyes of Hell.
When I bestrode its back, the beast unfurled
Its vast and mighty wings. Across dark seas
Of space we flew. Amid the Hyades
We reached at last that bleak and mythic world
To men forbidden and by gods abhorred,
Carcosa, where the great Hastur is Lord.

XXII. CARCOSA

It was a scene that I had known before,
This barren, desolate, and drear expanse
Through which I wandered in a dream-like trance.
And there in somber splendor by the shore
Of dark Hali the nameless city stood:
Black domes and monolithic towers loom
Stark and gigantic in the midnight gloom
Like druid menhirs in a haunted wood.
These streets and walls I seem to half-recall,
Wandering blindly through the winding ways
Beneath a sky with strange black stars ablaze,
From some mad dream ... or was it dream at all?
Aye, here it was I heard Cassilda sing,
Where flap the yellow tatters of The King!

XXIII. THE CANDIDATE

Down the dark street of monoliths I passed.
The shambling, faceless figure of my Guide
A voiceless thing that beckoned at my side.
And to the dreaded Gate I came at last.
Before the silent Guardian I made
The black unhallowed Sacrifice, and spoke
Names at whose sound forgotten echoes woke.
The portals gaped. I entered unafraid.
Fate, or my stars, or some accursed pride
Had brought me here. Naked, I stood alone
And took the Vow before the Elder Throne—
He *laughed*, and drew His tattered mantle wide—
O do not seek to learn nor ever ask
What horror hides behind ... *The Pallid Mask!*

XXIV. THE DREAM-DAEMON

In dreams the Daemon comes upon the hour
Of full moon over Arkham. And I see
The opal shores of seas unknown to me
Where Babel-tall, bizarre, the cities tower—
Black and basalt metropoli of myth
Athrong with ziggurat and pyramid
That scale dark skies where ebon moons are hid.
Is it a dream of Yaddath or of Ith?
Or some outré and undimensioned sphere
Beyond the cosmos? I seek not to learn
Upon what occult world those ruins rear,
Remembering those books I ought to burn.
This much I know: the cities and the shore
Were somewhere, somehow, known to me before ....

XXV. DARK YUGGOTH

There lies a world beyond the seas of night,
Past the last planet, on the farthest Rim
Of curving space, where by some cosmic whim
It reels and wheels beyond the shores of light,
Lost in the howling dark. The eye of man
Can never glimpse its lone imperial place,
Deep in the blackest depths of elder space,
Nor astronomic glass may ever scan.
This is the planet that Alhazred knew,
Beyond the measured, known, and numbered nine;
Lost and alone where never sun doth shine,
Nor soft winds blow, nor skies are ever blue.
Far in the midnight deeps beyond our sight,
There the black planet rides the tides of night.

XXVI. THE SILVER KEY

Dreams hold no dread for me, for I alone
Went down the Seven Hundred Steps and passed
The Gate of Deeper Slumber, till at last
I went beyond the limits of the Known ...
I have seen many-columned Y'ha-nthlei,
And talked with serpent-bearded Byatis,
And, flown on Night Gaunts to the last abyss,
Have glimpsed the foetid pits where Abhoth lay.
All worlds lie open to me ... time and space
Reveal their darkest secrets to the one
Who dares the nighted realm of They Who Shun
The Light, and comes to gaze into *His* face.
What I have seen would drive you mad; yet I
Cannot go mad; I cannot even ... *die*.

XXVII. THE PEAKS BEYOND THROK
Where ominous the mould-encumbered walls
Of riven citadels old as Mnar
Rise in their ruin, from a distant star
I wandered; now, nightmare alone recalls
Those greenly litten vales of writhing trees
Whose scaled and snaky limbs reached for my flesh;
And those black, hellish jungles beyond Kesh
Where I with ghouls conversed by foetid seas.
And there was one that shambled from the feast,
Whining with eagerness to scan my face,
A filth-encrusted, gaunt, hound-muzzled beast
Who sought to fold me in its vile embrace.
It spake those words at which I paled and fled:
"I was your Uncle, when I lived," it said.

XXVIII. SPAWN OF THE BLACK GOAT
They ride the night-wind when the Demon Star
Over the dim horizon burns bale-red,
Come from the charnel-pits of the undead,
Nadir of nightmare, where the shoggoths are.
Now, till the light of morning-litten east
Bids them return to the unbottomed slime,
Freely they roam the darkling earth a time
And from fresh graves abominably feast.
These are the spawn that nighted pits confine,
And shouldst thou sight them in the midnight gloom,
Then art thou lost! For not the Elder Sign
That seals the great Cthulhu in his tomb,
Canst save thee from the hunger-maddened wrath
Of the Begotten of Shub-Niggurath.

XXIX. BEYOND

I have seen Yith, and Yuggoth on the Rim,
And black Carcosa in the Hyades;
And in the slimy depths of certain seas,
I have beheld the tomb where lieth Him
Who Was And Who Shall Be; and I have flown
Astride the *shantak* or the *byakhee*
Where Kadath in the Cold Waste terribly
Bears up her onyx-castled crest unknown.
I have conversed with seer and archimage
In glacier-buried, drear Commoriom,
And traced the maggot-eaten parchment page
Of tomes that Tsathoggua carried from
Dim vast Cykranosh. I am no more sane,
For too much horror burns away the brain.

XXX. THE ACCURSED

Sometimes I dream that I was once a man
On some small planet in the deeps of night,
And not a mindless, mewling parasite.
And, with my brethren off Aldebaran
Or green Algol, I sometimes seem to trace
Against the dark a smiling, lovely thing ....
I half-recall a voice that used to sing
Old lullabies ... is it my mother's face?
Is it a vision, dream, or memory?
The chittering horde about me sweeps me on;
The half-remembered vision dims—is gone.
An ancient pain gnaws at the heart of me.
From this strange dream, this mystic cryptogram,
I wake to horror—*knowing what I am.*

XXXI. THE MILLION FAVORED ONES
From black Mnar, from Yuggoth on the Rim,
From those liquescent pits where shoggoths bloat,
Across the cosmic gulfs of spheres remote
—We come! We come! At the command of Him
Who is our Lord and Father. Bleak Kadath
And frozen Leng have known our awful tread;
Lost Yhe in the Pacific quailed in dread
Before our coming, and our Father's wrath ....
And some of us were human once, and some
Have never even heard the name of Earth,
Abominations of a monstrous birth
Out of the womb of nightmare. ... When we come,
The nations kneel in fear before our step ...
We are the Children of Nyarlathotep.

IN his working notes Carter dubbed this tale "Diary of a Madman." That fits the theme well enough, but of course it was the title of the famous tale by Guy de Maupassant, and Lin was no doubt planning to come up with a title of his own, which in due time he did. The result seems like a combination of Jack Chapman Miske's story "The Thing in the Moonlight" (credited to Lovecraft when Miske published it in his magazine *Bizarre* because Miske had added a few sentences onto either end of an account of a dream from one of Lovecraft's letters) and Derleth's "Something in Wood." Remember, Lin was not simply filching material from others, as unperceptive critics have often alleged. Rather, his point was to salute the originals by recombining their DNA, so to speak, into new patterns that would induce simultaneous reactions of both novelty and nostalgia in the reader.

"Something in the Moonlight", which appeared in *Weird Tales* #2 (Zebra Books, 1981), makes an interesting use of the "unreliable narrator" device (see Wayne Booth's discussion in *The Rhetoric of Fiction*). An unreliable narrator is a means of casting the whole story in an ironic mode, opening a gap between the narrator and the reader, who understands the situation better than the narrator does. Of course this is because the author has planned it this way. He has placed sufficient clues to alert the reader that the narrator is oblivious to certain important things that the reader will see. The author lets the reader in on the joke, while keeping the narrator in the dark. For instance, in Robert Bloch's "Notebook Found in a Deserted House", the child narrator's naiveté prevents him from understanding the ominous character of the events until too late, creating in the reader an acute sense of frustration and anxiety: He would like to warn the child but can't.

In "Something in the Moonlight", the main character is committed to a lunatic asylum for his beliefs about the imminent appearance of a Mythos demon. Of course, outsiders deem these beliefs delusions. The reader is already prepared to accept the reality of the Mythos in the Lovecraftian narrative universe, and so we at first regard the protagonist as something of a martyr, his confinement a product of the Inquisition conducted by the lords of the mainstream plausibility structure against those who dare take a dissenting view (see Thomas Szasz, *The Myth of Mental Illness*). Then, the more we read of the prisoner's diary, with its claustrophobic, margin-to-margin cataloguing of Mythos data, the more we begin to suspect that he actually has gone round the bend, has lost more than a few sanity points. It's supposed to be pretty common for Mythos protagonists, after all. So just how delusional is he? That's where the suspense element comes in. The reader, familiar with the Mythos, can not be sure just how reliable or unreliable the narrator is supposed to be, until ...

What is surprising is that Lin did not make the protagonist of this tale the hapless Arthur Wilcox Hodgkins from "The Horror in the Gallery." Having been committed to the very same loony bin for delusions of the same general character, he might well have been pictured seeking desperately to evade the revenge of Zoth-Ommog. We already know of Hodgkins' tendency to dump massive amounts of Mythos textual data into his diaries, so that, too, would have fit perfectly. So I will forgive you if you want to edit silently as you read, substituting Hodgkins' name for Horby's.

Something in the Moonlight

by Lin Carter

1. Statement of Charles Winslow Curtis, M.D.

QUITE early in the spring of 1949 I was fortunate enough to secure an appointment to the staff of the Dunhill Sanitarium in Santiago, California, as a psychiatric counselor working under the renowned Harrington J. Colby. The appointment was exciting and promising in the extreme, for it is seldom that a doctor as young as myself—the ink, as it were, hardly dry on his diploma—has the opportunity to work under so distinguished a member of the psychiatric profession as Dr. Colby.

Motoring up by taxi from Santiago, I enjoyed the glorious sunshine of Southern California and admired the almost tropical profusion of flowering shrubs and trees. I soon discovered the sanitarium to be a handsome group of buildings in the Spanish hacienda style, surrounded by spacious, well planted grounds. Gardens and tennis courts and even golf links were there for the recreation of the patients; there was, as well, a large lake behind the property from which at night the croaking of bullfrogs could be heard. The sanitarium was one of the finest, I had been given to understand, in this part of the state, and I looked forward eagerly to working under such excellent conditions.

Dr. Colby himself, spry and keen-eyed for all his silver hair, greeted me affably.

"I trust you will enjoy working with us here at Dunhill, my dear Curtis," he said while escorting me to my new office. "Your professors back at Miskatonic speak highly of you; I am given to understand that your primary interest in abnormal psychology is the several forms of acute paranoia. In that area, you will find one of your new patients, a fellow named Horby, singularly intriguing."

"I'm sure I will, doctor," I murmured politely. "What is the nature of his problem?"

"There is something in the moonlight that he abhors," Colby said. "He cannot tolerate moonlight, and the drapes in his room must always be closely drawn. Not only that, but he sleeps with all lights burning, so that not one ray of moonlight could enter his room."

"That seems harmless enough," I said thoughtfully. "There are several cases on record of—"

"There's more. He is afraid of lizards," said Colby succinctly.

I shrugged. "Well, sir, phobic reactions to various reptiles are certainly common enough—"

"Not Horby's," he said dryly.

Then in utter seriousness, and without even the slightest trace of comment by inflection or expression, he made the most extraordinary statement.

"The lizard Mr. Horby fears happens to inhabit the moon."

* * *

BEFORE very long I had met the rest of the staff, become acquainted with the layout of the sanatarium and familiar with its routine, and found myself "settling in" comfortably. For the most part, those patients to whom I was assigned were suffering from conditions depressingly common and ordinary. A lone exception was Uriah Horby: Even as my superior had predicted on the day of my arrival, Horby's case was singular and curious.

Paranoia, of course, is a mental disorder characterized by systematized delusions and the projection of inner conflicts, which are ascribed to the supposed hostility of others. Such, at least, is the textbook definition: I have found such cases more richly various and less simple of explanation.

Sometimes, paranoid patients believe themselves hounded by imaginary enemies (which can be anything from foreign spies to the Jesuits or some secret brotherhood of mystics). They believe themselves followed wherever they go and that they are spied upon continuously, and they assign to the malignancy of these shadowy foes every accident or mishap that chances to befall them.

The outward symptoms of paranoia are remarkably easy to discern: a tendency toward careless, disorderly dress, a neglect of personal cleanliness, rapid and disconnected patterns of speech, eyes that wander to and fro fearfully searching the shadowy corners of the room, and a furtive lowering of the voice so that hidden ears cannot overhear what is being said.

It is particularly in the eyes that paranoia can be detected, even by the layman. The gaze of a paranoid is either dim, glazed, unfocused, the attention being turned within to ruminating over one's endless and pitiful persecution—or it is afire with the febrile gleam of the fanatic.

When I first entered the room assigned to Uriah Horby, I felt the shock of surprise. He was a small man in his mid-fifties, lean of build and going bald, clean-shaven and seemingly in good health. He was seated at a small folding desk studying sheafs of notepaper written (I noticed) in a clear, tight, legible hand ... very unlike the hysteric scrawl of most cases of acute paranoia I have studied.

His person was scrupulously neat and so was his room. The narrow bed was neatly made, the small bookcase tidy, and the personal effects on his dresser and washstand effectively organized. When he raised his eyes to meet mine I was in for another shock of surprise.

For Uriah Horby had the clearest, most candid gaze of any man I have ever met. His eyes were shrewd and thoughtful, but their innocence and candor were those of a small child.

Before the tranquil sanity in his eyes, I felt myself amazed. To cover my lack of composure, I hurried to introduce myself. He smiled politely.

"How do you do, Dr. Curtis? Pardon me if I do not rise: To do so would disarrange these notes, and I have a passion for organization and deplore messiness. I have known you were about to join our little social circle here at Dunhill for some time, of course. I trust you have found your welcome adequate? As Menander said, 'The gentleman is at home in every circumstance,' but a madhouse *is* somewhat lacking in the amenities."

This was the man who went in mortal fear of lizards? A man whose chief and most deadly enemy lived in the moon? A paranoid who had been confined to Dunhill for over six years, and was believed incurable?

I could hardly believe it, yet it was indeed so ....

* * *

AT Dunhill, as I soon discovered, meetings between doctor and patient are informal and leisurely conversations, more like what my contemporaries call "rap sessions" than the usual clinical interrogations to which I had become accustomed. Uriah Horby was a deft and interesting conversationalist. His speech was coherent, his mind seemingly rational, his demeanor quiet and controlled.

He was an exceptionally intelligent man of obvious breeding and had enjoyed an excellent education. The son of a local merchant, he had studied abroad and traveled widely before settling in Santiago. He was of scholarly interests, learned in several abstruse fields, and, although absorbed by the nature of his peculiar fixation, able to converse easily upon a variety of subjects.

I conceived an intense curiosity concerning the man for several reasons, one of them being that he displayed in his manner and deportment and appearance none of the haunted, harried traits I had so often observed in other victims of paranoia. And his delusions of persecution were certainly novel.

"Why is it that you fear lizards, Mr. Horby?" I inquired bluntly on one of our first meetings. He considered his folded hands, lips pursed judiciously, as if carefully choosing his words.

"They ruled the earth before the earliest of our mammalian ancestors arose," he replied soberly. "In time, our kind replaced theirs, and they hate us for it. As well, they are utterly alien to our species—vicious and cold-blooded predators, devoid of emotion. That the highest order of sentience should reside in such loathsome reptiles is more than abhorrent, it is unholy."

Consistent with a formal, even pedantic, diction, as can be seen above, his speech was completely unemotional and lucid. Whatever fears tormented the man were obviously buried deeply within him.

"My understanding has always been that reptiles possess very little of what we should call intelligence, and operate on rudimentary instinct alone," I remarked. It is sometimes unwise to argue or to disagree with a mental patient, of course, but I meant to draw our man out, if possible.

He smiled dryly. "I gather, Dr. Curtis, that you have never encountered the *Necronomicon* in the range of your studies," he said, changing the subject, or so I thought. I shook my head.

"I don't believe I have," I admitted frankly. "A Greek work, I assume? Theological?"

"Translated into Greek from the original Arabic," he answered. "Also into Latin and Elizabethan English. The author, a Yemenite poet of the eighth century of the Christian era, was named Alhazred; his work has been dismissed by your colleagues in the formal sciences as the ravings of a diseased intelligence. Had there been asylums for the insane in Alhazred's day, as there are, unfortunately, in my own, I have no doubt he would have been locked up in one."

"I gather that this Alhazred discusses the intelligence of reptiles?"

"To complete my reply to your first query, it is a work of demonology rather than of theology," he said somberly. "It presents a theory, drawn from documents and sources of the most fabulous antiquity, that this planet was first inhabited by entities from other worlds and galaxies and planes of existence, countless ages before the evolution of man. The nature of these beings is such that they would seem like gods or demons to lesser creatures like ourselves: Immortal, indestructible, not constructed from matter as we know it, they are incomprehensible intelligences of pure, devouring evil—older than the world, and desirous of possessing it ...."

These words, spoken in quiet, sober tones, sent a chill through the warm afternoon sunlight. Despite myself, I could not suppress a shudder: The nature of Horby's paranoid delusions were, then, religious.

"In one section, during the first few chapters of Book IV," he continued, "Alhazred relates the history of a prehistoric town or settlement called 'Sarnath' which early men built in ominous proximity to 'the grey stone city Ib', where dwelt a race of aquatic nonhumans who worshiped the demon Bokrug in the form of a gigantic water lizard. Although Alhazred does not employ the term in the passages of which I speak, the aquatic beings are known as the Thunn'ha: They are green-skinned, batrachian, speechless. They worshiped their reptilian divinity with abominable rites—"

Recalling Dr. Colby's words, I hazarded aloud the guess that this devil-god of Ib resided in the moon. Disconcertingly, Uriah Horby paled and bit his lip.

"Not he ... not he," he whispered hoarsely. "But That which he serves ...."

His voice shook a little on these words, as if struggling to suppress some powerful emotion. Sensing my patient's perturbation, I changed the subject at this point and began to question him about his childhood experiences, seeking a possible trauma.

Our interview terminated not long thereafter.

2. Extract from the Notes of Uriah Horby

Tues. the 17th. Young Doctor Curtis is a likable fellow and keen enough on his work, but a blind, stubbornly ignorant fool nonetheless. As they all are. When my book is published, perhaps then the scientific community will recognize the value of my discovery and the dimensions of the enormous peril awaiting mankind in the near future.

Summer will soon be upon us, and the frogs will begin their hellish nightly serenade; I must strive to organize my notes, for the Hour Appointed cometh nigh and time is running out for me ... perhaps young Curtis will prove useful in at least one sense: he seems fascinated by my "case" and exhibits a pitiful eagerness to gain my confidence. Possibly I can persuade him to assist me in locating the complete text of the Zoan chant; if it is not to be found in Prinn or in von Junzt, perhaps it is in the *Cultes des Goules*, although Diedrich swears it is not. If only my father's *Necronomicon* had been complete! Well, I have long ago tried all of the nine formulae between the Ngg and the Hnnrr, and the Zhooric sign is obviously of no avail against them. What remains, but the Chian Pentagram and the Xao games? And if they fail, I have yet to employ the thirteen formulae between the Yaa and the Ghhgg ....

But time is running out for me, as the end of the Cycle nears. Running out for *me?*—it is running out for all mankind!

3. From the Statement of Charles Winslow Curtis

IT was not long before I learned that Uriah Horby was an enthusiastic lifelong student of archaeology and quite a talented, though an amateur, scholar in that field. It was this fascination which the ancient past held for him, it seemed, that had some connection to his present condition.

"I found my first clue in Alhazred, of course," he remarked during the course of one of our early conversations together. "In chapter iii of Book IV ... I am quoting from memory, of course, but my memory is most precise on certain subjects ... 'In the fullness of time a prophet arose among the men of Sarnath, by name Kish: even that one we remember as the Elder Prophet, for that They Who Reign From Betelgeuse made revelation unto him, saying, Beware the Ib-folk, O men of Sarnath! for that they were come down to this earth from certain cavernous places in the Moon, ere man rose out of the slime, and the Water-thing they worship in foul ways is Other than ye think, and the name Bokrug is but a mask, behind the which there lurketh an Elder Horror' ... now, following this clue, I delved into the pages of von Junzt—"

"Von Junzt?" I interposed. He brushed my query aside with a prim yet brusque gesture.

"Friedrich-Wilhelm von Junzt, the German occultist, author of the *Unaussprechlichen Kulten*," he said a trifle impatiently. "You should be able to find him in most of the standard biographical reference works. If you ever bother to check up on any of the things I tell you, Dr. Curtis, you will discover that I am inventing nothing: All of these data are valid and authentic, and may be found in print."

I forced a laugh. "It's just that these ancient mythologies seem to have little, if any, relevance to our own time!"

Uriah Horby fixed me with a clear, piercing gaze. His voice was firm and reasonable as he spoke.

"Things happened here on earth long ago. They are *still* happening ... why did the federal government destroy blocks of seemingly abandoned tenements in Innsmouth, Massachusetts during the winter of 1927-'28? Why did a naval submarine discharge torpedoes into Devil's Reef in the harbor? What really happened in the old Tuttle house on the Aylesbury Road near the Innsmouth Turnpike? What events actually took place at Navissa

Camp in Manitoba in late 1931 ... or, for that matter, what is the real story of what happened at Rick's Lake in north central Wisconsin in 1940? Why has the explorer Marsh never disclosed what happened to the ill-fated Hawks Expedition on the Sung Plateau region of mountainous Burma, after they reached the ruins of Alaozar?"

I looked at him nonplused; there was nothing that I could say. Some of the mysterious events he referred to had been noised abroad in the newspapers, and even I had hazy recollections of the matters to which he made reference.

With a slight shrug of his shoulders he moved on.

"But, to continue: Quoting from the *Cylinders of Kadatheron* and the *Ilarnek Papyrus*, which were Alhazred's principle sources for the Sarnath legend, von Junzt speculates most intriguingly on the *lunar* origin of Bokrug and of the creatures he commands, which are the Thunn'ha. It seems that when Alhazred transcribed from these very ancient sources, he was working from an apparently incomplete copy of the texts. Expanding on the hint given in the passage from the *Necronomicon* which I have already quoted to you, von Junzt postulates an extragalactic origin for Bokrug and his minions. In brief, he suggests that they came hither with the Great Old Ones through the star-spaces, or the dimensions which lie between them. But none of the ancient scriptures at our disposal mention Bokrug in the context of the Old Ones, which is odd, although the books which I have consulted are sadly fragmentary and are lacking many pages and even entire sections."

"I gather that these Great Old Ones are the demonic or godlike alien intelligences which Alhazred theorizes were the original inhabitants of our planet," I said. He smiled.

"That is precisely correct, Dr. Curtis."

Just at this interesting juncture, and most unfortunately, a male nurse interrupted our conversation, for one of my other patients was having a seizure. I was forced to bid a hasty adieu to Uriah Horby, postponing the remainder of our talk until some later time.

Interestingly enough, while I was striving to draw the man out with leading questions, I was not entirely ignorant of the matters which occupied him. For I remembered that I had indeed heard of this *Necronomicon* he quoted from and mentioned so frequently: When I had been an undergraduate at Miskatonic University there had been quite a bit written up about the ancient book in the local papers in connection with some bizarre murder or suicide. I forget the details of the case, but it seemed that my old alma mater had a copy of the incredibly rare book under lock and key, and was one of the few institutions of higher learning in this country to possess a copy. Odd that the title of the Arabic book had slipped my mind.

Later that afternoon, while recording my notes of the talk with Horby, I remembered what he had said about my checking his data. Within twenty minutes I found a capsule biography of the German scholar he had mentioned, whose pretensions to scholarship seemed authentic enough from the list of degrees recorded after his name in the entry.

Horby, it appeared, was not making it all up. He had stumbled upon some obscure, horrible mythology and had been drawn into it by his scholarly fascination with the ancient world, until at last it occupied the center of his interests.

The case was growing more intriguing all the time.

4. Extract from the Notes of Uriah Horby

Fri., the 21st. Last night, meditating on the Sign of Koth, I obtained a vision of Deep Dendo. It is unfortunate that Those who reside there either cannot or will not assist me in my search.

The Chian Pentagram has proved useless to my purposes, as have the Xao games. My correspondent in Paris has transcribed certain material from *Eibon* which he thought might have considerable bearing upon the situation, and I am translating the old Norman French—a slow and laborious job. And, I suspect, one ultimately futile. Lacking the relevant passage from the *Necronomicon* I feel frustratingly helpless. My knowledge of the Elder Lore is so dreadfully incomplete ... *I do not even know the name* of the Entity to whom I am opposed, nor the place where He abideth. Lacking these vital terms, I am without adequate means of defense: With them, I might be able to hurl the Zoan chant against Him, or to erect barriers of mental force in the manner taught me by the Nug-Soth.

Later: I used the Sign of Koth again, receiving transient glimpses of the inner city at the two magnetic poles, but to no avail. Have asked—entreated!—young Doctor Curtis to help me obtain the passages I need from Alhazred. The amiable fool thinks me mad, but may take pity on me and have the material copied. Mad, am I? When *They* come down again to reconquer Their ancient empire—when the earth is cleared off and the Eternal Reign begins—"madmen" like me will be mightier than emperors!

5. From the Statement of Charles Winslow Curtis

HORBY has asked me to help him with his work by securing the text of certain key passages from Alhazred to which he has not been able to gain access. Seems like a smart thing to do, gain his confidence by harmless favors such as this. I have sent a telegram to one of my professors back at Miskatonic; expect he will be able to get the material to me.

Horby has not been sleeping well of late. He complains about "the frogs", and it's true that in this marshy area behind the sanitarium they have been raising a hellish chorus of night. I declined to prescribe sleeping pills or tranquilizers for him, however, on Dr. Colby's advice. Horby's increasing agitation seems due to his conviction that some crucial time period is almost here when the "defenses" he has built up against his dreaded lunar enemy will fall. Exactly what he fears will happen then I cannot say, nor will he tell me.

I have learned the cause of the danger he believes himself to be in. His nameless enemy, the force behind the demon Bokrug, supposedly became aware of his existence when he rashly published as a scholarly monograph his conjectural translation of the *Ilarnek Papyrus* to which he has often referred, and therein speculated on Sarnath and its legendary doom. The town, by the way, seems completely mythical, for I can find nothing about it in history or in archaeology. But the cult to whom these matters are sacred—and, to his way of thinking, the dark divinities behind that cult—took sinister umbrage at the publication of the ancient text, which seems to have revealed more about their religion than they wished made part of public record.

At any rate, Horby's monograph discussed a means of employing another demon called "Cthugha" against the "dragon in the moon." According to his account, this Cthugha is a fire elemental and is, by his essential nature, in direct opposition to such water elementals as the devil-god of whom Bokrug and the Ib things are merely the minions and servitors. The Alhazredic demonology, I infer, argues that the Old Ones are divided into four groups of elementals, all opposed to one another.

Horby also explained to me that all of these ancient and evil gods have their secret cults of quasi-human or nonhuman worshipers which linger yet in certain remote backwoods and far places. His monograph came to the attention of the cult which worships the force behind Bokrug, which is why they and their god are "after" him.

Somehow, there is something *irresistibly plausible* about his fixation. I find myself unable to refute either it or his logic. He is a most extraordinary man.

6. Extract from the Notes of Uriah Horby

Mon., the 28th. It is horribly close now to the Time when the power of the moon waxeth to its height, and That which resides therein will be at the peak of His strength. Not even Cthugha and the Flame Creatures can aid me then: Curtis is my only hope.

The material from *Eibon* proved worthless; I believe that the information I so desperately need was most probably to be found in Eibon's third book, "Papyrus of the Dark Wisdom", which von Junzt only paraphrases. But it is too late now to write to my Parisian friend ....

The D'horna-ahn Energies will no longer protect me when the fatal night arrives. Through the use of the Ritual of the Silver Key I have been in communion with the fungoid intelligences of Nzoorl, and obtained precious glimpses of S'glhuo and Ymar. But nothing avails me .... They on Ktynga warn that I will not be able to call upon their strength when the time comes, but this I already know. Mighty Yhtill could stand between me and It, but I have never been to Carcosa or taken the Vow before the Elder Throne.

It is written: There are forty-eight Aklo unveilings known to mortal men, and a forty-ninth, whereof men knoweth naught, nor shall they know, until such time as Glaaki taketh them. If I could travel through the reversed angles of Tagh-Clatur, or employ the enormous energies of the Pnakotic Pentagram, I might survive. But there is little hope left to me, unless that procrastinating fool Curtis comes through.

7. From the Statement of Charles Winslow Curtis

THOMPSON at Miskatonic sent me a long letter today, including with it the material which Horby has asked me to help him obtain. I have read it through and see nothing in it that could conceivably be harmful—merely the ravings of a deranged and superstitious demonologist. Just for the sake of completeness, I shall copy it out for my notes on the case.

The passage occurs in Book III, Chapter xvii of the *Necronomicon*, and is quoted from the Elizabethan translation of Dr. John Dee, the notorious occultist. It reads as follows:

> But of the Great Old Ones begotten by *Azathoth* in the Prime, not all came down to this Earth, for Him Who Is Not To Be Named lurketh ever on that dark world near Aldebaran in the Hyades, and it was His Sons who descended hither in His stead. Likewise, *Cthugha* chose for His abode the star Fomalhaut, and the Fire-Vampires that serve Him; but, as for *Aphoom Zhah*, He descended to this Earth and dwelleth yet in His frozen lair. And terrible *Vulthoom*, that be brother to *Black Tsathoggua*, He descended upon dying Mars, which world he chose for His dominion; and He slumbers yet in the Deep of Ravormos 'neath aeon-crumbled Ignarh-Vath; and it is written that a day or a night to *Vulthoom* is as a thousand years to mortal men. And, as for great *Mnomquah*, He took for the place of His abiding those cavernous spaces which yawn beneath the Moon's crust; and there He abideth yet, wallowing amidst the slimy waves of the Black Lake of Ubboth in the Stygian darknesses of Nug-yaa; and it was them that serve Him, even the Thunn'ha whose leader is *Bokrug*, that came hither to this world and dwelt betimes in the grey stone city Ib in the land of Mnar.

That was all the passage Thompson quoted; the further piece Horby had wished to see—something called "the Zoan chant" from Book VII—he failed to include in his letter, saying the pages are utterly illegible.

Well, perhaps it's not too late to bring this material to Horby. True, evening has fallen and the moon is rising, but I doubt he is yet to bed.

8. Extract from the Notes of Uriah Horby

Wed., the 30th. I am doomed. I am lost. The time has come—is less than an hour away—and all my barriers are fading. My spirit shall be raped from my shuddering flesh, in ways I cringe to think upon, and I shall wander upon the black winds that blow between the stars forever, a nameless wraith lost in the wailing multitudes of the Million Favored Ones. ...

It is Curtis at the door! Perhaps all is not lost; I shall end this entry here and admit him. Shall I ever write another word of this journal?

9. From the Statement of Charles Winslow Curtis

IT is now my painful duty to record a sequence of events which I do not understand, and I write the following if only in the vain hope that somehow I will be able to sort these matters out to my own satisfaction.

On the night of the thirtieth, some time past moonrise, I brought the passages copied from the *Necronomicon* to Horby, who met me at the door and virtually snatched the paper from me. He was in the worst state of agitation I have yet seen him in, his face flushed, eyes bloodshot and feverishly bright, hands trembling like a leaf.

He scanned the quotation swiftly, then threw back his head and voiced a shrill cry of triumph.

"It *is* Mnomquah! Of course—how could I not have known? And the place of his imprisonment by the Elder Gods is the Black Lake of Ubboth, in the gulf of Nug-yaa, at the moon's heart! Ah, all becomes plain to me now ... those cryptic references I have tracked down in the old books—" Suddenly he broke off short, turning the paper from side to side in shaking hands, his flushed features paling to a sickly pallor.

"But there is more? Please, God, Curtis, there must be *more*! *Where is the Zoan chant, you fool?* How can I direct the energies against the Black Lake without the chant—?"

"I—I'm sorry," I stammered apologetically. "My old professor back at Miskatonic was unable to copy out the ritual you wanted, because the pages were not legible at that point in the book—"

He stared with unbelieving horror into my eyes. Never have I seen a look more piteous: It would have wrung the heart of a stone thing. Then his face crumbled, his shoulders sagged. The page from Thompson's letter fell from listless fingers to drift into a corner. He turned from me to face the window, and, absurdly, I felt myself dismissed. Tactfully, I withdrew, feeling he wished to be alone with his thoughts.

Would to God I had stayed.

* * *

LATER that night, just as I was undressing and making ready to retire, one of the attendants called me to say that Horby was loudly chanting or praying, and that he feared it might disturb the other patients.

"If they can even hear him, with that hellish frog-chorus booming from the marsh," I remarked wryly.

"Yes, doctor. But may I give him a sleeping pill?"

"Oh, I think so. A good night's sleep will do him a world of good. He is more distraught than usual. Ring me back if he proves uncooperative," I said. The male nurse agreed and hung up the phone.

Feeling some obscure premonition, perhaps, or merely restless, I went over to the window. The frogs were roaring away at full voice and the moon was high, glaring down at us frail, puny mortals like a gigantic eye of cold white fire. By its illumination, you could see the pools of the marsh behind the building, flashing like the mirrors they were.

Out of the corner of my eye I caught a glimpse of something moving out of the waters and through the reeds, up onto the rear lawn. Something black and huge and wet, moving in the moonlight with a strange, splay-footed, *hopping* gait. I blinked, rubbed my eyes, and it was gone. Probably a dog from one of the neighboring farms, I thought. But the lawn *glittered* from a slick deposit! It was like the slime-track left by a garden slug ....

Moments later I was jolted by a horrible, despairing cry—a shriek of unutterable terror, the sort of sound that the damned must make in the abysm of Hell.

I went out into the hall, which was suddenly full of people running. I followed them without words. The shrieking went on and on.

But the frogs had ceased their croaking song upon the instant Horby shrieked.

Yes, it was Horby. We burst into the room to view a scene of absolute chaos. The drapes were torn from the window and the glass of the panes lay in a thousand icy shards upon the carpet, which was soaked with slime and water. Moonlight poured coldly, triumphantly, through the open window.

Face down in the wreckage lay Uriah Horby, stone dead. The expression frozen upon his face was one of such intolerable fear that I hope never to see a similar expression upon a human visage.

There was not a mark on his body.

In the corner of the room crouched the attendant who had gone to sedate him. The man had suffered a ghastly shock. He was incoherent, his broken speech interspersed with fits of idiotic, horrible giggling. He was chewing and spitting out the pages from Horby's manuscript and journals. They were trampled and torn and smeared with some odd greenish slime that rotted the paper like diluted acid.

"What has happened here?" demanded Dr. Colby, shaking the male nurse by the shoulder. The fellow peered at him vaguely from a white, wet, working face. Spittle smeared his lips and dribbled down his chin.

"... There was something in the moonlight, hopping across the lawn," he babbled in a feeble voice. "It ... climbed the wall and broke through the window. ... It jumped on Mr. Horby. ... It was like ... it was like ...."

Then he began that hideous giggling again. Colby stared at me, shaken. I stared back.

"God, what a stench—that *smell!*" someone muttered, gagging. It was quite true. The whole room reeked of salt seawater gone stagnant and scummed with filth. It was indescribable.

"What do you think, Curtis?" Colby asked me in low tones, out in the hall again.

"I don't know what to think," I said numbly.

"Nor do I," he sighed. "But this was the night Horby feared, the night his private demon was in full strength. I believe there was something to his story, after all."

"I don't know, sir," I said. But I lied. Because I knew. Mnomquah had been revenged ....

Ever since then I've found myself avoiding the moonlight, too. It makes me feel uneasy. And I've been reading the *Necronomicon*. Looking for the Zoan chant, perhaps, I don't know.

Poor Horby ....

INSPIRED in large measure by Lovecraft's poem "The Outpost" and his revision tale "Winged Death", "The Fishers from Outside" (which first appeared in *Crypt of Cthulhu* #54, Eastertide 1988) is a fine instance of its type, the story of a seeker after ancient knowledge who experiments at the cost of his life to discover whether old legends may speak truly after all. Like its fellows in the genre, "The Fishers from Outside" creates the impression of a death wish on the part of its doomed protagonist. While other characters may scoff, the protagonist seems not merely to want to *know* one way or the other, but rather, like Heinrich Schliemann, to *prove*. Like Ouspensky, Professor Mayhew is "in search of the miraculous." This in full knowledge of the fact that, if the hoped-for revelation proves out, it will surely mean his own death! How can we explain this? Is it an inherent and irredeemable implausibility that must rend the fabric of verisimilitude in any and every such Faustian tale? No, not at all, though some unimaginative school marms may think so.

Dénis de Rougement (*Love in the Western World*) explains what's going on here, though I am extending and adapting his point somewhat. Faustian seekers in horror tales do not merely blunder into their fates. They are seeking an imagined "realer reality" higher than this mundane world. This is what Arthur Machen's character Ambrose (in "The White People") calls "real sin", the storming of heaven. What is the sharper, brighter, realer world "beyond this illusion" (Kansas, "Carry On My Wayward Son", 1975)? It is death. That is also the crucial key to the attraction of Anne Rice's vampire novels, I suspect. The shadowy existence of the vampire, life lived on the edge, at the extreme, ironically makes the waking world of the living seem like dusty death by contrast. The chic of the vampire is, like traditional religious faith in an afterlife, a wishful denial of Epicurus' truth: "When death comes, we are not." Both afterlife belief and vampire fiction posit that when we are dead we will be aware of it, and that in this way death will be the elevation of life. Life was the tedious rehearsal; death is the real thing.

Even so, Professor Mayhew (like so many others) seeks a truth that, once known, must necessarily translate him from this dull sphere into the rarefied atmosphere of what lies outside, and that is death. Ironically, it is he, not the giant vultures, who is the "fisher." He is casting his line out into the void, hoping to find the greater existence that overcomes the world: death. He might not know to put it into those words, but his actions speak louder than words. Like Richard Pickman, horror delvers such as Professor Mayhew finally slip back into that darkness they loved to haunt, because for them, like the avatar in "The Haunter of the Dark", darkness is as radiant light.

In the original version of this story, Lin had confused Golgoroth, the amorphous god of darkness, and Groth-Golka, the bird-god, both of whom appear in Robert E. Howard's "The Gods of Bal-Sagoth." He had intended to make the change to Groth-Golka, but did not get to it. In this publication of the story I have made the correction.

The Fishers from Outside

by Lin Carter

STATEMENT OF HARLOW SLOAN

WHEN Mayhew found the Black Stone beneath the ruins of Zimbabwe, it was the culmination of many long and weary years of work. His quest had begun twenty years before, when as a young student at Miskatonic he had first heard of the "Fishers from Outside" in the unpublished journals of the explorer Slauenwite. That odd and curious term was the name by which the Gallas of Uganda referred to a mysterious race that had ruled central Uganda—according to the legend—before the first mammals were.

Intrigued, Mayhew read on with growing excitement as Slauenwite told of certain hellishly old stone ruins which the local tribes dread and avoid, of jungle-grown megaliths believed to be "older than man", and of a certain stone city somewhere in the south which their witch doctors whispered was an abandoned outpost of creatures "flown down from the stars when the world was young."

I suppose it is hard for a scholar or a scientist to pin down exactly what first impelled him in the direction of his future work. But Mayhew always said it was the native stories Slauenwite recorded in 1932 in his journals. At any rate, he embarked on a search for more information about the Fishers from Outside. He found fragments of lore concerning the mystery race in such old books as the dubious *Unaussprechlichen Kulten* of von Junzt, the notorious *Book of Eibon*, Dostmann's questionable *Remnants of Lost Empires*, *De Vermis Mysteriis* by the Flemish wizard Ludvig Prinn, and the frightful *Ponape Scripture* that Abner Exekiel Hoag had found in the Pacific islands. In the fervor of his growing obsession, Mayhew even dared to look into the nightmarish pages of the *Necronomicon* of Abdul Alhazred, the Arabian demonologist.

According to Alhazred's account, the Fishers were the minions or servants of the demon Groth-golka, who had anciently been worshiped on Bal-Sagoth, which some rather questionable authorities claim to have been the last foundering remnant of the mythical Atlantis. On Bal-Sagoth he was worshiped in his "bird-god" avatar, wrote the Arab. Most scholars would dismiss the legend as idle tales, but Mayhew knew there was independent corroboration for at least part of the account, for Norse voyagers during the early Crusades had seen Bal-Sagoth, recording something of its strange gods in their sagas.

* * *

AFTER completing his doctorate, Mayhew obtained a grant and went to Africa. He followed the footsteps of Slauenwite, exploring central Uganda, studying native myths and stories. Tales came to his ears of an ancient stone city buried in the southern jungles of the Dark Continent, which some thought the ruins of the legendary King Solomon's mines but which others ascribed to the handiwork of Portuguese slavers or traders. Mayhew knew that the Egyptian geographer Ptolemy had written many centuries ago of "Agysimba", the stone city in the jungle. Doubtless the Ugandan myth and the old Egyptian story referred to the same ruin ... and that could hardly be anything else than old Zimbabwe itself, that immemorial and mysterious stone city deep in the jungled heart of Rhodesia ... Zimbabwe, whereof so much is whispered and so very little known for certain.

I joined him at the site of Zimbabwe in 1946. I had been studying at the University of Cape Town, and one of his papers—a monograph on Ugandan petroglyphs, still indecipherable—caught my eye. I wrote, applying for a job, and was promptly accepted.

I knew little of Zimbabwe. I knew it was the focal point of a vast system of mighty towers and ramparts spread out over something like three hundred thousand square miles of trackless jungle. The ruins are found in Mashonaland, the mining areas of Gwelo, Que-Que, and Selukwe. At the center, deep in southern Rhodesia, about two hundred and eighty miles from the sea in the valley of the Upper Metetkwe, lie the colossal fortifications of enigmatic Zimbabwe—greatest and most fabulous of the roughly five hundred stone structures found in this wide zone, which seem the work of a race unknown to history, and whose puzzling architecture has no parallel elsewhere on this planet, save in certain fearfully ancient ruins in Peru.

This little I had gleaned from that tantalizing book, Hall's *Great Zimbabwe*, which raises so many disturbing questions and settles so very few—if any—of them. And soon I was to see the fantastic city myself!

* * *

MY first sight of mysterious Zimbabwe came at dusk. The sky was one supernal blaze of carmine and vermilion flame, against which the titanic walls of the enclosure soared impressively, composed of massive blocks weighing each many tons, the wall extending hundreds of feet, enclosing the weird, uncanny "topless towers" of which I had heard. Mayhew's workmen had cleared away the vines and undergrowth which for ages had encumbered the gigantic rampart, but the jungle, I somehow knew, had not surrendered, but had merely retreated before superior force and was biding its time, waiting for the puny, ephemeral children of men to leave that it might inexorably regain its antique domain over the mighty walls and towers.

A shudder, as of eerie premonition, ran through me as I first gazed upon lost Zimbabwe drowsing the ages away. Then I forced a shaky laugh and put such trepidations from me; after all, night had nearly fallen, and the breeze was dank and wet.

Mayhew I found a devoted, even fanatic, scientist. His peculiar fixation on the legend of the "Fishers from Outside" set by, he was a learned and scholarly man. He told me something of the Groth-golka myth and discussed what scraps of knowledge had been accumulated as to the history of the stupendous ruin before us. The Portuguese had first glimpsed it about 1550, he told me, but the first explorer did not reach these parts until 1868.

"I understand no inscriptions have ever been found," I murmured. He nodded, his lean, ascetic face serious and troubled.

"Yes, and that's another mystery! A race that can build a stone wall fourteen feet thick, in an elliptical enclosure eight hundred feet in circumference, should surely have some form of writing, if only for the required mathematics," he mused.

"And no artifacts have ever been found?" I hazarded.

"Only these," he said somberly, holding out a wooden tray. Within I saw a number of small, oddly shaped objects of baked clay and carved stone. They resembled curiously stylized birds, but not like any birds I know ... there was something misshapen, deformed, even—*monstrous* about them. I repressed a shiver of distaste.

"Do you know what they represent?" I asked faintly.

For a long moment he peered down at the tray of tiny artifacts, gazing at them through his eyeglasses, a pair of pince-nez spectacles he wore always, looped about his throat on a long ribbon of black silk. These pince-nez were his most famous affectation, and I knew of them long before I ever came to know the man himself.

Then he turned and looked at me.

"Perhaps the Fishers from Outside," he said, his voice dropping to a faint, hoarse whisper. "Or, perhaps, their mighty Master ... *Groth-golka*."

Something in the uncouth, harsh gutturals of that strange name made me wish, obscurely, that he had not spoken it aloud. Not here, amid the immemorial ruins of elder Zimbabwe ....

* * *

I SHALL not bore you with any extended account of the many weeks it took to complete our excavations. First, we investigated the weird topless towers, which were devoid of any interior structure, save for thick stone piers jutting at intervals into the hollow, chimney-like interior. They were uncannily reminiscent of the pegs in an aviary, the perches in a bird cage, it seemed to me; but I said nothing, leaving the professor to his own conjectures.

Within a month I was sent upriver to obtain supplies. I was rather glad of this, for I would miss our work in the Plain of Megaliths. There was something about this vast and level field, covered with row on row of mammoth stone cubes, that made me think of hundreds of Druidic sacrificial altars. As the date of their excavation approached, my sleep was disturbed by dark dreams in which I seemed to see hundreds of squirming naked blacks bound to row after row of the altar stones ... while weirdly bird-masked shamans raised an eerie, cawing chant beneath the peering moon, whose cold eye was obscured by drifts of reeking smoke from many fires ....

Terrible dreams they were!

Upriver, I found the trading post and loitered there long enough for the excavations to be completed on the Plain of Megaliths. My host was a local tradesman of Boer descent, who questioned me intently about our work and eyed me furtively from time to time, as if there were questions he did not quite dare ask.

"Ever heard of the 'Great Old Ones'?" he blurted one night, his courage bolstered by rum. I shook my head.

"I don't think so," I said. "What are they, some native legend?"

"Yes ... but, *mein Gott*! ... native to what world, I could not say!"

I stared at him, baffled; before I could ask another question, he abruptly changed the subject and began to talk lewdly and disgustingly about the local native women. I left downriver the next day with the supplies.

It seems I had lingered at the Ushonga trading post longer than had been needful; the Plain of Megaliths had been excavated, and the diggers had turned up nothing more interesting than hundreds of the little bird-like stone images. Mayhew had therefore turned his attention to the great

Acropolis, and beneath the foundations of the huge center stone a remarkable discovery had been made.

He showed it to me by the wavering light of a hissing kerosene lamp, tenderly unwrapping the odd-shaped thing with hands that shook with excitement. I stared at it in awe and amazement ... yes, even as I had stared at Zimbabwe itself that first night ... and with a cold inward shudder of ghastly premonition, too.

The Black Stone.

It was a decahedron, a ten-sided mass of flinty, almost crystalline black stone which I could not at once identify. From the weight of it, I guessed it to be some sort of metal.

"Meteoric iron," Mayhew whispered, eyes alive with feral enthusiasm, behind the glinting lenses of his pince-nez, for once askew. "Cut from the heart of a fallen star ... *and look at the inscriptions!*"

I peered more closely: Each of the ten angled sides was a sleek plane of glistening black, covered with column on column of minute characters or hieroglyphs in a language unknown to me, though naggingly familiar. They in no slightest way resembled hieratic or demotic Egyptian, or any other form of writing I could remember having ever seen. I later copied some of them down in my notebook and can reproduce a few specimens here:

The professor reverently turned the metallic block over. "This side in particular," he said in a low voice.

I stared at the weird, stylized profile figure of a monstrous thing like a hideous bird with staring eyes and a gaping beak filled with fangs. There was a stark ugliness to the depiction that was quite unsettling.

I looked up at him, a mute question in my eyes.

"*Groth-golka,*" he breathed.

* * *

WITHIN the week we departed for the States. Nor was I at all loath to go, for all the excitement of our excavations and the discoveries they had unearthed. To tell the truth, ever since that night I had first set eyes on the Black Stone, I had not been sleeping at all well. A touch of jungle fever, perhaps, but night after night I tossed and turned, my dreams a mad turmoil of frightful nightmares ....

One night in particular, after I saw the Stone, I again dreamed of Zimbabwe as it might have looked at its height: the sacrificial smokes staining the sky and obscuring behind lucent veils the white face of the leering moon as it gloated down on scores of writhing blacks bound to the stone altars, grotesquely masked priests leaping in a wild and savage dance ....

I knew that they were trying to call down from the stars some monstrous horror-god, but how this knowledge came to me I cannot really say. Then the moon was hidden by black, flapping shapes that circled and swooped like enormous fishing-birds, darting down to the altars to pluck and tear at the wriggling bodies bound there ... and one of the huge, queerly deformed-looking bird-things emerged into the moonlight, and I stared with unbelieving horror at its hulking, horribly quasi-avian form, clothed with scales not feathers ... one glimpse of the repulsive thing with its one leg and glaring Cyclopean eye and hideous, hooked, fang-lined beak—

I woke screaming, with a bewildered Mayhew shaking me by the shoulders, demanding to know what was the matter.

No, I wasn't unhappy to be going home: I had had more than my fill of the sinister brooding silence of that thick, fetid jungle, crowding so ominously close to the ruins as if waiting, waiting ... of that horribly old stone city, whose mysterious past contains hideous secrets I did not wish to plumb ....

The reason for our abrupt departure was quite easily explained. It would seem that Professor Mayhew had found what he had been looking for. The discovery of the Black Stone from Zimbabwe would make him very famous—and his fame would be all the greater, of course, were he able to decipher the inscriptions.

For he, as well, had half-recognized them. My vague, teasing recollection of having somewhere once seen something very much like those queer glyphs tormented me; I could neither pin it down nor could I get it out of my mind.

It was Mayhew, however, who remembered where he had seen symbols very much like them, and the moment he spoke of it I felt certain that he was right. The *Ponape Scripture*! I must have seen the glyphs reproduced in some Sunday supplement article about the cryptic old book. But the professor, of course, had studied the actual *Ponape Scripture* itself, in its repository at the Kester Library in Salem, Massachusetts. He had examined the actual book, written in an unknown tongue, and had compared it against the debatable English version prepared by Abner Exekiel Hoag's bodyservant, a Polynesian half-breed from the isle of Ponape.

Mayhew hoped to find, somewhere, somehow, the key to the unknown language. On the boat, he fretted over that, sending radio-telegraph messages.

"Churchward would know, if he were alive, I'm sure of that," he muttered. "His *Naacal Key* has never been published, but I have seen his speculative work on Tsath-yo and R'lyehian. Somewhere among his notes there might be data on this Ponapian glyph system, whatever it is called ...."

One night, as we neared the coastline, he burst into my cabin, triumphantly waving a piece of yellow paper.

"Churchward's widow has given me permission to borrow his unpublished notebooks and papers!" he crowed, face unhealthily flushed, eyes bright with excitement. "A chance, at last!"

Privately, I doubted it. But I kept my reservations to myself.

We disembarked and went immediately to Salem, where the professor had reserved rooms for us at the University Club. The next morning, leaving me to unpack our notes, records, and sample artifacts, he was off to await the arrival of Churchward's papers. For days he pored through them in growing exasperation, for the author of *The Lost Continent of Mu* and other dubious works of pseudoscientific speculation had known nothing of the unknown language, it seemed.

"What about Hoag's papers?" I suggested. "Perhaps his servant left a glossary or something; I know it was back in the seventeen hundreds, but still, since the *Scripture* is right here at the Kester, perhaps they hold the remainder of his library, as well."

His eyes flashed and he smote his brow with a groan, dislodging his pince-nez from their perch. "A splendid idea, young fellow!" he cried. "My intuition on hiring you was right."

The next day, I accompanied the professor to the library, where his scholarly credentials quickly gained us access to a private reading cubicle and to the strange old book itself. While he pored over it eagerly, I regarded the volume with thinly disguised repugnance. I recalled what little was known of its curious history: The famous "Yankee trader", Abner Exekiel Hoag, of the Hoags of Arkham, had discovered the ancient book on one of his rum-and-copra trading ventures in the South Seas, back in 1734.

It was a weird document of many pages, inscribed with metallic inks of several colors on palm leaf parchment sheets, which were bound between boards of archaic wood, carved with grotesque designs ... the very reek of the ages rose from it, millennia made almost palpable, like the miasma of age-old rottenness ....

I had read what the famous Pacific archaeologist Harold Hadley Copeland had written of the book in his own shocking and controversial *The Prehistoric Pacific in the Light of the* Ponape Scripture, which only increased my repugnance. Poor Professor Copeland, that once-brilliant and pioneering scholar, had developed an uncanny fixation regarding the so-called "lost continent of Mu" which some occultists and pseudoscholars, like Colonel Churchward, consider to have been the original birthplace of humanity—the "Atlantis of the Pacific."

Suddenly I became aware that Mayhew had turned upon me a glittering eye, bright with excitement.

"What is it, Professor?"

"Sloan, my boy, it's here ... many of the identical symbols we traced and copied from the Black Stone! See—" he indicated several of the symbols on the crumbling, half-decayed sheets of leather-tough native parchment, "here—and here, and—here!"

"Odd that you didn't recognize them at once, when you first began making your tracings from the Stone," I murmured inanely, searching for something to say. He shrugged, restlessly.

"I only glanced over the original codex," he explained, "as I was more interested in the English version ... but look: I have tried as best I could to match the hieroglyph to the English text, with the following conjectural result—"

I glanced at the sheet of scribbled notepaper he brandished before me. I do not recall all of the symbols or their meanings, but of the three symbols I drew earlier in this statement, the first stood for the name or word "Yig", the second for "Mnomquah," and the third for—

"*Groth-golka!*" Mayhew breathed, almost reverently.

For some reason, I shuddered as if an icy wind were blowing upon my naked soul.

* * *

THE Curator of Manuscripts at the Kester Library was Professor Edwin Winslow Arnold, a chubby-faced man with a cherubic smile and piercing blue eyes. He had obviously heard of my employer and knew somewhat of his academic reputation, for we found no obstacle in our path which would prevent us from examining the miscellaneous diaries and papers of Abner Exekiel Hoag. A large number of these were in the Massachusetts Historical Archives, of course, but these could hardly be expected to contain the information Professor Mayhew desired. The documents which related to the *Ponape Scripture* were in the "sealed" files, and were made available only to reputable scholars.

Within a day or two, Mayhew found what he was looking for, in the form of a battered, water-stained notebook obviously kept by Hoag's man, Yogash. This Yogash was the bodyservant Hoag had "adopted" in the Pacific islands, a Polynesian/Oriental half-breed of some kind (weirdly there filtered into my memory a bit of nonsense poor mad Copeland had recorded in his book, *The Prehistoric Pacific*, in which he conjectured that this mysterious Yogash person might be, in his inexplicable phrase, "a human/Deep One hybrid", whatever *that* might mean).

Yogash had kept a workbook in which the English equivalents, often marked with an interrogation point in the margin, perhaps to indicate that the equivalency was dubious or uncertain, were aligned with columns of minutely inked glyphs. This was the key to the language of the *Scripture*, by perusal of which Mayhew hoped to be able to translate the secrets of the Black Stone.

"They are all here," gloated Mayhew, peering enthusiastically over the blurred, stained pages of the old notebook. "Nug, and Yeb, and their mother, Shub-Niggurath ... Yig and Mnomquah and Groth-golka himself—"

"Are these the gods of some Pacific mythology?" I hazarded.

"So they would appear to be, from their prominence in the *Ponape Scripture*," he murmured abstractedly.

"But—if that *is* true, then, how do you explain their recurrence on the other side of the globe, in the depths of South Africa?" I cried.

The Professor peered at me over his pince-nez.

"I cannot explain it," he said finally, after a moment's silence. "Any more than I can explain how virtually the same characters found on the Easter Island Tablets, whereof Churchward wrote, appear in the Mohenjo-Daro inscriptions, found in the northerly parts of India."

"Churchward was an occultist of sorts," I protested. "His reputation as a scientist has never been taken seriously!"

"Nevertheless, the Easter Island Tablets exist—you can find excellent photographs of them in back files of *National Geographic*, without needing to search more deeply into the scholarly periodicals. And I trust you are aware of the veracity, if not of the significance, of the inscriptions found at the site of Mohenjo-Daro?"

I nodded, my resistance to his arguments subsiding. But—how could this mystery be explained, save by postulating some worldwide prehistoric race or network of religious cults which have hitherto eluded the attention of scholars?

Baffled, I turned to other tasks, abandoning speculation.

* * *

WITH the help of the amiable Dr. Arnold, Professor Mayhew and I had clear and distinct photographic copies of the notebook made for further study and comparison with the inscriptions on the Black Stone, since obviously the Kester Library could not permit Yogash's notebook to leave the premises, as it was a part of the Hoag papers.

For days and weeks we compared the symbols, jotting down a rough rendering into English. The grammar and punctuation, of course, had to be supplied by the professor and myself, as it was not possible to deduce from the notes of Yogash what equivalents of these were in the unknown language of the *Scripture*. From a study of the notebook, many bits of data came to light which meant little to me at the time, but which excited the professor tremendously.

"So!" he exclaimed one evening, "the language is neither any known form of Naacal, nor is it R'lyehian or even Tsath-yo ... I had rather conjectured it might be a form of Tsath-yo ... but, no, Yogash refers to it in six places as 'the Elder Tongue' and in two places as 'the Elder Script'—"

"I've heard you mention that word 'Tsath-yo' before," I interjected. "What exactly does it refer to?"

"It was the language of ancient Hyperborea in prehistoric times," he muttered offhandedly.

"Hyperborea?" I exclaimed, skeptically. "The polar paradise of Greek mythology? I believe Pindar refers to it in—"

"The conjectural name—lacking a better one!—for a polar civilization which was the presumed link between elder Mu and the more recent civilizations of Atlantis, Valusia, Mnar, and so on. Although Cyron of Varaad, in his brief *Life of Eibon*, does indeed suggest that the first humans migrated from foundering Mu to Valusia and the Seven Empires, and Atlantis as well, then in its barbaric period, before traveling north to Hyperborea ...."

I could make little or nothing of these rambling explanations, but filed them away for future reference. My concepts of ancient history, I perceived, were going to require some extensive revisions if I must include therein, as true and veritable cultures, such fairy tales as Mu and Hyperborea and Atlantis.

That night my bad dreams bothered me again, and I awoke soaked in cold sweat and shivering like a leaf in a gale. Across the room I saw the white moonlight bathing the eerily inscribed facets of the Black Stone, and suddenly I felt an uncanny and inexplicable fear. Or was it—*foreboding*?

* * *

BEFORE many weeks had passed, Professor Mayhew gradually came to understand the purpose and nature of the mysterious inscriptions on the Black Stone from Zimbabwe.

They were nothing less than litanies and ceremonials for the summoning—the "calling down", to employ the ominous phrase of the Stone's language—of the Fishers from Outside which were the minions and servitors of the dark demon-god Groth-golka. Odd, how my weird dreams had seemed to predict this very discovery, for those horrible nightmares which had plagued me from the first day I laid eyes on the accursed Stone had been of rituals whereby the hideously masked priests had seemed to call down from the nighted skies those horrible bird-things (the professor had discovered, in deciphering the Stone, that they were properly termed "shantaks")! But here I caught myself beginning to take almost for granted that one's dreams can actually presage the future.

As for the dark divinity they served, Groth-golka was presumed by this mythology to dwell beneath the "black cone" of Antarktos, a mountain in Antarctica, at or very near to the South Pole. (Of course, I am translating these concepts: The actual text calls it "the anteboreal Pole", and the name "Antarktos" was supplied by the professor himself.)

When he had gotten to that portion of the translation, he seemed to hesitate, to become lost in dreams. I asked him if all was well, if he felt ill; he roused himself with an effort, and gave me a shadowed smile.

"It is nothing; a momentary qualm. No, Sloan ... I called to mind a scrap of verse I have somewhere read—I cannot think just where—but the name *Antarktos* was attached to it—"

And in a low, throbbing voice, he recited these strange lines:

Deep in my dream the great bird whispered queerly
Of the black cone amid the polar waste;
Pushing above the ice-sheet lone and drearly,
By storm-crazed aeons battered and defaced ....

Something in his hushed, hoarse voice—or was it in those grim and ominous lines of verse?—made me shudder uncontrollably. I thought again of my weird dreams of that Plain of Megaliths, of those naked bodies bound for sacrifice, and of the semi-avian monstrosities as they swooped, and plunged, and clutched and clawed, ripping and tearing the naked, writhing meat staked out for them ....

And again that night I had ... unwholesome dreams.

* * *

TWO days after this incident—and fear not, officers, my story is very nearly done—the professor seemed to have concluded the major portion of his researches. That is, as far as I could tell he had finished deciphering the last of the summoning rituals of the shantaks cut deep on the slick metallic planes of the Black Stone.

"Sloan, I want you to go to the Kester today," he told me that afternoon, just when I had assumed our day's toil was done. "I will need the text of this part of the *Book of Eibon*—" and here he handed me a scrap of paper torn from his pocket notebook, with page numerals scribbled down. I gave him a surprised look.

"But surely the library is closed by this time, Professor, and I could make the trip tomorrow morning—?"

He shook his head. "I need the text of that passage tonight. The library, staff are on hand and qualified scholars with passes signed by Dr. Arnold should be able to gain entry without difficulty. Take care of this at once, please."

Well, there was no refusing such a request—Professor Mayhew was my employer, after all—so I left the University Club and caught the streetcar on Banks Street to the library. The sky was lowering and gray; a fitful, uneasy wind, chill and dank as a breath from the very grave, prowled amid the dry leaves of early fall as I hurried between the granite pillars and into the bronze gateway.

I found no difficulty in securing the *Book of Eibon* from the files and began copying down the passage which the professor required. It consisted of certain matter from the seventh chapter of Part III of the *Eibon*, a lengthy mythological or cosmological treatise called "Papyrus of the Dark Wisdom." The passage read as follows:

> ... but great Mnomquah came not down to this Earth but chose for the place of His abiding the Black Lake of Ubboth which lieth deep in the impenetrable glooms of Nug-yaa beneath the Moon's crust; but, as for Groth-golka, that brother of Mnomquah, He descended to this Earth in the regions circumambient to the Austral Pole, where to this day He abideth the passage of the ages beneath the black cone of Mount Antarktos, aye, and all the hideous host of Shantaks that serve Him in His prisonment, they and their sire, Quumyagga, that is the first among the minions of Groth-golka, and that dwelleth either in the nighted chasms beneath black Antarktos or in the less inaccessible of the peaks of frightful Leng; where also did great Ithaqua, the Walker Upon the Wind, take for His earth-place the icy Arctic barrens, and mighty Chaugnar Faugn dwelleth thereabouts as well, and fearsome Aphoom Zhah, who haunteth the black bowels of Yaanek, the ice-mountain at the Boreal Pole, and all they that serve Him, even the Ylidheem, the Cold Ones, and their master, Rlim Shaikorth—

It was with a distinct shock that I realized suddenly that there was nothing—*nothing at all*—in this Eibonic material that the professor and I did not already have recorded in our notes, and that the only explanation for my being sent on this false errand was to get me out of the way while the professor did—*what*?

* * *

SEIZED by a nameless premonition, I snatched up the papers on which I had copied the passages from *Eibon*, returned the old book to the clerk, and left the grounds of the library. Dark clouds had come boiling up over the horizon, drowning the long narrow streets in gloom. The wind blew from the north, cold and dank as the panting breath of some predatory beast.

Abandoning the notion of waiting for the streetcar, I hailed a passing taxi and rode back to the University Club. I had the horrible feeling that every moment might count against life or death, and yet I could not have told you what it was that I feared. There are certain times in our lives when knowledge comes to us by unknown paths, and woe unto him who ignores the warnings explicit in that foreknowing!

Tossing a crumpled bill at the driver, I sprang from the cab and raced into the building. Plunging up the staircase, I entered the rooms assigned to us, only to find no sign of the professor.

Even as I turned to descend the stair and to seek for Mayhew in the club library, there came to my ears a weird, ragged, chanting ululation from the roof directly above our rooms, and among the weird vocables I recognized certain words—

"Iä! Iä! Groth-golka! Groth-golka Antarktos! Yaa-haa Quumyagga! Quumyagga! Quumyagga nng'h aargh—"

These were the opening words of one of the summoning litanies to the shantaks, for I clearly recalled them from the manuscript of Professor Mayhew's tentative translation of what he called the "Zimbabwe Rituals." Then I knew, with a surge of cold fear that closed like a vise about my heart, that the professor had employed a mere subterfuge to get me out of the way while he went up to the roof and tried out the summoning litany ... and I cried out; I cursed the unholy curiosity of the scholar that would dare such an enormity.

Up to the roof I ran, stumbling over the stairs, and burst out upon the rooftop to see before me a scene of horror!

A dome of leaden clouds hid the sky as if some immense lid of gray metal had been clamped down upon the world from horizon to horizon. The wan luminance that filtered through the roiling vapors was a lurid, unnatural, phosphoric, sulfurous yellow. For a fleeting instant I was reminded of the skies over Zimbabwe in my dreams—the flaring bale-fires, the drifting smokes, the bird-masked priests, the leering moon—then I shrieked and saw—*and saw*—

Down they came, the semi-avian hurtling shapes, all slimy scales where feathers ought by rights to be, hippocephalic clubbed heads hideously grinning ... and hovered on scaly, translucent wings: hovered and swooped and dipped, to tear and tear at the shrieking scarlet-splattered thing that jerked and jiggled prone on the rooftop, wallowing in a bath of blood—that shrieking thing that I could never have distinguished as having once been human, had it not been for the one detail to which my shuddering gaze clung with unbelieving terror—*the blood-spattered pince-nez on their sodden ribbon of black silk, about the crimson ruin of what had once been a man's head.*

HERE is the first of a pair of tales which are more or less direct sequels to August Derleth's seminal Mythos story "The Return of Hastur." In fact, so close is the relation between them that "Behind the Mask" (which appeared originally in *Crypt of Cthulhu* #47, Roodmas 1987) almost fails to stand on its own unless "The Return of Hastur" is pretty fresh in the reader's mind. Here we begin to sense Lin Carter having said about all he had to say in the Cthulhu Mythos subgenre.

Too often Carter's stories have the failing of merely rehearsing hackneyed Mythos gimmicks which are just too familiar by now to frighten. When the veil is drawn aside and we see the same old stuff, well, the story kind of falls flat. Such stories are written with a strange obliviousness to reader response. The implied reader (i.e., the audience who seems to be in view) of such tales is a first-time reader, a Mythos novice. Did Lin (or Derleth, etc.) really believe the bulk of their readers fell into that category? I doubt it. Rather, what has happened is that the author is working too hard to open up an ironic gap between the reader and the narrator/protagonist. The wide-eyed recitation of Mythos data by the narrator/character who has just discovered it (Paul Tuttle, Arthur Wilcox Hodgkins, etc.) is not intended to educate us, the readers, about the Mythos. Just the opposite: These seemingly inevitable Mythos catechisms are intended to show us what novices these characters are, otherwise it would not be plausible for them to come to the nasty ends they do. They are ill-prepared for the challenge (even, apparently, after having learned all the Mythos data they throw at us!).

Tedious as these Mythos lectures are, they may be necessary; it may work. But what if the bulk of the tale is taken up with it, and even the climactic revelation is old news to us? I suppose we are being asked to see something familiar through new eyes, those of this Mythos greenhorn, and maybe we will experience a small share of vicarious horror. But this does not often seem to work. Instead, we are tempted to conclude: "Too bad! He should have checked with me first! I could have saved him some sanity points."

You will form your own judgment concerning this particular story, but I think Lin just manages to avoid the pitfall, or at least to climb back out of it momentarily, at the point of his description of the masked hierophant of Leng. Here he has taken the traditional picture just enough farther to make us do a double-take.

Behind the Mask

by Lin Carter

1.

IN July of 1928, the library of Miskatonic University in Arkham, Massachusetts, received a rare and unusual gift. It arrived as part of the Tuttle bequest, one of a number of suppressed works of occultism and demonology. The book to which I refer was known as the *R'lyeh Text*.

Dr. Cyrus Llanfer, the director of the library at that time, looked over the collection in a cursory manner before handing the volumes over to one of the junior librarians, a young man named Bryant Hoskins, for cataloguing. Some of the books were in printed form, such as the sinister *De Vermis Mysteriis* of Ludvig Prinn and von Junzt's *Unaussprechlichen Kulten*, while others were manuscript copies, often in fragmentary condition, such as the obscure *Book of Eibon*, the mysterious *Pnakotic Manuscripts*, and the *R'lyeh Text* itself.

Most of these rare works were known to Dr. Llanfer, if only by reputation. He was fully cognizant of the extraordinary rarity and priceless value of the bequest and he privately resolved to write personally to the nephew of the late Amos Tuttle, who had given his uncle's superb collection to the library. Admonishing his assistant to handle the precious volumes with care, he saw them safely stowed away.

Young Hoskins was less familiar with these little-known works than was Llanfer, but as a librarian by profession and a collector in a small way, rumors of some of these fabulous titles had filtered into his knowledge. The *R'lyeh Text* in particular interested him. He knew the curious old book had never been published in any language, having been circulated in manuscript form for generations, perhaps for centuries, among certain secret sects of occultists and devil-worshipers.

Despite his interest, he found the very appearance of the book oddly repugnant. Opening it, he was appalled at the reek of decay which arose from its crumbling pages. Mastering his repugnance, he examined it gingerly and found that, while the codex was written in English characters, the actual language was unfamiliar to him and bore little if any resemblance to the several tongues, ancient and modern, with which he was acquainted. It was inscribed in faded inks upon thick leaves of yellowed parchment which were flaking and crumbling, as if from curious morbidity. Here along the Atlantic coast, he knew, the damp salt air breeds mildew and mold which often attacks books and papers; the condition of the *R'lyeh Text*, however, stemmed from some other kind of decay which he could not at once identify.

While the odor of the disintegrating pages was bad enough, Hoskins found the binding repellent in the extreme. It was a tan or brownish leather whose soft, finely grained texture had an unwholesome resemblance to that of *human skin*. Some of the witch cults of the Dark Ages, he knew, had bound their hellish testaments and grimoires in the tanned skin of human sacrifices ... but, surely, this could not be the case with the *Text* ....

Everything about the queer old book repelled the young librarian and aroused a squeamish revulsion within him. Its aura of unnatural ancientry and inexplicable decay, the very odor which exuded from the rotting pages, the shuddersome *feel* of the soft, smooth binding, aroused a certain revulsion within the young man which he could neither deny nor quite explain.

It was as if some uncanny, seldom-awakened sense within his innermost being detected a frightful danger within the ancient book ... and was trying to warn him to leave it alone.

But this was sheer nonsense, of course.

2.

DURING the following weeks, Bryant Hoskins discovered quite a bit about the history of the *R'lyeh Text* and the other queer old volumes contained in the Tuttle bequest. The book in question had been purchased by the library's benefactor, Amos Tuttle, for a reputedly enormous price. He had got it somewhere from the dark interior of Asia, obtained from a Chinese priest or shaman in inner Tibet. There was some scandal or other connected with Amos Tuttle's acquisition of the *R'lyeh Text*: The less reputable newspapers of the time were full of rumors concerning queer and fearful things which had, supposedly, recently occurred in the old Tuttle house on Aylesbury Road near the Innsmouth Turnpike. There were hints of a ghastly sequence of events surrounding the death of Amos Tuttle, things too starkly dreadful *not* to be hushed up and quickly forgotten ....

To all such furtive and whispered horrors, Hoskins turned a deaf ear. He was a scientist first and foremost: a scholar, known for his lucid and rational intelligence, a man not given to poking into weird legends and stories based on flimsy or insubstantial evidence. Queer things were happening among the ancient, crumbling seaports of coastal Massachusetts these days which might have given him pause, had he bothered to listen much to the tales going about. Only a few months before, during the hard winter of 1927-1928, there had been mysterious goings-on in the neighboring town of Innsmouth. Agents of the federal government had apparently been conducting a strange and secret investigation of some sort in that vicinity, as a result of which a surprisingly large number of raids and arrests had been made in February of 1928, and certain blocks of crumbling tenements along the abandoned waterfront had been burned and dynamited. There were even stories that a U.S. naval submarine had discharged explosive torpedoes *down* into the marine chasms off Devil Reef, although sober and sensible local citizens dismissed this wild tale as mere rumor, or, this being the era of Prohibition, as part of the continuing battle against liquor smuggling.

To none of these fanciful stories did Bryant Hoskins bother listening. Doubtless, the government knew what it was doing, he reasoned. Equally certain, whatever events had actually taken place in Innsmouth had been expanded by whispered rumor entirely out of all proportion to the facts.

What fascinated him about the old book was the mysterious language in which it had been originally written, and the reason why the redactor of this particular copy had rendered the strange tongue into English characters. The only conceivable reason was so that it might be read or chanted aloud by persons or cults to whom the original glyphs or characters would otherwise have been illegible.

Among the letters and papers of the late Amos Tuttle were references to a portion of central Asia known as *Leng*. Whether or not Leng was part of inner Tibet was unknown to Hoskins, nor could he find reference to it in any of the standard atlases or geographical works to hand. One of his former teachers at Miskatonic, however, had heard of Leng in one or another shadowy old Asian mythology.

"Yes, of course, the so-called 'shunned and forbidden' Plateau of Leng, where the Ancient Ones supposedly ruled long before the first men evolved; you will find information concerning it in Alhazred," his teacher friend remarked. Alhazred, Hoskins vaguely knew, was the author of a work called the *Necronomicon*, and the *Necronomicon* was another of the old, little-known books which the Miskatonic Library possessed. It was, in fact, one of the library's chief treasures.

"Who were these Ancient Ones?" he inquired interestedly. "Some pantheon of Asiatic gods?"

"Demons, rather, I should say," commented the other. "In Alhazred they are called the 'Old Ones', or the 'Great Old Ones', in contrast to the leaders of their minions, whom Alhazred names as the 'Lesser Old Ones'—Dagon and Hydra, Bokrug, Rlim Shaikorth, and so on."

These names meant nothing to Hoskins at the time, of course.

3.

AMONG the copies of Tuttle's letters, Hoskins found several addressed to the Gupchong Lamasery on the fringes of northern Tibet. These letters entreated that a sealed document be carried by hand through the mountain passes into Tcho-Tcho country and delivered, if possible, to someone or something called "the Tcho-Tcho lama." Hoskins' informant, an enthusiastic amateur anthropologist and student of folklore, had information about this item, too.

"The Tcho-Tcho people are a tribe in Burma," he explained. "Some authorities consider them purely legendary; supposedly, their cultus is centered in the ruins of Alaozar in the Sung Plateau region ... nobody knows what's there, I'm afraid. Only the Hawks Expedition got that far, and you know what happened to *it*."

"But Burma is not beyond the mountain passes of northern Tibet, but entirely in another direction," argued Hoskins. His informant nodded.

"I said the Tcho-Tcho people were *centered* in the Sung Plateau country. Actually, they are a religion, or at least a cult, found scattered through the mystic heart of Asia. Since they worship the Great Old Ones, it's not surprising to find a Tcho-Tcho lama in the Plateau of Leng. All that country was under the dark dominion of the Old Ones ... in the Alhazredic mythology, that is."

"What kind of a place is Leng?" Hoskins asked.

His friend shook his head. "Cold; barren; dead—sterile. Nothing lives there. Nothing *could* live there. The place is under the eternal curse of the Elder Gods, that is, the beneficent divinities opposed to the evil demons called the Old Ones."

"If nothing lives there, how do the Tcho-Tcho survive?" Hoskins persisted. He could tell that, for some reason, his colleague was uneasy at continuing this conversation. He couldn't guess why.

"I meant that nothing *human* lives there, or could live there," his friend said in oddly hushed tones. "I never said the Tcho-Tcho were human." With that strange comment, Wilmarth abruptly terminated the discussion. He left Hoskins puzzled and unsatisfied, and more intrigued than ever.

Nothing human ....

4.

HOSKINS succeeded in identifying the original language of the book as "R'lyehian." This proved to be a mythical tongue spoken only in R'lyeh itself, which was a lost city sunken under the sea like Atlantis. But R'lyeh was believed to have been submerged beneath the Pacific Ocean, not the Atlantic, and this in itself was a curious item of information, since at the time Hoskins now thought the *Text* to have been transliterated into English letters, the first explorers had yet to reach the Pacific.

Following Wilmarth's advice, he consulted the *Necronomicon*. To his surprise, he found therein a sentence or versicle directly quoted from the *R'lyeh Text*; it was as much a jumble of unpronounceable consonants and vowels as the rest of the *Text*, but with a certain difference.

The line read: *Ph'nglui mglw'nafh Cthulhu R'lyeh wgah'nagl fhtagn.*

The difference lay in the fact that in Alhazred the sentence was actually translated. It meant: *In his house in R'lyeh dead Cthulhu waits dreaming.*

This very line Hoskins found in the *Text*, very near the beginning. In fact, it was on the third page of the bound manuscript. What seemed important about this to Hoskins was that, obviously, the R'lyehian language was, or had been, known and understood, or otherwise neither Alhazred nor anybody else could possibly have translated it. But the language had no direct connection to any Arabic or Arabic-related language whatsoever; this Hoskins learned by consulting a linguist in the Eastern Languages Department of the university.

What most excited Hoskins about this point was that Tuttle himself had scribbled a marginal note on the third page where the line appeared. In a crabbed hand, he had written what appeared to be his own translation of the cryptic sentences: "His minions preparing the way, and he no longer dreaming?" The marginal gloss was followed by other scribbled notations whose meaning so eluded Hoskins that he dismissed them.

The implications of the marginal entry were astounding. It could only mean that Amos Tuttle *himself* knew, or could at least partially decipher, the mysterious language of ancient and legendary R'lyeh. That meant that somewhere among Tuttle's papers, Hoskins might conceivably find a glossary or dictionary of R'lyehian, with whose aid Hoskins himself could read the strange old book.

At this point it becomes obvious that the young librarian had developed an unhealthy fixation on the mysterious volume and yearned to penetrate its hidden lore. Had his superior, Dr. Llanfer, been aware of this development, he doubtless would have swiftly put an end to Hoskins' work with the *R'lyeh Text*. Busied with other matters, however, he unfortunately remained oblivious to the strange fascination which the old book exerted on the young scholar.

A search through the Tuttle papers proved fruitless. Further perusal of the *Necronomicon*, however, provided Hoskins with a remarkable discovery. The passage which contained the information read as follows, in the Elizabethan English version by Dr. John Dee, the notorious British wizard and astrologer, and comprised the entirety of Chapter xvi of Book III, the "Book of the Gates":

> *Of Leng, and the Mysteries Thereof*: Concerning this Leng, 'tis said by some to lie in Earth's dreamlands to be thus only visited in sleep by power of the Sign of Koth, but I have heard yet others tell that it lieth afar off in the frozen wastes of the anti-boreal Pole, and there be those that hint of Leng that it may be found within the black and secret heart of Asia. But, while many differ on the place thereof, I have heard no man say aught of Leng that is wholesome to the ears of men.
>
> Now of this Leng, 'tis written that in that dark and frigid land many worlds meet, for it is coterminous with dimensions alternate to our own; and amidst those bleak, untrodden sands, and frozen hills, and black and horror-haunted peaks, there be strange Portals to Beyond; and Things from Outside that sometimes stray through the Gates to stalk through earthly snows, returning thence to Their unknown and nameless Spheres, glutted on horrid feasts whereof I dread to think upon. So they say: but, as for myself, I believe me well that cold and frightful Leng as much be part of other worlds as part of this, and representeth but a half-world, as it were, a bridge between the worlds.
>
> They say of old ventured Ilathos there, a wizard of Lomar, beyond the Bnazic Desert and through the Vale of Pnor, taking great care to avoid the dreadful Vaults thereof, and that in time he came upon a crude stone tower amidst the Waste wherein there dwelt from of old a certain Priest whose unseen visage went ever veiled behind a mask of yellow silk. It is written upon the Cylinder of Kadatheron that long they conversed together there in that lonely and ill-rumored tower, the Lomarian mage and Him they call the Elder Hierophant, but of that which was spoken all record has been expunged therefrom, and the Cylinders of Kadatheron are blank, and no man knoweth why.
>
> But I have not seen Leng in all my wanderings or travels, save only in my dreams, and but repeat here the idle tales which others have hinted at within my hearing. He who would know the secret of Leng, he who would plumb the mysteries of Leng, he who would walk the bleak and lonely paths of Leng, let him venture thereunto if he knoweth the Way.

Hoskins stared at the page of the *Necronomicon* filled with a strange, tremulous excitement that he could neither name nor explain. That night he had the first of many dreams ....

5.

It was in the early days of September that Bryant Hoskins at last found that for which he had searched so assiduously. Amos Tuttle had, after all, compiled or perhaps copied from some other source a "R'lyehian Key" (as he had entitled the document); the reason why Hoskins had not found it before was that the glossary had been bound toward the end of a volume of miscellaneous pieces which bore the overall title *Celaeno Fragments*.

As it was not permitted to remove volumes from the "locked files" of the library, Hoskins rashly purloined the book, concealing it among the papers in his valise. Later that night in his rooms in Darley Street, he studied the Key with trembling hands. He had long ago copied out extended portions from the *Text*; now he compared the unknown words to Tuttle's glossary. In particular, he compared those lines upon the third page of the codex which began with the enigmatic phrase which earlier had caught his attention.

The entire passage contained only seven lines divided into three verses. Hoskins recopied them upon a blank sheet of writing paper, leaving a space between each line, and laboriously attempted a full translation with the use of Tuttle's "R'lyehian Key."

When he was finished some hours later, the page read as follows:

> *Ph'nglui mglw'nafh Cthulhu R'lyeh wgah'nagl fhtagn.*
> (In His House at R'lyeh dead Cthulhu waits dreaming.)
> *Y'ai 'ng'ngah cf'ayak shugg-yaah Cthulhu nafl fhtagn.*
> (But in the Hour which cometh when Cthulhu no longer
>   waits dreaming,)
> *N'gha-uaaah 'nygh glag'ng aargh-cf'ayah y'haa mgl'gn.*
> (Then let the world beware the coming-hence of its Master.)
> ***
> *Ygnaiih! Ygnaiih! S'sathagua dy'uth aiih-cf'ayagh!*
> (I rise! I rise! Up from the depths I come!)
> *Mgw-ygna! Mgw-ygna! S'sathagua mglw'nafh ph' R'lyeh!*
> (He rises! He rises! Up from His House in R'lyeh!)
> *Mgw-cf'ayak! G'ngah mglw' aargh-cf'ayah n'gh yafl.*
> (He cometh! The Hour of His coming-hence is at hand.)
> ***
> *Ygnaiih! Aiih-cf'ayagh-ngwa! Uaaah 'nygh sh'uggua mng mgl'gn.*
> (I rise! I come forth! Let the world tremble before its Master.)

Hoskins stared at the result of his labors, curiously rapt with a fascination such as he had never felt before. It seemed to him that he was on the brink of recovering an incredible trove of wisdom lost for centuries or ages.

To his surprise, he noticed that it was dawn. He had toiled all night over the "R'lyehian Key", not even noticing the hours as they raced by. No wonder he was shaking with fatigue and exhaustion!

That day he did not report to work at the library, pleading a temporary indisposition. Instead, he slept the deep sleep of physical and nervous exhaustion.

And again there were dreams ....

6.

ON previous such occasions, the dreams of Hoskins had been filled with dark desert landscapes framed with sharp-fanged peaks whereon untrodden snows gleamed palely beneath the cold eye of the peering moon. His dreams were tumultuous with glimpses of crumbling slopes of awesomely ancient stone, the parched and wrinkled floors of prehistoric seas—grim and frightful vistas which reeked of bleak desolation, barrenness, utter sterility and absence of life.

Now during his day-long slumber, Hoskins dreamed of a squat, ugly turret or tower crudely cut from dark porous stone, which stood alone in a frightful waste. Darkness hung over this scene, nor could even the curious eye of the inquisitive moon penetrate the sky, obscured as it was with a film of lowering vapors ... but, now and again, rifts appeared in the clouded firmament, wherethrough glittered icily stars.

Not the known, familiar stars and constellations that Hoskins knew from his childhood: No, these weird stars were formed into constellations unknown to him yet strangely *meaningful*, as if they shaped enormous symbols vaguely familiar to his dreaming intellect. The sensation was one of unearthly strangeness; yet it was also hugely portentous, as if vast realms of knowledge were contained in those starry symbols which he could—*almost*—discern.

Of the stone tower amid the desolation he could make out few details, so gloomy was the umbrage which shrouded its rearing bulk and so obscure and fitful the wan luminance shed by those unknown constellations. There radiated from the uncouth angles of that squat, misshapen tower a cold and timeless malignancy ... an implacable and cunning hatred of ... of what? Of living things? Of life itself, perhaps?

In an upper, circular window of the turret-like tower, a ruddy light came and went, like unto the revolving beam of a lighthouse. There drifted through the dreaming brain of Bryant Hoskins a cryptic phrase he had come across in the mad pages of the *Necronomicon*—

The Elder Pharos ....

Odd, how in dreams the mind picks up wisps and shards of scattered memories and fits them together into a new pattern whose significance, upon awakening, we dismiss.

He woke in twilight, pervaded with a curious languor, as if made weary by his own dream-venturings.

7.

DURING the weeks that followed, Bryant Hoskins paid scant attention to his duties at the library, devoting as many of his waking moments as he could possibly do to translating the whole of the *R'lyeh Text*. Tuttle's glossary proved flawed and many of the meanings Tuttle had recorded Hoskins replaced with more correct definitions ... although how he came by them even he could not have said. Intuition, perhaps.

Gradually, however, the pattern of meaning buried in the mysterious language began to emerge into view. The *Text* was a melange of chants and prayers, litanies and incantations to several divinities which bore names like Cthulhu, Idh-yaa, Zoth-Ommog, Ubb, Ghatanothoa, Ythogtha, Dagon, Hydra, and Yeb. These were all, it appeared from the context, elemental spirits of the waters of the earth, demon-godlings of the sea. They were, he deduced, severally imprisoned at various sites along the ocean's floor— Cthulhu in the sunken stone city of R'lyeh, his son Ythogtha at Yhe, Zoth-Ommog in a submarine abyss near the "Island of the Stone Cities" (a term which, for some reason, again perhaps intuition, reminded Hoskins of the island of Ponape, with its colossal ruins of Nan-Matal), and Ghatanothoa in a sealed crypt atop the submerged mountain of Yaddith-Gho.

Each of these sea demons was served by tribes of minions, Cthulhu by the deep ones whose leaders were "Father Dagon and Mother Hydra"— names, of course, familiar to Hoskins from earlier reading. For example, Dagon was the sea god of the Philistines and Hydra a monster-goddess from Greek mythology. Ythogtha and Zoth-Ommog, on the other hand, were served by a race called the Yuggs, whose leader was Ubb, "Father of Worms"; and Ghatanothoa had the dark ones as his servitors, under their leader, Yeb.

These last three, it seems, were the sons (or "spawn," as the *R'lyeh Text* phrased it) of Cthulhu himself, sons which he had begotten in forgotten aeons upon the final member of this grim pantheon, Idh-yaa. According to what Hoskins was slowly piecing together from these rituals and incantations, these entities had all descended to this earth from the stars when the world was newly made, long ages before the rise of humankind. All of them, apparently, except for Idh-yaa the Mighty Mother, who abided yet upon a distant star or world called "Xoth", which was her natal place, as Cthulhu himself had been spawned upon another world called "Vhoorl."

It was difficult to know exactly what to make of this weird mythology, which dealt with such advanced cosmological notions as distant galaxies and travel through the dimensions. Indeed, it sounded like the scientific romances of H. G. Wells which Hoskins had devoured in his 'teens, or like some of the stories he had glanced at in the pages of a pulp fiction magazine called *Amazing Stories*, which had begun appearing on the newsstands only two years before.

And there was another mystery.

Not every night, to be sure, but often enough for their frequency to become vaguely frightening, Hoskins in his dreams returned again and again to those bleak and gloom-shrouded vistas of a frigid, desolate wasteland he had come to think of as *Leng*. And to within sight of that misshapen and lonely tower, that squat and crudely carven turret, which brooded on the plain, ever casting its flicker of ruddy luminance from the upmost circular window ....

What could this dead plateau have to do with the tombs of imprisoned gods upon the floor of the Pacific? Why did his sleeping brain—as apparently it did—draw a connection between a frozen and lifeless plateau and the black sea-bottoms? Was it only because of his knowledge that Amos Tuttle had bought the old book from the dark and cryptic heart of Asia, through the medium of a Chinese priest in a lamasery on the northern borders of Tibet?

The "Tcho-Tcho lama" ... *was* he one and the same as the "Elder Hierophant" mentioned in the *Necronomicon* in the chapter on Leng ... the nameless one whose face was forever hidden behind a mask or veil of yellow silk?

One possible connection between Leng and the Pacific which had already occurred to Hoskins had been casually mentioned early on by his former literature instructor at Miskatonic, the amateur folklorist and anthropologist, Professor Wilmarth.

The shunned and forbidden Plateau of Leng, where the Ancient Ones supposedly ruled long before the first men evolved .... Wilmarth's very words echoed unforgotten in Hoskins' memory.

The "Ancient Ones" were the same as "the Great Old Ones", and Cthulhu and his spawn were great powers among the Great Old Ones, he knew from his research in the pages of Alhazred. If they came down from the stars so long ago that the first men (or first *mammals*!) had not even evolved, perhaps the plateau or desert of Leng had been then submerged beneath the primal seas of that age ... and, also perhaps, Cthulhu and his spawn and their minions had ruled the prehistoric world from Leng, before the seas drained away and the dry land emerged, whereupon they migrated to the vast Pacific—well, it wasn't much of a theory, but it did satisfy Hoskins in that it answered the problems and contradictions which baffled him, and which robbed him of his rest.

Something else was robbing Hoskins of his rest during those last weeks of September and early October, 1928. *His dreams* ....

Ever, the same recurring dream ... that blank and desolate expanse of sterile, frozen waste ... that squat and ugly stone tower thrusting against the weirdly deformed constellations ... that circling, bloody beam of light that flashed and flashed and ever and again flashed from the topmost circular window.

In his dreams, night after night, Hoskins floated bodiless across the plateau ... and always, when the dream-spell broke and he awoke, shaking like a leaf and drenched in icy perspiration, *he had come ever nearer to the portal of the tower.*

What might happen when the dream-sequence ended he could not guess, but he feared it mightily. For something within the tower aroused in him a primal sense of fear ... an inarticulate and dreadful *loathing*.

Desperate to find surcease of dreams, Hoskins purchased opiates from pharmacies in his neighborhood, and even consulted a physician, Dr. Ephraim Sprague, who came highly recommended. Dr. Sprague listened to Hoskins' rambling account of his nightly excursion into dreamland without comment, his expression wryly skeptical, and prescribed a sleeping powder which proved as ineffective as the opiates Hoskins had already tried.

The doctor must have told Hoskins' superior at the library something of his condition, because the next morning Cyrus Llanfer called the young man into his office, inquired sympathetically about his health, and suggested a brief vacation.

"I've noticed you seem drawn and haggard recently, as if you weren't getting enough rest, Hoskins," he said. "You seem run down, as if your nerves were bothering you. These New England winters can be dangerous for someone with as little resistance as you seem to have, so ... what do you say? A few weeks in a warmer climate, eh? Do you a world of good!"

Hoskins left Dr. Llanfer's office, trembling uncontrollably. He couldn't recall just what he had said by way of counter-argument, and on the whole he rather feared he had become belligerent, almost hysterical, and certainly rather incoherent. But—the very thought of breaking off his work at this point filled him with a cold and depthless horror ... he was so close to the Ultimate Secret which he knew was concealed within the *R'lyeh Text*, that to break his concentration by accepting a vacation now would be disastrous.

He hoped that he had neither insulted nor affronted Dr. Llanfer, but—couldn't the senile old idiot see that the world *needed* the wisdom he would soon be able to bestow upon the multitudes of hapless mankind?

If needful, he would steal the *Text* itself, as he had already stolen the "R'lyehian Key", and flee from Arkham and from the interference of others. There was a cabin in the woods that had belonged to his father, and where the family had vacationed during the long summers of his boyhood ... it would provide a perfect refuge in which he could complete his work without being pestered by meddling outsiders ....

If only he could find surcease from those terrible dreams as easily!

8.

DURING the late fall of 1928, Bryant Hoskins fell into a serious decline. The nervous affliction which he suffered from soon became blatantly obvious to everyone. His features were drawn and haggard, his eyes bloodshot, his form wasted as from some debilitating disease.

In part, this was assigned to the insomnia which, it was believed, he suffered from. In actuality, of course, it was Hoskins himself who strove to refrain from sleeping ... because of those ghastly dreams which now preyed upon him almost nightly ... those dreams in which he floated stealthily nearer and nearer to that horrible stone tower which brooded enigmatically amid the wastes of frozen Leng.

When neither the panaceas available at the pharmacy nor the medicines prescribed by Dr. Ephraim Sprague availed him in his struggle to cease dreaming, Hoskins turned to certain furtive folk who lurked in disreputable dives along the rotting waterfront of Arkham—dark, foreign men who purveyed obscure narcotics from squalid bars and fetid alleyways.

These drugs, indeed, kept him from dreaming, but at a grisly price. For his strength declined even as his mind lost its wonted lucidity, and his health began to crumble. Cognizant of Hoskins' rapid decline, Dr. Llanfer finally insisted that he take the undesired vacation he had earlier offered. Hoskins could only accept, but he stole the *R'lyeh Text* and vanished into the thick woodlands to the north of Arkham.

The New England winters were hard and cruel in those parts, and backwoods farmers were often snowed in for months. Hoskins brought with him, therefore, sufficient supplies of food and coffee and kerosene for the stove, together with clean clothing, blankets, and writing paper. That very night, his first in the little cabin in the woods, the snow fell heavily; when he awoke from a dreamless sleep at dawn, it was to find himself completely isolated, surrounded on all sides with a smooth field of unbroken snow.

The isolation, however, was exactly what he most desired. Not Dr. Llanfer nor any other could pester him here ... here he could accomplish his great work, which was to translate the whole of the *R'lyeh Text*, and to reveal its secrets to the ignorant and unsuspecting world.

One thing, however, Bryant Hoskins had forgotten in his haste. The narcotics he had purchased from the furtive, foreign men in the crumbling dives along the waterfront would soon be exhausted ....

9.

ON the night of November 11, 1928, lacking the drugs which alone could protect him from his dreams, Bryant Hoskins fell at last into an exhausted slumber toward dawn. No longer able to resist the urge to sleep, he took the precautions of putting a tablet and a pencil by his bedside, so that he could, upon awakening, record the substance of his dreams—a practice into which he had fallen.

The note found later by his bedside, scribbled by a hand so palsied as to be virtually illegible, reads as follows:

> Again, the dreary waste, the opaque skies, the uncanny stars! Nearer than ever have I drifted, unto the very portal of the stone tower. The doorway looms before me, the lintel thereof inscribed with signs carved into the crumbling stone ... signs which I cannot read, but which I have seen in the frightful pages of the *Necronomicon*.
>
> The door itself is a massive slab of stone through which I pass unopposed, and unwilling, as if helplessly borne along by some invisible current of force. Unresistingly, I enter a dark chamber whose gaunt, bare walls are hung with woven tapestries depicting hideous shapes lording it over groveling naked human slaves.
>
> Against the further wall of this chamber (which is frigid as the Pole, and pervaded by an unclean stench of indescribable foetor) a Being sits, or squats, or lolls, in an ancient chair of carved black wood. Larger and more corpulent than the common run of humankind, its curiously misshapen limbs and torso are swathed in robes of lustrous silk. Behind these garments I sense a body oddly deformed, perhaps with more limbs than are normal, or with limbs of multiple jointage.
>
> The face of the being is entirely hidden behind a veil or mask of yellow silk, through which nothing of the visage thus concealed can be discerned. But I notice, even in the paralysis of ultimate horror which freezes my mind and will, that the silken mask *twitches* oddly, and bulges in the wrong places. ...
>
> I do not wish to know what the face of the Tcho-Tcho lama looks like. But, against my numb and frozen will, the hands of my dream self reach out to pluck the mask aside—

Those were the last words written by Bryant Hoskins.

10.

BY mid-November, it was discovered that the *R'lyeh Text* had been purloined from the locked shelves of the Miskatonic Library, and that another volume from the Tuttle bequest, one known as the *Celaeno Fragments*, was also missing. In light of the fascination these two books had exerted on Hoskins, it did not take Dr. Cyrus Llanfer very long to deduce who had appropriated the two books. Hoskins' landlady, Mrs. Mullins, quickly divulged the location of his cabin in the woods; as the priceless volumes were the lawful possessions of the Library, Dr. Llanfer had no other recourse but to inform the local authorities of the theft.

Two constables were dispatched to recover the stolen property. They found the country roads nearly impassable due to the heavy snows, but managed to reach the cabin.

What they found within was then immured in the County Sanitarium, safely locked up in a padded cell. It laughs and howls and sometimes weeps, but when it speaks, which is seldom, it only repeats the same phrases over and over.

"... The face! ... the face! ... Those putrid holes where eyes are wont to be! ... that pink and squirming tentacle-like proboscis, where a face should have a nose and mouth and chin ... and the *laughter*, the mocking and malignant, gurgling *laughter* ... God! God! *How can a thing laugh without a mouth?*"

The thing in the cell died raving the following spring, in early March of 1929. The stolen books were returned to the locked shelves of the Miskatonic University Library, and very, very seldom does Dr. Llanfer permit even established scholars to consult them.

In explanation of this, he says, quite simply, "There are some things man is not meant to know, and some books man is not meant to read." Perhaps he is right, after all.

SURELY the most outrageous absurdity in the history of weird fiction (and let's hope it *is* history by now) is the story which ends with the narrator writing his last words as he is being dragged away by a monster. I don't know which ending is more stupidly hilarious, that of Lovecraft's "The Diary of Alonzo Typer", Frank Belknap Long's "The Hounds of Tindalos", or Robert Bloch's "Notebook Found in a Deserted House." All commit the same mortal sin: When the narrator finds himself abruptly overtaken by the horror, his last act is to continue to write, even if he finds himself so petrified as to be unable to flee. Had the doomed narrator actually been writing down the tale up to that point, surely the narrative would have broken earlier, and we would be left to guess why. Since the author (e.g., Lovecraft, not Alonzo Typer) fears that would not allow for sufficiently definitive closure, "the sense of an ending" (Frank Kermode), he must venture some way of letting the reader hear the other shoe drop. There are better ways. Hence the kindred device of a subjoined note from the authorities: "The foregoing narrative was found tightly rolled and stuffed up the rear of the late occultist Poindexter P. Poe."

A genuine effort to maintain the suspension of reader disbelief would leave the jagged edge of the "unfinished" account, thus keeping open the vital ambiguity of "the fantastic" (Tzvetan Todorov), whereby we are left forever suspended between the mundane possibility and a suggested but unverified supernatural explanation. For an example of a Lovecraftian tale that does dare to go the way Todorov has marked out, see Jorge Luis Borges' "There Are More Things" in his collection *The Book of Sand* or in my forthcoming anthology *Acolytes of Cthulhu* (Fedogan & Bremer). The general reluctance to leave the loose ends dangling strikes me as yet another confirmation of Käte Hamburger's contention that first-person narrative fiction is essentially a deceptive attempt (formally if not intentionally, of course) to hijack the literary form proper to autobiographical nonfiction. The fictive character of the work finally betrays itself by insistence upon a resolution within the text, something characteristic of fiction and notoriously absent from reality, which is why we love to take refuge in fiction and try to model our lives on this or that particular story (Don Cupitt, *What Is a Story?*).

It is this same anxiety for a finale that has led many writers to try their hand at supplying an ending for a fragment left unfinished by an author. Why did Lin Carter leave "The Strange Doom of Enos Harker" dangling? Perhaps he just never got around to finishing it. Perhaps he felt he had come to a dead end. Nonetheless, proverbially, the author's own judgment is often the last we should accept about his work, and reading the substantial fragment, I can see a number of arteries severed that may be sewn back together, so that the story may live again. So now let us see if we can rescue "Enos Harker" from a premature burial and keep him going long enough to meet with the doom appointed him. For those purists among you, Lin's fragment ends with section 5, and my continuation picks up with section 6.

The fragment in its unfinished state was first published in *Crypt of Cthulhu* #69, Yuletide, 1989.

The Strange Doom of Enos Harker

by Lin Carter and Robert M. Price

STATEMENT OF PAXTON BLAINE

1.

IN 1931 I graduated, with modest honors, from Miskatonic University in Arkham, Massachusetts, and for some months thereafter sought gainful employment without success. It was my intention to continue my studies and seek a degree upon the completion of my thesis, which was concerned with obscure cult survivals in certain parts of the East. Very much research remained undone, however, and employment in those Depression years was scarce and seldom remunerative; since I required part-time employment, my search was futile.

At length, however, I noticed an item in the personal columns of the *Arkham Advertiser*, placed therein by Dr. Enos Harker. He offered a comfortable subsistence and free room and board in his home for a private secretary able to organize his notes and prepare a manuscript for publication. The opportunity seemed nothing less than a godsend, and I applied forthwith.

Dr. Harker had rented a seaside house, barely more than a cottage, on Cairn's Point. Once a fashionable oceanfront resort for the wealthy merchants and older families of the seaport town, the neighborhood was largely deserted by now, and even rather desolate. But the streetcar connected the suburb with the downtown area, and it was not difficult to find my way.

My potential employer was an unusual figure of a man in his late sixties, I assumed. Inclined to corpulence, he affected a severe clerical suit of drab black, and even a clerical collar. I soon discovered that he was, or had been (I never quite learned which), a preacher in one of the more obscure of the Pentecostal sects—a missionary, in fact, who had spent many years in India and parts of Burma and Tibet. Portions of his face and hands were curiously swathed in surgical bandages, and he informed me at our first meeting that he suffered from a skin condition similar to scrofula or eczema, for which a local physician was treating him. It was this disability that necessitated the hiring of someone to handle the paperwork, for I gathered that it was his hands which were most seriously affected by the disease.

"Blaine, Blaine," he murmured, with a slight, thoughtful frown. "I wonder if you are by any chance a relative of Dr. H. Stephenson Blaine of the Sanbourne Institute for Pacific Antiquities, in Santiago, California?"

"I have that honor," I acknowledged, "for he is my uncle."

"Excellent, excellent!" Dr. Harker made reply, in that oddly hushed, almost whispering voice of his, which made me wonder, a bit squeamishly, if his peculiar affliction had not somehow affected his vocal cords as well as his face and hands. "I have read a monograph or two of his. A scholar of some reputation, I believe."

Our conversation soon terminated. Dr. Harker seemed to be satisfied with my credentials and I was, as I have already stated, happy with the terms of his employment. I was to begin my work the following Monday. We parted and I returned to my small flat on Parker Street in a mood of considerable elation.

Over the following weekend, it occurred to me that perhaps it would be wise to look up my employer in the various reference works available in the library at Miskatonic, which I did. He had been a graduate of the Byram Theological Seminary in Kingsport, had traveled and lectured widely, and, as I have already remarked, had spent many years as a missionary in the East. An amateur anthropologist of some note, he had published a number of papers on certain aspects of Asian archaeology and upon certain of the cults of the Far East, which interested me greatly, as my own interests, of course, lay much in that area of study.

Apparently an explorer of some repute, he had penetrated into portions of inner Asia seen by few white men, and had been one of the first to explore the ruined stone city of Alaozar in the Sung region of Burma. He had also traveled extensively, it would seem, in the more northerly parts of Tibet.

All of these things made me certain that we should enjoy a mutually profitable and interesting relationship.

Why, then, did I feel an uneasy qualm that warned me to shun this unusual personage?

A qualm almost to be named as ... *fear?*

2.

MY tasks were simple enough, and did not require extensive labor. Until his progressive disability had robbed my employer of the fullest use of his hands, he had been compiling notes toward a scholarly work of great length and complexity. It became my primary duty to organize these items of information into some sort of order, to take down by dictation further data as he gave it in his soft, weak voice, and also to journey to the library of Miskatonic University and the Kester Library in nearby Salem for further research.

Many of the books I delved into for this purpose were tomes I had already consulted in the course of preparing my own thesis. I refer to certain volumes such as the *Unaussprechlichen Kulten* by the German occultist von Junzt, the Comte d'Erlette's *Cultes des Goules*, von Heller's *Black Cults*, the original German text of the *Unter-Zee Kulten*, and the heavily expurgated treatise, *Le Culte des Morts*. I had also to look into the abhorrent pages of the old *Necronomicon* of Alhazred for certain references to a singular corpse-eating cult in a place called Leng.

This particular volume is as notorious as it is rare, and its rarity is nigh fabulous. Generally kept under lock and key, my connections among the faculty of the university gave me free access to the damnable volume, although some of the ravings I glimpsed within its thickly written pages were to haunt my dreams thereafter.

In general, my employer was seeking references to a cult or tribe called the "Tcho-Tcho people", rumored to linger on in certain of the more inaccessible parts of jungled Burma and in Leng—wherever Leng was supposed to be, for I could not find it in any atlas. They were believed to worship gods or devils with names like "Zhar" and "Lloigor", but so little about them was known for certain that many authorities seemed to consider them to be merely legendary.

I was also to search for any and every reference to Leng itself; to a certain Tcho-Tcho lama who veiled his visage behind a mask of yellow silk and dwelt in a "prehistoric" stone monastery; to Inquanok, which seemed to be both a people and a place, the place being adjacent to the plateau of Leng; and to certain sea divinities or maritime demons with uncouth, unpronounceable names like "Cthulhu", "Idh-yaa", "Zoth-Ommog", "Yeb", "Ghatanothoa", "Ubb, Father of Worms", "Ythogtha", and so on.

None of this research was particularly demanding of my time, but it was oddly disturbing. This was not only because my own researches had led me to many of these same sources, but because of certain events in the recent past which were still whispered of by the townspeople, but which had been hurriedly hushed up in the newspapers—the effect being that no one quite knew whether they were wild fables or contained a germ of horrible truth.

What really happened in the old Tuttle house on Aylesbury Road near the Innsmouth Turnpike, and why was the account published in the local papers so oddly cursory? For what reason did federal agents dynamite and burn several blocks of decaying waterfront tenements in nearby Innsmouth back in the winter of 1927-1928, and why did a U.S. naval submarine discharge torpedoes into the underwater chasm off Devil's Reef? And what really happened to poor Bryant Hoskins in that cabin in the woods to the north of Arkham, that led to his death as a raving madman in the County Sanitarium in March 1929?

Nobody really knew; or, if they knew, they didn't speak of it.

And why was Enos Harker so interested in this obscure, damnably ancient mythology?

3.

SOME of the information I extracted from the old, crumbling books excited my employer to a pitch of feverish intensity. For example, I returned from one such trip to the library at Miskatonic with two quotations which seemed to me to be little more than innocuous, but which kept him up all night, pawing through his sheaves of notations with those bandaged hands of his, muttering under his breath, the visible portions of his features flushed with unhealthy and febrile exultation. For the sake of me, I could not guess why!

The first passage from the *Necronomicon* read thusly:

> It was from fabled Sarkomand the Tcho-Tcho people first came into the Waking World, that time-forgotten city whose ruins bleached for a million years before the first true human saw the light of day; and its twin titan lions guard eternally the steps that lead from the Dreamland into the Great Abyss, wherever Nodens reigns as Lord, and the Night-Gaunts that serve Him, under dread Yegg-ha, their master.

The second was a fragmentary ritual, apparently quoted from another source, which went thusly:

> Aye, was it not written of old in R'lyeh that the Deep Ones await their followers, and we must not fail to be present at the Great Awakening? It is written that all shall arise and join with them, we who carry the Emblem and those who have merely looked upon it. From the ends of the earth cometh the Summons and the Call, and we dare not delay. For in watery R'lyeh Great Cthulhu is stirring. *Shub-Niggurath! Yog-Sothoth! Iä!* The Goat with a Thousand Young! Are we not all Her children?

When I delivered these notes to Enos Harker he virtually snatched them from my hand, holding the pages close to his face (for his eyesight had recently grown weakened, perhaps due to the progressive degeneration caused by his disease) and scanned them with fierce intensity.

"Of course!" he mumbled in that weak voice of his. "From Sarkomand they came ... all the way to the Sung plateau, to build their ghastly stone city in the jungles! I should have guessed it from—" but here his voice broke off and he glared at me with wary suspicion, almost as if he thought me spying upon some private thing. Then he went into the screened front room, which faced the beach, to scan the notes in private.

When I retired, a little past midnight, his light was still burning.

4.

IT had by now become quite obvious to me that my employer's health was failing very rapidly, although I still did not understand the nature of his complaint. I knew that a local physician, a Dr. Sprague, had been treating his scrofula—or whatever it was—with zinc ointment and with a substance called cortisone, then generally unavailable, as it was still in the experimental stage of being tested and had not yet been released to the general market.

None of the medications seemed to halt the spread of the skin condition. In addition, his features became bloated and puffy, and his person, which had been normally corpulent when I had first begun working with him, soon became grossly obese. He had difficulty in walking at times, and gradually the white bandages spread over his swollen, pasty visage until he was virtually masked with bandages, like an Egyptian mummy. There was also a peculiar *smell* about him that was singularly repulsive ... a nauseating stench, as of sea-water gone foul and rancid, or like the bloated, rotting corpse of some marine creature exposed to the harsh air and the cruel sun.

But perhaps I exaggerate. The cottage stood so close to the empty, deserted beach that the salt wind penetrated every part of it, and the reek of the stagnant seawater in the tidal pools and among the gaunt rocks filled my nostrils night and day.

Harker became increasingly dependent upon me for many of the small necessities of everyday life. It was no trouble for me to ride my bicycle into the edge of town and buy groceries, nor to wash the dishes and remove the garbage and handle his bills as already I was handling his correspondence.

This correspondence ranged all over the world, for Enos Harker was continually in touch with certain scholars in places like France, Peru, India, and even China, who had made a special study of the weird old mythology that had become his life's work. This mythology, by the way, had as its central belief the notion that the earth had been visited by strange and demonic intelligences from other worlds and galaxies, and even from beyond the universe itself, from the very remotest of ages, long before the evolution of humankind. Not being made of matter as we know it, these "Ancient Ones" or "Old Ones", as they were known, were deathless and unaging.

Aeons before man, they were pursued to this part of space and time by their former masters, a race known only as the "Elder Gods." A titanic conflict ensued, and at its terminus, the Elder Gods were victorious over the rebels who had been their former servants. Unable to destroy the Old Ones, they imprisoned them with powerful spells—and, in particular, with a potent talisman called the "Elder Sign"—and in their charmed imprisonment they, presumably, rage and roar to this latter day, for all the world like Fenris the wolf and the Midgard serpent in the Norse legends.

They are served, even in their imprisonment, however, by their minions or subject races, few of which are to be considered even remotely human. The devils which mostly concerned Enos Harker were the sea entities, Cthulhu and Ythogtha and the rest; their minions are called the Deep Ones and the ancient books of this system of superstition describe them shudderingly as huge and bloated things, half frog-like, half fish-like, partly squamous and partly rugose, with ghastly protuberant eyes, and gills.

The Tcho-Tcho people, also among his prime interests, are followers of another group of divinities, not sea elementals at all. They are associated with the "shunned and evil" plateau of Leng, which some texts discuss as though located in "the black heart of Secret Asia", and elsewhere mentioned as near the South Pole. This doubtless makes as little sense to the reader of this statement as it did to me at the time.

But there was an uncanny *coherence* to all of this. On the surface it seemed a mad, chaotic jumble of nightmarish legend, but underneath it all was a basis of something sinister, age-old and time-forgot ... but hideously *suggestive*.

For who would expect myths centuries, even millennia, old to concern themselves with intelligent creatures from other planets, distant stars, remote galaxies, or weird dimensions beyond the three we know?

5.

MOST of the correspondence concerned a particularly rare book called the *R'lyeh Text*, for which my employer was searching with a furious need that went far beyond mere scholarly or scientific curiosity, and approached the proportions of a fixation.

Copies of this curious old book, while rare, were not unknown; indeed, several redactions (for the book had never been printed and existed only in manuscript copies, furtively circulated between the members of obscure cults) were to be found right on the closed shelves of the library at Miskatonic. The problem was that, while the *R'lyeh Text* was written in the letters of the common alphabet, the language itself was no longer known or understood. It apparently consisted of rituals or invocations to the devil-gods of this mythology, which were read or chanted aloud by their worshipers; hence they needed only to be able to pronounce the uncouth verses, but did not really need to understand what they meant.

Few scholars, if any, could read the "R'lyehian" language, and it was for one of those that Enos Harker was so desperately searching ....

I have previously alluded to the strange mystery surrounding the death of Bryant Hoskins, who died in a madhouse in 1929. While the case attracted considerable attention in the public press, the authorities seemed to have hushed the whole affair up, but it had taken place so very recently, that there were still people about who possessed information concerning what had really happened in that secluded cabin in the woods to the north of Arkham.

By purest chance, one day about six months after I began my employment as the secretary of Enos Harker, a clue to the mystery came to light. A muckraking journalist on one of the less reputable Boston papers began digging into the case and turned up a sensational story which most people, I suspect, dismissed out of hand as wild speculation.

One item of information emerged from the newspaper story which sent my employer into a frenzy of excitement. Young Hoskins had been employed at Miskatonic in the capacity of private secretary to the director of the library, Dr. Cyrus Llanfer. In July of 1928, the library had received, as part of the Tuttle bequest, not only a priceless copy of the *R'lyeh Text*, but a document in what was believed to be Amos Tuttle's own hand called the *R'lyehian Key*. The very existence of the *Key* went unnoticed for some time, until Bryant Hoskins chanced upon it by accident. It had been bound at the end of another manuscript volume, something called the *Celaeno Fragments*.

It would seem that the late Amos Tuttle had been one of those few scholars on Earth who was still able to decipher the mysterious, ancient language in which the *R'lyeh Text* was written, for his *R'lyehian Key* was none other than a glossary of the ancient language, together with some speculations on verb forms and grammatical structure.

Hoskins, who had become fascinated by the mysterious *Text*, spent the last months of his life translating it into English. The labor had broken his health, both in mind and body, but when he was taken away to die raving in the asylum, the manuscript of his version of the *Text* was salvaged from the cabin.

According to the reporter's account, the "Hoskins Translation" now reposed in the secret shelves of the Miskatonic University Library.

Thither I went, bright and early, the very next morning.

6.

I WAS ushered into Dr. Llanfer's office and he greeted me amicably enough, for we had had dealings over the past few months, during which my employer had sought access to the *Necronomicon* and other books. While these abhorrent old volumes are strictly forbidden to the general public, they *are* accessible to qualified scholars. Moreover, I was by this time well acquainted with Dr. Llanfer, so I imagined I should encounter no difficulty in gaining access to the Hoskins translation. I was in for a surprise.

"Mr. Blaine," the white-haired archivist said to me with a troubled note in his weary voice, "come with me if you will." He motioned me to follow him into the Special Collections room, then through a double-locked door. Proceeding across the carpeted floor to a metal set of shelves, he unlocked this, too, and displaced two or three metal strongboxes of various shapes and sizes (some of which could hardly contain books, I mentally remarked). He turned toward me with one of these metal cases, unlocked it, and opened it as gingerly as if he were a lion tamer parting the jaws of a ferocious beast.

"Here it is. Not much to look at, is it? Just a set of scribbled notes on pad paper not a year old. No ancient artifact, though God knows we house enough of those. This is the translation you're looking for. I have no plausible pretext under which to bar you from reading it, though I half-wish I did! This text has meant madness and death to at least three men of my own acquaintance. And so far as I know, all they did was to read it. As for myself, I have not perused its contents, not even after young Mr. Hoskins made reading it so much easier. Do not misunderstand me. I have the love of learning, of recovering lost knowledge even as these men did. But unlike Amos and Paul Tuttle and Bryant Hoskins, I do not have a suicide urge. I hope that you do not have it, either."

Taken aback by this monologue, I scarcely knew how to reply. "What of Dr. Harker? It is he who has sent me. I am only his emissary. If the book is not available to him, it will be my duty to tell him so. This I will do without qualm. But you must realize that he will not rest until he has had a chance to consult that book. Especially since, as you say, you can hardly deny a qualified scholar access to the official holdings of the library."

"Yes, all that you say is quite true, Mr. Blaine. Quite true. Only promise me that you will play your role as disinterested stenographer well. Read and transcribe what you must. But hold it within you only as long as it may take you to get back to Harker's home and tell him. I fear he has already progressed too far down his path to be helped. And it would be cruel to prolong his agony. May the forbidden knowledge of the text of R'lyeh deliver the inevitable blow swiftly and mercifully. Here. Take what you need."

I proceeded to avail myself of Dr. Llanfer's oddly grudging generosity, intimidated by now at the prospect of whatever shocking revelations I should meet with. What could a mere text, however ancient and recondite, contain? I opened my notebook and commenced jotting down the greater part of the translation, feeling more and more a sense of anticlimax the further I went. At long last, after a couple of hours, I finished my task with something akin to a sense of disappointment, almost as if I had failed to find something I had sought within the text. Of course, I had no idea what it was my employer might be looking for. I knew not whether he should recognize whatever he sought in these strange litanies, nor whether disappointment might not be better than satisfaction, given Dr. Llanfer's manifest opinion of the ancient screed.

When I returned to Dr. Harker's manse that evening, it was plain he had been waiting with intense agitation, for he fairly grabbed the notebook from me and, without a word, turned and closed the door of his study. I was half-minded to linger just outside and listen for any demonstrative reaction within, but I rebuked myself for such juvenile scheming and retired for the night.

My curiosity had by now reached a zenith, its fires only banked by the silence in which the old clergyman shrouded the whole business. He only grew less and less communicative as his baffling condition worsened, seeking to make himself understood chiefly by monotone mutterings and waves of his bandage-mittened hands. Yet even such charades as these made it evident to me that somehow we were running a race against time. Was it a race to attain some goal, still unknown to me? Or was the race to escape some frightful doom worse even than the physical debilitation that seemed rapidly and steadily to be consuming him? Strictly speaking, it was no business of mine. Certainly Dr. Harker never sought to share his burden with me.

I had more than an inkling that the reticent Dr. Sprague knew more than he dared say. He approached his ministrations with what appeared to me a hint of fear, though mixed with a greater dose of resignation, this made no sense to me at the time.

On one occasion I had exchanged pleasantries with the elderly physician as I made to leave the house and make another bicycle trip into Arkham to consult again the volumes in the university library. Upon learning my destination, Dr. Sprague offered to drive me into town on his way back. I felt some revelation to be at hand, but as it happened I was disappointed. As he seemed to expect, I asked him about the precise nature of my employer's mysterious malady. Contrary to my own expectation, he had little to tell me.

"Beyond the physical symptoms which are as evident to you as they are to me, I can only say that what plagues Dr. Harker is something more in the nature of a *spiritual* affliction." He plainly wished not to discuss the matter at greater length, but I had the very definite feeling that he had meant by his cryptic words to warn me of some danger. Could the old missionary's pestilence be somehow contagious?

7.

AS the days passed, I began to mark new symptoms plaguing Dr. Harker, chiefly an inability to sleep through the night. Though he denied it, it was clear that nightmares were displacing his nocturnal respite. Once I believed I heard him chanting one of the Psalms, as if to ward off his nightly nemesis: "He giveth to his beloved sleep ...."

Once his agitation passed over the line into actual screaming, and of such urgency as to awaken me, asleep as I was at the opposite end of the house. He himself remained asleep, and seemed to calm somewhat as I crept softly to his bedside, knowing that, despite my good intentions, such an invasion of his privacy might lead to my immediate dismissal. But I had to be sure the old man was all right. His breathing had slowed somewhat, but I noted that his nightmare flailings of a few moments previously had disarranged the gauzy wrappings of his face. The disturbance was but slight, and yet what I saw disturbed me profoundly. I have said that Dr. Harker had been quite plump on my first sight of him and had, with the progress of his disease, continued to bloat in a most unwholesome fashion. This I vaguely attributed to the side effects of some medicine he must be taking, since otherwise one would expect advancing degeneration to shrink and wither the body. Nothing I had seen prepared me for what I saw now.

His face, which he had lately taken to veiling almost completely, was partially visible, and it had suffered shocking disfigurement. His eyes were almost totally obscured by grotesquely swollen puffs of blue-veined pasty flesh. His nose, which admittedly I had never seen unswathed, seemed to have expanded to an astonishing degree. Here the change was not due to swelling—the very structure seemed to have been altered, the bridge oddly broadened, the nose itself, still covered at the top, absurdly elongated. His hair, always thin and wispy, was mostly gone, some of it visibly scattered around the pillow.

Though I felt utter repulsion, my curiosity was stronger still, and I actually found myself reaching hesitantly to pull away yet more of the loose bandaging. As I stood frozen with indecision, startlement shook me: The muffled voice spoke. "It appears I am found out. But I think you have discovered enough for one night." As he spoke, he made to rearrange his futile disguise, and he sat up.

"I am most sorry to have disturbed your sleep, my young friend. Return to your bed. I doubt that sleep will return with you, but try to get some rest.

We will talk, and talk plainly, on the morrow. I would have taken you into my confidence ere now, save that I feared you might become drawn into the web that holds me fast." With that, he turned his obese form over on its side, shaking the bed frame as he did.

There was nothing more to be said for the moment, so I turned and found my bed again. I resigned myself to some sleepless hours before the dawn and gazed out of the window to the cold white orb of the moon, which, I fancied, looked down upon secrets it knew but, like the intimidated Dr. Sprague, would not, or perhaps dared not, reveal.

Yet, despite my shock, I fell asleep almost at once. As if the moon had been the swaying watch of a hypnotist, I seemed to have passed without noticing into a dreaming state. The wan, bluish radiance of the lunar disc seemed to narrow and to gather in intensity. It seemed even to go on and off periodically, though at very long intervals, as I watched and watched, seemingly for endless hours. The contrast with the surrounding darkness was great, so that the strange light illuminated nothing but itself. I seemed to know that the unseen landscape was not that which I would recognize in the light of day. As with a false memory, I felt I knew the lay of the shrouded land and that it must be a vast, bleak mountainous plateau. With equal tacit certainty I felt that the light I watched was set to guide the path of someone or something on its way home.

With this ... glimpse, I awoke to find the sun streaming on my face. Ordinarily I should have awakened with the light much sooner, and I found I shook off Morpheus with unaccustomed difficulty. I arose, showered, and dressed with a lingering sense of oppression. At the same time I eagerly anticipated whatever Dr. Harker might have to tell me. It was with some distraction that I made my way through the assigned tasks of the morning. My researches had come increasingly to seem like a charade. Of what import could fine points of exegesis of obscure old texts possibly be in the face of my employer's obviously impending collapse? Mustn't there be more significant things I could do to make his remaining weeks or days more pleasant? I resolved to make the suggestion whenever Dr. Harker should summon me. The day waned, and I suspected the old clergyman's lack of sleep had taken its toll, and that I should have to wait till the next day for our promised conversation.

To my surprise, the buzzer sounded in the library to summon me to his bedside at 9:45 in the evening. I rose with haste and paced rapidly to his door, knocking before I should venture to enter. Some moan from within I took as my invitation and turned the handle, opening the door into almost total darkness. After what I had seen the previous night, I did not wonder at the reason.

A tired but surprisingly steady voice began to recount the strangest tale I had ever had occasion to marvel at. It is possible the disorientation I felt was due in some measure to the altogether unaccustomed tone and timber of what should have been a familiar voice. I could not imagine what tumorous occlusions could have grown so quickly so to affect his formerly clear and rather comforting voice. I will report as accurately as I can what the doomed man confided in me, as there no longer seems to be any point in keeping it to myself. The essentials are right, I am sure of that, though I will hardly blame you if you wish to accuse me of exaggerating.

8.

ENOS Harker entered into the study of divinity at Byram Theological Seminary rather later in life than most of his classmates, having felt a dramatic "call" to the ministry in early middle age. Previously he had earned a wide reputation as an explorer, amateur archaeologist, and lecturer. Rather in the manner of Richard Haliburton, he would regale lecture-hall audiences with titillating exotica and tall tales from far corners of the globe. In fact, it was while returning to his hotel from one such engagement that his life had changed forever. While crossing town, he had felt strangely drawn to one of the storefront congregations of a small Pentecostal denomination. What attracted his attention was the sound of the sobbing hymns and shouted "prophecies" emerging from behind the painted glass of the large windows that had once displayed merchandise in the days before the neighborhood had run down. Wandering through the door and down the central aisle, he knelt with the circle of moaning seekers in what revivalists call a tarrying meeting.

Suddenly the Holy Ghost struck one of those present like lightning. She seemed to explode into almost orgasmic ecstasy, her arms flung skyward, her head thrown back, and unleashing a torrent of nonsense syllables, what Harker would learn was called "speaking in tongues", ostensibly divinely inspired oracles in genuine foreign languages unknown to the speaker in a normal waking state. Harker watched in growing alarm and yet unable to turn away. One by one, all those in the circle succumbed to the spittle-spewing frenzy, as if electrically wired in series, until it finally and ineluctably reached him.

When, in the wee hours, Harker found himself back outside on the street, he was a changed man. He began to pore over the scriptures, the copy provided him by the elders of his new religious fellowship. Not the King James Version, this Bible had been newly translated by the founder of the sect, himself under prophetic inspiration.

He returned to the shabby sanctuary every night for the next month or so, his speaking schedule forgotten and his conviction of new purpose and new destiny reinforced and focused. One midnight, the sweating, straining knot of believers, their hands clasping him about the head and shoulders, began to shudder and sway, and one of them blurted out a prophetic declamation. Brother Enos, it announced, had been set apart by the Lord to take the Full Gospel message to foreign climes as a missionary.

This duty the earnest new convert did not shirk. The sect was tiny and militant, eschewing, as is the manner of such conventicles, any cooperation with other churches varying from their own doctrine by the slightest degree. By themselves the sect, its name a jumble something like "the Fire-Baptized Temple of the Apostle of God", had neither the numbers nor the resources to maintain a theological college or a missions board. Thus his attendance at the staid Byram Seminary, theological training being a prerequisite for any reputable missionary agency.

The years of dreary dogmatics, homiletics, and biblical languages did little to dampen the fires of Enos Harker's zeal, and upon graduation and ordination he lost no time in choosing his mission field. In truth, it was not really his choice, the location being divulged to him, as he assumed, by the Holy Ghost during a dream. His destination would be a little-known recess of darkest Asia, a place of which he had never heard, a high and airless plateau called Leng.

Dr. Harker did not pause to explain how he managed to gain the cooperation of a missionary agency to journey to such a remote outpost without demonstrating any competence in the local languages. I gather, however, that with the mountain-moving (some would say "fanatical") faith of the Pentecostalist, he simply dared to believe that the "gift of tongues" would suffice him, that when the moment came to speak the words of the gospel message, the Holy Ghost would quite literally supply the words.

He knew it would be no easy thing even to gain access to his goal. He knew how the first Christian missionaries to China and Tibet were cruelly tortured and martyred, but should this be his eventual fate, he would not shrink from it, welcoming the martyr's crown for the glory of his Lord. He had then imagined, you see, that such might be the ultimate sacrifice in the service of God. He was later to discover horrors far worse.

As the night grew deeper at the old man's bedside and I found myself, ironically, taking the role of father confessor, I was no longer so certain I cared to plumb the mystery further, but I knew it was too late to withdraw. I had the curious feeling that something more ominous awaited me than even the severest shock a mere story, even a true one, might deliver.

Enos Harker's reading while in theological school had been wider than the narrowly prescribed list of standard works drawn up by his professors. Before his abrupt conversion it had of course been wider still. He knew that other Westerners had managed to penetrate into the secret heart of Asia without molestation. Showing the proper respect for a culture in which they were visitors, and which they plainly admired, pilgrims like Madame Alexandra David-Neel and the artist Nicholas Roerich had actually been welcomed and given generous freedom in the usually off-limits regions north of the Himalayas. But they had come to learn the esoteric wisdom of the East, and he had come for quite a different purpose: to teach and to preach the glad tidings of the Holy Ghost. Still, if he came as a holy man seeking out holy men, he was sure he could make himself understood, and that he might even find a ready hearing. Such was his faith.

Dr. Harker, whose wasted constitution forbade him to enlarge upon any point not absolutely needful to relate, passed over the no doubt colorful details of the long sea voyages and difficult treks over land by the most primitive conveyances. He never expected divine inspiration to make it any easier to arrange for transportation or knowledgeable guides without him knowing the tongue-twisting languages of the many tribes and clans along his path. His earlier, purely secular travels had given him a facility for making connections, and somehow he made his way to the shunned Plateau of Leng.

Then a man of hardy physique and robust health, he had found the climb up to the frigid tableland a bracing challenge. He had picked up a smattering of Tibetan and Nepalese phrases necessary to make certain rudiments understood, but his grasp of these languages utterly failed him to understand the sudden reluctance of his guides and bearers to complete the journey up and across the plateau itself. Apparently the man who had hired them for the missionary had withheld the fact of their ultimate destination in order to get them to agree to go even this far. So all fled him. This, too, thinking of the missionary travails of Saint Paul, he took in stride.

On he pressed, finding that the way to his object was after all clearly marked, at least at night, when, from a distant structure, vague against the mist-shrouded horizon, there emerged periodically a beam of light like a beacon, he assumed, to welcome distant pilgrims to a place of holy retreat. As soon as he saw it he thought of Moses and of how God had guided the children of Israel through the wilderness as a pillar of fire by night. The redoubtable Dr. Harker took it as a good omen.

It took several days to cross the plateau, the total flatness of the place robbing him of any sense of distance. He trudged on for hours, but the squat complex of buildings never seemed to get any closer, until all at once it loomed on the horizon. Structures began to dot the blasted landscape as he approached. Most were the broken teeth of once-proud pillars and obelisks which bore wind-eroded carvings. Upon examining one of these in the light of his lamp, Dr. Harker found long vertical columns of letters remotely resembling Tibetan, of which he had seen quite a bit during his recent journeys. But this was not precisely Tibetan. Subsequent research would disclose that what he had seen was a linguistic ancestor of the Naacal language of fabled Mu. Alternating with these mute stelae were queer carvings of unrecognizable marine creatures, some of which suggested nothing so much as the submarine behemoths of the Permian Age. But surely these glyphs had represented no actual models, but only recounted heathen myths native to the region. Still, it was singularly improbable for marine motifs to occur in the religion of a plateau in the mountainous heart of Asia.

A stiff wind suddenly blew up from out of nowhere and pummeled the intrepid missionary as if Aeolus himself would prevent him from nearing the grim pile of brooding buildings. Harker, however, had an inner drive of his own and would not be kept from his destiny. He pressed on indefatigably. He had nearly reached the nearest of the buildings, a low, unadorned structure made of huge stone blocks that had so settled together and been smoothed by the howling winds of countless generations that they seemed almost the natural mass of a megalith. Then, without warning, a pair of stocky humanoid shapes loomed up through the ubiquitous gloom that seemed to hold daylight forever at bay. The men, for such they must have been, were completely swathed in great fur cloaks and cowls against the ripping talons of the plateau wind. They accosted the weary traveler, whether in hostility or in rescue, he could not yet surmise, and half-guided, half-carried him the rest of the way into their compound. Though the windy torrent whipped away their words like autumn leaves in a hurricane, Harker believed he caught the word "Leng."

He remembered little else until he awoke inside a dimly lit cell whose only illumination came from a small butter lamp on the floor in a corner. Of comfort there was none, save for a threadbare yak hide beneath him, which hardly softened the naked stone floor. For a moment he feared he had been consigned to some already-forgotten dungeon reserved for any so foolish as to violate the chaste isolation of the place. Then he realized the inhabitants must be a monastic fellowship of ascetics, and that they had no doubt assigned him quarters no more Spartan than their own. He resolved to try to communicate his gratitude for their rough-hewn hospitality—provided he ever saw another of his hosts.

9.

SEVERAL days might have passed. The absolute silence, together with the lack of any hint of sunlight, made it impossible for him to gauge the passing of time. Sometimes when he would awaken from a longer or shorter period of sleep there would be a meager portion of food awaiting him, which he gratefully consumed.

Then one day, he guessed some two or three months later, he awoke to find himself not in his accustomed cell, but in the center of a circle of silent, seated forms in a large meeting hall. Butter lamps provided the only light here, too. None of the shapes could he see distinctly. It was disorienting to behold a robed figure seeming to sit or recline, then to begin to move laterally without rising. Movements were few, and bodily outlines were mostly obscured by generous folds of draping cloth, but something in the perspective suggested that occasional arm or hand motions presupposed the wrong anatomical angles.

Once in a while, there were low exchanges of unfamiliar words, though sometimes he could not be sure whether they were sounds of intelligent conversation he heard, or rather the hypnotic drone of distant insects. The ring of the men of Leng held thus for some hours, apparently in the performance of some spiritual exercise.

Looking about him at what little the soft hazy light revealed, Harker was taken aback to notice what looked like a shadowy dais off to one end of the low but vast chamber. Atop this structure, which seemed imperceptibly to merge with an outcropping of stalagmites rising from the natural stone floor, there sprawled a shifting heap of living matter. Upon this figure Harker tried now to focus, hoping that as his eyes adjusted to the gloom he might be able to scrutinize the form more clearly.

All at once he became aware of a low sussuration that had only just broached his threshold of hearing while very gradually increasing in volume. The monks were chanting. The illumination began to grow the least bit brighter, though nowhere could Harker spy anyone adding fuel to the many small lamps or otherwise adjusting the light.

No matter; at least a better glimpse of the figure on the throne had become possible. Still his head mildly ached with the frustrated effort to put some familiar construal upon what his eyes reported. For the shape shrouded in luxuriant layers of yellow silk seemed amorphous. He had once or twice seen individuals with thyroid conditions that made them dangerously obese, women from whose limbs sagging pouches of redundant flesh depended. In these cases the conventional lineaments of the human body had become obscured like an ancient fossil encased in mud. But this comparison only began to hint at the appearance of the Hooded Thing before him. Three great bell-like funnels of lemon-yellow silk veiled thick and stumpy protrusions, presumably a head and two arms, though no recognizable flesh was visible. There were strange ... *shiftings* among the folds of the massive cassock that Harker found himself wishing the shadow still hid.

The chanting died away as quickly as it had begun. Now Harker felt that the still-unseen visages awaited some word from him. Sooner or later he would have to speak, else why had he come among these strange heathen people at all? So he up and spoke, knowing that in no case could his audience possibly know his language, but trusting in the promise of scripture that the Holy Ghost should fill the mouth of the one who preached the gospel. "My friends, you whose lives, like mine, are given unto spiritual things; I have journeyed far to bring you glad tidings of great joy. For unto you has come this day a Savior, who is Chr—"

"*Ta tvam asi!*" came back a voice, as if to punctuate his words. He knew from his seminary studies in Comparative Religion the meaning of this phrase. It was a famous quote from the Hindu *Upanishads*. It meant "That, thou art" and referred to the identity of the individual self with the divine Brahman. Did one of those present mean to refute his preaching with a counter-gospel? Or had the Spirit made them understand his English syllables, even as God had translated for the multitude at Pentecost so that each heard the gospel in his own native language? Did they indeed understand him? If so, what was the sense of the Hindu formula?

He had barely a moment to ask himself these questions before he felt a spiritual onrush such as he had not felt since that first night in the storefront temple. His tongue and vocal cords were no longer his own as he yielded to the impulse of the Spirit. He blanked his conscious volition and uttered forth the glossolalic syllables: *Pnglui ngah Cthulhu fhtagn!*

In a moment all the figures seated about him were bowing and prostrating themselves before him, or at least that was what he thought. Given the confusing body shapes and motions, he could not be sure what they were doing, but it seemed like obeisance more than anything else. He had been merely the mouthpiece for his God, no more than a messenger handing over the sealed message. It was not for him to know what words the message contained. But he thought and hoped he had somehow prophesied the glad tidings of salvation, and that his audience had found themselves cut to the quick even as Simon Peter's hearers at Pentecost. He would soon find it was not so simple as that, but whatever he had said, it had certainly met with their approval, and their attitude toward him was henceforth of the most positive and even reverential.

The Reverend Harker had made his apostolic journey to distant Leng to plant the banner of the gospel where it had never flown before. He had come to teach, and yet henceforth he found himself playing the role of learner. His mysterious hosts made that much clear, providing him with scrolls and block-print codices in great numbers.

He had, as I have said, already picked up a smattering of the central Asian languages required to make his way into the remote hinterlands, but this proved a meager basis on which to plod through lengthy and turgid volumes of metaphysics and yogic disciplines. Once or twice the monks of Leng managed to secure the temporary services of Nepalese or Chinese outsiders who might facilitate the missionary's progress in learning, but nothing was systematic.

Nonetheless, after many days (it later turned out to have been years!), Harker found he could understand something of the spoken language of the men of Leng—less than one might expect given the time spent among them, for it was a strange whistling, buzzing, even grinding sound hard for a Westerner to understand or reproduce. The written languages, particularly the proto-Naacal, were easier to grasp.

These studies supplied the key to a vast repository of ancient and esoteric learning. Dr. Harker was soon amazed at the wealth of lore that slept in the vast subterranean libraries of the monastery. Heathen lore it might be, but he was not such a boor as to scoff at the gathered wisdom of a civilization ancient when his own ancestors were still huddling in caves. Some of what he read betrayed fairly close kinship with certain Hindu-Buddhist doctrines just then becoming more widely known in the West through Max Müller's *Sacred Books of the East* translation library. Others held surprising parallels to the familiar doctrines and commandments of his own faith.

10.

THE turning point came, the light dawned, when at length he was presented with a very ancient parchment which, as his widening eyes deciphered line upon line, purported to be a contemporary account of the apprenticeship of Jesus of Nazareth among the adepts of Leng. Here appeared to be the answer to the long-standing riddle of the "lost" years of Jesus between his youth and his baptism in the Jordan. Everything the bemused Harker had learned up to now, no matter how *outré*, had not really touched him personally. *This* ... this struck at the heart of his faith.

Yet was it a threat to his belief? Or a *supplement*? Was it possible that he might be on the verge of discovering a new, or long-forgotten, dimension of the gospel? Was this why he had been so strangely drawn to the virtually unknown frontier of Leng? Was he preaching the gospel to these people? Or were *they* preaching it to *him*? It did not take him long to resolve that providence had vouchsafed him a unique opportunity to learn, and that he had best take full advantage of it.

They brought him more scrolls, more scriptures, which he devoured with a newly stoked spiritual hunger. He mastered the *Upa-Puranas* almost effortlessly now, and the *Black Sutra* of the legendary avatar U Pao opened its secrets to him. *The Book of the Sayings of Tsiang Samdup* remained stubbornly mute to him no longer.

Throughout the years he was allowed but brief and rare glimpses of the shrouded figure he surmised to be the abbot of this arcane fraternity. Never a word did he hear from that almost amorphous personage. It appeared that he spent most of his time in mystic contemplation. Then one day Brother Enos (as he had come to think of himself) was startled to hear the shimmering crash of a great gong reverberating throughout the nitrous low walls of the monastery. He knew something momentous must have occurred, and he half-expected one of the brethren would come to his cell to inform him what had happened. Yet it was with a mounting sense of alarm verging on panic that he roused to the bitter whine of the bone trumpet summoning him at the midnight hour to join the brethren for a procession down unfamiliar halls and ramps leading to an obscure quarter of the vast hive-like complex, the full extent of which he had never been given to suspect.

Butter lamps rested in niches along the halls, giving scarcely any illumination at all, though perhaps it was enough for eyes long accustomed to the byways of the night. The monks carried on a low chanting in some language that seemed alien to Harker even after all his studies. Once a great deal of this had transpired, the group, numbering a dozen or so, filed into a chamber that rose a good deal higher than almost any other he had seen. In the middle was a broad wooden table ringed with candles. At the center of this was a veiled heap of irregular outline. He wondered that the old abbot did not preside over what looked more and more to be a sacramental feast. Then he realized what the silken veil must cover. The masked hierophant had finished his business in this incarnation.

What would happen next? What was the nature of this ceremony? Was it a simple memorial, designed to speed the soul of the late lama to his next incarnation? Or would it somehow decide the succession to the holy throne? He would have to wait and watch.

One of the hunched, cowled shapes now held a book whose opened pages shadowed his spread hands. A new chant rose, this time in the more familiar tongue of Tibet. "Fly, fly, O Nobly Born, from this house of clay, and thou shalt behold the Obsidian Night! The Maw of Chaos! From it thou camest; tend thou unto it! Know it for the Void of thine inmost Self! Skirt thou the perilous slopes of Sumeru and seek instead the gates of Sarkomand. Shun the ravishing sights of the Elder Deities, and know thyself as one of the Wrathful Deities." On and on it went, and Harker began to recognize it as a hellish parody of the notorious *Bardo Thödöl*, the Tibetan *Book of the Dead*.

At last silence returned. Now the celebrant, having put down the book, held aloft the inscribed and rusty blade of a ceremonial knife a foot long. Others lifted up a section of the silken cloth, and the priest began to cut, to slice. Enos Harker grew increasingly terrified, sensing what was coming, yet unable even to consider the possibility with his conscious mind.

The gloved hand held out the quivering, putrescent flesh to him, with a few muttered syllables. Involuntarily, Harker's mind supplied the gospel words, "This is my body; take, eat." *And he did.* It seemed inevitable, and he even felt ashamed of his qualms, thinking of Father Abraham obeying God's command to slay his firstborn son.

(As my employer related these shocking events, I could not help but recall vividly how he had earlier required me to fetch for him the disgusting passage from the *Necronomicon* concerning the "corpse-eating cult of Leng." Apparently he was quite well informed on the subject already.)

11.

IN the months that followed, the destiny of Enos Harker was made clear to him. Since his return to the States, Dr. Harker's researches had been devoted in the main to corroborating the secrets of his initiation from Western occult sources, and to finding some way of understanding them in light of Western thought, which again formed the inescapable atmosphere of his thinking.

First of all, he had managed plausibly to locate the mystical philosophy of the men of Leng as an apparent hybridizing of Manichean Gnosticism, which, as is well known, penetrated both China and central Asia well before the tenth century, and the shamanistic Bönpa faith of Tibet and Mongolia. This accounted for the strange, inverted parallels to Vajrayana Buddhism, which had largely supplanted the Bönpa in neighboring Tibet, as well as the striking dualism that opposed a set of elder deities with another set of wrathful deities.

It seemed that, on a penultimate level of being, higher than that of waking perception but lower than the Ultimate Oneness of the Void, there existed a whole geography of dream continents and oceans, with exotic names like Sarkomand, Ikranos, and Mount Sumeru. It was from this strange realm, the home of the Ancient Old Ones, the Undying Masters of the Leng sect, that dreams and revelations came.

The highest point of the bizarre pseudo-Buddhistic cosmology was the universal void in which all supposed truths were revealed to be half-truths and fell away. Here chaos without form or name, beyond *Namarupa*, held sway. All beings were considered illusory, momentary refractions of this Bliss-void, which certain scriptures named Azathoth, others Achamoth, or Vach-Viraj. But there was a series of divine demiurges, half-real personifications of the Chaos to provide a face to whom mere humans might relate as worshipers to a god. Of these there might be many or few, depending upon the tasks and the needs of the time.

The most important of these were a pair of entities called Lloigor and Zhar, though their secret names were Nug and Yeb, and they were also known, when the stars were in certain configurations, *which they now approached*, by the names Klulu and Nyarlathotep. These were the avatars they would assume to ring down the curtain on each world-cycle. They might walk among men in human form, sowing madness and chaos, for these were deemed by them spiritual enlightenment. Nyarlathotep had appeared once in human form as the Egyptian pharaoh Nephren-Ka, while Klulu strode the doomed shores of Atlantis with the gaunt visage of the priest-king Kathulos. This was long ago, but at the end they would emerge again, Klulu rising from the subconscious depths of hapless human minds in a torrent of fatally maddening night terrors, while Nyarlathotep would come forth in human form again. In the meantime he would by no means leave his sons, the men of Leng, as orphans. In every generation he would live among them, psychically projecting his essence (or *tulku*) into a chosen vessel. This, of course, was the hierophant of Leng.

The indwelling of the deity caused a gradual transformation of the natural flesh into an exalted substance which took on more and more of the original likeness of the entity within, which was not to be seen by men. Upon the death of each vessel, the successor would be chosen by manifest signs. The sacred essence would be passed to the new avatar by means of physical ingestion. Then the acolytes would present to him the Yellow Sign, the Pallid Mask, and the Silken Mantle. He would pursue a life of telepathic linkage with the Klulu avatar on the Dream-Bardo, so as to know when the end of the age was imminent. The time had to be soon, for the faith of the cult of Leng, which had once (as they believed) spanned the globe, had now retreated to this single monastery, a predestined ebb such as occurs toward the end of every cosmic cycle.

There were other Byzantine complexities, such as the multitiered organization of the men of Leng; many of them were not privy to the deepest secrets and doctrines of the sect but acted chiefly as passive mediums for the voices of the Ancient Old Ones who made their directives known from time to time. The great revelation, which the reader will by now have surmised, is that Enos Harker had been chosen as the latest, and apparently the final, avatar bearing the *tulku* of Nyarlathotep.

12.

HE had returned to the West only a few short years ago now, feeling the desperate need to think upon all he had heard, upon the responsibilities that now rested upon his shoulders. Those devoted to him as their priest-king, indeed as their living god, dared not question his departure, though they cannot have been very enthusiastic about it. For all they knew, he might have sensed the call to go forth into the world again, even as former avatars had done in times past, to prepare things for the final advent of Chaos when mad auroras should roll forth and blast all things with merciless, wasting light.

As I should imagine it, the very sophistication of the vessel, an educated man of the West, which made this incarnation of the *tulku* so very potent, also made it less predictable, less manageable than previous pontiffs, who had all been ignorant Asians born and raised in the back of beyond, dwellers in a virtual stone age bereft of culture or human contact.

We are all of us, to an unsettlingly large extent, creatures of peer opinion. The world we live in is like an atmosphere we breathe, and it is notoriously difficult not to do as the Romans do when in Rome. Thus Dr. Harker's confusions and nagging doubts, once he returned westward, quickly blossomed into a crisis of indecision in which his loyalties to rival pictures of reality nearly tore him asunder. He tried to control his thoughts through the preparation of the scholarly monograph which I had been hired to put into final shape. His urgent wish to consult texts like the *Necronomicon* and the translated *R'lyeh Text* was really a last-ditch effort to *dis*confirm his own beliefs and experiences as illusions and delusions. Perhaps he had been brainwashed by the cult. He now hoped so! Better that than that the insane things he had come to believe should prove true!

But prove true they did. He had hoped that the utterances he had once thought bits of the uncouth tongue of R'lyeh would turn out to have nothing in common with what appeared to be a tangible relic of that language, translated by an objective third party. The terrible truth was that some of the same phrases he remembered hearing (and saying!) were there, and were defined exactly as he had come to understand them. There was no chance now that it was *not* true.

As for me, I must admit I found myself one step behind the elderly clergyman. I felt very afraid that the noose of the truth was closing about my neck as well. I desperately hoped that of which at any other time I should have felt unquestionably certain: that the man before me, plainly suffering from delirium, was raving insane. But I, too, realized it was too late for that, too late for sanity.

13.

I NOW knew well enough the nature of the affliction that was fast ravaging the physical form of Dr. Harker. He was not after all degenerating. He was *transforming, transfiguring* into the likeness of the Apostle of the Last

Hour, Nyarlathotep. When that transformation was complete, that hour would have struck. The Kaliyuga was at an end. Whether the apostle emerged on this side of the world or that made little difference. Once he had sloughed off the last clinging vestige of his host Enos Harker, a human being with a human conscience, the last hopes of preventing his apocalyptic mission would vanish, too.

Silent until this point, I stammered a question to my employer, though to think of him in such terms now seemed frivolous. How could he be so strangely calm? Had he simply resigned himself to his fate? And to the grim fate to be meted out to all mankind? Or was there some last shred of hope that he had thus far kept from me?

"It may be. It may be. Earlier this evening I had a visitor. It was his coming that made me delay so long to call you here to my side. He is a man who is knowledgeable in these matters, in some ways more knowledgeable than myself despite all I have seen. He is the Swami Sunand Chandraputra, or at least that is what he requests to be called. He understands the situation quite well. He left me this."

The bandaged, paw-like protuberance held forth an abnormally large key of tarnished and elaborately carved silver. "With this, I may venture to escape. I cannot save my life. My fate was sealed the moment I partook of the blasphemous sacrament. But it may be possible to go where the emergence of the Thing inside me will do no harm. I shall take hold of the Key, and I shall enter a state of dream more real than the illusion we now share. There I shall pass through a door, the mountain portal of Sarkomand. The Tcho-Tcho devils will be waiting for me and will try to bar the way. But if I may hold firmly to this, that they are but the groundless phantoms of my own mind, then I may win through. What will happen then, I do not know. But the way back for the avatar will be long, too long for him, having assumed the cumbersome mantle of gross flesh. *Listen!* The time is at hand! *His* dreams begin to impinge on the waking world!"

I had been vacantly aware of some increasing reverberation for some minutes, but it had not yet obtruded upon my conscious mind. Now the sound, if hard to put into words, was plainly to be heard. There seemed to be a slow and steady tread as of great steps, the steps of Leviathan shaking the earth, though I felt no physical tremor. They resounded from deep below the ground, as if from some unsuspected caverns under the earth. As the minutes passed, the echoing steps seemed to rise gradually along the bending curve of the firmament till they were close to reaching the zenith. I sat thus, my eyes fixed upon nothing in particular, waiting, listening. I jumped as the mantel clock sounded midnight. I turned to look to Dr. Harker, I suppose for some signal of guidance, *only to find an empty bed.*

Not entirely empty. A key, of blackened silver and of outlandish proportions, pressed its bulk into the disheveled bed sheets. Instinctively I grasped it, turned, and made for the door. I paused not, nor entered my room again to retrieve any of my few belongings, but headed inland with all the desperate speed I could muster. I had little thought of what might happen next, only that I must flee like Lot from Sodom.

I must have found my way back to my old lodgings on Parker Street, where the landlady, hearing my frantic knocking, gave me admittance. I can remember little of what passed that night or the next day, nor was I a witness of what happened at Cairn's Point, of whatever *could* have happened there. As I have said, the district is largely deserted, and that is merciful, in light of what finally transpired. A derelict who chanced to be staggering down the streetcar tracks toward the beach related how he had seen first a strange flash of bluish light erupting from the top of what I am sure was Dr. Harker's rented cabin, as if it were a lighthouse on the shore. Then there was a widening flash in which there appeared to be a knot of several figures struggling in shadowed silhouette, one larger than the rest. The authorities put that part of it down to alcoholic delusions. Not even they can deny that *something* turned the whole of the beach into a great sheet of glass.

Whatever agency, whatever force, was responsible, something the chemists at Miskatonic are still debating, it also reduced the beach house of Enos Harker to a thin layer of wind-scattered soot. No search has been conducted for the missing Dr. Harker, since his infirmity was well known, and Dr. Sprague has assured the police that he could have been nowhere but in bed when disaster struck. The drifting ashes must therefore include his own.

However, I know better, and I am not alone. Dr. Sprague, not for the first time, seems to know more than he is willing to say, and Dr. Llanfer seems not to be alarmed, but rather almost relieved, as if a drama had reached its denouement. All the others are naturally upset at not being able to file away a mystery they cannot solve. The greater mystery is that of which they have no inkling, that of the strange doom of Enos Harker.

HOW strange that the works of H. P. Lovecraft should include a "canon" of unfinished fragments, a phenomenon reminiscent of *A Canticle for Liebowitz*. How much stranger that August Derleth, he of the "posthumous collaborations" with Lovecraft (something reminiscent of Herbert West), never ventured to finish up any of these tantalizing bits and pieces, these Pnakotic fragments. That didn't stop other writers from forcing HPL to participate in a necromantic round-robin.

Brian Lumley undertook a continuation of "The Thing in the Moonlight", though, strictly speaking, this one wasn't originally even a fragment, at least not in the same sense, since it began as an excerpt from a letter in which HPL described one of his dreams. Editor Jack Chapman Miske added the three opening mini-paragraphs and the last two closing ones, publishing it as a makeshift tale in his magazine *Bizarre*, Vol. 4, #1, January 1941. (He had first called the mag *Scienti-Snaps*, if you can believe it!).

"The Book" represents Lovecraft's abortive attempt to make the "Fungi from Yuggoth" sonnet "The Book" into a prose tale. Martin Warnes picked up where HPL left off and finished it up as "The Black Tome of Alsophocus" (which, forgive me!, always makes me think of "esophagus", as if the tome were a monograph on the Heimlich maneuver!). You may find this fine story in Ramsey Campbell's *New Tales of the Cthulhu Mythos*.

Lin Carter decided to try his hand at "The Descendent." The present tale, "The Bell in the Tower", is the result. He had planned to include it in a collection to be called *The Black Brotherhood*, a volume of marginal Lovecraft revision tales and posthumous collaborations. After his death I tried to press on with the project with the cooperation of Ted Dikty, but the Grim Reaper took Starmont House away along with Ted, and that was that for *The Black Brotherhood*.

A related idea, also regrettably cut short by the scythe, was for Lin Carter to finish up August Derleth's own Celaeno fragment "The Watchers out of Time", which would have been not only poetic justice, but terrific fun. (Derleth had already incorporated some of Lin's Mythos lore into the story.) Lin's eyes widened with the possibility when I mentioned it to him one afternoon at a meeting of our New Kalem Club, but he never got around to it. I have a feeling, however, that someone yet may.

The first appearance of "The Bell in the Tower" was in *Crypt of Cthulhu* #69, Yuletide 1989.

The Bell in the Tower

H. P. Lovecraft and Lin Carter

THERE was a man in London once who screamed when the church bells rang. He lived all alone with his streaked cat in Gray's Inn, and people called him harmlessly mad. His room was filled with books of the tamest and most puerile kind, and hour after hour he tried to lose himself in their feeble pages. All that he apparently sought from life was *not to think*. For some strange reason, thought was very horrible to him, and anything that stirred the depths of the imagination he fled as from the plague.

He was very thin and grey and wrinkled, but there were those who declared that he was not nearly so old as he looked. Fear had its grisly claws upon his heart, and any sudden sound would make him start with staring eyes and a sweat-beaded forehead. Friends and companions, if in truth he possessed any, he shunned, for he wished to answer no questions regarding his strange condition. Those who once knew him as scholar and aesthete said that it was very pitiful to see him in this state. He had dropped them all years before, and no one of them knew for certain whether or not he had left the country or had merely sunk from sight in some hidden byway.

At the time of which I write, it had been a decade since he had taken rooms in Gray's Inn, and of where he had been in the interval he would say nothing—until the night when young Williams bought the *Necronomicon*.

This Williams was a dreamer, and only twenty-three, and when first he had moved into the ancient house he had felt a strangeness and the chill breath of cosmic winds about the grey, wizened man who dwelt in the next room. Curious, he forced his friendship upon his neighbour, where old friends dared not force theirs, and marvelled at the fright that sat upon this gaunt, haggard watcher and listener. For that the man always watched and listened no one could doubt. He watched and listened with his mind more than with his ears and eyes, and strove every waking moment to drown *something* with his ceaseless poring over gay, insipid, popular novels. And when the church bells rang he would stop his ears and scream, and the grey cat that dwelt with him would yowl in unison until the last peal would die reverberantly away.

Try as Williams would, he could not make his neighbour speak of anything profound or hidden. The old man would not live up to his aspect or his manner, but would feign a smile and a light tone and would prattle feverishly and frantically of cheerful trifles, his voice every moment rising and thickening until at last it would break in a piping and incoherent falsetto. That his learning was deep and thorough, his most trivial remarks made abundantly clear; Williams was not surprised to discover that he had attended Harrow and Oxford.

Later, it developed that he was none other than Lord Northam, of whose ancient hereditary castle on the Yorkshire coast so many odd tales were told; but when Williams tried to talk of the castle, and of its reputed Roman and even pre-Roman origin, the old man refused to admit that there was anything unusual about the edifice. And he but tittered shrilly when the subject of the supposed under-crypts, believed hewn out of the solid granite crags which frown on the stormy waters of the North Sea, was raised by his young visitor.

So matters went between the two until that night when Williams brought home the infamous *Necronomicon* of the mad Arab, Abdul Alhazred. He had known of the dreaded volume since his sixteenth year, when his dawning love of the bizarre had led him to ask certain questions of a bent and furtive old bookseller who kept a queer and dusty little shop in Chandos Street; and he had always wondered why men went pale when it was mentioned. The old bookseller had told him that only five copies were rumoured to have survived the shocked edicts of the priests and the rigid suppression of the lawgivers, and that all of these were believed safely locked away with frightened care by those custodians or archivists who had dared to glimpse into the hateful black-letter.

But now, at last, Williams had not only found an accessible copy of the notorious volume but had made it his own at a price so low that it seemed ridiculous. He had purchased the old book at a Jew's shop in the more squalid precincts of Clare Market, where he had occasionally purchased odd curios and obscure artifacts before; and he almost fancied that the gnarled old Levite had smiled as if with *relief* amidst the tangles of his beard, when Williams discovered the volume and announced his desire to purchase it. Indeed, the flaking leather bindings with their verdigris-eaten clasps of brass had been placed on the shelf so prominently, and the price was set at such an absurdly slight figure, as to almost make him suspect that the bookseller was eager—even *anxious*—to be rid of the accursed tome.

A single glimpse of the title was sufficient to send Williams into transports, and some of the diagrams inserted into the vague Latin text excited the tensest and most disquieting recollections in his brain. He could not bear to waste a moment, but was possessed with impatience to take the ponderous volume home and to plunge into the decyphering of its pages, and he departed with the book in such precipitous haste that he hardly heard the old Jew chuckle disturbingly as he left the bookshop. But when at length he had borne the book safely to his room, had secured and locked the door behind him, and had begun to scan the yellowed pages, he found to his dismay that the combination of the clumsy black-letter, which was nigh-illegible, and the debased idiom in which the book was indited resisted such linguistic abilities as he possessed. Then he bethought him of his strange neighbour, whose scholarly attainments by far exceeded his own, and knocked upon the door of his mysterious, frightened friend for assistance in unravelling the twisted, medieval Latin.

Lord Northam was simpering inanities to his streaked cat when the younger man entered, and he started violently at the appearance of his unexpected visitor. Then he saw the volume and shuddered wildly, and when Williams uttered aloud its title he fainted altogether. It was when he had fully regained his senses that he began to relate his own story, or figment of madness, in a frantic, whispering voice, eager to have it told so that he could make certain that Williams would not delay but would hasten to burn those abominable pages, and scatter their ashes wide.

Lord Northam's Story

THERE must (Lord Northam whispered) have been something very wrong at the start; but it would never have come to a head had I not explored too far into the mystery. I am the nineteenth baron of a line whose beginnings extend disquietingly far into the distant past—unbelievably far back, if family traditions may be credited, for there are ancestral tales of our descent from pre-Saxon times, when a certain Luneus Gabinius Capito, military tribune of the Third Augustan Legion, then stationed at Lindum in Roman Britain, had been summarily expelled from his command for his participation in certain secret rites unconnected with any known and recognised religion.

This Gabinius had, or so the rumours ran, come upon a cavern hollowed out of the cliffs which fronted upon the stormy waters of the sea, and where strange furtive folk met together and made the Elder Sign in the dark; an odd, old folk whom the Britons knew not, but whom they greatly feared, and of whom they whispered that they were the last lingering few to survive from a great land amidst the Western Ocean, long since sunken beneath the hungry waves, leaving behind only those isles with their rathes and menhirs and circles of standing stones, of which Stonehenge was the greatest.

There was no certain evidence, of course, that Gabinius had built an impregnable fortress *above* that forbidden cave, and had thereafter established a line which Pict or Saxon, Dane or Norman, Roman or Briton, were equally powerless to obliterate. Nor was there any certainty in the tacit assumption that from that uncannily protected line had sprung that bold companion and staunch lieutenant of the Black Prince whom Edward Third created first Baron of Northam. These legends were unsupported by any form of substantial evidence, but they were often whispered; and, in very truth, the stonework of Northam Keep, at least in the older portions of its masonry, bore disturbing and even alarming resemblances to the Roman stonework of Hadrian's Wall.

As a child (continued Northam after a pause), I always experienced the most peculiar dreams whenever I chanced to sleep in the more ancient parts of the castle, and I acquired a nervous habit of continuously searching back through my memories for certain half-amorphous scenes or inexplicable patterns or the oddly significant impressions created by certain effects of landscape vistas and odd cloud formations—none of which seemed to form any part of my conscious recollection of waking experience. By degrees, I became a dreamer who found life tame and unsatisfying, a searcher after weird realms and inexplicable relationships once familiar as in some prior life, but seemingly discoverable nowhere in the visible regions of this world.

I became filled with a feeling our tangible world is only one strand— one fibre—in a fabric vast and ominous, and that unknown demesnes impinge upon and permeate the sphere of the known at every point. In my youth and early manhood, having drained dry the fonts of formal religion and mysticism, I turned to the intense perusal of the occult mysteries and the arcana of ceremonial and ritual magic. Nowhere, however, could I discover that for which I hungered—the means to penetrate beyond the vast illusion we call Reality, thereby to obtain the vision of those enthralling worlds of remote and unutterable alienage that dimly haunted my dreams, and the knowledge of whose intangible and ineluctable splendours obsessed my every waking moment and made bland and pallid every pain or pleasure to which the body and its senses may attain. In absinthe and hasheesh, in opium and laudanum, in a myriad of dangerous drugs and illegal or poisonous alkaloids I sought, through the deliberate and systematic derangement of the rational mind and the senses, that supernal and transcendent vision; but in no opiate did I find the key to that revelation of worlds and planes of existence ineffably superior to our own, which was the guerdon of my labours.

In lieu of ease and content I found only restlessness and ennui, and as I grew older the staleness and limitations of life became ever more tedious and maddening to me. During the 'nineties I sought surcease from the insipidity of existence by delving into Satanism, by dabbling with every theory and devouring avidly any doctrine which might offer a palliative to the close and stifling vistas of unimaginative science and philosophy and the dully unvarying so-called Laws of Nature. Books like Ignatius Donnelly's fabulous account of Atlantis I absorbed with zest, and a dozen obscure precursors of Charles Fort enthralled me for a time with their meticulous documentation of inexplicable occurrences ... but in naught could I find a path to the *utterly unplumbed* gulfs beyond the reach of the astronomers or the cognizance of mundane cosmographers—the nameless vortices of never-dreamed-of strangeness, where form and symmetry, light and heat, even matter and energy themselves, may be unthinkably metamorphosed or totally wanting—the ultimate, unguessable regions beyond the strictures of time and space, where the laws of Euclidean geometry or of cause and effect or of sequential time itself are bent awry, and where the chimerical and the self-contradictory are the norm, while the rational and the tangible are but idle fancies.

In despair, I sought in travel the alleviation of my discomfiture; I would traverse leagues to trace down some furtive village tale of an abnormal wonder, and once I ventured farther off and into the deserts of Araby in search of a certain Nameless City of vague and unsubstantiated rumour, which no man is known ever to have beheld. There rose within me the tantalising faith that somewhere an easily accessible Gate existed, which if once found would admit me freely to those outer deeps whose echoes faintly reverberated in the ancestral adyts of my memory.

The Gate I sought might well be within the compass of the visible and waking world, yet it might exist only within the depths of my mind or soul. Perhaps (I mused) I held within my own half-explored brain that cryptic link which would unlock the innermost portal or awaken my dormant senses to elder or to future lives in forgotten dimensions of reality; which would give me access to the stars, and to the infinities and eternities which lie beyond them, and to states of being or modes of apprehension fabulous to me now.

Pursuant to this notion, I searched yet again through that mouldering library of ancient tomes accumulated over the span of centuries by the barons of my line, amongst which were treatises on daemonology and the alchemical science, abstruse and recondite philosophies, works which discussed the Eleusinian and the Orphic Mysteries, and innumerable histories of witchcraft and diabolism, the writings of the Kabballah and of the Gnostic mages. Although I had winnowed the library thoroughly in my youth, it yet remained within the bounds of possibility that there remained some rare and occult tome or monograph which I had scanned inattentively, or even overlooked, and which might hold the key that would open those supernal Gates to the astounding vistas and incredible marvels which lay Outside.

It was, I remember clearly, on a rainy evening in November when I found wedged and thus hidden behind a formidable row of tomes devoted to theological disquisitions, a secret book which, even as I had half-guessed, half-hoped, I had previously overlooked. It was none other than a copy of that abhorrent and frightful *Necronomicon*, another copy of which you so imprudently purchased this very day, young Williams. I had read shuddersome references to Alhazred's book in other volumes which reposed on these very shelves—in the infamous *Cultes des Goules* of Comte d'Erlette, the *Unaussprechlichen Kulten* of von Junzt, and old Ludvig Prinn's hellish *De Vermis Mysteriis*—but never heretofore had I chanced to encounter a copy. Bound in rotting leather it was, and locked with clasps of rusty iron which I prised open with my pen-knife. The pages were crumbling with age and foxed with mildew, and a palpable reek of decay rose to assail my nostrils as I opened the volume and began to peruse its pages.

Unlike the printed copy you now hold, the book I had found concealed behind the shelves was a holograph manuscript, to which many different hands had contributed, as was patently evident from the different kinds of parchment, vellum, or paper upon which it was inscribed, and the variegated handwriting, and which of my ancestors had compiled the manuscript and had caused it to be bound in leather I could scarce conjecture. Indeed, it was not until I began to notice the occasional marginal gloss inscribed with fresher ink and by a more recent hand than the redactors of the pages themselves, that I gained cognizance of his identity: *for it was in the unmistakable hand of my great-great-grandfather*, the sixteenth baron of my ancient line—he who had so narrowly escaped the assizes and the consequent gallows in the last days of the maniacal witchcraft persecutions.

The copy of the *Necronomicon* was immensely long, well over one thousand pages, and for the following week I merely leafed through it, my febrile imagination seizing here and there upon an individual passage or phrase which titillated my fancy with hints of Gateways that opened to other worlds than these, to the abysses of anterior cycles of time, and to unimaginable regions beyond the bourne of space and time. At length it occurred to me that there might be other books or papers secreted behind that stolid row of interminable theological puerilities, and thus it was that I found a recessed latch sunk into the ancient mahogany of the bookcase. In pressing it, a groan as of the creaking of rusty hinges thrilled my senses, and in the next moment one entire section of shelving slid slowly and ponderously open, revealing a dark and dusty passageway and a flight of steep stairs leading *upwards* into the impenetrable gloom, all swathed and festooned with the ghostly webs of untold generations of spiders.

The great library of Northam Keep was on the topmost storey and I well knew that there was nothing above the room, save for an ancient stone

The Bell in the Tower

tower whose casement windows had been tightly shuttered from within and whose only entrance had been sealed with brickwork long before I was born. Therefore, the mystery of where that steep and hidden stair might lead intrigued my curiosity immensely. Pausing only to prop the concealed doorway open with a heavy tome and to snatch up from the library table an oil lamp, I entered the dusty alcove and began to ascend the stair with a mingled feeling of cautiousness, trepidation, and adventurous expectancy which is hardly describable in mere prosaic words. The steps of the stair were of wood, thick with generations or centuries of dust and mouldering with neglect. At the top I found a trapdoor which I forced open with a squeal of protest from rust-gnawed hinges.

I discovered a queer, octagonal room almost completely bare of furnishings. My lamp disclosed nothing more than a table of heavy wood and a great carved oaken chair of Jacobean or, perhaps, Tudor craftsmanship, which reposed in the very center of the chamber. Upon the table there lay the stub of a candle in a brass holder, a dusty inkwell which contained the dark scum of long-dried ink, and several quills, arranged neatly beside a folio into which was thrust a sheaf of parchment written all over in a spidery hand. The only oddity which the tower chamber housed beyond these ordinary articles of furniture was a huge, ancient bell of age-blackened silver which was suspended from the rafters directly above the chair. It was the size of a church bell and stamped or otherwise incised about its rim was a series of angular characters which I vaguely recognised from my extensive readings in the occult as the "Nug-Soth runes", concerning which I knew little more than the name itself. The clapper of the bell was in the shape of an inverted trident, and it was tied by a length of tarry twine to a curious clockwork mechanism of coiled springs, heavily coated with some oily lubricant. The obvious purpose of this quaint mechanism was to enable the bell to be rung without the need of human hands to swing it.

As I could make nothing of the utility of this, I went at once to the table in the centre of the room, placed my lamp upon the dusty surface, and seated myself and began to examine the sheaf of manuscript, which was in the unmistakable hand of my great-great-grandsire—that Ruthven, Lord Northam, of which so many dubious legends are still whispered hereabouts, and whose age-dimmed oil portrait, with its heavy brow ridges and jutting cheekbones, harsh, angular jaw and severely aquiline nose, repeat the identical features which heredity has graven on the visages of every member of my line since the days of our remotest ancestor. The entries were dated in the seventeen hundreds and seemed to be the records of a series of experiments, but, alas, these were set down in some cypher which employed letters and numerals according to some code or system which I could not at once unravel. Leafing impatiently through the manuscript I found at length a certain passage towards the end which was written in plain English, and which read:

> Even as ye Brachmans of Hindoostan employ'd the repetitive ring'g of small Bells as an adjunct to their Meditations, so doe ye Shamans of Tartary and ye Red Priests of Thibet, for a similar Purpose, that is, to benumb ye Rational Minde and purify ye Senses so as to apperceive ye Higher Planes. See Abdool Al-Hazred his III Booke, chap.viii.

Thereupon followed certain instructions concerning the winding of the clockwork mechanism, the rhythm and timing of the ringing of the bell, and the duration deemed most advisable for the experiment.

At this point I began to notice that my head was aching and my heart pounding rapidly, to the point where it seemed likely I would swoon like a woman if I remained any longer in this enclosed space and continued to breathe the stifling and stale and vitiated air of the tower chamber. The wooden shutters which sealed the long windows resisted my efforts to open them; indeed, they were locked and barred so stoutly that it would take a crowbar to open them and admit the fresh air of open day. I took my lamp and the folio and descended the steep and narrow stair again to the library, and turned at once to perusal of the *Necronomicon*. I found without difficulty the passage to which my ancestor had alluded; it was in the third book of the *Necronomicon*, which bore the title "The Book of the Gates", and it read thusly:

> And alsoe ther remaineth yet Another Mode by whiche ye may at least perceive That which lieth beyond ye strictures of ye Naturall Worlde, withouten daring ye Riskes attendant upon yr entry thereinto in ye Bodie; a means whereby ye may thrust aside ye Veil and peer into those oth'r Realms of Beinge the whiche pervade and inter-penetrate with our owne Plane, yet whiche remaine invisible and imperceptible to mortall Men, and by them Unknowne. Ye Ritual of ye Bell this mode is call'd, and it employeth a certaine Bell of Silver inscrib'd about ye Rim thereof with ye IX Spatial Key, the whiche shouldst be writ accordingly either in ye Runnes of Ye Nugge-Sothe or in ye antient Aklo letters. Yet be wary that ye not over-doe yr usage of this Mode; for him who sees Beyonde, he may betimes alsoe be seene by Them that make of that Realm the Place of Their abiding.

I read this passage over and over, possessed with a feverish sense of excitement and discovery which you may easily imagine. From the antique form of the writing, spelling, and grammar, I hazarded the guess that this was a transcription from Dr. Dee's own English translation of Alhazred's book, of which I had often read in my studies; at least, the form of the language seemed as old as the reign of that Tudor queen in which Dee had flourished.

In my great-great-grandsire's hand there was scribbled a marginal gloss to this passage which sent a thrill through my inner being. He had written—

It worketh well.

* * *

MY impatience to attempt the Ritual of the Bell would brook no delay, so I began the experiment that very evening. According to the notes of my ancestor, a certain potion must be imbibed in preparation, the recipe for which was given in those portions of his papers which were not encoded. The formula involved certain drugs and poisonous alkaloids such as belladonna and aconite, but as I had sampled these and other potent narcotics earlier while striving to systematically derange my senses, I fortunately had liberal supplies of such chemicals on hand.

With some little labour I managed to open the shutters which effectively sealed the casement windows, permitting a cold wind from the tossing waves of the sea to clear the stale air from the tower chamber; then, setting the mechanisms according to the instructions, and imbibing the elixir, I seated myself directly beneath the bell of age-tarnished silver and the Ritual commenced. The slow tolling of the bell was deep-toned and mellow, and as the ringing continued I became aware of a drowsy numbness stealing over my senses, but whether this was due to the drugs I had taken or to the monotonous music of the bell was difficult to say with any precision.

Through the open casement I could see the houses of the old town below the Keep and the low hills beyond, and the crags which affronted upon the waves which glittered in the luminance of the rising moon. Gradually—imperceptibly—an uncanny *change* began to take place, transforming the scenery which lay below me. At first, the outlines of the old houses *blurred* and became indistinct; in time they faded away altogether and were replaced by another and very different set of images which seemed to have been *superimposed* upon them as if by some mysterious enchantment. The ancient houses, most of which dated from the day of Elizabeth, and which were crumbling with age and long neglect, became new and fresh, as if rejuvenated; the street of glistening cobblestones was gradually replaced by a meandering path that seemed strewn with glittering mica, and the rounded hills and rugged crags beyond the town of Northam were changed, by slow and minute gradations, into a fang-like row of stone spires, as harsh and unweathered by the ages of wind and rain as must be the mountains of the moon themselves.

Beyond the needle-like spires of naked stone now drove no longer the billows of the sea; in their place, a seething and viscous black *vapour* boiled and smoked, seemingly heavier than the air itself, and irisated with fugitive glints of strange and unfamiliar hues to which I could assign no name. The moon had long since faded from the firmament, which had changed from depthless black to a peculiar shade of fulgurant purple, upon which now floated moon after moon of luminous nacre and pallid opal. By the shifting rays of the many moons I perceived that the mica-strewn street or path, which had been empty, was now thronged with a strange and shadowy company who wore the habiliments of many lands and distant ages. Here strode a soldier in the brazen greaves and breastplate of a Roman legionary, and by his side a portly figure in the sober broadcloth and peaked hat of a Puritan divine; a shuffling Oriental in mandarin robes of shimmering silk went accompanied by Saxon peasants in coarse smocks of homespun, with shocks of straw-yellow hair and thong-bound cloth leggings; swarthy-visaged individuals paced the glittering path in turbans and tarboosh, their lower limbs clothed in voluminous pantaloons, scimitars thrust through sash and cummerbund.

As I gazed enthralled upon this fantastic promenade drawn, it seemed, from every nation and epoch, I became gradually aware that *Others* more shadowy and indistinct accompanied them—strange gaunt naked figures with beaked heads and folded membranous wings like Chinese fans. But there was some curious quality about these Others that made it exceedingly difficult for my vision to ascertain the details of their alienage, as if the very matter of which their bodies were composed defied the light of the many opalescent moons, or as if my organs of sight were too gross to discern their lineaments with clarity.

This uncanny multitude seemed bound for a common destination, as if embarked upon some nameless pilgrimage whose nature I could not name, but ere long I became uneasily aware that the *goal* of their pilgrimage was no other than the very castle in whose tower chamber I sat enthroned—or whatever bizarre and unguessable edifice occupied its same position in this alternate reality or weird, unearthly dimension. It was only then that I bethought me of those eldritch crypts rumoured to exist far below the bottommost cellars of Northam Keep, that cavern hewn by unknown hands before mundane history began, for some arcane and hidden purpose unknown to me. The mood of disquietude which came over me at this juncture I could not account for, but it sufficed to disturb my tranquility to such a degree that the vision blurred and faded, and the strangely *new* houses and the mica-dusted paths and sharp spires of naked rock were replaced by their known and familiar counterparts on this plane. And I awoke from my trance-like state, the tolling of the great bell having ceased, to a numbed and drowsy awareness of my surroundings, uncertain as to whether I had been awake all the while, or deep in drug-induced dreams.

Nightly thereafter I repeated the experience, each time discovering to my delight and marvel something previously unglimpsed in the unearthly landscape. Where gnarled and ancient oaks grew beyond the village, the dream-world of my visions sprouted monstrous and ichthyphallic fungoid growths with obscene, nodding bulbous heads all striped or splotched or mottled with surly crimson, febrile nacarat-orange, sinister purples, virulent and venomous greens; beyond the fungi grove I perceived curious, twisted trees whose serpentine and rugous trunks *writhed* with unwholesome vitality like undulating vipers, as if striving to reach the pale and leprous moons that drifted across the purpureal skies where strange stars flared and flickered in odd alignments, very alien to the constellations of our earthly skies. And once I glimpsed, far off across that ultra-telluric sea of coiling vapours, a stately ship with sails of lambent luxurious tapestry, so different from any vessel that ever plied our earthly seas as to hint at ports of origin beyond the moon, as if it had floated here across the unguessable abysses of space itself.

But ever, during these nocturnal visions, were the glittering paths thronged with a motley horde of pilgrims come hither from every era and nation: druidic priests in sombre robes, the oak-leaf chaplet bound about their brows, the golden sickle in their hands; Cro-Magnon hunters clad in hairy hides of beasts, bearing long stone-tipped spears in their grasp; Scythian archers; slender and beslippered Persians in mitred caps; Egyptian hierophants, their heads covered in *klafts* of starched linen, the mystic uraeus bound about their brows; half-naked savage Picts; tall Normans in sparkling chainmail half-covered with long surcoats emblazoned with scarlet heraldries ... and ever there loped or shambled amongst these more familiar figures, who had seemingly stepped from the pages of history, those gaunt and ungainly *Others* who bore no resemblance to terrene lifeforms, but were ghastly hybrids, mingling the likeness of men and beasts, lizards and insects, in their persons.

And each time I repeated the Ritual of the Bell, it seemed that my ability to perceive these *Others* was subtly incremented, until at length I beheld their alien anatomies, which seemed sprung from the divergent biologies of supra-mundane spheres, as clearly and distinctly as I behold you now. But it was not until the eleventh repetition of the experiment that something occurred which gave me pause and which drove icy terror into my very soul. I had been leaning from the tower window, staring with rapt and fascinated gaze upon the surging crowd, when one of the Others—a plodding and ungainly, brutish thing whose obese and pulpy corpulence was hideously pustuled with swollen and abnormal growths, like rudimentary tentacles or truncated proboscises—paused in its shambling progress, and craned its flat-browed and multi-eyed head skywards *and stared directly into my eyes.*

* * *

I SHRANK back from the window, shaken to the heart with a sudden and nameless fear—but fear of *what*, I could not say!—and returned tremblingly to the great, carven chair and cowered therein. The tolling of the ancient silver bell had ceased and a tense, uncanny silence brooded over the room, even as those leprous moons of cold and nacreous light brooded over the limitless vistas of the weird and wonderful and yet horrible world beyond my tower chamber. Then it was that I recalled with a chill of foreboding the words of admonition with which Abdul Alhazred had terminated his passage—the passage to which that reputed warlock, my great-great-grandsire, had drawn my attention:

> *Yet be wary that ye not over-doe yr usage of this Mode; for him who sees Beyonde, he may betimes alsoe be seene by Them that make of that Realm the Place of Their abiding.*

Had I, in truth, continued my experiments beyond the proscribed limit? I had no way of knowing whether or not this was true, but I resolved to discontinue using the drugged potion and the tolling of the bell hereafter; but first, I could not restrain my curiosity as to the nature of the goal of that ultra-mundane and trans-temporal nightly pilgrimage I had watched so many times—the crypts or cavern beneath the very foundations of Northam Keep, which had been so inexplicably protected from all attempts to destroy it over so many numberless decades and generations and centuries. Thus it was that the next morning, upon arising from restless and intermittent slumbers made unspeakably hideous by shadowy and half-remembered dreams, I descended into the cellars below the castle and found at length the sealed and barred portal of ancient black wood which for untold ages had guarded its secret from the knowledge of men.

The keys to the crypt were antique and cumbersome, and the locks were eaten with rust and decay, but with perseverance I at last managed to unseal the portal and ventured within, holding aloft an oil lamp to afford some illumination. The age of the crypt was unguessable, hewn as it was by crude, primitive implements from the solid granite of the crag upon which my remotest ancestors had reared Northam Keep, and the gloom which pervaded it, and which had perchance for centuries known not the benison of light, was Stygian and profound. In the outer chambers I discovered the stone sepulchres of my ancestors, whose dates marched backwards, generation by generation, into the abysm of time; but nowhere in these antechambers did I descry aught that could have been the goal or shrine of that mysterious pilgrimage which I had watched file by below my eyrie night after unforgettable night. Indeed, it was not until I chanced to discover the *innermost* crypt that I came upon what proved the ultimate guerdon of my quest into the horrible history of my ancient line ... that great coffin crudely hacked from black basalt, whose ponderous lid I prised away, tilting the lamp so that I might peer within ... and from one terrible glimpse of *that* which the ages had mercifully hidden from the sight and knowledge of men ... that gaunt and glistening and all-but fleshless Thing that squirmed and wriggled in the stinking foetor of its own putrid slime ... that bony and naked and undead Thing whose skull-like and mewling head reared suddenly as if to stare with blind eyes into my own ... that slick, white, unclean Abnormality upon whose lineaments I stared with a soul-sickening sense of *recognition* ... at which I screamed and let fall the burning lamps from nerveless hands, to fall and shatter within the sarcophagus, to drench with liquid flame the writhing monstrosity which squealed and shrilled with torment from the flames, *but neither burned nor died* ... and, screaming, I flung myself in panic-maddened flight from that unspeakable crypt of nethermost horrors ... sealed and locked the ponderous portals behind me with palsied hands ... and fled stumbling up the winding stair to the safety and sanity of the normal, everyday world.

* * *

THAT night I flung the abhorrent *Necronomicon* upon the fire in the grate and burned as well the papers I had found in that accursed tower chamber, and poured every last drop of the vile and hideous potion down the drain, vowing never to risk my soul or sanity again to feed the thirst of my imagination on that penumbral, nightmarish world beyond the Veil.

The next day, hungry for the sight and sound of men, I left the castle for the first time in weeks and sought out the public house in town, where I sought surcease from my unendurable memories in strong ale and noisy companionship. From the tavern I wended my homewards way in the gloaming, and had all but reached the foot of the drive that ascends the steep to the gates of the castle, when the bells in the village church began to toll the hour. That dreadful music, so horribly alike to the monotonous tolling of that gruesome and sinister silver bell, made me shudder to the roots of my soul, and I was about to scramble up the drive to Northam Keep, when suddenly an inexplicable vertigo seized me and I was forced to lean against the corner of the nearest building in my giddy sickness. I shut my eyes, trying to master the strange weakness which had assailed me, and opened them at length to stare down at the slick cobbles beneath my feet, *but saw only powdery and glinting mica*. In a panic of utter terror, I looked around with dazed, uncomprehending eyes, noting the peculiar *newness* of the old, old houses ... looked skywards into depths of fathomless purple, where pallid moons of ghostly opals leered down as if in ghastly mockery at my plight. Now all about me moved a throng of curiously garbed strangers, bound for a goal which horribly I knew; and one of them, a pulpy and bloated, corpse-like thing with more limbs than was normal, turned to grin directly into my eyes, which widened with unbelieving horror. And all the time, the church bells tolled and tolled; and I knew myself to be hopelessly and irretrievably lost to a damnation more shuddersome than that threatened by any merely earthly creed ....

In that very hour I left forever the ancient castle of my ancestors, and fled to London, vowing never to return to that haunt of horror where I had rashly and imprudently dared the ultimate blasphemy of striving to pierce the Veil that separates our sane and mundane sphere from regions of unguessable loathsomeness that lie beyond, yet dreadfully near to hand. I am glad that I burnt the *Necronomicon*, and you should do the same, young Williams, for there are things men were not meant to know and sights of the very Pit upon which no sane man should dare to gaze. And still I shriek and cower when the church bells chance to ring, and ever are my dreams and my every waking hour rendered unspeakable by that last sight I had in the crypt, when the undying thing reared its fleshless head to peer with blinded eyes into my own, and I saw—*and knew*—those heavy brow ridges, those jutting cheekbones, that harsh and angular jaw and severely aquiline nose ... *the very features that heredity has stamped upon every member of my line since time immemorial and the days of my remotest ancestors!*

NOW that you've been introduced to Winfield Phillips, Hiram Stokely, and Anton Zarnak, I suppose you're ready for the following gloss on the Xothic cycle. If Lin Carter himself liked to write new Mythos tales to plug gaps in the system of the Mythos, some of us find it irresistible to write them to plug gaps left by writers like Lin himself. If he implied a sequel but did not provide one, then, well, it may be a dirty job, but some ill-omened acolyte has to do it.

Where is the Oriental Quarter, the stomping grounds of Dr. Anton Zarnak? You will note that in "Perchance to Dream" Lin Carter placed it in New York. He borrowed the locale from Robert E. Howard's Steve Harrison detective stories. Where did Howard envision River Street, China Alley, etc.? It's hard to say! In "The Mystery of Taannernoe Lodge", River Street seems to be in New York City, but in "The Silver Heel" we are told that a character who had left the city might be in New York *instead*, while another character is said to have recently relocated from San Francisco, as if it were perhaps nearby. The West Coast has always seemed to me the most natural setting for the adventures of Steve Harrison and Anton Zarnak, and so it is in the present story.

The first appearance of "The Soul of the Devil-Bought" was in *Cthulhu Cultus* #5, 1996.

The Soul of the Devil-Bought

by Robert M. Price

I

THE telephone rang with a sound one does not typically expect telephones to make. This one sounded like a gong, and was in fact attached, in an arcane manner recalling the hammer and tympanum arrangement of the human ear, to a medium-sized brass gong somewhere in the surprisingly vast interior of the apartment. Muffled as it was by the many Oriental rugs and elaborate tapestries that insulated nearly the whole layout of the place, the mellow depth of the sound still managed to penetrate every inch of the strange domain. There would be but a single ring in any case, but this time a dusky hand reached out to the dumbbell-like receiver in a second flat, as the giant possessor of the hand, a turbaned and taciturn Sikh, had been standing like a posted guard next to the intricately carved teakwood pillar-table on which the telephone sat like a museum antiquity. Akbar Singh spoke the monosyllable with something suggesting imperious urgency: "Yes?" Then, "What is your business with my Master?"

The statuesque Sikh stood apparently alone in the book-lined study, as if he were a cigar-store Indian included among the exotic collection of antiques, curiosities, and finely bound books crowding the place. It was not his own sanctum sanctorum, and yet he seemed alone in it—till all at once the high-backed leather swivel chair behind the great mahogany desk spun around to face him. The face he saw was an accustomed one for all its peculiarity in the eyes of most of the few who had seen it. His subtle Eurasian face remained as passive as the Buddha's, yet his obliquely slanted eyes beneath a high, unfurrowed brow seemed to smolder with adventurous expectancy. It was almost as if he were following the telephone conversation telepathically, as perhaps he was.

Dr. Anton Zarnak rose and reached across the cluttered desk top to receive the telephone from his servant. His eyes closed as he listened, as if meditating, as if seeking to pick up signals from his caller that the other was not intentionally sending. The silver-white lightning zigzag that mounted up from his widow's peak to disperse through his otherwise jet-black hair might have suggested the drawing of psychic forces to his magnet-like brain.

"Yes, Mr. Maitland ... soon to be *Dr.* Maitland, is it not? Yes, I thought so. I was expecting your call. Never mind how, but it was the next natural development. No, that's all right. I assume you are calling with reference to the Winfield inheritance? ... I am not without my sources."

Through all this, the giant Sikh let a small grin draw up the corners of his mouth. He was amused at the obvious confusion his master's prescience produced in such inquirers. He was no stranger to the feeling himself. If he felt a hint of amused superiority now, it was not because he understood Zarnak's secret any better than the nonplused caller; he had simply become accustomed to the inexplicable. Now Dr. Zarnak was handing him back the receiver.

"We will depart at once, my friend. I felt it best not to require our scholarly caller to leave his ivory tower to venture the shadowed courts of our Oriental Quarter. The Sanbourne Institute is no appreciable distance by car, and I suspect it will do us both good to get some fresh air." Akbar Singh nodded as he stepped away to fetch his master's coat. Fresh air indeed—he had breathed little but drifting incense for some months now, half-suspecting that the fumes were meant to instill in him some psychic sensitivity, or else protection. He did not really care to know more.

II

AS the black sedan purred its way beyond the cobbled labyrinths of the Oriental Quarter and up the Southern California coast to Santiago, its driver felt relieved to open up the throttle till the county roadways brought them to the Sanbourne Institute of Pacific Antiquities. To this institution the renowned Dr. Zarnak was no stranger. Indeed, it was from this place that he had earned the latest of his several doctoral degrees. His association with his alma mater was congenial, though he was scarcely the average alumnus.

Zarnak was not infrequently called upon to date or authenticate certain relics purchased by the Institute from various questionable vendors on River Street, where the wharves disgorged all manner of strange cargo brought in from obscure ports of call throughout the Pacific and Indian Oceans. There was no use in scrupling over how such items were obtained, since legality meant little in most of the places these traders frequented. The antique objects might as well have been freshly exhumed from Davey Jones' locker as far as any Westerner could tell. If one or one's institution did not take advantage of such opportunities, it was not to be doubted that others would.

It was in connection with quite a different matter that Zarnak was calling on Jacob Maitland, a zealous young graduate assistant at Sanbourne just nearing the end of his doctoral work and about to get his thesis in final shape to defend before his committee. He had done his work on a curious old document called the *Ponape Scripture*, a palm papyrus manuscript brought to the Sanbourne Institute not long before by the ill-fated scholar-explorer Harold Hadley Copeland. Maitland had had occasion before now to contact Dr. Zarnak, whose acquaintance he had made during the last months of Zarnak's own work at Sanbourne. He had read Zarnak's dissertation, *A New Scrutiny of the Polynesian Genesis according to the* Cthäat Aquadingen. Young Maitland had at once perceived the crucial utility of some of his elder colleague's methods as applied to his own project, for he suspected that the obscure pages of the *Ponape Scripture* might be written in some lost variant of the Naacal language of fabled Mu. But these matters had been far from his mind when he had telephoned Zarnak an hour earlier.

Jacob Maitland's story, and his dire suspicions, began to unfurl as he welcomed Dr. Zarnak and his manservant into his tiny office. His name was stenciled onto a cardboard plaque taped to the pebbled glass of the door. As a graduate assistant he had little status and few prerogatives, and those few did not include spacious accommodations. Glancing at the massive frame of the Sikh, Maitland suggested perhaps the faculty club or even the library might be more conducive, but Zarnak insisted privacy was the more important consideration, and Akbar Singh modestly retired from the scene, announcing his intention to stay with their automobile outside.

It seemed that Maitland had been highly annoyed at a duty assigned him by his supervisor, manifestly because no one else with the right to delegate the matter had hesitated to exercise that right. He was to seek out a Mr. Winfield Phillips, heir to the property of one Hiram Stokely, an eccentric recluse for whom no living contemporary had had any use—save for the famous Harold Hadley Copeland, himself the great benefactor of the Sanbourne Institute. Copeland had at some point managed the unthinkable, to purchase from the cantankerous Stokely two priceless old volumes, *Die Unaussprechlichen Kulten* of F. W. von Junzt and the *R'lyeh Text*, with which Maitland knew Zarnak to be more than familiar, together with some manuscript pages from an oddity called the *Yuggya Chants*. How he had been able to persuade old Hiram to yield up these volumes no one at the Institute could even guess, unless, as some suggested, Hiram had mastered all that these books had had to teach him.

Copeland had eventually bequeathed his own vast collection of idols, manuscripts, modern volumes, maps, diaries, and what not to the Sanbourne Institute of Pacific Antiquities. Once it had been discovered among his diaries that his copies of von Junzt and of the *R'lyeh Text* had come to him from Stokely's collection, the trustees of the Institute naturally wondered what else of similar scholarly importance might lie moldering in the late eccentric's library. Could not some arrangement be made with the heirs, a pair of the old man's nephews, Bryan Winfield and Winfield Phillips? According to the local scandal mill, the two had moved into the decaying hacienda-style estate of the hated Hiram Stokely some weeks before to set up an openly homosexual household, to the outraged consternation of the poor white trash of the nearby town of Durnham Beach, whose Puritanical scruples apparently did little to hinder their own squalid depravities.

Soon a new scandal had replaced the old. Perhaps rumor had merely substituted a new lie for one that had become stale, but it was noised about that, whereas formerly the two young men had been inseparable on the few occasions they had ventured forth into town, now one caught sight only of Winfield Phillips, whose air seemed distracted in an ominous way, though no one, not even the gossips, could point to any specific evidence of foul play. Perhaps some lovers' spat between the two dandies had driven the offended cousin away under cover of night, or perhaps he had taken his own life in a moment of maudlin despair, as homosexuals were wont (or thought) to do.

Jacob Maitland had found these reports half-plausible, having read somewhere of Phillips' keen interest in the Decadents. He judged no man for his private affairs, but the Durnham Beach gossip was more than casually interesting to him simply because it had fallen to him to make the first cordial contact with Winfield Phillips, and he feared on the basis of these reports that the man might be arbitrary and unreasonable in his dealings. When Maitland soon discovered, in addition, that Phillips had for a number of years been associated with Miskatonic University in an analogous capacity to his own at the Sanbourne Institute, he began to dread that his counterpart might have designs on whatever of his uncle's precious volumes might remain, intending to donate the books to the Hoag Library of Miskatonic, and thus to strengthen his own prospects of gaining a choice faculty position. This possibility sounded all the more likely to Maitland because he had hoped, by securing any such rare books for the Sanbourne's collection, to advance his own scholarly career. There had been nothing to do but drive up to the Hiram Stokely property and discuss matters as amicably as he could with Winfield Phillips himself.

Phillips had not bothered to restore telephone service to his uncle's house, apparently sharing some of the old man's eremitic inclinations. So Jacob Maitland had had little choice but to make the long drive through the dreary mudflats and acres of stunted scrub pines to the old hacienda—and just hope that Phillips would be home. Given the desolation of Durnham Beach and the surrounding acres, Maitland had considered it unlikely Phillips would be busy at anything away from home. The peculiar look of the midget forest of scrub pine had made him think of the New Jersey Pine Barrens which, according to local superstition, housed the fantastic Jersey Devil. Looking at the local equivalent of the Barrens, he could well understand how the desolation of a place like this would incarnate itself in legendary form.

He had grimaced as he had realized he was driving past the blasted acres of the infamous Hubble's Field, the routine excavation of which some years previously had yielded shocking revelations of many ages' worth of human sacrifice and mass murder. These ghastly revelations had effectively doomed the adjacent town to eventual desertion, as no one would move there. Even the surly denizens of Durnham Beach seemed to despise their ancestral habitat, though no appreciable number had ever sought to leave, not even a few years back when there had been a rash of strange disappearances, mostly of children. It seemed to Maitland that something kept the Durnham people rooted to their poisoned land, so that the thought of fleeing never even seemed to cross the minds of most. What could keep an outsider like Phillips here? It was no wonder that his boyfriend had left, no doubt deciding that he had had quite enough of these surroundings.

III

ZARNAK listened with inscrutable silence as Maitland continued to fill the narrow confines of his office cubicle with details of his story. The younger man more than once paused to reprove himself for boring his guest with over-ample detail, but the latter assured him that no fact ought to be neglected. "Sometimes, my young friend, the memory is but a camera which records details which mean nothing to us but which may speak volumes to another who examines the picture it has taken. Go on."

Maitland had had no idea what to expect when his knock was finally about to be answered. What would Phillips look like? Maitland had seen a poor photo of the man, standing literally in the shadow of his erstwhile employer, Dr. Seneca Lapham, a professor at Miskatonic, the subject of the photograph. That had been from some years ago, in the aftermath of some queer business at Billington's Woods in rural Massachusetts.

The sight that had greeted him was even more unexpected. It was not Winfield Phillips, nor even his reputedly vanished cousin. The figure before him, despite his undistinguished manner of dress, had plainly been an American Indian (of the once-local Hippaway people, as Maitland would later learn). This taciturn man, whose prominent cheekbones shaded curious scar patterns, must have been taken on by Winfield Phillips, with some of his new-found wealth, as a factotum. That the man was an Indian might imply that none of the nearby townspeople would willingly work for Phillips, though, God knew, there were few enough employment opportunities in the ghost-town community.

Each man had momentarily contemplated the other in silence, Maitland at a loss for words, the Indian awaiting some remark to which he might reply. Finally, as Maitland had begun to sputter false starts of embarrassed cliché, the Indian, a much older man, simply pointed to himself, saying "E-choc-taqus."

Maitland had managed to get out his own name, albeit stumblingly, as if he were not quite sure of it, and then a third figure had joined them. This man had introduced himself as Winfield Phillips. He had at least matched the general impression of the man in the photograph, though he had had somehow the appearance of being substantially older than his thirty years should have made him. Perhaps the unaccustomed duties of settling his late uncle's affairs had worn on him. The burdens of everyday life often took a greater toll on those whose minds were characteristically at home with scholarly abstractions, as Jacob Maitland knew only too well.

Maitland had extended a hand and received a shake with a hint of reluctance. "Pleased to meet you, Mr. Phillips. I wonder if I might come in to discuss something with you. About your inheritance, you see."

The other's eyes had narrowed in suspicion. "The assessor's office? But I thought—"

"Oh, no, nothing like that, Mr. Phillips. I'm from the Sanbourne Institute."

"All right. Do come in. I'm afraid I've had quite enough of federal, state, and local jackals appearing out of the woodwork, each expecting a share of the carrion. Forgive the imagery."

"Uh, surely," Maitland had said, removing his hat and handing it to the Indian servant, who at first had seemed not quite sure what to do with it.

The place had been sumptuously furnished, mostly in Victorian style, something Maitland had noted with a subliminal note of relief, for he hated to see homes where the inner decor belied the outer facade, or, worse yet, where the oblivious new homeowner had no sense of propriety and would mix styles haphazardly. Then he had realized that Mr. Phillips must simply have had the interior of the old place cleaned out and repaired as necessary, not bothering to second-guess his ancestor's tastes in furnishings. Still, that very effort implied Phillips's intent to stay and make the home his own.

Phillips had led his guest into the second floor library and indicated a seat on one of the couches facing the fireplace, while his servant had stoked the fire in the grate. Taking a seat in a wing-back leather chair opposite

Maitland's perch, Phillips had sat comfortably, like the lord of the manor settling into the familiar contours of a favorite chair.

"At first, as you may know, Mr. Maitland, I came here from back east, thinking merely to attend my uncle Hiram's funeral and to take care of a few items of business over at the Sanbourne. I'm afraid I haven't got around to that yet. Affairs here have kept me unexpectedly ... busy." He had gazed emptily up at the high ceiling, as if looking through it to greater expanses beyond. "I had planned to sell the old place, but the longer I stayed here, the more I began to feel at home, I can't say just why. In fact, I almost had the feeling, silly isn't it, that I had returned home here after being away. No, I had never been here to visit Uncle Hiram, though I confess to feeling that I know him better now, living among his things this way."

Maitland had not been able to help noticing that in all this garrulous speech, Phillips had made no mention of his cousin and companion Bryan Winfield. It had sounded as if his cousin had formed no part of the events. Maitland had wondered what else Phillips might be strategically omitting. Then again, Maitland's role was simply to negotiate for some old books, not to play the role of detective.

"Well, to come to the point, Mr. Phillips, speaking of your late uncle's possessions, I am here to tell you that the trustees of the Sanbourne Institute are curious to know whether his, that is, your library might contain any more old volumes like those Harold Hadley Copeland once purchased from Hiram Stokely—"

"Yes," Phillips had interrupted, "I know the ones you mean. And frankly, I can't imagine what it was that possessed Uncle Hiram to part with them in the first place. In fact, I'd been considering asking for their return, so that the Stokely Collection, as I've begun to think of it, might be complete again. Of course you must have had photographic facsimiles made of them by now, you've had them long enough."

There was a blow! Maitland had come to add to the rare book holdings of the Sanbourne, and here he was, about to lose some of the crown jewels of the Institute. He should, he silently rebuked himself, never have come!

"This comes as something of a surprise, Mr. Phillips, but I can understand your viewpoint. I'm sure the trustees will be willing to consider the matter. I'm sure it can be settled amicably. Before I go, is there something I might help you with over at the Institute? You mentioned some errand you had there—"

"To be sure, Mr. Maitland, I did. But I really don't think I'll bother seeing it through. You see, it had to do with a fellow named Arthur Wilcox Hodgkins, a rather distraught man who appeared one day at Miskatonic, having come all the way across country from your own Sanbourne Institute. It seems he had a peculiar dread of one of the old Melanesian idols from the Copeland bequest. He sounded more than a little paranoid, if you want my impression. Nonetheless, some of our faculty heard him out and thought it the most compassionate thing to let him take home with him one of our own lesser museum pieces, a star-shaped stone of curious workmanship, which he was convinced would function as some sort of apotropaic device to protect him from the occult doom he feared.

"Newspapers not long afterward reported that his terrors had gotten the best of him at last, that he had gone wild in the Sanbourne Museum gallery, murdering a night-watchman and trying to set the place ablaze. All this transpired some eight years ago.

"My employer at Miskatonic, a Dr. Lapham, asked me, while I was out here for Uncle Hiram's funeral, to check into the matter, wondering if there were something more to the tragedy than the papers thought best to let on. But since coming into my inheritance, I have decided not to return east after all, and as for the Hodgkins case, I rather imagine it best to let sleeping dogs lie, don't you? The Sanbourne is hardly likely to relish the prospect of the whole messy business being stirred up again for prurient public consumption, are they?"

Maitland had indeed heard of the bizarre tragedy of the unstable Hodgkins, whose days at the Institute had not overlapped his own. He knew there was more to the case, though what it might be he neither knew nor cared to find out. Phillips was right: It would be a blessing for the Sanbourne Institute not to have to deal with that publicity nightmare all over again.

"Your point is well taken, Mr. Phillips. Little is to be gained that way. We appreciate Professor Lapham's concern, but to be honest, we would appreciate your own more!" Both men had laughed, thawing the stiff politeness of the conversation, though only in time for it to draw to its close. Phillips had risen as the old Indian had entered the room.

"Echoctaqus, would you please show our guest out?" The Indian's features had remained impassive, but something in his bearing had said that the role of underling did not come easily to him. "I'll be looking forward to hearing from you about those books, and please reassure your trustees that I'll be more than happy to reimburse the Institute for at least the amount Copeland paid my uncle for them. You won't forget? Good."

A bemused Jacob Maitland had followed the Indian servant down the winding staircase to the entry hall and had been halfway out the door when behind him he had heard the raised voice of Winfield Phillips calling him back.

"Oh, and, ah, one other thing, Maitland, if you please! If you should happen to hear from Dr. Lapham or anyone else at Miskatonic, please be sure to give them my regards and to convey my apologies for what I now realize was a joke in rather bad taste. Thanks so much, old man."

Maitland had felt surprisingly relieved to be behind the wheel again and retracing his path through the dismal acres of Durnham Beach and

Hubble's Field, silently eating up the miles back to the palm-girded campus of the Sanbourne Institute of Pacific Antiquities.

IV

THERE his tale ended as well, as his voice trailed off into a question mark. He had asked Dr. Zarnak nothing specific, but both men knew that the whole story was in fact a question, a puzzle, the beginning of a story and not the end of one.

"First, my young colleague, tell me, have you brought Phillips' request before the trustees yet?"

"No, all this happened little more than a week ago, and the trustees won't be meeting for another month and a half."

"Good, good," nodded the other. "You must never relay that request, for Phillips must never regain those volumes. I am sure that his uncle never yielded them up to Harold Hadley Copeland willingly in the first place."

"Then how ...?" The rounding eyes and rising brows of the younger man finished his question for him.

"I am not at full liberty to say, Mr. Maitland. Suffice it to say that Professor Copeland possessed something well beyond a theoretical knowledge of certain matters that had occasioned his acquaintance with Hiram Stokely in the first place. Let us say that there were at his service certain resources that enabled him to drive a hard bargain and to get what he wanted. Though you can see the good it did poor Copeland in the end."

"All right, sir, but what about the business of the 'joke' Phillips had made? That struck me as odd, hardly characteristic of the man's general mien."

"You are to be congratulated. You have the keen eye of the researcher. As for the so-called joke, I think I can provide a comprehensive answer there." So saying, Zarnak reached down for a leather valise he had carried in with him, opened it, and deposited before Jacob Maitland a neatly typed manuscript of some forty pages. Alone on the top sheet, like a voice crying in the wilderness, stood the single terse line "Statement of Winfield Phillips."

"Go ahead, read it now. It will not take long, and it contains a number of things you will need to know for our conversation to continue. I shall meditate in the meantime."

So Maitland read, unperturbed at first, then with a growing sense of subtle alarm. The typescript began on a somber note, anticipating the writer's own imminent death. Phillips had composed the narrative in the very same house, no doubt in the same room, in which Maitland had interviewed him less than a week ago. He told of his mission to Santiago, his meeting with his cousin (and here Maitland could read between the lines some possible justification for the rumors of the pair's homosexuality), and their initial exploration of their uncle's mansion. Phillips' breathless description of his chance discovery of a shelf full of little-known classics of the Decadent movement left Maitland cold, as his own interests ran decidedly toward the scientific, not the literary, much less the polluted tributary of the Decadents. When he got to the subsequent disclosure of centuried copies of John Dee's *Necronomicon* and Gaspard du Nord's edition of the *Livre d'Ivon*, his pulses quickened; here were the books whose hypothesized presence had motivated his trip out to the Stokely, now Phillips, estate. He was aghast at the implied death of Bryan Winfield and half-suspected that the narrator protested too much his innocence in the affair. All in all, much that had been unclear was explained in these mad pages, and yet somehow everything seemed even more mysterious than before.

Zarnak's eyes met his as Maitland looked up from the last page. "You are perhaps wondering whether Phillips gave in to the voices that beckoned to him in the end. Deep down, from what you have told me, I think we both know the answer to that."

"Then this is no joke? I was afraid it wasn't. What *was* the 'joke in poor taste', then? And how did you manage to get hold of this manuscript, Dr. Zarnak?"

"I came by it through unexceptional means. It seems that Winfield Phillips mailed the manuscript to his old mentor, Seneca Lapham, no doubt immediately after typing it. It was his last act while in reasonable possession of his faculties. It was not long before he regretted having sent it off and wanted very much to allay the fears and questions his shocking account must have occasioned at Miskatonic. He wrote again, assuring Dr. Lapham that the earlier parcel had simply been an endeavor to fictionalize his visit to Durnham Beach. It was the discovery of the various chapbooks and manuscripts of Henquist, Gordon, Ariel Prescott, and the rest that had inspired him to seize upon the macabre qualities of his visit, the funeral, the old, mildewed mansion, and so forth, and utilize them in a pastiche of his own. He claimed he realized only after having mailed it off that he had omitted a cover letter explaining the fictional nature of the whole thing and wanted to supply that lack now."

"To tell you the truth, Dr. Zarnak, I'm not sure I wouldn't have been satisfied with that explanation. But I take it Professor Lapham was not?"

"Correct. He had ample reason to know that truth is often very much stranger than fiction. Then there was the complete surprise of young Winfield abandoning his position at Miskatonic. Besides, even if the manuscript had been a piece of fiction, why on earth would Phillips ever have thought the serious-minded Seneca Lapham would have wanted to read its disgusting contents? He is not a man for such trifles, as Phillips knew better than most.

"Dr. Lapham did not reply to either mailing from his former assistant but instead passed the manuscript on to me for my opinion. When I heard from you, I knew you must see it as well. It is certain that the narrative contains elements that the secretive Phillips now wishes had never been revealed, facts that presumably may be used against him. For instance, did you notice Phillips' initial puzzlement over the unaccountable fact that his uncle, whom he did not know and had not met, should make him and his cousin his sole beneficiaries? Hiram Stokely had become estranged from both branches of the family to which the two young men belonged. What could have been his motivation? Something else: What was the reason for the hasty, closed-casket funeral?"

Maitland lowered his eyes, shading his features with his hand. "Frankly, I'd rather not guess. But why bother with Phillips? If he turns out to be every bit as mad as that fellow Hodgkins, it's his own business, surely? Why appoint ourselves his inquisitors?"

Zarnak knew that the younger man was having second thoughts. His earlier forebodings were now giving way to fear, and this he sought to rationalize as much as to disguise. "Mr. Maitland, Jacob, why then did you call me into the matter, if not to get to the bottom of it?"

"My only interest in Winfield Phillips was in the rare books his uncle left him. I've told you, even in that errand I was only carrying out the wishes of my superiors here at the Institute."

"Come, Jacob, you don't even believe that yourself. I am quite a good judge of first impressions, and I realized when we met that you were a true delver into secrets. And we both know that most secret things are concealed for their danger. The righteous hide them away lest their disclosure prove dangerous, while the wicked hide them only till an opportune time, when the secret things would do the most damage. You knew that from the start, and I believe you know what is at stake here, specifically."

"*Hubble's Field.* That's the problem, isn't it? The locals think the disappearances will start again, and they'll be next. And it will be Phillips who starts it all up. He'll keep his new allies, the yuggya?, well sated with their blood in return for who knows what rewards?"

"Very astute, Jacob Maitland. I see I was right about you. What you have outlined is but the beginning of sorrows that will ensue if our friend Phillips is not stopped straightway. For I am convinced that he was lured out to his uncle's property in order to continue the old sorcerer's terrible work. My guess is that, while his vampiric allies had no concerns beyond ensuring a fresh supply of human sacrifices, Hiram Stokely had rather bigger things in mind, things hard for a sane mind to conceive of, though I have a few guesses.

"It would be a complex plan entailing much effort. His devil's bargain caught up with him before he could finish his tasks. More than likely,

Professor Copeland had thrown Stokely's plans awry by forcing him to part with certain crucial volumes he required. You saw how eager his nephew Phillips was to regain them. Somehow, perhaps through the lingering psychic influence in the house itself, young Phillips has been enlisted to carry old Hiram's blasphemous schemes to their completion. At least that is my fear."

"What of the Indian?" asked Maitland, suddenly recalling how strange his presence had seemed. "Is it no more than Phillips having to go outside the town for help?"

"Would that it were so, friend Jacob. In that case, one would still have to ask why Phillips would trouble himself to locate an Indian, of the Hippaway tribe, I believe. There are none of them to be found in a radius of many miles nowadays. I cannot imagine there would be one on the list of any nearby employment agency. Especially not for such work. His name is the real signal. Does it strike a familiar note with you?"

Maitland rose, put one fist to his hip, touching the index digit of the other hand to his chin, unconsciously striking the contemplative pose. "Yes ... yes, it does, now that you mention it, though I was sure at the time I'd not heard the outlandish jumble before."

"No, it would be something you have heard, or rather read, since your visit."

About to give up on the game, Maitland suddenly turned a quarter circle to face him and, with light dawning in his eyes, he almost spoke, then grabbed up the typescript and began shuffling through the pages. "Here it is! The old devil is named for the Place of the Conqueror Worm, *E-choc-tah* in the tongue of the Hippaway. Hubble's Field. Good Christ! Why would anyone ...?"

Zarnak had stood to his feet now and was shaking the pile of pages together to even up their edges once more. "It is a very old legacy, Jacob. Our local burying ground, Hubble's Field, is only one of many such honeycombed horrors. The children of Ubb, Lord of Maggots and Corruption, are active the world over, as many traditions attest. The holy city Jerusalem, now part of the British Mandate of Palestine, had once been a center of the cult of Yog-Sothoth, and it was erected in olden times next to an unclean place of Ubb. The Bible curses that place as Tophet, Gehenna, and Akeldama, the Field of Blood. Of it Isaiah writes, 'the worm dieth not and the fire is never quenched.' The demon Ubb eventually seduced Solomon to his fealty, whose great treasures and sorcerous powers are well known, though their true source remains unsuspected. In return, Solomon caused Ubb's cult to be established in the Jerusalem temple itself, where it remained till the reforming zeal of King Josiah swept the whole gallery of abominations away."

Zarnak fell silent as the shadow of his man Akbar Singh loomed against the pebbled glass window. The occultist lifted his valise and motioned for Jacob Maitland to precede him. Maitland had not planned on any outings today, but he felt he had little choice but to accompany the strange and almost spectral figure to his waiting sedan. All were silent as the tall Sikh, whose turbaned head brushed the ceiling of the automobile, made the night-black vehicle glide through the urban jungle like a panther on the prowl.

V

SEVERAL hours later, the road-weary Maitland found himself standing in the entrance hall of number 13 China Alley, the dwelling of Anton Zarnak. The master of the house himself had quietly disappeared for the moment, and the wide-eyed guest handed his coat to Akbar Singh, who seemed to him as improbable a manservant as the old Indian Echoctaqus.

Poor Maitland scarcely knew whether he stood in an embassy of some Far Eastern empire or in a compact and overflowing museum whose collection of exotica far surpassed anything the museum of the Sanbourne Institute had to show. Beneath his feet lay the huge skin of a white Siberian tiger. Suits of gilded armor stood to either side of a door frame, and their make suggested no conventional armorial style, no particular country or era he knew. He strained to read the small placard mounted on the base of one and thought he made out the odd word "Nemedian."

Everywhere his eyes met wonders. From the walls of the corridor mounted animal heads gazed glassily at one another. One was avian, though far too large to represent any ordinary species of bird; the other had to be some kind of boar, but it had altogether too many tusks. He caught sight of what he first took to be a stuffed bat, but closer inspection showed it to be a flying reptile of an unknown type. In a daze, Maitland stepped closer and extended a finger. Yes, the stitching was that of the taxidermist, not of the toy maker.

The gentle touch of the mighty hand of Akbar Singh brought him to his senses once again. He shook his head and followed the direction the giant indicated and soon found himself sinking into a plush chair facing that of Anton Zarnak, who sat with his hands together, like a tripod, his goateed chin resting on their apex. On the desk before him was an old book.

Zarnak took it up, saying simply, "Let me read you something."

> The nethermost caverns are not
> for the fathoming of living eyes;
> it is written in the Scroll of Thoth
> how terrible is the price of a single glimpse,
> for that the marvels thereof

are strange and awful.
Nor may those who pass ever return,
for in that transcendent Vastness
lurk Shapes of darkness
that seize and bind.
Cursed the ground where dead thoughts live
new and oddly bodied,
and the wakeful mind
that is held by no head.
Wisely did Ibn Mushachab bless the tomb
where no wizard hath lain.
Happy the town by night
whose wizards are all ashes!
But woe to that place
whose folk omit to burn the poisoner
and the enchanter at the stake.
I tell you, it will go easier for Sodom
and Gomorrah than for that town.
For it is rumored of old
that the soul of the devil-bought
hastes not from his charnel clay,
but fats and instructs the gnawing worm;
till out of corruption horrid life springs,
and the dull scavengers of earth
wax crafty to vex it
and swell monstrous to plague it.
Great holes are digged in secret,
where earth's pores once sufficed
and things have learnt to walk
that once did crawl:
The Affair that shambleth about in the night,
the Evil that defieth the Elder Sign,
the Herd that do stand watch
at the secret portal of every tomb,
and feast unwholesomely therein.
All these Blacknesses
slither but seldom from the moist
and fetid burrows of their loathsome lair.
Less shall ye fear them than
Him That Guardeth the Gateway;
that guideth the dead beyond all worlds
into the Abyss of Unnamable Devourers.
For he is that Ubb,
the worm that dieth not.
These are the words of al-Hazrat,
Imam of al-Illah.
The wise shall heed them.

"Well, what do you make of *that*, my friend?" Zarnak let the massive book fall closed.

The other's eyes had closed during the reading but now sprang open. "But wasn't the author of the *Necronomicon* himself something of a wizard? So Ibn Khallikan attests. And the *Al-Azif* has the reputation of a kind of occult Bible. I'm afraid I don't understand, Dr. Zarnak."

"I have thought long and hard on the very matter you mention. Here is what I have discovered, or at any rate surmised. To put it perhaps oversimply for the moment, I have concluded that the *Al-Azif* and the *Necronomicon* are not in fact one and the same. The former was the work of an eighth-century Yemenite demonologist, Abd al-Hazrat. The more notorious *Necronomicon*, while it incorporates various bits and pieces of lore filched from the older *Azif*, is substantially a new work, a series of mediumistic revelations made to Dr. John Dee while he gazed into his scrying crystal.

"Once he had transcribed the visionary material, he stood aghast at the character of it. Suspecting demonic inspiration for the larger part of it, he tried to disguise its true origin by fathering the work on the obscure Arab al-Hazrat. It was a day when Christians commonly believed their Saracen rivals to worship idols and monsters such as Termagant and Iblis, so the attribution seemed natural. Dr. Dee dared not simply destroy the blasphemous text outright for fear of what vengeance might be wrought upon him by whatever alien influences had imparted the revelations to him. Afterward he petitioned his God for the gift of the tongue of angels, that spoken by the antediluvian revealer Enoch, that henceforth he might receive the oracles of God without admixture.

"What I have just read you comes from the original work of al-Hazrat. I do not care to say how it came into my hands. But I am fairly certain that in this passage we have some clues to our mystery. I will keep my own counsel about some of it till events corroborate my guesses, but I will tell you this. It would be a waste of time to approach our Mr. Phillips again. He would surely grow suspicious, no matter what pretext we used to cloak the reason for our interest in his affairs. We must retain the element of surprise, and here is how we shall do it ...."

VI

MIDNIGHT found a lonely trio trudging through an even lonelier landscape, as Anton Zarnak, accompanied by his servant Akbar Singh and the somewhat reluctant young scholar Jacob Maitland, made their way through Hubble's Field, trying to get as near as they dared to the old Hiram Stokely mansion without being seen in the wan moonlight.

The farthest quarter of the vast and desolate expanse harbored a very old cemetery, with headstones dating in some cases to pioneer days. Excavations some years before had disclosed the shocking fact that pretty much the whole of Hubble's Field had long been honeycombed with clandestine burials dating back further still, but of course none of those makeshift graves was marked.

Work at the site had been suspended while the appropriate county boards had met to decide what to do next. Finally, two considerations had persuaded them to discontinue the operation and to reroute the planned utility lines elsewhere. First, the presence there of ancient Indian remains made the place sacred in the eyes of the surviving Hippaway, who appeared as if from nowhere to make their case quite vociferously. Second, since there was no possibility of identifying any of the skeletal carcasses, some of them seemingly mummified, it was thought best not to bother reinterring them elsewhere. Best to let the place alone, dreaming of its enigmatic past. No one came there any more, not even to lay flowers at the graves in the tiny cemetery that lay close to the mansion. Most of these graves were so old that no one survived to memorialize dead relatives resting there.

It was here that Zarnak chose to start digging. To Maitland's nervous questioning the unflappable occultist replied, "It is always easier when paying a visit to begin by locating the door. These even have their residents' names listed. Rather like your apartment house." It was a grim jest, but neither man laughed.

Akbar Singh's huge muscles swelled as he attacked the moldy mound of graveyard soil, unearthing the rotting lid of a coffin in surprisingly few minutes. They seemed long to Maitland, who was in constant terror, not of the supernatural, but simply of being apprehended by the local police—as if any were likely to be patrolling the God-forsaken area. He winced at every blow of the Sikh's shovel against the yielding wood of the old casket. Wood splintered as Akbar Singh pulled free what was left of the lid.

"Just as you surmised, my Master—nothing!"

Maitland and Zarnak both advanced to the lip of the emptied grave. Maitland spoke first. "You mean we've taken all this insane risk for *nothing*? I *told* you—"

"No, young Mister Maitland; please take a closer look. Don't be afraid. Indeed, the coffin is untenanted. That is as I suspected. I believe we will find something else instead. Now, let Akbar Singh finish his work." The Sikh set to work again, this time roughly tapping this and that section of the exposed coffin bottom, shredding what was left of the once-fine silken lining. Then a sudden splintering sound.

"The false bottom, sahib." Zarnak joined him, drawing forth an electric torch.

"And the steps? Yes, there they are. Not much, barely more than an uneven incline, I fear, but we ought to be able to make it. Come, gentlemen."

Jacob Maitland's reaction to this development may readily be imagined. With a quick prayer, the first he had uttered in many a year, the young scholar followed Akbar Singh, Zarnak bringing up the rear, down the stairs in the crypt.

When they finally reached the end of the slippery ramp, which seemed to be a huge mud hill lent what little stable structure it possessed by an underlying heap of yellowed bones, the three venturers were glad to attain level ground again—until, that is, their descending feet splashed through fully a foot of scummy standing water. As they made their slow way forward, feet emerging from the mire with a sucking *pop!* each time, they tried hard to gain a sense of their bearings in case a speedy retreat should prove necessary. That was of no use: The place was a labyrinth. Echoes defined the height of the ceiling variously the further they went. Once or twice their heads bumped the rock above them, but then they would shortly hear the distinct sounds of leathery wings fluttering stickily far above them. Once they had to retrace their steps, losing an hour or two, when the ceiling began to close over their heads again and finally lowered to such a degree that passage was impossible.

Eventually, they judged, they must be in more or less close proximity to the mansion. If so, there would soon be visible piles of gemstones, ancient coins and treasures: the gathered loot of the centuries, mined and excavated by the wriggling scavengers who served the repellent Ubb, blasphemous totem of the eaters of the dead.

Though none cared to point out the fact, it would also be soon that they would encounter one of the nonhuman subjects of Father Ubb, unless of course the statement of Winfield Phillips had indeed been a fiction or a macabre joke after all. Too much of it had proven out already for that welcome alternative to hold out much hope.

The moment delayed no longer, as fearful anticipation incarnated itself in the form of an obscenely glistening wave of corpulent viscosity, suddenly rising up before them from the underlying ooze. The thing, which held its ungainly position for several seconds unmoving, had no visible countenance. In general shape it might have borne comparison to a single severed octopus tentacle endowed with a life of its own. Great circular sucker-mouths quivered along its exposed underside, no doubt in eager throes of appetite.

All three men had crouched, bracing themselves for fight or flight, though each seemed equally futile. It was then, in the midst of the cool detachment deadly danger brings, that Jacob Maitland realized what it must mean that the disgusting creature towered motionlessly, with its presumably more vulnerable underside exposed. It was trying in the only way it might to indicate peaceful intentions. He thought of the passage from the *Azif* which ascribed some manner of craftiness, hence intelligence, to the servitors of Ubb. Without thinking, he blurted out his hunch to the others. Even with the echoes Maitland thus let loose, the posture of the hideous denizen did not change.

"Well done, Maitland!" cried the mud-smeared Zarnak, a ridiculous caricature of his usually impeccable appearance. "I believe our host is satisfied that you have understood him. Look, there he goes, and I'd swear he means us to follow. *Come!*"

The bloated maggot-thing slid slowly through the muck and slime that covered the cavern floor, apparently troubling to keep the upper portion of its segmented jelly above the surface, so they could track and follow it. Fully aware that they might well be following along like sheep to the slaughter, the three men saw little in the way of alternatives. If the yuggya, for such they must be, had sought their destruction, a sudden and fatal ambush would have been a simple matter.

Before long they began to recognize familiar-looking landmarks. They must, they now realized, have strayed far from their goal, and the beast before them had perhaps been sent to guide them to their destination. Soon the feeble glow of the waning flashlight began to magnify itself a thousandfold as its pale rays fell upon sudden heaps of ancient treasure. Here it was! The mysterious source of the wealth of Winfield Phillips, of Hiram Stokely before him, and of who knew how many corrupted souls in the ages before them?

As Zarnak had warned them, the real treasures of temptation were the promised secrets of elder blasphemy that lay beyond the veils of human ignorance. They were already getting more of those secrets than Maitland, for one, would have wished. He only hoped he might survive this adventure with a fair measure of blissful ignorance intact.

VII

MORE than once nearly losing their footing, as their clumsy waterlogged steps landed on piles of underwater coins or fell on the open hinges of old chests that closed like toothless bear traps on their numb feet, the weary party finally arrived at the chosen destination to which their nightmare sheep dog had guided them. All alike strained and squinted to grasp the outlines of a shadowed image pressed against the rocky cave wall in front of them. Was it some sort of statue? It seemed motionless enough, but then a low moan crept eerily from where its lips would be. Emboldened, the men came nearer, semi-circling the pathetic creature fastened to the rocks with a combination of rusty manacles and too-tight cords.

It hardly stirred, and anyone could see it had severe anemia. Half-healed scars showed that the man had been often and deeply bled. It was a marvel that any spark of life lingered. Perhaps whoever, or whatever, had done this to him knew ways of prolonging life. Or, more to the point, prolonging death. Zarnak knew that, in any case, life could not keep its toehold here for long. He bent close, gesturing for the others to do the same. The flesh-scarecrow somehow rallied. A whisper struggled forth.

"Bryan ... Winfield ... still alive ... wish I weren't, damn them—"

Suddenly the great worm-thing rose up again, splashing noisome ooze in all directions. Again it remained upright, directly across from the crucified man, with Zarnak, Akbar Singh, and Maitland between them. As the three involuntarily turned their heads to see the thing standing behind them, the dying man spoke again, this time with a greater steadiness called forth from some unknown reserve.

"My cousin ... Winfield ... yes, *that!*"

Zarnak's whisper punctuated the other's: "... fats and instructs the very worm that gnaws ...."

Maitland was turning greener. "But ... who was it I saw? Surely ...." He trailed off into dumbfoundment, passive and resigned before one paradox too many. He began to totter, and the tireless Sikh reached out to steady him. Zarnak turned to him.

"Jacob, *sahib* Singh, unless I miss my guess, the man living in the house somewhere above is not Winfield Phillips, though he bears his face and form. It is in fact none other than *Hiram Stokely!*"

The wasted form manacled to the nitrous wall nodded with as much emphasis as it could manage.

"He had read the *Necronomicon* and must have reasoned that he could cheat death by willing himself to linger in his decaying physical form till the maggots got to him. He must have arranged to let his 'impending' death be known, left instructions not to embalm him, and mandated an immediate burial. The sooner he reached the moist and tainted earth of Hubble's Field the better. He had already begun to change in a hideous way, hence the closed coffin ceremony. He exerted his fading will on the loathsome carrion-eaters, till they had consumed him. Somehow"—(here Zarnak indicated the swaying bulk of the yugg-creature)—"somehow *this* was the result. But who could abide the thought of living on in such a form? This is where the ill-fated Winfield Phillips and his cousin Bryan came in."

Maitland, ringing wet and already chilled to the bone, nonetheless discovered his spine was capable of even deeper freezes. Zarnak went on.

"As young relatives and strangers to him, they could be assumed not to harbor the old family grudges, nor to know the reasons behind them. Old Hiram had chosen them as his heirs for no other reason, hoping to lure them to the old hacienda. His logic was flawless, I must admit. He trusted that they would not be long in discovering the secret of the cavern below the house, probably reasoning that sheer greed, if not curiosity, would impel them on a thorough search of the place for hidden caches of the old man's fortune. The thing that had been Hiram Stokely simply resolved to wait at the foot of the stairway till the boys should sooner or later discover the secret closet in the library, and he would seize the first that came within his reach.

"This was the 'Red Offering', the blood his new body needed to maintain it. The first doomed interloper turned out to be poor Bryan here. The Stokely-thing expected to be able to establish a telepathic link with whichever cousin remained, counting on a certain psychic predisposition that ran in their witchcraft-blighted line. It worked, and under the guise of promising him Faustian knowledge and wealth untold, he lured the immature Phillips to his damnation. In the end, he worked the wonder of supplanting Phillips' very consciousness, trapping it forever in his own slime-coated body. His plan worked perfectly—until now. We must see to it that the old wizard does not live on to bring his terrible schemes to ultimate fruition, or the whole earth will become one vast Hubble's Field."

"That, as you know, would be only the start." This was a new voice, and it came from above, no doubt from further up the same staircase the two cousins had perilously descended many months before. It was Winfield Phillips' voice, though again it was not. None of them knew what Hiram Stokely's voice had sounded like, but if they had, there would be no mistaking it now.

A flood light, or so it seemed to the sensitive eyes of the three below, enveloped them, making them easy targets for an unseen gunman. Maitland went down at once, though there was no way to judge how severe the wound might be. The impact would have knocked him over, weakened as he was, in any case. Zarnak and Akbar Singh both made for the outer circumference of the beam as fast as they could stumble, while another shot shattered the lolling head of Bryan Winfield. If he had not already succumbed in the previous moments, his message delivered to someone at last, the bullet, meant for Zarnak, freed him. Other shots echoed and ricocheted, competing in volume with Stokely's outraged cries; he had apparently hoped to drain Bryan of a bit more blood.

As Zarnak and the Sikh each found shallow niches to provide a moment's shelter, neither could readily think of what to do next. They had few options as long as the Indian Echoctaqus, for it must be he, held his rifle. There was one variable in the equation everyone was overlooking—until, that is, it broke the surface of the slime lake and glided with amazing swiftness to the landing where the newly bodied Hiram and his confederate stood, the latter desperately firing futile rounds at the oncoming behemoth.

"Don't waste your shots, you old fool!" Hiram screamed, the voice of the younger Phillips cracking with the unaccustomed emphasis. As the wriggling missile bore in on them, it became clear that its object was Hiram alone, and the Indian, casting aside his empty rifle, sailed from the rocky precipice, half thrown, half jumping, into the darkness. To his misfortune, he managed to land atop the waiting form of Akbar Singh, who proceeded to provide an appropriate welcome—with his fists.

Meanwhile, Hiram, wearing the form of his nephew, was struggling against a second, grossly pulpy layer of flesh, as the greasy slime of the yuggya body engulfed him. The great invertebrate gained new strength as its kissing suckers popped open dozens of veins and arteries all over the now-limp form of his enemy. The screams died down, the eyes glazed; the usurped body of Winfield Phillips shrank like a dried fruit rind. The vengeance of Winfield Phillips was complete.

All this Zarnak saw as he crept from concealment and ascended the stairs unnoticed. Below him, the Sikh and the Indian fought with surprising fury, Akbar Singh's titan strength dampened somewhat by many hours of dull exertion, the Indian's adrenaline pumping away to even up the odds. Still, Zarnak entertained no doubt of the eventual outcome.

As he ventured to approach the quivering mass of translucent, stinking jelly, lapping and bubbling over the desiccated form it had vanquished, Zarnak sensed a sudden and subtle change—for the worse. Something terrible was happening. The yugg-maggot was regaining its form, its strength, its stature. It seemed somehow different.

Zarnak's sensitive instincts told him what had surely happened: In the moment of death, the demon-soul of Hiram Stokely had *again displaced the psyche of Winfield Phillips and regained control of its previous host*. Now it meant to pass into the body of Anton Zarnak himself! The occultist seemed unable to thwart the other's design. He began to feel the separation, the drifting, the—

Then he went down, struck by something hard and wet smacking into the back of his nodding head. As he struggled to hold onto consciousness, he saw from the corner of his eye what had hit him, breaking the mesmeric hold the Hiram-thing had exerted upon him: the severed head of the Indian shaman Echoctaqus! Akbar Singh had wrenched it free of its moorings in one great effort and used it as the only instrument available to disrupt the horror he could see transpiring above.

The desperate maneuver had worked, and now Akbar Singh came charging up the steps, dangerously slippery with splattered blood and ooze. He had seized a torch out of its wall bracket as he passed, and now he thrust it over the head of Zarnak, just rising slowly to his knees, and into the midst of the viscous larva before him.

The thing made no sound except for the echoes of stones knocked loose by its flailing, ropy tentacles, the pseudopods randomly erupting from all over its violently quivering bulk. Then came the sound of bubbling and nauseous popping as molten pustules formed and vomited forth their unwholesomeness. Cleansing, obliterating flame swept in seconds over the glistening form of the thing, reducing it swiftly to a crumbling heap of caked ash, which kept collapsing as hidden pockets of mephitic gas imploded one by one.

Glad to turn away from the sickening spectacle, Zarnak and his rescuer made their way gingerly down the precarious steps to see to their third companion. Before they reached bottom, however, they met the staggering figure of Maitland, clutching the ripped flesh of a surface wound on one arm, but otherwise almost cheerful, given the circumstances. "What say we vacate the premises before any of Ubb's colleagues get wind of what's happened and come looking to settle the score? And this time, let's go through the house!"

So they did, taking one further precaution. After a quick search, Akbar Singh located a quantity of flammable liquids left over from the cleaning and renovation of the old hacienda. These he dispensed in liberal amounts over most of the extent of the interior. He had saved one of the torches from below the house. Once he was a safe distance from the front door, he warned the others, ignited the torch, and pitched it onto the verandah. Then he turned and ran as if the demons of hell were on his tail. Truth to tell, he wasn't entirely sure they *weren't*. Rejoining the others, he turned and watched the growing inferno. Beside him, Zarnak whispered, as if speaking to himself, "Happy the town by night whose wizards are all ashes."

ADDITIONAL CALL OF CTHULHU® FICTION TITLES

THE COMPLETE PEGANA

Lord Dunsany's fantasy writing had a profound impact on the Dreamlands stories of H. P. Lovecraft. This original collection is composed of newly edited versions of Lord Dunsany's first two books, *The Gods of Pegana* (1905) and *Time and the Gods* (1906). Three additional stories round out the book, the first time that all the Pegana stories have appeared within one book. Edited and introduced by S. T. Joshi.

5 3/8" x 8 3/8", 242 pages, $14.95. Stock #6016; ISBN 1-56882-190-5.

THE HASTUR CYCLE
Second Revised Edition

The stories in this book represent the evolving trajectory of such notions as Hastur, the King in Yellow, Carcosa, the Yellow Sign, Yuggoth, and the Lake of Hali. A succession of writers from Ambrose Bierce to Ramsey Campbell and Karl Edward Wagner have explored and embellished these concepts so that the sum of the tales has become an evocative tapestry of hypnotic dread and terror, a mythology distinct from yet overlapping the Cthulhu Mythos. Here for the first time is a comprehensive collection of all the relevant tales. Selected and introduced by Robert M. Price.

5 3/8" x 8 3/8", 320 pages, $17.95. Stock #6020; ISBN 1-56882-192-1.

THE ITHAQUA CYCLE

The elusive, supernatural Ithaqua roams the North Woods and the wastes beyond, as invisible as the wind. Hunters and travelers fear the cold and isolation of the North; they fear the advent of the mysterious, malignant Wind-Walker even more. This collection includes the progenitor tale "The Wendigo" by Algernon Blackwood, three stories by August Derleth, and ten more from a spectrum of contemporary authors including Brian Lumley, Stephen Mark Rainey, and Pierre Comtois.

5 3/8" x 8 3/8", 260 pages, $15.95. Stock #6021; ISBN 1-56882-191-3.

All titles are available from bookstores and game stores. You can also order directly from **www.Chaosium.com**, your source for Cthulhiana and more. To order by credit card via the net, visit our web site, 24 hours a day. To order via phone, call 1-510-583-1000, 9 A.M. to 4 P.M. Pacific time.

ABOUT THE SERIES EDITOR

ROBERT M. PRICE has edited *Crypt of Cthulhu* for fourteen years. His essays on Lovecraft have appeared in *Lovecraft Studies, The Lovecrafter, Cerebretron, Dagon, Étude Lovecraftienne, Mater Tenebrarum,* and in *An Epicure in the Terrible* and *Twentieth Century Literary Criticism.* His horror fiction has appeared in *Nyctalops, Eldritch Tales, Etchings & Odysseys, Grue, Footsteps, Deathrealm, Weirdbook, Fantasy Book, Vollmond,* and elsewhere. He has edited *Tales of the Lovecraft Mythos* and *The New Lovecraft Circle* for Fedogan & Bremer, as well as *The Horror of It All* and *Black Forbidden Things* for Starmont House. His books include *H. P. Lovecraft and the Cthulhu Mythos* (Borgo Press) and *Lin Carter: A Look behind His Imaginary Worlds* (Starmont). By day he is a theologian, New Testament scholar, editor of *The Journal of Higher Criticism,* and pastor of the Church of the Holy Grail.

CPSIA information can be obtained
at www.ICGtesting.com
Printed in the USA
BVHW07s1148190518
516621BV00001B/52/P